TITAN SONG

**DAW BOOKS PROUDLY PRESENTS
THE NOVELS OF DAN STOUT**

TITAN SONG

Book Three of the Carter Archives

DAN STOUT

DAW BOOKS, INC.
DONALD A. WOLLHEIM, FOUNDER
1745 Broadway, New York, NY 10019
ELIZABETH R. WOLLHEIM
SHEILA E. GILBERT
PUBLISHERS
www.dawbooks.com

DAW TRADEMARK REGISTERED
U.S. PAT. AND TM. OFF. AND FOREIGN COUNTRIES
—MARCA REGISTRADA
HECHO EN U.S.A.

PRINTED IN THE U.S.A.

Dear Reader,

*It's all just words on a page
until you bring the story to life.*

*This book is dedicated
to you.*

LOOK, IT'S NOT THAT I hate disco.

    There are plenty of things that I do hate. Predators who lurk in shadows, targeting the weak and the weary; villains who find joy in snuffing out the tiny lights of individual kindness and stealing the warmth that makes life worth living. Those are the people I've dedicated my life to finding and dragging into the light of justice. Compared to them, why would I be bothered by a garish, repetitive squeal of synthesized sludge pawned off onto vapid club-dwellers too tweaked out to recognize a decent melody if it walked up and bit them in the ass?

So no, I don't hate disco. But I sure as Hells don't like it, either.

Despite that fact, I'd been listening to the radio blare overproduced bilge for the better part of an hour as I drove across the ice plains. The reason for that was the cop who shared my ride; he loved the stuff. Jax drummed his hands on the dashboard of the snow-runner, roughly matching what passed for a beat as I gripped the steering wheel tighter and hoped that the radio signal would hurry up and die. My partner's biting jaws were slightly open, reverberating a hum past jagged tusks the size of my fingers, self-harmonizing with the whistle from his speaking mouth, a hole set low in his throat, just above his necktie. It would have been impressive, if he hadn't been off-beat and out of tune.

"Can you not do that?" I raised my voice above the rumble of treads on densely packed snow. We were due north of the city, the profile of the Mount retreating in our sideview mirrors, and with it the warmth of the geo-vents that made Titanshade an oasis on the snow-swept ice plains. The vents' continuous output of sulfur-scented heat was the only thing that allowed the city to exist and cloak itself in something akin to civilization.

"Do what?" Jax's eyes were concealed behind wraparound shades, making it impossible to see if they were crinkled with amusement, and nothing so expressive as a smile would ever grace the rigid bones of his biting jaws. Southerners were often intimidated by Mollen-kampi faces and the frozen mask of perpetual aggression they conveyed to human eyes. Some people thought they looked dangerous, but I held no such uncertainty—the fact that my left hand was two fingers short of the usual allotment proved that a Mollenkampi's bite was far worse than their appearance.

I peered at the ice plains through my own sunglasses. Shades were obligatory on the ice plains in daylight. While the sun was out the vast, unbroken white expanse was as blinding as it was deadly.

The fuzzy radio signal brought us a track from Dinah McIntire, the pop queen whose heavily processed voice had dominated the city's radio playlists since she'd announced she was bringing a music festival to our town. Big-name artists rarely toured in Titanshade. It was too far to travel, the climate too inhospitable. The rest of the world had always been content to forget about us, as long as we supplied them with oil. That was one more thing that had changed in recent months.

"It's not my fault you can't feel the music in your heart," Jax said.

In fact, I felt it too deeply. The blend of static and song echoed the buzzing sounds and the overwhelming, aching hunger that came when I crossed the invisible spiderwebs of sorcery. Sensations that I needed to keep secret.

I snapped back to reality when Jax stretched a hand in front of me, pointing at a speck on the horizon I'd been eyeing for the last little while.

"Is that it?" he asked.

"Yeah, kid. That's it."

The Shelter in the Bend rig site grew larger with each second, and soon we were able to make out the outline of the temporary tents nestled in its shadow like the city's buildings nestled against the Mount. The entire structure had been thrown up in the last two weeks, amidst much speculation and excitement. As much as I thought they were crazy, I had to admire the organizers' audacity. If we rarely had big-name concerts in Titanshade, the thought of a dozen playing for more than a week *outside* the city was unheard of.

The Titanshade city leadership was thrilled about it. A festival located hours from the city would cause no traffic jams and require no police coordination. It was even far enough from the manna strike that the military encampment wasn't concerned about accidental tourists. The festival made headlines for hiring furloughed rig workers for the structural work and security. The short-term salve for the unemployed made it an easy sell. It was a win for everyone.

It was a shame they needed a pair of Homicide detectives.

I'd never been to Shelter in the Bend before, but it had clearly been transformed into a tiny village of commerce. Signs welcomed us to Dinah McIntire's "Ice on Her Fingers" festival. In a bold move, she'd made Titanshade the crown jewel of her promotions, a two-week-long festival with a large number of bands and events. The airwaves had been inundated with announcements: *Ten Days of Dancing, Decadence, and the Divine D.M.* Now that we were on site, we were confronted with larger-than-life banners commanding us to look for her new single, "Titan's Song," in stores.

The site belonged to Rediron Drilling, who'd loaned out the facility to the pop star for her special event. Like all the rigs on the ice plains, its operations had been frozen two months earlier when the raw essence of magic had been discovered below the ice plains. The man who'd struck manna, Harlan Cedrow, had been willing to pay any price to find his treasure. Things had ended badly for him, and for all of us who'd been at the rig where the manna strike occurred.

I parked near a pair of snow-runners identical to ours, the TPD shields on their sides a match for the badges in our pockets. One of them had a light dusting of snow while the other was clean, as if it had arrived recently, its engine still warm. Probably the crime scene techs or patrol cops there to secure the scene. Our response time to this call was much longer than usual. Most drill rigs were far enough from Titanshade that they fell outside our jurisdiction. The oil fields kept their own rough laws, only turning to the authorities in cases of emergency. But maybe a bunch of southern musicians were more inclined to call in the police than a crew of roughnecks.

"Alright," I said. "Let's gear up."

Jax and I began securing the heavy coats customary for travel on the ice plains. Department-issue coats had only a few nods to utility, such as the heavy mitten tops that folded back to allow access to weapons. It was a struggle in the cramped quarters of the snowrunner, and the vehicle swayed as the wind drove into it, creeping through cracks and stripping away the interior warmth even in the short time we'd been there.

Jax peered at the festival signs. "You think the band is already here? They'd have to be, right?" He was excited, but also dragging a bit more than his usual eager young self.

"What's wrong, kid?" I said. "Another late night alone with your books?"

It was usually fun to watch his reaction when I prodded him about his college education and academic bent. Instead, Jax pointed at the central spire of the derrick. "Really impressive what they've done here!" The high-toned clicks in his voice were artificially chipper.

I frowned at the sudden change of subject. I knew he'd been spending an increasing amount of time with Talena, my daughter for all purposes, if not by blood or legal marriage. I'd helped raise her, or at least had done my best not to screw up too bad while I was with her mom. I shot a look his way, and found he'd pulled out a handkerchief and taken a sudden interest in polishing his tusks.

I grunted and peered out the window, studying the layout of the site. The prospect of a ten-day festival on the ice plains was mindbogglingly stupid. Even with our layers, Jax and I could only spend a limited time in the frigid air. But the marvels of engineering never ceased to amaze, and the transformation of the drill site certainly fell into that category. Structures of various sizes littered the area, but they were dwarfed by the central tent. It was a massive swell of tan-and-green-striped fabric, and the tip of the derrick rose through the center spire like the pole of a monstrous circus big top.

"They hung it right on the thribble board," I said.

"Huh?"

"Pipes sections stack," I said. "This derrick's a big one. It can stack three. A single, a double, a thribble."

"You mean a triple."

I clapped my hands together, making sure the fit of the gloves was proper. "Did your old man work the rigs? Mine did, and that's a thribble board."

Jax sighed. He was a newcomer to Titanshade, and didn't have oil in his blood. "Should I even ask what they call the fourth level?"

"A fourble."

"I genuinely don't know if you're messing with me or not."

We stared at one another for a moment, then I killed the engine and opened the door. The wind grabbed hold of it, yanking it from my grasp and making the hinges squeal even as it snatched the warmth from the car and the air from my lungs. I climbed out of the snow-runner and slammed the door shut, eager to keep moving. Each inhalation was a sharp jab to the ribs as the cold bit me from the inside. I was instantly grateful for all those bulky layers.

Jax came around the vehicle and stood by my side. "You're the expert," he said. "Which way do we go now?"

I considered our options. To one side of the parking area was a wide field of smaller tents and domed huts. These were rentals, heavily advertised as the perfect option for fans who didn't want to miss a single moment of the show. The whole thing seemed like a guarantee for frostbite.

But the main tent held the most promise. There was a stream of heavily cloaked people with safety vests and tool belts flowing in and out of the tent opening.

"When in doubt, follow the people fleeing for warmth," I said, and we moved in that direction, away from the hum of a small army of gas-powered generators that kept the lights and equipment boards running.

A human woman in a heavy coat stood apart from the foot traffic and waved us down as we approached. Only her eyes and a single lock of brown hair were visible beneath her hood and mask.

"Are you the cops?" The fabric of her face mask muffled her voice. "You look like cops."

Jax nodded. "Can we go inside?" Mollenkampi may have more innate cold resistance than humans, but they don't enjoy exposure to the elements any more than we do.

Our escort hustled us into the big tent, which turned out to actually be a series of smaller tents, roughly the size of my apartment, each separated by thick curtains, and each getting progressively warmer than the last. By the third entrance, flooring was laid out over the ice, providing better footing and adding a layer of insulation that would keep the snow from melting below us. That was impressive, but when we crossed into the main area I couldn't help but draw in a shocked breath. They'd managed to re-create an entire arena inside the tent. A construction crew was putting the finishing touches on the stage, positioned so the performers would have their back to the city.

It was time to shed the elaborate coats. There was a temporary coatrack set up near the entrance. A few paces away were lockers, row after row of them, along with signs indicating the price: *two taels*. The concertgoers would pay to store their coats, eliminating the need for a coat check.

As we all peeled off our own layers of protection, our escort proved to be a young woman, her hair tucked under a knit cap. "Name's Vandie," she said, draping her coat across an open rack. "You want a tour, or a soda or something? Or do you want to meet Cavanaugh?"

"We'd rather go straight to where the incident occurred," I said, avoiding the loaded term *crime scene*. "Where're the patrol officers whose vehicles are outside?"

"The patrolman is by the dressing room, and the others, um . . ." She trailed off, eyes widening as I removed my face mask. I'd gotten accustomed to reactions like that since our photos had begun appearing in the papers. I braced myself for a quick barrage of questions, but was saved when another woman's voice called out from behind us.

"Hello, gentlemen."

I turned to find a pair of plainclothes cops making their way across the massive open space. They were both human, a man and woman, the fabric of their dark cloaks swaying with each step, lined by shifting symbols stitched in iridescent thread. Outfits that marked them as divination officers.

The woman had an elaborate up-swept haircut, though a few casual wisps had escaped to tumble onto her shoulders. She smirked and said, "Appearing by popular demand, huh?"

Her name was Guyer, and she'd been a friendly ear more than once. I'd even taken my greatest secret to her, only to have her dismiss it out of hand. From the way she stared at me now, I guessed she was starting to rethink her skepticism.

The male divination officer outpaced her, grinning as he approached us with hand extended.

"Harris," he introduced himself. "I hear McIntire made serious noise to get the two of you sent out here."

He didn't know the half of it. Our public profile was a source of great contention within City Hall and the TPD. With the influx of cash and public relations that the concert brought, we'd never have been allowed near the site of such an important event if McIntire herself hadn't demanded we be present.

The male divination officer peered down at Jax as they shook hands. "You're much younger than you look in photos," he said. "Here I thought I was the freshest face in plainclothes!"

Harris was broad shouldered and tall, with dark skin and a wide, friendly grin that showed off a set of front teeth large enough to make an ice hare jealous. His hair was a neatly trimmed halo of natural curls, and his handshake was firm, with the kind of calluses you didn't get from police sorcery.

"And you must be Carter!" He pumped my hand with an abundance of enthusiasm. He didn't tell me how young I looked.

"Carter." Behind us, the woman who'd led us inside muttered my name. I ignored it. Over the last two months I'd been caught up in a series of high-profile investigations, and I got the occasional starstruck civilian.

"Why'd this case rate a pair of DOs?" Ajax asked, glancing from

Harris to Guyer. It was a good question. Divination officers relied on manna to force details from the remains of the departed, either through reading entrails or through more direct methods. For my entire lifetime manna had been so precious that it was only used in the most extreme of circumstances. Or at least it had been, until the last few months when the manna strike turned the global economy upside down. Now we were walking onto a crime scene that apparently warranted not one but *two* divination officers.

From farther in the tent, a pair of human men in security jackets walked over to us, but our guide intercepted them. She answered whatever concerns they had and they retreated. Maybe she was more than a junior intern after all.

"It's high profile," Guyer said. "But Harris is the only DO officially on this case. I'm merely here for the view." She swung an arm as she said it, as if she were there for the concert setting, but her eyes were locked on me. She felt I owed her a conversation, and I felt she owed me an apology. As a result we hadn't spoken much in the two weeks since Titan's Day. We'd have to talk sooner or later, but when exactly is the right time to have a talk about developing an inexplicable talent for magic, especially when there were so many additional ears around? A fact underscored by the way the woman who'd welcomed us inside now hovered close, listening in on our conversation. It's a common experience when wearing a badge. If someone isn't a victim or potential arrest, they like to hang around and observe things go down.

"The problem is that there's a whole structure behind the tents," Harris was saying. "Not to mention the wider scope of the drill site. There's still tons of people running around here."

"I can get you whatever access you need." Our guide's voice broke through our conversation, loud and confident. "The rig, the outbuildings, the fields."

"You can?" Harris asked. "Not the stage and tent, but the rig itself? That'll probably be off limits."

"Not for me," she said. "I own it. I'm Vandra Cedrow." She turned from Harris to me and her smile hardened into something less than friendly. "You killed my uncle."

OUR ESCORT HELD MY EYE, waiting for a reaction. Built with the slender musculature of a rock climber, she wore limited makeup, mostly dark eyeliner that terminated in elaborate flourishes. She wore her hair styled up and over her scalp, a dirty blond wave breaking on the beaches of her temples. The sides of her head had been shaved down to a sandy fuzz, and a gold chain wove through one ear's multiple piercings like an expensive golden thread. I could see the resemblance to Harlan Cedrow, if I imagined the former head of Rediron Drilling without his head plucked free of hair in the Therreau tradition. Or the bloody wounds from when I'd ended his life with a length of metal rebar.

Doing my best to keep my voice neutral, I said, "He didn't give me much of a choice."

And that was true. I'd chased her uncle onto the ice plains, pursuing him for crimes ranging from murder to more murder. I didn't regret my actions, but I regretted that day—when her uncle struck manna and started the chain of events that had caused the near-complete halt to oil drilling on the plains and put Titanshade on either a path to riches or a long road to irrelevance. But in the moment, none of that had mattered. In the moment, I'd simply been fighting to bring in a killer, and to stay alive.

Vandie's head bobbed up and down. Not a nod, more like the motions of someone listening to a song they'd heard many times before. "You managed to walk away just fine."

"I was carried out," I said. "And I was luckier than most." One of our sister officers hadn't made it out alive. And even I had left two fingers lying on the floor, severed by a Mollenkampi's bite. I suppose they'd been collected by crime-scene techs. It'd never occurred to me to ask.

"I'm sorry for your loss." Jax reinforced his words with a soothing hum. "The use of force is a last resort. On that day there wasn't another solution."

I bit my tongue, fighting the urge to lay out exactly why that force had been needed. Crimes needed to be punished, victims needed to be remembered, and a monster like Harlan Cedrow didn't deserve a free pass, even in death.

Over Vandie's shoulder I got a view of a man moving in our direction at a steady amble.

"I don't defend what my uncle did," Vandie said. "I don't know if my family will ever make amends for what happened. But I know that a mentally ill man ran onto the ice plains, and instead of calling in support, you chased after him and clubbed him to death." She worked her jaw, as if chewing on gristle. "So tell me again how force is a last resort."

The man headed our way was a deeply tanned human. Around Titanshade, that usually indicated an old roughneck, someone who'd spent long hours exposed to the glare of the ice plains sun. He had a full head of white hair, wind-chapped cheeks, and a face with more crags and crevices than the ice plains themselves.

Vandie wasn't letting up. "What's the matter? You forget the details of that particular murder?"

"Your uncle poisoned his workers and set them on us like attack dogs. He condemned innocent people to madness and destruction. Hells, he almost created an international incident. And he didn't care who knew. He left a trail of physical evidence and witnesses, because he was sick enough to be proud of it."

Cedrow's elbows drew in tighter. "It's amazing what witnesses will say with a bunch of cops on their doorstep."

The man had finally reached our position. He rested a wrinkled hand on Cedrow's shoulder, but spoke to us.

"Murphy CaDell, officers. I'm so glad you came." The man moved as if he were walking through molasses, and his speech was equally drawn out.

Cedrow tilted her head, addressing the older man while keeping her eyes locked on me. "We don't need them here."

"But here they are," said CaDell. "So maybe we ought to take him to see Dinah."

"Maybe he ought to get his ass off my property."

The man's eyes sought hers, and he hazarded a smile. "Vandie . . ."

"I mean it." The younger woman jabbed a finger at the scuffed floor coverings and held my eye. "This is private land, outside the city. Leave my property." Her voice was firm, accustomed to being obeyed.

I wagged my head. "That is not how this works."

Her jaw clenched, and the man had dropped his hand. But he took a step forward, as if ready to intercede in a physical escalation. "Let's not be petty, Vandie."

"Petty?" The younger woman turned, eyebrow raised. "If someone butchered your uncle and called himself a hero, how'd you react?"

CaDell tilted his head to indicate me. "He saved the city."

"*We* did what we had to," I corrected, before turning my attention back to Vandra. "And the only people using the word 'hero' weren't there to see what happened."

"And as for today, we're already on the scene." Guyer crossed her arms, displaying the glyphs that danced along the edges of her cloak. "You can't un-call the police once we show up."

Like all the city-state members of the Assembly of Free States, the legal authority of Titanshade extended only to its sphere of influence, the area immediately around the city limits. Areas in between jurisdictional spheres were treated like international waters: whatever authority arrived first controlled the situation. Most of the oil rigs fell into the category.

CaDell leaned closer to Cedrow. His cheeks and nose tip were red, and he had clear tan lines along his forehead, marking the spot he wore his hat while on the plains. I'd initially thought him much older than me, but I revised my estimate. The man had the wind-bitten, prematurely aged face of a rig worker.

"Vandie," his voice low, eyes half closed. "This is a bad scene. Let's not make it worse."

"Worse?" She parroted the word, lips puckering as if tasting its flavor.

"They were asked to come," he said. "And we certainly want a speedy resolution to this tragedy."

"Sure we do," she muttered, then faced the older man full-on. "Okay. I'll leave it in your hands. Take them backstage and get this mess cleaned up."

She pushed her way past us, shoulder clipping mine, not bothering to look at me as she added, "Try not to kill anyone while you're here, okay?"

CaDell waited for her to be out of earshot, then pasted a smile on his wind-chapped face. "Follow me, please."

He led us through a series of tented tunnels and temporary walls, laid out in a convoluted nest structure probably chosen for a mixture of security and insulation. It was like walking through a beehive or animal warren—our path lit by strands of overhead lights that intertwined through the tent framework like the younger Cedrow's ear piercings.

I tried not to obsess on her anger. Vandie's uncle had left a string of bodies and sacrificed the sanity of his workers in order to preserve the status quo. I didn't regret my actions, and I'd have done it again if I needed to. I breathed through clenched teeth, counting to ten as I told myself to let it go.

Happily, the slow-moving man who was our guide seemed to share none of his counterpart's ill-will. Instead, he provided a steady stream of information about the tent construction and how the various layers created air pockets, an insulated bubble that, while expensive, would keep the concertgoers and performers warm enough for the festival. He even spec'd out the type of material that allowed all that to happen, and in what order it was installed.

My lack of interest ran deep.

We finally emerged into a larger space, this one occupied by dozens of performers and roadies. We were in front of one of the oil rig's administrative buildings, built into the tent system like a dollhouse consumed by a wasps' nest. Standing in the middle of this space were a pair of humans in mid-argument. One of them was so famous that even I recognized her.

Tall and slender, Dinah McIntire carried herself like royalty. She wore a thigh-length dress gilded with sequins so large they looked like fish scales, each one a burnished yellow that brought out the gold flake in her eye makeup. The dark, thick swirls of her hair were accentuated by streaks of silver. Her dark brown leggings were an exact match for her skin tone, no doubt designed to make them invisible from the stage while still providing protection against the chill. She had cover-model features and a burning intensity in her eyes. It was no wonder she was a star. I wondered if she was also a killer.

She didn't acknowledge our approach. Her attention was focused on a petite man in a green-and-red-striped sweater, the object of her anger.

"I don't give two shits about difficulty, Cavanaugh. I want it done fast and I want it done right. You want a star on your stage, you better make it safe for me to be out there."

"Of course we want it safe, Dinah. But getting things done fast? It's Titanshade—we gotta grease some palms."

She peeled the fake eyelash from her right eye and frowned, tone unyielding. "You're a manager. Go manage it."

CaDell cleared his throat and I held my badge aloft. The argument ceased, and we got the pair's full attention.

"Sorry for interrupting," I said. "Are you Miss McIntire?"

"I am." The singer was all resonant voice and statuesque good looks. Two graceful strides with her hand extended. "And you don't need to introduce yourself. I'm so pleased to meet you, Detective."

I shrugged, pocketing my badge as I tilted my head toward Jax. "This is my partner, Detective Ajax. We—"

Jax stepped forward, gripping McIntire's hand, and pumped it as he gushed. "I loved 'My Tears Are Diamonds.' I listened to it so much I wore out the 8-track. I'm really excited for the show and already have tickets for opening night, thank you so much for coming to town." He was still shaking her hand, and McIntire withdrew hers a little forcefully.

"Thanks." She raised an eyebrow, then looked at his hand. "You, uh . . ."

Jax glanced down. Her fake eyelash lay crumpled in his palm. He held it out, and she plucked it up with a grimace.

"I'll let you get at it, then." She waggled her fingers in a farewell and turned her attention back to her manager. "Cavanaugh, start from the beginning and walk me through it."

CaDell headed back across the hall, gesturing for us to follow.

I hesitated. "We'll need to speak with you later," I told the pop star. But McIntire's attention had already turned to one of her other assistants.

We stepped after CaDell, and Jax leaned in, muttering, "Did I make a fool out of myself?"

"Don't worry, kid, you did fine." I let him enjoy that for a few paces before adding, "We'll just have to wait and see if she files a restraining order."

We followed CaDell through another stretch of tented tunnels, the striped material lighting up in the sunlight, which at least told me what direction was south. He gave us the background on how fast the tent had been raised.

"Vandie took the reins and ran with it," he said. "Hired a full crew of rig workers, every one of us out of work since the damned feds put a freeze on drilling. We're all better off now, too. We get medical expenses, more time off, and we rub elbows with celebrities. She's a practical saint of the Path, that Vandie." I respected his need to defend his boss, but I wasn't about to change my opinion about the young Cedrow.

After a short time we came to a wider hallway with a number of doors. They had been a cluster of steel-framed outbuildings before being consumed by the festival's labyrinth of tents. A red-uniformed patrolman lounged against the door frame. The patrol was a stocky human male with a baby face, and he was deep in conversation with a human woman who looked to be a dancer. His thumbs were hooked in his duty belt as he told some story that sent the dancer into laughter, one hand covering her mouth.

His own smile dropped away when he saw us, any small talk forgotten. Behind him, the dancer's eyes widened, and I could track her gaze as she stared at Jax's fearsome jaws. I suppressed a chuckle. *Southerners.*

"Anyone inside?" Jax asked, the small hole in his throat working carefully. I suspected he was aware of the dancer's scrutiny, as he added less musical tonality than he normally did to the human words.

"No sir," said the patrol, whose tag indicated his name was Worthington.

"What about the tech team?"

"Come and gone," he said. "Cleared the site for access, when you're ready. Body's still on site."

I glanced around the area. There were no other patrol cops in sight. "Where's your partner?" I asked.

"She got sick."

Jax pointed at the door, mandibles spread with surprise. "Is it that bad?"

"Nah, not that. Normal sick. Said she was light-headed, queasy. Ringing in her ears. That kind of thing. I'll probably catch it in a day or two. You know how it goes. She caught a ride back to town with the tech team."

I nodded. "It happens."

"Oh," he added, stooping to pick up a sealed folder propped against the bottom of the door. "They left this for you."

I accepted the folder. CaDell rubbed his hands and said, "Well, now. Looks like you've got this in hand. You need me, flag down someone wearing an orange vest. They're with our site management staff."

The aging roughneck departed, and we entered the crime scene.

The room beyond was spacious, and more luxuriously decked out than the other backstage areas we'd seen. There were a few rolling stands of costumes, four mirrored desks, a pair of couches, a nice television set, and a dead body shoved into the far corner.

I broke open the documents left by the techs, carbon copies with faded writing that only revealed itself when I squinted. I tossed it on the dressing table and turned to the divination officers. Now that we were alone, we could speak more freely. "You got here before us. Hear anything worth repeating?"

Harris pointed at the body. "Bobby Kearn. McIntire's drummer. Seems he was mostly respected, according to the people who kept volunteering their opinion."

"What kind of people?" I asked. "Came with the festival crew, or hired-on locals?"

Harris shrugged. "Mostly people who want in here to do their makeup or get costumes. Haven't heard much beyond that; we got here not too long before you." His fingers danced, a cartilage-popping warm-up for the gruesome brand of sorcery known as divination. "I'm ready to get started if you are?"

"No," I said. "We need to walk the scene first. Even with the techs' write-up, it's not the same as being hands-on."

Harris sighed assent, and Guyer watched without comment as Jax and I established the scene. It was time to get to know Bobby Kearn so that we could find him justice.

The victim was neither human nor Mollenkampi, but another of the eight Families. Bobby Kearn was a Gillmyn. A Family not uncommon in Titanshade, Gillmyn were built bigger than an average human or Mollenkampi. While some Gillmyn had fins along their cranium, others had smooth, domed heads. Our victim fell into the latter category. Kearn had a vivid green skin tone. Buccal sacs traced his throat, and webbed hands curled half closed on the carpet. All trademarks of the Gillmyn's amphibious ancestry. He wore denim jeans and a thin silk shirt in a muted blue. Judging from the flashy outfits I'd seen so far backstage, Kearn was not dressed for his performance. One foot had slid underneath the couch, but the other was exposed and barefoot. I crouched down and peered under the couch, confirming my suspicion—the other foot still wore a sock and shoe.

Jax hummed, mostly to himself. "Stab marks evident across his back."

I counted a dozen or more blows from a wide-bladed implement, but the pathologists back at the Medical Examiner's Office would let us know for sure.

"Direction of the strikes and his lack of one shoe indicate he was changing clothes—or at least shoes—when attacked. From the layout of the body . . ." I stood and took two steps away from Kearn, then turned back. "The attacker entered through the door and crept up behind the victim."

It also told me that the killer probably knew Kearn would be in the room, likely alone and unsuspecting.

Ajax scratched a note on his pad. "Start a search spiral?"

I glanced around. "Nah, too much clutter in here. Let's break it into sectors."

A quick consultation with the carbon-paper sheet the techs had left listing everything they'd cataloged showed that they'd also used a sector-based search pattern. Jax and I used their nomenclature for our own walk-through to make the later write-up easier.

The search was fairly uneventful, turning up only the things you might expect in a rock band's dressing room. Some booze, some un-labeled pills, and a ridiculous amount of gaudy clothing that probably cost far more than it should have. There were also a few assorted spare instruments along with a stack of reading materials and two separate phone lines, each relatively new, since the pigtail cords on the receivers hadn't yet begun to bunch up onto themselves. The trash held an assortment of proposed set lists and discarded wrap-pers of Black Gold candy bars. We found one dressing table drawer half open, with one lone candy bar left behind, the same brand name on display. I made a mental note that something may have been taken, possibly hidden behind the candy.

When I reached the television I flipped on the power to see what they had been watching. Once the tube warmed up, the news faded into view, a solemn-faced anchor talking about furthering tensions between Titanshade and the Assembly of Free States, the confedera-tion of city-states to which it belonged. I flipped the power off.

"Only one way in or out," Ajax said, indicating the single door.

I grunted my agreement and kept strolling through the sectors. From where Bobby Kearn had sat, he had line of sight to at least two mirrors. I crouched again, and confirmed that at least one of them would have shown him the door. Another sign that he knew the killer.

Jax stood by the mirrors themselves. He reached behind one— they were mounted a hand's-breadth from the wall—and a moment later the sound of Dinah McIntire's voice filled the room. *"Well then get a tape of the drum track and play that. We're three days from curtains up, so get your shit together!"* That was followed by shuffling feet and what sounded like heavy objects being dragged across a floor while someone noodled a riff across a synthesizer keyboard.

Guyer frowned. "Is that an intercom? Can they hear us?"

"Stage monitors," I said. "So the band can track what's going on during opening acts, between sets—stuff like that. It's strictly one-way."

From onstage there was a squeal of feedback as someone let a mic drift too close to an amplifier. Jax killed the sound and returned us to the quiet of the dressing room.

I took a breath, and stared at the floor. "The blood's contained."

Jax considered that. "Blood pooled around the victim," he stepped sideways, pivoted at the waist, "but no traces of it further into the room. The killer wiped off the blade?"

"I don't see a wipe pattern on Kearn's clothes. And no discarded piece of fabric on the floor."

"They could have bundled the blade inside something else as they left the room."

"Or . . ." I crouched closer to the body. "Maybe the blade snapped off and is still inside."

I reached for the victim's shirt with my left hand, the one missing two fingers. The second I touched the fabric, a painful, tingling jolt traveled up my arm. Invisible, sticky threads clung to my fingers like spiderwebs. I recognized the sensation immediately: the ties that bound disparate objects together through magic. As far as I knew, I was the only person alive who could sense them. The threads were tangled around the victim's body, in no clear design. It was a pattern

I'd seen before: Bobby Kearn had been using a hallucinogen mixed with a trace amount of manna.

I leaned back, carefully extracting myself from the invisible tangle of energy. For me, the manna bonds held a narcotic allure of their own. One I couldn't risk giving in to.

"Carter?" Jax's voice brought me back to the present moment.

I blinked rapidly and glanced around the room. "Yeah?"

"Anything in the wounds?"

"Um, no." I stood, hands resting on my hips as I took a gulp of air. "And I can't think of what kind of weapon would be strong enough to kill the Gillmyn but still break off cleanly." In truth, I could barely think at all. My mind was racing, and I stepped far back from the body, careful not to tug on any of the threads. As long as I didn't draw the energy they contained into myself, it would be fine. It *had* to be fine.

I reviewed the list the techs had left. Kearn had carried an ID, some cash, and a candy wrapper. All those items, along with the other physical evidence, were already on a snow-runner headed back to Titanshade, where they'd be processed into evidence. I glanced at my partner, still recording details in his notepad. "You have anything else?"

"Nope." He flipped the notebook shut.

I sighed, then looked over at Harris. "I guess you're up."

Guyer strolled to the door, letting the patrol cop know that there were to be absolutely no interruptions until she said otherwise. She closed the door and flipped the handle lock, for a bit of added privacy.

"Well," she said. "Let's see what the victim has to say for himself."

3

WITH THE DOOR CLOSED, THE two divination officers paced across the room, circling the body and eyeing it as if they were divvying up a newfound treasure.

Guyer slowed her pace. "What are you thinking?" she asked Harris.

The taller DO tilted his head, staring at the corpse. "Probably a pulse code."

Guyer grunted. "Using the stab wounds? Could work."

"If it doesn't, it'd still leave me plenty of wiggle room on the allocation."

Manna was strictly tracked and controlled, like the precious substance it was. The sorcerers' vials would be carefully weighed upon their return to make sure not a drop beyond the preapproved expenditure had been used. And just like a regular officer faced pages of reports to account for a bullet fired, the divination officers would have to account for their use of magic. Harris was making the most of what he'd been approved to use.

With a nod to her companion, Guyer stepped to the far wall, crossing her arms and growing still. This was Harris's show through and through.

The taller sorcerer knelt and reached into the folds of his cloak. He emerged with a small glass vial in hand, its contents a swirling iridescent liquid that had fueled the first industrial revolution and inspired wars, strife, and theft through the ages. The exact use of manna was a blend of mystery and technology. Anyone could use manna-bound objects, but it took a sorcerer's aptitude and training to create those bonds that defied the obstacles of distance and nature.

Harris squirted a fine mist of the liquid across his thumb and forefinger, which he then pressed into the dead man's stab wounds, tracing the jagged holes left in Kearn's back. Stepping away, Harris pressed the same manna-slick digits against his nose, the iridescence momentarily shining on his skin like the glyphs on the dark fabric of his cloak. His free hand moved through the air in rapid jerks, a mad tailor joining two pieces of invisible cloth. He was attempting to create a connection between the real world and the echo that Kearn had left behind.

I edged closer, curiosity overwhelming me. As casually as possible, I reached between the sorcerer and the corpse, feeling for invisible threads. Their absence indicated that Harris was using traditional manna, the remnants of the liquid retrieved from the bellies of whales, before those animals were hunted to extinction. DO Guyer's eyes narrowed with suspicion, and I fell back, reminding myself that she hadn't really come to observe Harris. She'd come to observe me, and that was dangerous.

I didn't fully understand how I'd gotten the ability to interact with manna, how to control it, or what the implications were. But I knew that talking about it put me at risk. If the government realized I had picked up this connection, then at best I'd be exploited for PR purposes. Much more likely was that I'd disappear into a secure medical facility, like the other first responders who'd shown the slightest hint of ill effects from being present at the manna strike. There were too many unknowns to risk my own safety and the safety of those close to me. I avoided Guyer not because of what she might do, but for fear that I'd say or do something that filtered up to the powers that be.

Determined to be uninteresting, I stayed put and focused on the ritual at hand. As Harris worked his spell, the glyphs on his cloak became easier to see, each one sparking and fading, pretty lights signifying danger, a sparkling fuse burning its path to an explosive charge.

The victim's body began to shake as though someone had run a few thousand volts through it. The stab wounds on Bobby's back contracted and relaxed, the opening and closing moving in time with Harris's breathing.

Harris muttered, "Bobby Kearn, I call to you from the Path." He paused, then said again, louder, "Bobby Kearn, I speak your name. Do you hear me?"

The corpse stopped quivering, the wounds no longer moving. Then, one by one, the gaps of the wounds began to pull closed and reopen. A dozen tiny mouths on vivid green flesh, stretching open in silent cries of dismay. Beside Harris, Guyer recorded the rhythms of the pulses on a notepad. The spell was similar to sorcery I'd seen Guyer use, although hers seemed more powerful than Harris's.

"I hear . . . I hear," she translated. "Let me go. . . ."

Harris spoke again, louder. "Name your killer!"

He stepped closer to the body. Arms raised, voice raised, anger slipping into his words. "Name your killer, Bobby Kearn, and let justice take its path." The body shook and writhed. This time its movements were underscored by a hiss of static.

I told myself that I was imagining it, that I wasn't hearing the same electric buzz that haunted my dreams. I glanced around the room, searching for the source. My gaze settled on the mirror that hid the PA system. Jax must not have turned it all the way off. I moved to the mirror, running my hand along its back, searching for the volume or power control. As I did, an ear-splitting howl of feedback came through the PA system, along with a hissing whisper directly in my ear. "Reprise . . ."

Fumbling, stretching, I finally located the dial. But as I began to twist, the flesh at the base of my thumb twitched and spasmed as a sticky, invisible thread traced a line across my palm, sending a manna-driven tingle up my forearm.

The pale flesh of the dead man swelled out and released in time with Harris's breath, slightly quicker now that something unexpected was happening. I fought to stay still, to not interact with the manna thread in any way. Again the voice, both from Guyer as she translated and the speaker on the wall, a single shattered word, "Reprisal."

A howl of static burst from the speakers, so loud that I clapped my hands over my ears and backed away. The rushing swirling buzz of static mixed with the band's rehearsal, disco beats and pulsing rhythms filling the air and numbing my mind. Sudden pressure cloaked my body, as if I'd plunged to a great depth, accompanied by a painful chill that bore through me. The shivering was profound and immediate. But even that paled to the hunger. I recognized the feeling instantly, the manic appetite that came with consuming manna threads. But I hadn't drawn on the threads around Bobby—I *knew* I hadn't. And Harris had been using traditional manna. Everything I'd learned told me that I should be fine. But I wasn't. I felt angry, even betrayed, though I couldn't say why. The whole situation was on the edge of spiraling out of control.

Desperate to ground myself, I focused on the chittering buzz that echoed all around me. The monitor continued to blare the rehearsal, but the buzz was a scalpel and the music offered no more resistance than Bobby's silk shirt had to the killer's blade. The sound wasn't normal, wasn't natural. It was a hundred whispering voices emerging from my dreams and bringing my terrors to reality. And it had rung in my ears since I first discovered my strange bond with manna. But now it was also accompanied by a perverse relief. Because for the first time, I wasn't going through it alone.

Whatever the source of the sound, it was audible to everyone in that room.

Kearn's body trembled, then shook. Harris stepped forward, accompanied by Guyer, both of them weaving their hands in the air, making manna connections and chanting words of focus. Behind me came pounding, and voices raised in alarm. Then the buzzing cut off abruptly, and the resulting quiet was overwhelming and off-putting, like the sudden silence of a home plunged into a power outage.

But it was short-lived, shattered by a series of pops, like an invisible bouncer cracking his knuckles. I glanced around, uncertain of where the sound came from. A moment later it came again, an echo that was louder than the original. This time, it was accompanied by a ripple of motion across the victim's torso. I raised my hands but stayed rooted to the spot. Something was going horribly wrong.

The buzzing swelled once more, quieter now, but sharper, more focused. There was a sound like balloons popping, and the crooked white tips of Bobby Kearn's ribs tore out of his back. They pierced the fabric of his shirt and stretched outward in a rough circle, like ornaments on a grotesque crown. With no heartbeat to supply pressure, the blood didn't squirt, but it did drip, and was flung from the jagged ribs as they flapped and strained. A spray of droplets struck my cheek, but I couldn't look away. I was dimly aware of shouts and pounding behind me, the noise muffled by the waves of cold and the buzzing that echoed in my ears. The room hummed with pent-up power, and the broken ribs pushed further out, extending from the dead man's back until it seemed their full length was exposed to the light. But even then it didn't stop. The ribs kept growing, spreading and unfurling like skeletal wings.

Impossibly, the corpse rose off the ground. Its back rose first, as though being tugged by an invisible rope. The body hovered, the tips of its fingers and single bare foot kissing the floor. With the ribcage protruding from its back, the broken curve of the body folded in on itself. Then, with a flap of its skeletal wings, it shot upward. Another painfully loud burst of static accompanied the motion, and Harris threw back his head and howled, his voice echoing in the air and over the loudspeakers. The corpse of Bobby Kearn stretched and jerked, looming over us as he hung near the ceiling. I felt like an ice hare, frozen in place as a great bird of prey descended from the sky.

The body darted forward, arms raised, straight at me. I stood rooted to the spot, staring stupidly as the body bore down, accelerating toward me until a police baton flashed across the room, connecting with the thing's temple and snapping the head to one side. Jax slammed into my ribs, lifting me up and dropping me to the floor as it hurled past us.

The buzzing ceased completely, and there was no noise to cover the wet thump of the body striking the floor, a toy dropped by a forgetful child. The tension in the air released, and Harris took a loud, shaky breath. It was over.

A loud crash behind me caused us to turn. The door flew open, shattered latch swinging loosely in the frame. The patrol officer and a pair of security guards filled the doorway, eyes glued on the grotesque heap of bones and blood in the corner of the room.

4

GUYER WHEELED ON THE INTRUDERS. "What the Hells are you doing!"

Across the room, Harris stared at Bobby Kearn's twisted remains. The impossibly long ribs had folded in on themselves, draping over the corpse like the wings of a sleeping bird. Harris looked unsteady, and Jax supported him with one hand as he guided the DO away from the body.

I knew we had to get control of the situation, but I couldn't make myself turn from the sight in the corner. As far as I knew, there was only one recorded instance of a body transforming like that after death. The previous time had been a few weeks earlier, and I'd been to blame—that body had transformed when I'd accidentally tapped into the invisible threads of magic connected to his body, so similar to the threads that now hummed in the air around us. Had I done this? Was it about to happen again? Afraid to move, I stood where I was and pressed my hands over my eyes, the stubs of my two missing fingers grazing my lips. I tasted blood. The drummer's blood.

My stomach clenched and I stumbled toward one of the mirrored dressers. In the light-rimmed reflection, my face was speckled with red gore thrown off by the corpse's pseudo-wings. I grabbed a random piece of clothing from the wardrobe and dragged it across my flesh, doing my best to scour away the tainted liquid. It clung to my cheeks, old acne scars holding on to the dead man's blood. I scrubbed harder. Behind me, the argument between Guyer and the security guards was getting more heated. I wasn't sure if the security guys had been friends of Kearn, or if they were driven by a more primitive sense of disgust at what they'd seen. The patrol cop, Worthington, did his best to lower tempers and justify his intrusion.

"There was—there was screaming," he said. As if divination rituals normally were performed with tea and polite conversation.

One of the security guards stood staring at the body, but the other had already taken two strides toward the exit.

"Stop!" I barked it out, and the guard's head snapped around.

"We gotta tell someone." The man was plaintive, the desperate tone of someone who wanted to wash his hands of responsibility, and forget what he'd seen. That was fine by me.

"You already told someone. You told us, and we're dealing with it." I softened my voice and walked toward them with my arms out wide, like a shepherd guiding a flock. "You interfered with a police ritual in progress, but we're gonna let that slide." With gentle herding gestures, I was able to usher them to the door and into the hallway.

"You're going to let it slide?" The other guard, the one who'd initially looked away from the body, spoke up. "What about whatever the Hells those sorcerers were doing in there? You going to let *that* slide, too?"

"Let us do our job, and we'll let you get back to yours." I pulled the door shut, but with the damaged latch, it began to swing open once more.

"And what, exactly," a new voice interrupted, "is your job?" Vandie Cedrow had appeared in the hallway, along with a few more security personnel. This was going from bad to worse. She peered at my face, her eyes tracing the streaks of blood I'd missed when cleaning up. "Because from what I see, you don't have any idea what's going on in here."

Cedrow's appearance was a reminder that the entire security crew answered to her. Big events would frequently have a few off-duty cops working security. But the selling point of the festival had been providing employment for furloughed roughnecks. And the fact that the Titanshade PD didn't have jurisdictional authority was a plus for festivalgoers who wanted to consume substances without being hassled. In short, we were on our own.

The door opened and Harris slipped through to stand at my side, one hand on the knob, holding the door closed. But even that brief opening had given Vandie a glimpse of Bobby's transformed body. She turned away, blinking rapidly as the color drained from her face.

"Divination isn't pretty," said Harris. "It's not sweet and sentimental like it is on the TV cop shows. It's difficult and painful, and it's a private experience for the victims."

I had to hand it to Harris, he was really selling the idea. Even the guards who'd been inside the room looked like they were having second thoughts. Of course, I knew that he was exaggerating. What happened to Bobby Kearn was a long way from normal. The closest I'd ever seen had been a man named Dale Turner I'd found dying in an alley. When I tried to come to his aid, his body had warped beneath my hands. But those changes were a faint shadow of the monstrous transformation we'd just witnessed.

Cedrow straightened her shoulders, drew a breath, and turned back to face us. When she did, I felt a pair of fragile threads brush my shoulder, stretching from her to the door, and the murdered drummer beyond. I didn't know what had happened to poor Bobby Kearn, or what had transformed and mutilated his corpse. But it sure as Hells looked like Vandie Cedrow was involved.

"We'll need you to help cordon off this hallway," I told her, and indicated the guards who'd arrived with her. "Station someone at either end of the hall."

The set of her jaw said she was ready to argue further, but I was saved when one of Dinah McIntire's assistants jogged up to her. "Miss Cedrow? Can you come to the stage, please?"

With a half-concealed snarl, Vandie waved the security guards into place, then turned and followed the assistant back into the maze of tented corridors.

I looked at the two guards who'd come into the room. "We're going to need to get statements." Their faces dropped, and I added, "Don't worry, it'll be painless."

The newly arrived security guards had followed Vandie's command and moved to the far end of the hall. That was good.

"You," I said, pointing at Worthington. "Find an empty room. If there isn't an empty room, then claim one and empty the people out of it."

The patrol officer nodded, and set off with the two witnesses in tow.

That left me alone with Harris. I eyed the sorcerer. Some life had returned to his face, and he seemed steadier on his feet than he had in the aftermath of the transformation.

"I should debrief them," he said. "We need to know if they saw something that might be useful," he glanced over his shoulder, "for figuring out whatever the Hells that was."

I opened the door to the crime scene and asked Jax to accompany Harris.

"Yeah, sure," said Jax. "I could use a minute out of here, anyway."

As Jax passed me, I entered the crime scene with my eyes on the floor, bracing myself to view the carnage once more. I swung the door shut, but it didn't quite catch on the broken latch. I half stepped toward it, meaning to shut it and protect the scene from any more prying eyes.

"Where do you think you're going?"

I turned, task forgotten.

Guyer stood over the body, her face still speckled with blood. She jabbed a finger at the transfigured remains. "Was that you?"

"Are you kidding?"

"Was that you?"

"No!"

"You don't have to hide it," she said. "We'll figure it out. But it's dangerous. Look at what just happened."

"If you're looking for someone to blame for batshit magic, why don't you start with the two sorcerers in the room?"

"The last time I saw a dead body transform, it was one of your cases." She stepped forward. "That man changed while you were tending his wounds."

"Dale Turner." I'd gone to his aid before I understood my effect on magical bonds. "And I remember that you spent a lot of time convincing me that I didn't have anything to do with it. That it was all a coincidence."

Guyer crossed her arms, slender wrists disappearing beneath the soft fabric of her robes. "A good cop knows when to admit she was wrong."

I grimaced, and looked at our reflections in the mirror. Just like Kearn would have done as a killer slipped toward his back. A few weeks ago, I'd have welcomed her acceptance. I practically begged for it. But since then I'd learned more about what I was experiencing, and I knew that I had to keep it secret, at least until I knew I was safe from discovery by the government. And that meant that no one else on the force could know about me, and what I could do.

I grabbed a decorative scarf off the wardrobe and held it out. "Here. You've got stuff on you."

She took the scarf and dabbed at her blood-streaked face.

"Carter, look . . ." Her voice softened. "I was wrong. We both know what you did two weeks ago." She didn't need to go into details. The confusion and chaos of that election eve had been captured by television crews and broadcast across the nation. Most people watching would have assumed any unnatural events were the result of the two sorcerers dueling on a rooftop. Guyer had guessed the truth. So I clenched my jaw and doubled down.

"I didn't do anything. Then or now." Lies are best served with a twist of truth.

She scowled, her grip on the scarf tightening. "This is bullshit, and you know it."

A different voice answered on my behalf. "It's not."

Guyer and I both turned. Jax had returned, slipping silently through the unlatched door. He shut it now, with a click that commented on my failed attempt to close it earlier. Back to the door, he stood with hands on hips, glowering at Guyer.

"You don't know what you're talking about," he said.

Guyer raised her hands. "Ajax—"

"You weren't there," he said. "But I was, fighting for my life while you were sitting across town, trying to make out the details on a television."

She barely started to shake her head before he continued.

"I saw it happen. The water creature and the clay transformation.

All of it. It was . . ." He gathered himself. "It was a nightmare. Like this," he nodded toward the body, "and you don't expect all of us to blame you for this, do you?"

"Well," I said, "maybe some of us do blame her for it."

"Is this how you want to play it?" A muscle along her jaw twitched as she stared me down. "Do you really want to piss off the one person willing to help you out?"

I shrugged. I'd spent most of my life doing exactly that.

The indifference seemed to be the final straw. Guyer drew to her full height and walked out, slamming the door behind her. I rolled onto my heels and swallowed, looking sidelong at Jax, not quite having the courage to face him directly. Every reason I'd given myself for not confiding in him the last few weeks came rushing back, but now, instead of seeming like reasonable, rational ideas, they dripped with self-pity and deceit. My partner had gone to the mat for me, and I'd left him hanging without the information he needed to make an honest decision.

I cleared my throat and glanced around quickly, verifying that we were alone.

"So," I managed.

"So."

I had to tell him. No matter how stupidly dangerous it was, I had to tell him.

"Guyer's wrong about this," I indicated the mangled body in the corner, "but not about everything." I stood as straight as I could. "I've got something going on, and I don't fully understand it."

"I know."

"You need to understand—" I cut off, as my brain caught up with my mouth, processing what he'd said. "Wait. You what?"

Jax let out a series of exasperated clicks. "I'm not clueless. I knew something was going on, even if I didn't know what. Besides," he shoved his hands into his pockets, "you kept trying to tell me you felt something, and every time you did, I told you it was in your head. I don't entirely blame you for holding your cards tight."

"Thanks."

"I don't entirely *not* blame you either. We all need friends, Carter. I don't know why you always make it difficult for people to help you out."

I looked at Bobby Kearn, at the coagulated gore and monstrous, skeletal wings. Had I done that? Would I do it again? And what would happen when the people in the halls of power realized that I represented an unknown force? I held in a shudder, and faked a smile. The walls were closing in on me, and I had to readjust my thoughts about who'd realized I had a secret. I needed a moment on my own.

"I'll be right back." I headed for the door. "I'm gonna go find the communications station."

"What are you doing, Carter?"

I didn't answer. I'd almost made it to the door when he spoke again, his voice louder, commanding.

"You need to make peace with Guyer."

I paused, but shrugged off the suggestion. "We need to radio this in, and get the techs back out here."

"Okay, fine. But you'll have to tell them why." He pointed a thumb at Bobby Kearn's body. "And we can't talk about this over open air."

I grunted. There were no phone lines this far from the city, so any message sent from the rig would be overheard by both the communications staff and anyone who happened to be tuned in. "I'll take the snow-runner back south far enough to get a signal on police band."

"Right. But there's something else." Jax wove a whistle in between his words, in an attempt to calm me. "One of the DOs will have to call this in to ARC division."

That also made sense. Arcane Regulation and Containment teams had been instituted after the manna strike to deal with events that indicated manna usage. They'd definitely need to be brought up to speed on this situation. "So?"

"So, Harris is going to want to stay with the body. And we need a DO to make that call."

I ground my teeth and wished that I couldn't see where he was headed. He still felt the need to say it out loud.

"You need to make peace with Guyer, because you and she are about to take a long drive together."

AS MUCH AS I'D DISLIKED Ajax's insistence on a disco soundtrack for the ride out, the grating silence with Guyer was worse. We drove south on the ice plains, the rumble of the snow-runner's tracks generating not quite enough rhythm to forget my troubles.

I turned on the radio to distract from the uncomfortable silence. The DJ was between tracks, talking about the concert and the other major news, the arrival of the Barekusu caravan. I reached for the tuner, but Guyer stopped me. "I want to hear this."

I dropped my hand. The reception faded in and out, but the story was simple enough to follow. The city was about to receive a visit from a large caravan of Barekusu. I'd seen them on the news, a long column of pilgrims, each of them the mass of two or three humans, thick layers of ice clinging to the long hair covering their bodies as they made the impossibly difficult trek by foot. Barekusu rarely traveled by any method other than walking, devouring the distance between their stops with long quadrupedal strides as their delicate sly hands stroked their fur and plucked the hair that made their fortunes. This caravan was of particular note, as at its head walked Weylan, one of the most prominent guides on Eyjan. There were other religious leaders who matched his stature, but it was hard to find one this side of the equator.

Halfway to the city limits I stopped, idling the vehicle as I tried the police band. It squealed a protest, but after repeated attempts, the voice of a dispatcher called a response. "SR-212 go ahead." The dispatcher had the brisk, clipped tones of someone accustomed to juggling a dozen potential emergencies.

Releasing the talk button, I glanced at Guyer. "You okay going second?"

She indicated her acceptance with a nod.

"We need a rush sheet on the 187 decedent," I said, not naming the victim. Open air communication was frequently monitored by reporters, or anyone with a police band radio. "Notify on secure channel." There were a few bands not accessible on civilian police monitors.

"Copy that. Channel L7 for further information."

The static pulsed, and interference shattered the dispatcher's voice. A tinny singing came through, bleed-over from another radio band that shouldn't have been possible—emergency bands are far enough removed from public airwaves specifically to prevent that from happening.

There was a familiarity to the rise and fall of the static's hiss that chilled my blood. A muffled buzzing, as if someone were trying to smother a beehive with a pillow. When the dispatcher's voice came back, I asked if they'd heard it, too.

"Static," they said, as if it were the most normal thing in the world. I put it out of my mind as I handed the radio over to Guyer and waited for the results of the pull sheet.

Guyer thumbed the talk button. "Dispatch, can you get Captain Auberjois on that secure channel as well?"

Auberjois was the Arcane Regulation and Containment team coordinator. Since the rediscovery of manna, the media had stoked fears of manna-wielding magicians posing a threat to the public. The reality was that manna was far too precious a resource to be used to mug passersby for pocket change. But when the sorcerous duel between Ambassador Paulus and the murderer dubbed "The Jaw-Stealer" appeared on live television, the mayor's office had passed the word to the brass back at the Bunker: the ARC teams were here to stay.

I flipped to L7 and we sat in silence, listening to the ping of the engine, until a dual-toned male voice came over the air. "Auberjois here."

Guyer relayed the importance of the events without disclosing any of the more salacious details. Even the Bunker's communications room wasn't immune to stray whispers. She used terms like "corporeal displacement" and "unanticipated occult surge" to describe the events we'd seen at the oil rig. But it seemed to get the point across.

When she was done, Auberjois said, "That's enough. DO Guyer, I'm placing you on this case as support for DO Harris. Wait on the rearrival of a tech team to process the change in the crime scene, then oversee the relocation of the body back to custody. It's vital to clear the scene ASAP." There was a static-filled pause. "Manna expenditure authorized as you and Harris see fit."

The idea of a sorcerer who suspected my involvement being given a blank check on her investigation wasn't good news. It was clear that Jax was right—I'd have to make peace with Guyer one way or another.

After Auberjois signed off, Dispatch came back with info on Bobby Kearn's record. He didn't have anything on file in Titanshade proper, but they were putting in a request to his last known address in Cloudswar. Expected delivery time of two or three days. Cross-department cooperation at its finest.

"Copy that," I said, and glanced at Guyer. "You need anything else?"

She shook her head, looking out the window, her eyes tracing the swirl of snow and sleet across the ice plains in the rapidly fading afternoon daylight.

I revved the engine and turned the snow-runner around for the return trip to Shelter in the Bend, calculating how best to break the silence.

It turned out that I didn't need to.

"I've been wondering," she said, "how much of your hard-luck persona is an act?"

"Hard-luck?" I kept my hands easy on the wheel.

"The 'poor me' angle you pull all the time. How much of that is an act, and how much is you actually believing that you're the victim in all of this?"

I scratched my nose, eyes still on the almost-invisible white horizon. "The only victim I saw today was a Gillmyn with knife wounds in his back."

"As long as I've known you—"

"Which is what, two months?"

"Three." She tugged on her coat zipper, pulling it halfway open then closed. "Feels longer, though."

Her coat was rugged and well-worn, with reinforced patches on the shoulders and elbows, far nicer than the ones provided to us by the TPD. I wondered why a divination officer would spring the cash on something like that. She was far more likely to be mingling in the warmer zones closer to the Mount, where the geo-vents were more densely packed, the cost of living was sky-high, and the deaths were considered more urgent to solve. Then again, Guyer never had been one for sticking to convention and safety.

"So." She settled further into her seat. "Tell me, how much of your beleaguered detective act is real, and how much is a defense mechanism?"

"Defense mechanisms would require a plan. I'm more of a figure it out over a beer and a sandwich kind of guy," I said. "I just move forward, doing the best I can."

"Oh, sure." She tapped the nails of one hand against the window, a rat-tat-tat that kept time to the rumble of the snow-runner's treads. "You're practically an open book."

"Pretty much," I said.

"Too bad about the typos."

"Cute." I tried changing the subject. "What do you think about the victim?"

"I think he's dead." She still watched the featureless ice plains roll by, only occasionally broken by the dark gray of a rock outcropping thrust up from the freeze, or the even more infrequent shape of a waypoint shed. "I think he was murdered, and someone prevented Harris from figuring out who did it. What I'm trying to decide," she turned to me, "is whether someone did that on purpose, or accidentally."

"You think someone influenced the manna connection between Harris and the victim's body?" I asked.

"Could be," she said. "Or it could've been someone closer. Someone who didn't mean to have that effect."

It wasn't exactly a subtle accusation. Okay, I thought, here goes.

"You know when I came to you, telling you that I could affect manna?"

"Yeah." She looked at me from the corner of her eye, still tugging on her coat zipper. "You claimed you could boost the magic that ties my baton to my brooch pin. It didn't seem to work."

"No," I agreed. "It didn't." Because that link had been made with official department-issued manna, stolen from the belly of an unfortunate whale a century or more ago. I'd learned the hard way that my connection was only with "next gen" manna pumped from below ground, the first manna source found since whales had been hunted to extinction. A discovery that had turned my life upside down.

"Because I thought what you claimed is impossible. But then I saw you on television, fighting beside Ambassador Paulus."

"Not beside her," I said. "We had a common enemy. That's all."

"She's a powerful sorcerer."

I didn't respond. I'd seen evidence of Paulus's strength firsthand, so close that it had almost cost me my life. If Gellica, Paulus's lieutenant, hadn't intervened, it likely would have been the end of my story. I owed Gellica my life.

Guyer was still talking. "But even a sorcerer that powerful has limits. And what she did, turning a man into clay? That's impossible, too. Unless her magic was boosted somehow."

"And?"

"And how do you think that happened?" She stared at me as I drove.

I swallowed, ignoring the bitter taste in my mouth. But there was no avoiding this. If Jax had figured out that I was keeping my connection to next gen manna a secret, then there'd be no keeping it from a smart and determined DO like Guyer.

"That was me," I said. "Not all of it, but . . . yeah. That was me."

"I need to know more than that."

"Okay."

"I need to know what you can do, why you can do it—"

"Okay."

"I need dates and times and something I can wrap my head around—"

"Okay! Imp's blade, I get it. I'll tell you all about it. I don't have all the answers you want, but I'll give you what I have." I puffed out my cheeks and exhaled. "You'd think the least you could do would be to wait until you could buy me a meal while we talk."

"I owe you a beer and a sandwich. Duly noted. Now keep talking."

The tent-draped shape of Shelter in the Bend was approaching fast.

"Whatever it is, it happened at the manna strike," I said. "With Vandie's uncle."

"Harlan Cedrow."

"Yeah." I clenched my left fist, missing the feel of my pinkie and ring fingers. "Since then I can feel the threads between enchanted items. I can pull on those connections, drawing energy out and dumping it into others. Don't ask me how, because I don't know."

She blinked, swallowed, then blinked again. She shook her head slightly, and seemed to struggle for words. "That's . . ."

"Impossible, I know. You told me the same thing a few weeks ago, before you sent me home like a kid making up stories in class."

"I was going to say hard to wrap my head around. The idea of sensing the actual connections between manna-bound objects is . . ." She shook her head.

"Whatever. When I first came to you I didn't understand that I only had a connection to next gen manna. Traditionally sourced manna I've got no ability to affect."

"That's why you couldn't affect my baton." She looked thoughtful. "But say I'd recharged that link with a bit of next gen manna. Could you reach over right now and alter it?"

I glanced at her. "Not while I'm driving."

"Why? Is it difficult?"

"Dangerous. Consuming. And," I hesitated, "it isn't something I understand. So I don't like the idea of being, I don't know, frivolous with it."

"Okay," she said, and something in her voice made me believe it. "But later, we'll have to do it."

When I didn't respond, she pointed at the waypoint shed, a wood and concrete shack with a steeply angled roof and chimney, barely big enough for two people. "Have you ever spent time in one of those things?" They were scattered along the ice roads, oases of shelter for any travelers unlucky enough to have a broken-down vehicle.

"Yes. Overnight."

She frowned, as though my tone had been dour enough to short-circuit any follow-up questions.

"I'll tell you the story sometime," I said, "in exchange for a beer and a sandwich."

Guyer's lips quivered as she held in a chuckle. We weren't back to where we needed to be, but we'd at least called a ceasefire.

A temporary peace was okay. I'd take that as a win.

Arriving back at the concert site, we parked in a side lot populated by a number of bulky box trucks. Vandie Cedrow's work fleet, I assumed. Unlike the professional touring buses and semitrailers belonging to the bands playing the festival, most of the box trucks had clearly been bought used, with overly clean outlines of recently removed business logos.

From there we flagged down a worker and pressed him into being our guide. Following his lead, we entered through a cleverly disguised tent flap intended only for staff use. I filed the entrance away in my head, thinking it might be of future use, as our new guide led us through the mazes of tent corridors. But it was a lost cause. The simple map in my head didn't come close to capturing the labyrinthine chaos, and I was lost long before our guide delivered us to the room that held Kearn's body. Ajax and Harris were holding a hushed conversation by the closed door. Jax waved a hello, and Harris beamed at us.

I chewed my lip and mentally reviewed what we had to work with. A body transformed in death, making it useless for forensic purposes. A crime scene stripped of its physical objects of interest, with only a carbon copy of the tech report listing what had been sent back to town. We had two divination officers, two Homicide detectives, and one patrol cop, all at a potential madhouse if the dancers, builders, and associated hangers-on got wind of the state of Bobby Kearn's corpse. A murder was bad enough—word of what had happened afterward would push tensions even higher. Of course, there was no reason not to start canvassing potential witnesses, assuming we could find them.

I glanced over my shoulder, down the tented corridor. "This place is a warren of tunnels, wrapping through the existing rig buildings. I can't even get my head around the layout."

"I know." Jax tapped my shoulder with a thickly folded stack of papers. "That's why—"

"We need to know where the physical buildings are, as well." I pointed at the closed door to the murder scene. "What's on the other side of that far wall? Could something have been moved between rooms? What if there's something messing with the DOs' magic from over there? We have to assume that we're looking for a sorcerer as much as we're looking for a killer."

"Carter . . ."

"We need to talk to the contractors. Whoever's building the stage and setting up the tents. They'd have to know where everything was in order to build the series of tents, and they'd never have thrown it away—even if it's trashed, there's a blueprint around here somewhere."

Jax let out a series of exasperated whistles and clicks. He waved the paper he was holding and said, "We got it."

"We went and talked to the construction crew." Harris patted Ajax on the back. "Turns out this guy is a bigger hero around here than I thought."

Although my partner's jaw was rigid and expressionless, his eyes crinkled with amusement. "Apparently I had my photo in the paper often enough that they recognized me."

"Good for you, kid." I twirled my fingers, hurrying him along. "Now let's see that map."

Not willing to reenter the crime scene, we crouched down where we were. Jax spread the blueprints over the floor, flattening the folds the best we could and ignoring the mystery stains that ringed the edges.

"We came through this entrance." Jax drew the nub of his pencil eraser across the main entry hall and the winding tented tunnels we'd traversed, ending at one of the oil rig outbuildings that had been consumed by the tents. "And we're here."

"So the double lines are the preexisting structure," I said, "and the singles are the tents . . ."

Guyer reached past us both and traced a well-manicured nail along a particularly serpentine path.

"If someone was panicked, and wanted to get out as fast as possible, this is the most direct route and takes them past the fewest doors." She tapped the other outbuilding.

"That's not the only connection," said Jax.

"But it is the only one that doesn't traverse an open, public space." Guyer indicated the larger areas off the route she'd indicated. "Whoever killed Kearn wouldn't have wanted to cross though a potential crowd, especially if they were marked with blood or carrying a weapon."

Harris grinned at Guyer. "There was no weapon recovered on the scene."

I pulled the techs' report out and riffled through the carbon paper once more. "That's right. There was almost nothing in the victim's pockets. Only unusual items on the floor were some Black Gold candy bar wrappers."

"Killer with a sweet tooth?" asked Jax.

"Or a litterbug," I said.

Worthington flagged us down as we approached the end of the hallway. He nodded at the pair of rooms where the security guards had been sequestered. "These guys are getting antsy. When are you gonna cut them loose?"

We didn't have any reason to hold them, other than the fact that we wanted to keep them from panicking others and Vandie Cedrow had grudgingly given her assent to having them sit for a time.

Guyer sighed. "I'll go talk to them. It'll be useful to know what they thought they saw, and I'll point out they're getting paid to sit around for a few hours."

Harris started to protest, but she waved him off. "I need a break from you boys, anyway. I'll catch up with you when I'm done."

She slipped past Worthington and into the first of the rooms. Ajax, Harris, and I made our way back through the maze of corridors, following the lights and billowing tent fabric until we came to the spot Guyer had indicated. Here the tents expanded into an area large enough to cover another of the rig's outbuildings. We headed toward the door of the buildings, but I slowed as I spotted a human flipping through a call sheet and munching on a candy bar as he meandered down the hall. The wrapper was rolled back, but the *-OLD* of the logo was enough to draw my attention.

"Hey buddy," I called. It took a second call before the roadie noticed me. "Where'd you get the snack?"

He glanced at the Black Gold candy bar, as if he'd forgotten it was there. "This? Sheena had a bunch."

"Where is she? I'm dying for something and I'm not gonna get a chance to eat anytime soon."

He blinked, mind clearly debating whether it was considered a social failure to direct a cop toward a friend, even for a snack. "There's a cafeteria—"

"That's for staff only, and the vending machine's out of order." I layered on the lies before ending with a plea. "C'mon. Be a pal, huh?"

He pointed toward a tent face I'd missed before, nestled against the side of the outbuilding.

"Thanks," I said, and waved toward my companions. We had a new destination.

WE APPROACHED THE ZIP-UP WALL, the conversation inside clearly evident from our position as we approached.

Unsure where to knock, I tapped the metal door zipper and announced ourselves. "Titanshade PD. We need a word with you."

Silence, then a deep voice demanding, "About what?"

It was a foolish question, considering that a murder investigation was in full swing. I answered with a single word.

"Bobby."

There was whispered conversation, then quick, light steps across the plywood flooring as someone approached the door and drew open the zipper. A young Gillmyn's face appeared, below a head fin that quivered with nervous energy. "Yes?"

Jax took over. "We're looking into Bobby's death." He'd latched on to the success I'd had using the victim's first name. A reminder to any potential witnesses that the victim was a real person, and the real focus of the conversation, not the resultant investigation or whatever short-term concerns they might have had. "Can we come in and talk?"

We'd already been given permission to search the property, but it's always a good idea to get permission to walk into a new area where someone feels defensive. Playing the psychology of every potential suspect or witness is a key part of uncovering the truth.

"I don't know . . ." The man glanced back into the room, lean corded muscles dancing along his neck and shoulder beneath his tight shirt.

"We can talk right here," I said, "but that means anyone walking by will overhear it."

It may have been enough to convince them, but Harris chimed in. "I'm sure you want to help us find out what happened to your friend."

I suppressed a wince. I didn't like dropping in the term "friend" quite yet. It carried implications that could be easily misconstrued.

The man frowned and his shoulders inched back, as if he were moving from uncertainty to anger, but he stepped away from the door. His shirt was tucked into pants that were tight at the waist and flared dramatically at the legs. The tailoring meant that the fabric echoed and amplified his movements as he stalked back into the room. He moved with a dancer's grace.

The other occupant was farther in the room. She was also a Gillmyn, and also had a head fin. They looked to have been hired at least in part because of their physical similarities. All the better for symmetrical dance routines.

The pair of Gillmyn eyed us, curious and cautious, the way people tend to look at cops when they think that if they say the wrong thing they'll end the conversation in handcuffs. Sometimes that's for a good reason. Often times it's not—we're not out to bust people for standing around and talking, we're interested in the dangerous sources of violence and confusion that can take a person's sanity and crumple it like yesterday's newspaper. Whether these two had something to share with us or not still stood to be seen.

I walked to the far side of the tented room, poking at the billowing fabric with the edge of my notepad. Harris and Jax took up seats closer to the dancers, all the better to peer into their eyes and track their stray glances. It was clear that I'd be playing the heavy from across the room.

"So," Jax began, "you've heard what happened to Bobby?"

The woman nodded. "Everyone has by now."

"What's your name, and when exactly did you hear?"

"Sheena Kathreese," she said. "I don't know when. Do you?" She looked at her companion, who shook his head with vigor, as if that would make him seem more cooperative. It was too late for that. He'd reacted poorly when we introduced ourselves, and he leaned in and angled his body protectively when Jax asked for the woman's name. Everything about the guy screamed that he was hiding something, and damn nervous about it.

"And what was your name, sir?"

"Michael." He gave no last name. That may have been because he used a single name, a Mollenkampi tradition that had spread to many other Families in the AFS, or because he was being coy. My money was on the latter.

"Michael what?"

"Kathreese," he said. His voice ascended at the end of each sentence, turning every statement into a question.

"He's my brother," Sheena said, her arms pulled tight to her body. As if she were cold or scared.

"Okay." I made a show of writing down their names, pressing home that this was official business. "So, Sheena and Michael, you're not sure when you found out, but can you tell me what you heard?"

Michael said, "We heard he was dead, but, you know, not in some kind of natural way? More like something had happened to him?"

Harris leaned forward, face serious. "We just came from the room where Bobby passed." He and Jax kept using the victim's name. If the witnesses cared for the decedent, then that would make them more inclined to help us solve the case. If they were guilty, it would burn their conscience or raise their anger. Anything to help personalize the crime was a benefit.

Michael tossed his head, fin rising and falling, and his shoulders twitched as he spoke. For a dancer who crossed the room with a cat-like grace, he had a certain jerkiness about him as he sat on the couch. That could be from a guilty conscience, or it could be simply his nature. "We don't really know him?"

It was an obvious lie, and that was the wrong move. Harris sat back and crossed his legs, billowing his cloak with a flourish that made a show of the runes that danced in and out of sight along its edges, symbols of his power. The dancers blanched, and I knew how they felt.

Sheena looked to her brother. The buccal sacs along her neck flared, and her breathing was quick, shallow, and nervous. Sheena was the weak link. And weak links were worth testing.

"We've been out here for hours," I said, "and we still haven't eaten anything. Any chance one of you has a snack?"

"What?" Sheena sounded confused by my sudden request.

"You know, something to munch on."

Sheena nodded toward the far end of the room. "There's snacks on the dresser."

I strolled in that direction, noting the glass dome and metal base of a gumball machine. I rested my hand on it and looked at Sheena.

"Sweet tooth, huh? You got any candy bars? I like Black Gold."

Michael sprang upright, flipping the low table onto Jax. My partner sprawled backward, head hitting the floor with a crack. I had a moment of alarm, but had to focus on the Gillmyn sprinting in my direction.

The dancer moved with extraordinary grace, every movement fluid as dry snow swirling across ice. He lashed out at Harris, the heel of his hand catching the DO on the jaw, sending him sprawling out of his seat.

To the side, Jax rose on wobbling legs, but managed to drive forward, planting his shoulder into the bigger man's sternum. He hadn't drawn his sidearm, likely not wanting to give the larger Gillmyn the opportunity to wrest it out of his hand. But Michael rolled with Jax's charge, spinning aside and sweeping a leg between my partner's shins. Jax tumbled, prone once again, and Sheena sprang on him, hands scurrying over his chest and struggling to keep him pinned to the ground as her brother charged me.

I didn't draw either, as any shots fired would tear through the tent fabric and endanger anyone in the adjoining rooms or corridors. Instead, I closed my hands around the gumball machine, pulling the glass top from the base and spilling the hard candy spheres across the floor. Michael pulled back, confused, hesitating for a heartbeat before continuing his advance, loose gumballs crunching beneath his heel. But that fractional hesitation was the opening I needed. I hurled the glass globe at Sheena.

Michael's head whipped around, tracing the arc of the glass sphere as it missed his sister by a handbreadth. Sheena reared back, distracted by the globe, and Jax caught her wrist and pivoted, throwing her to the floor. Michael's shoulders and hips aligned with his gaze, all his attention focusing on the sibling he'd been so eager to protect. Perfect.

I closed the gap and swung the metal base as hard as I could, connecting with his upper back, immobilizing one arm and sending him to his knees. I followed up with a strike to his head, a solid thump that dropped him to the floor. Before I could do anything else, Jax was on him, blood dripping from the back of his head.

"Stay down!" he snarled, snaking a pair of cuffs onto the Gillmyn's wrists.

Sheena was the first to start talking.

"He didn't *do* anything." She spoke mostly to herself. Her eyes were downcast, the buccal sacs along her neck deflated.

"Who?" We'd already stabilized the situation and explained her rights, so I was more than happy to let her keep talking.

"Bobby. He was—" Her voice hitched, and she swallowed. She sat on the floor, feet stretched out and hands behind her. A deep breath, then she continued. "He sampled the goods, then finished getting dressed while we talked. I asked for a candy bar. He said no, and I got so damn *angry*."

"That's why you killed him?" said Jax. "Over a candy bar?" His clothes were rumpled, and he swayed slightly on his feet. The tumble with Michael had left him physically scuffed and mentally shaken.

"I don't know. I just . . . did." Her feet tapped together, a staccato rhythm, the dancer trying to find release. I decided to reroute her before she got too distracted.

"You said he sampled the goods. What were you selling him?"

"What everyone wanted when they heard we were coming up here. Snake oil."

I chewed my lip. That explained so much. Snake oil was a modified hallucinogen, cut with just enough black market manna to give it an iridescent sheen. A cheap pipe dream, it had far too little manna to affect users. Unless I was around. Though I couldn't use manna to connect distant objects the way a sorcerer could, I had the unique ability to drain those threadlike connections, then infuse that energy back into another manna thread. If Bobby Kearn had been using snake oil, I may have been involved in his corpse's transformation without knowing it.

I forced myself back into the present. Sheena was responding to Jax, though I'd missed the original question.

"Are you kidding?" She let out a dry chuckle. "The chance to get high with manna? It's too good to pass up. Especially for a celebrity. Remember last year when people were dissolving pearls in wine vinegar and making cocktails? Dinah was all about that."

I had no idea what she was talking about, but then I didn't read celebrity tabloids. Jax, however, seemed to know exactly what she meant. "Are you saying Dinah McIntire wanted snake oil?"

Sheena shrugged. "Maybe. I don't know. I'd never sell straight to her, anyway. That's what Bobby did. He took care of the hookups for everyone. I was trying to get on his good side, you know?"

"Where'd you get the snake oil?"

"One of the security guards. All these oil guys have been out of work, and they're looking for ways to make cash."

"And what's this guard's name?"

"Saul Petrevisch. He hooked us up."

Jax recorded the connection's name.

"Sheena." I squatted down, getting my eyes to her level. "Why did you take the candy bars?"

Her voice dropped lower. "I don't know. I'd been so angry when he said no. So I grabbed all of them after I . . . you know."

Harris exhaled, seemingly more disappointed than disgusted. "You killed a man and stopped for a snack?"

"You don't understand." Sheena blinked away tears. "I wasn't even hungry. I asked for the candy bar because I saw it, and wanted to make conversation. Get on his good side, like I said. But when he said no, it was like . . ."

"Like what?" I said.

"Like I wanted to tear apart the whole world."

Worthington shuffled the prisoners outside, to the back of his snow-runner. Harris headed out as well, so that he could warm up his vehicle. Jax and I stood in the entry area, along with Guyer, all three of us putting on our coats. Across the room, Vandie Cedrow and a crew of burly figures in security jackets stared daggers our way. Never one to shy away from people who hate me, I strolled over.

The guards tightened into a half circle between me and Vandie. I stared past their shoulder muscles at the woman who had bought their loyalty.

"You got your killer." She spoke loudly, putting on a show for her crew. "Now you can get out."

"My job's not done, Miss Cedrow. I need contact information for one of your workers. Saul Petrevisch."

She widened her stance, arms crossed. "Why are you harassing my men?"

"Is Saul one of your men? I was led to believe he'd been let go?"

"He moved on. You want to talk to Petrevisch, go back to the squalor of the city."

She turned away and walked back into the hive of the tents. One by one, the former rig workers followed her. The arrest of out-of-town dancers was one thing, but they had little interest in talking to cops about one of their own.

Eventually, only a single man was left. The wind-battered rigger, Murphy CaDell.

"She's done amazing things, Vandie has."

"Is that so?" I said.

"She's put furloughed rig workers back to work, after the government was happy to let them starve. She's advocating for safety requirements, pensions, and stronger unions. Hells, if it were up to her, she'd rerun all the geo-vents in Titanshade to bring warmth to the outer edges of town. I'm telling you, when the wells open up, they'll be a better, safer place because of Vandie Cedrow."

I glanced down the corridor Vandie had taken. The tent fabric pulsed and fluttered like a living thing. "So about Saul Petrevisch . . ."

"A good worker," he said. "Chemical engineer, before the furloughs. But he struggled with personal issues. I'll send you his information."

I gave him my card. "I'll be expecting it tomorrow morning."

"It'll be there." He dug into a pocket and handed over a card in return. "Be seeing you, Detective."

I stalked back across the room to rejoin my peers. The politicians may have liked the idea of putting furloughed roughnecks back to work, and the concert promoters liked the idea of a setting outside police jurisdiction, but the waters around us teemed with sharks.

"I'm glad to be out of here," I muttered.

Guyer frowned. "Speak for yourself."

"What do you mean?" said Jax. "Everything about this crime indicates Sheena killed Bobby, then got assistance from her brother. Everything backs that up, including Sheena herself." He ran a hand over his head, gingerly probing the damage along his head plates where he'd hit the floor.

"I mean you're the homicide guys. You solve that and go home. My job is to worry about who caused the victim's transformation."

Guyer's eyes were on me as she spoke, and for a long moment I thought we'd have to rehash the whole question again. Then Jax chimed in.

"Do you need help? We can stay if you need us." He winced, and reached a hand to his head plates. The poor SOB needed a doctor, not an all-night hunt for magic.

Guyer's expression softened. "No. But thanks for the offer."

"But—"

"It's Titanshade, Jax. Money and magic outrank simple murder every time." Drawing my coat tighter, I prepared to reenter the frigid cold.

Jax headed out, but I hesitated, catching Guyer's eye once more. "Let's talk about it when we have that beer and sandwich?"

After a moment she gave me a brusque nod. The truce was holding. I could flap my mouth all I wanted, but the truth was that the transformations were far more my problem than hers. I had to find out what had caused that transformation and drag it into the light. Prove that it wasn't me. And to do that, I'd have to track down the man who supplied the snake oil, Saul Petrevisch.

Beyond the entrance, Sheena and Michael were heading back to Titanshade. At least this was one death that hadn't gone unsolved, and one case that we could cross off our list and forget.

That, of course, turned out to be a lie.

7

IT WAS LATE INTO THE night when we arrived back in Titan-shade, but I insisted we head downtown. I'd learned the hard way that it was vital to get paperwork drawn up and done as soon as possible. Jax made an effort to follow me to the Bunker, but I held up an arm.

"Go home, kid. But first, get someone to look at your head. I don't need you bleeding to death and leaving me with even more forms to fill out."

He assured me he would, and left me to finalize the reports that would clear the case to the City Attorney's Office. Already, Sheena and Michael were making their way through the gears of the justice system. It was neither efficient nor pleasant, but it was part of the job.

I ended my day and staggered past the glass doors of the Bunker, waving a hand in the thermal vent by the entrance, mumbling the prayer of departure. *For your suffering, which brings us safety and warmth, we thank you.*

It didn't matter to me if the Titan could hear it, I was grateful for the sacrifice all the same. By the time I got home I wanted nothing more than to feed the cat and drink a beer. I was successful at the former, but my empty fridge meant I went to bed unsatiated and angry.

My dreams that night were full of buzzing, ominous voices echoing from the static. When I awoke, the buzzing was simply my alarm clock's persistent drone and I found that once it was silenced, I could finally get some rest. I stumbled in to the Bunker by late morning, coffee in one hand and newspaper in the other. I wove my way through the hallways of general processing, greeted by the usual array of shouts, screams, swearing, and sobbing. A never-ending fugue of victims lodging complaints and perpetrators being booked. The noise receded as the elevator doors closed and I ascended to the third floor. I made my way down the hall to the Bullpen, the open-office layout space in the center of the Homicide department. It was where Homicide detectives researched, worked the phones, and procrastinated doing their most unpleasant tasks. I took a breath and enjoyed the relative silence. Our victims were silent, the next of kin were visited in their homes. We worked apart from the public, and the only sound of broken lives was our own.

On the edge of the Bullpen I stopped by my mailbox and found a trio of messages. Two were garbage memos, but the third was golden. Saul Petrevisch's contact info had been delivered as promised. I broke into a grin and headed toward the pair of desks that Ajax and I called our own.

It was immediately apparent something was wrong. Instead of his usual tidy stacks of forms and reference material, Ajax's desk was in disarray. As I approached, he crawled out from under the knee well. His head was bandaged, his eyes were wide, and his mandibles were quivering like a junkie in need of a fix.

I set down my paper and inbox messages, and sipped the coffee. "Lose something?"

His eyes darted around the room and he leaned closer before speaking in a low whisper. "My badge."

"Okay." I matched his hushed tone. "Walk me through it."

"I had it at the concert site. I know I had it then. And I always put my badge and gun in a lockbox below my dresser when I go to bed. But this morning I opened the box and only my weapon was in there. I turned my apartment upside down, and the nurses' station said I didn't leave it when I got bandaged. If it's not here, then I lost it in the snow-runner, the bus, or the festival site."

"Was it your real badge?"

He stared at me. "What kind of question is that?"

"Kid, you need to get a copy made. Keep your real shield in a safe at home, and carry the dupe with you."

He glanced around again, as if Captain Bryyh was going to jump out from behind a desk and write him up. "That's not policy, is it?"

Jax was so good at his job, it was easy to forget how fresh he was to the city and the force.

"No, but it's common sense. Look how panicked you are right now."

"Wait, what good would that do? Someone will still be out with my badge."

"Yeah, but anyone can go to a shady pawnshop and pick up a fake badge with a random number on it. Collectors, wanna-bes, you name it. The original shield, though, that's one of a kind. I don't know what the actual penalty for a lost badge is, but it can't be—"

"Ten days suspension and a two hundred tael fine," he said. "I looked it up this morning."

I whistled. "Okay, that's bad. But relax. It's probably at the festival site. You got pretty ruffled during the arrest, and it dropped off your jacket. We'll get it from the old rig worker, CaDell. He's already been helpful."

I dug into my stack of papers on my desk, somehow still messier than Ajax's even after his desperate search, and retrieved the business card Murphy CaDell had given me the night before. It read Director of Operations, Tremby Property Management, with the letters TPM braiding together to form a distinctive logo. But what really caught my eye was the mailing address. "The Estante district. That's a ritzy address for a management company."

Jax snatched the card out of my hand.

"Calm down," I said. "There's no phone service to the rig site. We'll need to radio him, and you don't want to ask for a police shield over the air."

"So what do we do?"

"We'll have to make a trip, or get word to him. But first, we get you covered for today."

He stared at me blankly. "How?"

"We're gonna do like everyone else—go to a shady pawnshop and pick up a fake badge."

Tomorrow's Treasures was a pawn shop on Gaius Street. It was owned and operated by Big Mike, a gregarious fin-headed Gillmyn who'd forgotten more about weapons and antiques than most people learned in a lifetime. He was a source of expertise and information.

When he saw me he flared his buccal sacs and jabbed a finger at the door.

"We're closed!"

Jax shoved his hands in his pockets and looked at me. "A friend of yours?" He was trying to be funny, but the nervous shake in his voice betrayed him.

I gestured at the other shoppers browsing the aisles of used guitars and power tools, trading cards and family heirlooms. "Someone oughta explain that to them."

Mike threw his head back and slammed a palm on the counter. "I'm just pulling your leg! Good to see some of Titanshade's finest in here." Mike always spoke loudly, but this he practically bellowed. From the corner of my eye, I watched a teenager set something back on the shelf and make a path for the exit.

Mike tracked the kid's path until he was out the door, and asked, "What can I do you for, officers?"

"This is my partner," I said.

"No kiddin'." Mike jerked his chin in greeting. "Ajax, right? I recognize you from the papers. What happened to your head?"

"Well, um . . ." Jax touched the bandage on his head, and sounded embarrassed. "A pair of dancers."

"Ah, yeah." Mike nodded sympathetically, hands resting on his belly. "Hit your head on the pole?"

Jax blinked, and I stepped in to salvage the conversation.

"Need a word," I said. "A private word."

"Fine. Reg! Watch the front." He lifted the gate in the counter and let us into the back.

We filed after him into the back, where shelves brimmed with pawned items that hadn't yet been forfeited or claimed. Each once was something that people had desired, maybe loved, now converted into collateral for short-term loans. The city's faded dreams transformed to tomorrow's treasures.

Big Mike guided us through a dented steel door into a cluttered office space. Mike claimed the room's sole chair, while Jax and I hovered, trying not to topple the stacks of merchandise and paperwork.

He looked at me and rubbed his palms together. "Well?"

"Need a dupe made," I said. "Rush job."

Mike waggled webbed fingers. "I'm a little behind."

"So charge a little more." I figured Ajax would see it as an investment. Mike named a figure and Jax agreed without haggling. One more sign the kid hadn't fully caught on to how things work in Titanshade.

"Badge number?"

Ajax hesitated. "It's okay," I said.

My partner shook his head. "Maybe I can get something off the shelf instead?"

"It won't match your badge number."

"I'm not going to keep it," he said. "I won't need it for more than a day."

Mike shrugged. "Suit yourself." He made the words seem more affable than indifferent.

"You got a TPD detective badge sitting around?" I asked.

He huffed, thinking, and I blinked against the sudden swampy odor. "Pretty sure I do." He focused on Jax. "You want me to put out feelers, see if anyone's trying to pawn a legit shield?"

Jax hummed a note of gratitude. "That'd be great."

"Wait here." Mike lifted himself out of the chair with a grunt. "I'll go see what I can turn up."

As he departed, I claimed Mike's vacant seat for my own.

"Once we're done here, we can tie up some loose ends on the Bobby Kearn case."

"What loose ends?"

I pulled out the message from Murphy CaDell that had been waiting in my inbox. "Saul Petrevisch."

Jax rubbed his bandage, probably trying to place the name. "The guy who supplied Sheena and Michael with snake oil?"

"You got it."

"That's not relevant to the murder. The fact that there was a drug buy is important. But where it came from?" He spread his hands. "Why stop there? Are you going to track it back to the driver who smuggled it into town?"

"Trust me, we need to do this." I tapped Saul's name on the message. "How many open cases do we have right now?"

He paused, doing a brief tally. "A half dozen, if you count the CaMachio double homicide as two cases."

"A little on the light side, then. And we're waiting for info or stalled on all of them."

"So?"

"So we've got time." I dropped my voice. "And you wanted me to tell you about any manna-related stuff, right? Well, this is a manna thing."

He looked at me, silent and skeptical.

"We'll just run out, see what Saul has to say for himself, and then we'll look up this property management company and find your real badge. Deal?"

His eyes narrowed. "Fine. But I'm driving, and you're talking."

I spun Mike's desk chair, swiveling around and watching the pawned dreams spin by. "Whatever you say."

After Mike came back with a temporary detective's badge for Jax, we piled back into the Hasam and made our way to the outer rings of Titanshade. Saul Petrevisch lived in Beggar's Delight, a neighborhood near the Borderlands that skirted the edges of town. Here the thermal vents were sparser, resulting in colder temperatures. Less chance of nicking a thermal vent meant taller buildings, since crews could sink footers deeper in the ground, something they'd never be allowed to risk in more well-heated neighborhoods. Disrupting the flow of warmth that kept the city alive would be considered a personal affront to the entire population of Titanshade. In a city known for corruption, there were precious few things that could get a wealthy person thrown in jail; damaging the network of thermal vents that snaked beneath the city streets topped the list.

Traffic was slow, with several roads rerouted to account for the arrival of the Barekusu. Because the geo-vents appeared organically, buildings and blocks were constructed to take advantage of their presence. As a result, streets rarely followed anything resembling a consistent pattern. It was worse in the city center, but even in more leeward areas like Beggar's Delight, streets wound unpredictably, narrowed and widened at random, and terminated in abrupt dead ends. Any amount of road work or detours resulted in traffic jams that took a degree in advanced mathematics and abstract geography to untangle.

We advanced a few car lengths, then came to another stop, this time in front of a television store. The front window displayed a wall of screens, all tuned to the same station. A dozen various-sized images of the same reporter bundled up against the cold, standing in the Borderlands, on the wide streets of Secor Boulevard, where the Barekusu caravan was expected to roll in.

Jax inched the car forward. Another bit of progress, as I stared out the window.

"Not getting that duplicate made," he said. "Does that make me . . ."

"What?"

"I don't know, naive?"

"No, kid. It makes you principled." I rubbed the underside of my chin, looking at my pale reflection in the window, and wondered at the flesh that had grown loose since the days I was young and idealistic like Ajax. "You do what you gotta do. There's worse things in this world than sticking to your beliefs." Beyond my faded reflection people shuffled past the wall of screens, heads down, their breath leaving trails of steam in their wake.

He didn't respond, so I continued. "Look, I've seen cops do terrible things and I've seen cops be braver than anyone would ever give them credit for. Most of us are just trying to get by and make the world a little bit better before we hit retirement."

Jax pointed at a group of kids in matching denim and fur-trimmed leather jackets. They walked with a collective swagger, taking up most of the sidewalk.

"You think they say the same things about themselves?" he asked. "I don't mean the dangerous ones. I mean the small-time criminals we arrest and see back on the streets the next day. You think they're simply trying to get by, seeing terrible things and feeling like the good they do is underreported?"

The teens approached an elderly lady with a walker. As they came up on her, two of the group shoved the others aside to allow her plenty of space to pass unmolested.

I frowned. "I know they do."

Jax gripped the steering wheel, eyes back on the creep of traffic. "I didn't get the dupe made because while I was in that pawnshop I kept hearing my training officer from Kohinoor." Jax had seen his home-town overcome by organized crime and street drugs. "He told us that every dirty cop starts with something small. A free coffee, a better seat at a restaurant. Small things offered as thank-yous. Nothing that'd hurt anyone. But after a while, the cop thinks they *deserve* that coffee, they *deserve* the better seat. And the first time they walk in and they don't get it, they get angry." Jax hummed a low note. "Angry, entitled people with power are dangerous."

"Getting a dupe badge isn't a power trip," I said. "Your original fell out of your pocket, probably while you were arresting a killer. Does a ten-day suspension for that sound fair?"

"No. And free coffee doesn't sound like corruption."

I didn't respond, awkwardly aware of the wallet in my pocket, and the duplicate badge it held.

Jax was the one to break the silence.

"So when you're doing your magic thing," he said. "What exactly can you do?"

I hesitated, gnawing on my bottom lip. But I'd agreed to tell him, and I didn't see any way out of it.

"I mean," he was actually starting to sound excited, "can you fly or turn invisible?"

"Don't be stupid." I made a show of looking at the foot traffic. "So how long do you think the Barekusu will stay? You want to make a wager on when they can't handle this town anymore?"

His windchime laugh was obnoxiously loud in the confined quarters of the Hasam. "Sure, if I was interested in changing the topic. Which I'm not. Tell me what you can do."

"Fine." I stretched my legs as far as possible in the Hasam's tight quarters. "You know how manna connects things, right? Like if you bind a pebble to a boulder, then spin the pebble, the boulder will move, too?"

He nodded. "Or bind the pebble to a hat, and make one as soft or hard as the other. I'm familiar with the concept, Carter."

"Well, there's lines of force that connect them, like threads. Since the manna strike . . . I can feel them."

"Like they're real things?" he said. "I was always taught that connecting threads are a conceptual construct. There's nothing there to interact with. That's what makes magic . . ." He waved a hand, searching for the right word. ". . . magic."

"Hey, you're the one who wanted to hear this," I said. "I was happy to talk about the caravan coming to town. Speaking of which, are you gonna go see them?"

Jax rolled his eyes, as if walking a particularly moody child down a candy aisle. "I'm asking questions because that's how I learn. And to answer *your* question, no, I'm not planning to go see them. I saw a Barekusu caravan once. I think I'll pass on this one." He inched the car forward. "So you can sense the invisible threads of magic. And then what, you can weave them together?"

"No, they stick to me. But back up a minute. You've seen Barekusu in person?" I glanced at him. "When? What's it like?" Nomads, teachers, philosophers, the Barekusu were the eldest of the eight Families, and had introduced each of the other sentient species to the world as they awoke. Traveling in caravans the size of small towns, they had taught the world the One True Path, and helped negotiate peace and prosperity among the other Families. They also made really great sweaters.

"Stop changing the subject. We're talking about you being a secret sorcerer."

"It's not sorcery. Sorcerers create the ties that connect manna-bound objects. I can't do that, but I can feel them, you know?" I shifted in my seat, wishing I hadn't let him drive. "Like spider silk sticking to your hair when you walk through a web." I looked at the thick plates covering his scalp. "Do you need me to explain hair, too?"

"I do not get paid enough for this," he muttered, before raising his voice slightly. "Okay, so you can feel them but not create them. You're like the opposite of a sorcerer."

I opened my mouth, then paused. "I guess so. I hadn't thought of it like that before."

"Okay. I understand that, I think. So what do you do to these threads?"

"The problem's what they do to me," I said. He started to respond, but I cut him off. "If I pull on the threads—or maybe it's more like squeezing on them? It's hard to explain. Anyway, it drains the strength of that manna bond. Everything gets cold, and the world sounds far away. Like being underwater. Then I can redirect that . . ." I shook my head. "That energy, I guess? I don't know what it is, but I can dump it into another manna bond."

"Like a sponge," he said. "Or a battery. You're a battery for magic!"

"Whatever. Anyway, it's your turn," I said. "When did you see the Barekusu?"

"I was on my way home from college," he said. "I'd stopped to get food, and couldn't figure out why the whole town was out on the streets. Then they arrived."

"And?"

"And it was a procession." He showed no sign of elaborating.

"What do you think about them?"

The Barekusu meant a lot of things to different people, and my partner was no exception. Jax had been educated in a religious school, though he focused on political science. I hoped he'd have a unique view on the eldest of the Families.

But instead of answering, he asked, "What do you think they're like?"

"I don't know. They're just people." I rolled down the window and tried to ignore the exhaust fumes. "Quiet, hairy people the size of a pickup truck, but people."

"Wait till you see them up close," he said, indicating the dark shapes on the wall of televisions. "It's a little harder to convince yourself that they're just people then."

"I might do that," I said.

"Gellica could get you in to meet them," he said.

"She and I aren't really communicating right now." Like Guyer, Gellica was another former ally whose trust I'd lost. "Now that I need friends more than ever, I seem to be losing them as fast as I ever have. Maybe it's fate, maybe it's something else. It's impossible to say."

We jerked to an abrupt stop as we were cut off by a dingy white box truck, the panels on the side a slightly different sheen where an old logo had been peeled off. I snarled at Jax. "Shortcuts! You trying to kill me?"

"Right," he said. "Impossible to say why you're losing friends."

At least I could always count on him.

Jax parked the Hasam and turned to me.

"That's everything you want to talk about?"

"No. But that's it for now." Whatever was happening to me, it was complicated by the secrets Gellica and I shared. But her secrets weren't mine to share. Not even with Jax.

"And you don't want to go to anyone about this?"

"I already did. Guyer didn't believe me, until she did, and now she thinks I'm creating chaos in my wake. Gellica knows, but . . ." I rubbed my jaw. "Like I said, the important thing is that this stays between us for right now."

"Just for right now."

"Absolutely."

He looked at me for a long moment, then his eyes wrinkled, as if he was laughing at some private joke. "Let's go follow this lead of yours. The faster we close it out, the faster we can get back to real work."

W E EXITED THE HASAM AND began making our way through the crowd. I pulled a scarf from my overcoat pocket and draped it around my neck. The fog was especially thick, and the chill bit into us as we zigzagged across the blocks to get to our destination. Here at the edges of the city, the fog hit the cold air from the ice plains and froze, turning into small particles of ice that pricked my wrists and neck as they fell to the street, doomed by their own weight.

We had to badge our way in past the patrol on the fringes of the caravan's route. Jax was particularly quick to put his replacement badge back in his pocket. I'd expected to see patrol cops, but as we got closer to the route, the security was military. The soldiers didn't give a damn about investigations or witnesses or laws. We ended up circling around until we found another pair of patrol cops we could badge past.

"Asshole soldiers didn't let us through," I said.

"Screw those guys," one of them said, indicating that we were free to pass with a jerk of his thumb.

I muttered to Jax as we walked. "The military's making a presence in the city itself. As if we didn't have enough trouble getting across town in an emergency. How much of a fight do you think our fine aldermen in City Hall put up over that?"

"From what I read, somewhere between the resistance of a sleeping puppy and a wet paper bag. Read the news sometime," he said. "You're not the only one bothered by it."

I curled a lip. Bothered was one thing. People were *bothered* all the time—they just couldn't be bothered enough to do something about it. Of course, most people didn't have the time or money to make a difference. And the ones who did? They had every reason in the world to leave things exactly as they were.

After an infuriating walk past further checkpoints and milling pedestrians, we entered the building and climbed to the sixth floor of a seven-story walk up. The Borderlands were cold and I was glad for my overcoat, even after six flights of stairs. Our knock was answered promptly by a middle-aged human woman with tears in her eyes.

"I didn't think you'd get here so quick." She stepped back and away from the door. I moved forward but Jax, ever the stickler, asked, "Can we come in?"

She twitched her arms, a hopeless, sad gesture. "Yeah. I guess you're gonna have to."

We followed her inside. I recognized the layout immediately. It was standard enough for a two-room apartment. A separate bedroom and bathroom to the rear, while the common room had a countertop barely big enough for the hotplate and single-basin sink needed to legally qualify as a "kitchenette."

"Why did you think we were on the way?" It was possible that word had gotten back to her about the murder, the arrest, and she'd made the connection.

"I called."

"Who did you call?"

She scrunched her nose. "You."

The woman walked to a wooden chair with one leg held together by packing tape and picked up the telephone receiver from the seat. "They're here."

She hung up and sat down, placing her hands over her mouth. She wore a knit cap, and hair tumbled out on either side, forming side blinders as she stared at a section of carpet a few paces in front of her.

"What, exactly," I said, "did you call in about?"

She pressed the heel of one hand against her jaw. "Shortcuts. Didn't they tell you before they sent you out here?"

I swung out my hands, as if I were helpless in the face of bureaucracy. "Try us again."

"Saulie's dead. Killed."

"Wait, wait, wait . . . Who killed him?"

"Me." She shook her head.

Jax and I shifted our postures immediately. The woman before us didn't seem aggressive, but anyone who mentions in passing that they just got done murdering someone needs to be taken seriously.

"Is that true?" I said. "We don't have time for jokes."

"You think this is a joke?" Her breathing was hoarse, her head cradled in her hands, hair spilling over her face. "Didn't they tell you anything before they sent you out here?"

"We'll need to make a report," I said, picking my way through a minefield. We had no idea how she'd react to any of this, or even if this Saulie person was really dead. "Do you have ID?"

She dug a hand into her back pocket and pulled out a wallet. Jax took it, then tossed it to me.

I glanced at the card. Her name was listed as Donna Raun.

I made my way to the woman, making enough noise to ensure she heard me coming. I didn't want to spook her. "I'm a Homicide detective." I left out my name. With my recent notoriety, there was no reason to make her more uncomfortable or distract her from the information I needed. "You're Donna?"

She nodded, and I asked, "How do you pronounce your last name?"

Always start them off with softball questions. Teach them it's okay to tell you things. Ask questions you know the answers to, and watch what they look like when they tell the truth or lie. Then use those to gauge later answers. It's all in a detective's bag of tricks. People are puzzle boxes, and we're trained to find the solution as quickly and accurately as possible. It required putting a certain distance between us and the people we spoke to. But despite my partner's earlier protestations, we weren't there for the living. We were there to bring justice to the dead.

She gave me her pronunciation—"Rhymes with Brown"—and I made a note.

"Why don't you tell me what happened, Miss Raun."

Donna's nose dripped and her eyes leaked, and it didn't take me long to mark her as someone who hadn't meant for things to go the way they had. She didn't sidetrack, just set in on what had happened and why it wasn't her fault.

"I came back from the grocery and Saulie was all smug. He'd scored while I was gone, you know?"

"Scored what?"

"Angel tears," she said. "But with a little extra."

A tingle of fear danced along my spine, and I traded a look of concern with Jax. Angel tears was a popular street drug, a hallucinogen delivered via eye drops. The "something extra" was a promise of manna slipped into the mix. Maybe it was a lie, maybe it was real, maybe it was anything that would make users believe that they were engaging in some kind of magic ritual. Anything to escape the doldrums of their lives. Either way, that something extra was what differentiated angel tears from its manna-laced upgrade: snake oil. And if there was active next-generation manna in the apartment, I risked crossing the threads, risked giving in to the hunger and coldness that marked my connection with the strange world of manna.

I reexamined the apartment, though it was a useless gesture. Threads were invisible; I'd only know they were present if I felt their tug on my flesh. The place had an unpleasant odor to it, like too-ripe fruit, and the ash cones sitting on a plate in the kitchenette indicated that the occupants had tried to mask it in their own way. All in all it wasn't too bad, not like the homes of those well and truly consumed by their drug of choice—something I'd seen more than enough of in my time on Vice. In those situations I was mostly concerned about the bug infestations that were usually present in places like that. Saul and Donna were either relatively new to A-list drugs, or they had extraordinary self-control, or someone who cared about them enough to make sure their basic needs were met.

"So Saulie, he's your partner?"

"Roomie."

I pulled a frown. "There's only one bedroom."

"There's two beds, if you bothered to look."

I raised my hands, immediately acknowledging my mistake.

"Okay," I said. "Saulie got snake oil. Did he do that often?"

"Sometimes. Not often. It's hard to get. He got some last week, and he didn't touch the stuff. Just moved it. He sold it to a guy he knows, someone with connections. Said they were gonna dilute it and move it on the street. I'm not involved, but I knew about it, you know?"

"I do." Snake oil and angel tears were usually sold as eye drops. That made it easier to dilute, as long as the iridescent sheen of manna didn't fade too much to make it less valuable. And CaDell had said Saul had been a chemical engineer. "He didn't keep any for the two of you?"

"Course he did. But some out-of-towner asked him for a hookup, and was willing to pay stupid cash. Saul was in a bad way. Money-wise, I mean. Like, I'd let him slide on his half of the rent when he got furloughed from the rig. Thought his luck changed with a job from Vandie Cedrow up at the festival. Then he got laid off from there . . ." She clenched her eyes shut and fell silent. I wasn't sure if she was angry with herself or her former roommate.

We waited silently for Donna to find her story once more.

"Saul sold what we had to the out-of-town lady, then bought a little back from the dealer he'd sold the rest to."

"The dealer whose name you don't know."

She sniffled. "It's not healthy to know the names of people like that."

"Who was the out-of-town buyer?" I already knew, of course. Sheena the dancer, who'd passed it on to Bobby Kearn.

"Not sure. Someone who was willing to pay premium, you know? But Saul didn't drop any of it himself."

Jax spoke up, his voice more melodic and comforting than mine could ever be. "You came home and Saul had scored from his dealer friend. Did you use right away?"

"No," she said, burrowing a little deeper into her sweatshirt. "We just had it, you know? I came in the door and he was all, 'Hey, let's have some food and then we'll see the stars.'"

Seeing the stars was another new phrase, one that hinted at the investor at the center of the snake oil plague. I inhaled deeply. No smell of burning food. A glance at the hotplate confirmed that there was no breakfast cooking, though the dirty dishes in the sink looked to be relatively recent, holding the remnants of leftover red sauce.

"But you never got around to food, did you?" I moved to her side.

I didn't feel any threads there, either. That was even more of an indication that she wasn't using snake oil. Of course, it could still be on the other side, or her back, or only wrapped around herself.

"Nah, we didn't." She trailed off, as if pining for that last meal together with a friend.

"What happened?"

"I walked in and he was dropping on his own."

He'd been sneaking in a quick hit.

"And then?" I said.

"We started arguing. About him dropping, but mostly the dishes."

I glanced back at the dish pile, confirming my earlier observations. It was small, smaller than my own pile at home, which served just one person and a cat. For two, it was even more discreet. "What about the dishes?"

Donna worked her lips. "It was . . . I don't know. It just really got under my skin, like there was something he should've been doing." She pulled her hair away from red-rimmed eyes and sat up straighter. "My mom used to warn me about running into a hade on the ice plains."

"A hade," said Jax. "Like the spirit?"

"Yeah." Donna's shoulders shook, though from sorrow or agreement, I couldn't tell. "The ones that whisper and lie, the unforgiving dead who try to lead you off your Path."

I knew what they were. A Barekusean word, "hade" carried two meanings, a type of ghost and the sound of newly thawed water trickling through a snowbank. That whispering sound of liquid moving behind a frozen mass was said by the Barekusu to mimic the murmurs of lost spirits. It was the old joke about the city name. Titanshade or Titan's Hade, depending on how you said it. Every Titanshader knew the legends of wanderers on the ice plains being led to their death by the whispering dead.

But the legends were lies.

"The dead aren't unforgiving," I said. "They only want closure. And," I spoke slowly, attempting to give my words gravity, "they want the living to admit to what they've done."

Donna's shoulders rose, defensive, about to share something she wasn't proud of. "I got mad." She glanced at Jax as he joined us, keeping a discreet distance. "Real mad, like I'd been drinking. I don't drink no more, because of my temper."

"Sure," I said. "That's smart."

"Like I said, I got mad. But Saulie, he wouldn't listen, no matter what I said, he wouldn't listen, and the buzzing in my head kept growing—"

"Wait." I felt Jax tense beside me. "Buzzing?"

"Yeah, like a . . . radio station out of tune."

"You ever have that before, when you get angry? When you're drinking, maybe?"

"Nah. Never." Her shoulders slumped, defeated. "I don't know why it happened now, either. I really don't. I just—I was so *mad*, you know? Like he'd done real bad by me. And it got so bad so fast, it was like I had to hit something or I'd burst. And when I hit him once, I couldn't stop."

"What'd you hit him with?"

"A book."

"Okay."

"One of them carabella record books. Great players, famous matches, that kind of thing. Saulie got it at the secondhand store. He loves carabella. *Loved*, I guess—" She broke off, swallowing a cry, and Jax hummed some words of comfort.

"Donna," he said, "you can take all the time you need. But first we need to look in the other room, okay?"

My eyes met Jax's, and he nodded. I stepped away and he moved ever so slightly to her side, one hand drawing closer to his belt. I was glad my partner had the foresight to carry cuffs. One benefit of working plainclothes is that we didn't have to carry the utility belt full of items that a patrol cop did. The downside was that we weren't as prepared for any eventuality, and the rarity with which we made arrests meant that most days my cuffs were sitting back in the Hasam or on my dresser at home.

I moved as well, more conspicuously than my partner, like a stage magician's distraction. "So you know what happened to Saul is serious, and we have to take you into custody, right? Do you understand that?"

She nodded, and I followed with, "Can you put your hands behind your back?" the agreement to the questions priming her for the agreement to be handcuffed, and laying out the implicit agreement be-tween her and us. "My partner's going to take hold of your hands now, okay?" Sometimes you need to bark orders, and sometimes you need to take a softer touch. Jax slipped her hands together and bound them in handcuffs, linked metal bracelets designed to restrain and protect.

With Donna controlled, I walked to the bedroom. I slipped open the door and saw the splattered evidence of Donna's blind rage.

The victim—Saulie, apparently—was wedged in between the beds. There were two of them, just as Donna had said. Both were relatively neat and tidy, one made with a flower-print bed cloth, the other more rumpled, like I usually left mine. Both of them were spattered with blood.

The murder weapon was evident, a book with red-soaked pages warping and curling in on themselves, abandoned on the floor. She'd simply dropped it when she walked back to the front room to call it in. But her hands weren't red-slicked when she'd let us in the room. I glanced over my shoulder. The kitchenette was out of my line of sight, but I remembered the layout and the dish-filled sink.

I slipped back out the door and into the living area, where Jax crouched beside Donna, his voice calming as he told her she'd done the right thing by calling us.

"We both wanted to see the Barekusu come to town," she said. "Now Saulie's not gonna be there, and it's my fault. We were gonna go down the street and be there when the procession came in."

The phone sat on an end table. There wasn't any blood on it. From what I'd seen in the bedroom, she'd have gotten gore all over the phone. She must have cleaned her hands after coming out of the bedroom.

"They're beautiful," she said. "All them Barekusu, coming in from the ice plains. They're finally gonna make sense of this town."

I stared at the sink. The liquid that covered the dishes wasn't red sauce.

"It's gonna be beautiful," Donna said, "just beautiful."

She closed her eyes, letting her hair hang down like a curtain. Jax looked at me. I nodded, and in a softly musical voice, he told Donna her rights.

AFTER SHE'D HEARD HER RIGHTS, Donna sat quietly in her chair, head low, hair obscuring her eyes, hands restrained.

I exhaled, and said, "Okay. Let's talk about your friend Sheena from down south."

Donna didn't respond. I stepped closer. "My partner explained your rights, and you don't have to answer me." Slowly, I dropped to a crouch, bringing my face to her eye level. "But I don't think you wanted to hurt Saul, did you?"

Through strands of hair, Donna stared at me with red, tear-filled eyes.

"And I don't think you want to see anyone else get hurt either." I waited, and she answered with the slightest shake of her head.

"So I want to ask you," I said, voice gentle as possible, "how do you know Sheena, and where did you get the snake oil you gave her?"

Donna's jaw worked, but her voice was too soft to hear. I leaned closer, almost holding my breath. As she was about to speak, someone pounded on the door to the apartment, and a nasally voice commanded, "Titanshade PD! Open up!"

Jax crossed the room in a few quick strides and threw open the door, displaying his badge. But it was too late. Donna had retreated back into whatever mental prison she'd sought refuge in, and showed no further interest in talking to me.

The two patrol cops who'd responded to Donna's emergency call were happy enough to see us, until they realized that the homicide meant they'd be babysitting the crime scene for the immediate future.

One of them was a younger officer named Chandler, who I figured had a few years on the streets. The other was an older guy, probably about ready to put in his transfer to an administrative position. His name was Dixon, and I'd run into him at cop bars like Hammer Head's. I'd never cared for him much, until he started treating me better when I was all over the papers during the manna strike mess. After that, I really disliked him.

"Suspect's in custody," I said. "Get her downtown."

The patrol cops traded a look. "That'll be a while."

"I don't care about a damn parade, we need to secure this scene."

Jax interjected. "It's more than a parade," he said. "The caravan is going to attract a ton of people, along with media."

"And the military," Chandler added. "Soldiers from the strike site are all over the streets."

"Great." The AFS military had occupied the site of the manna strike since the discovery had been made. They'd taken a serious PR blow when it was discovered that the feds were throttling manna production. The reasons why were for the talking heads on TV, but the lack of other drilling had made tensions flare on the streets and in homes across Titanshade. If there was a military escort for the Barekusu, it was both a PR move and show of force. Sooner or later, everything was a prop for the powerful to move around on the game board.

I peered out the dingy windows. The place didn't have much of a view, but it was high enough that I could see the crowds and closed-off streets. I didn't like it, but Dixon was right.

"Fine, we'll stay here for now. But we still need to call it in."

Since our suspect had used the phone, I instructed Dixon to keep the site secure as Jax, Chandler, and I headed outside. By the time we hit the sidewalk, there was clearly more foot traffic than when we arrived. The Barekusu caravan was getting closer.

Chandler led the way to her vehicle, to pick up crime scene material and allow us to use their car radio to call in a tech team and get the red tape rolling. The street had been emptied of moving vehicles, leaving only the occasional parallel-parked car or mopeds pulled onto the sidewalk. The crowd was thicker than a busy lunch-hour rush, but oddly still. Instead of rushing to the next meeting, or trying to get to work or home to the kids, everyone was almost motionless as they held their spot and waited for the arrival of the Barekusu.

The caravan came into view gradually. The crowd's silent excitement grew. They were a cross section of the city, huddled together in heavy coats to protect against the deep chill of the Borderlands. Day laborers and shop owners stood with retirees and schoolchildren. All of them craning their necks and staring down the road like impatient public transit riders waiting for the next bus.

The first shapes to emerge were military vehicles, soldiers with fur-rimmed jackets riding in open-top vehicles. They must have come from the manna strike site, brought in on trucks since they clearly wouldn't have lasted on the ice plains. They came down the street in two columns of four, rumbling along and waving to the citizens. As if anyone was there to see them, instead of the caravan behind them.

After the trucks, a new sound emerged. A low hum, harmonizing and reverberating like a chorus, deep and ominous and beautiful. The song swelled until I felt it in my chest. A contrabass prelude to the main event. Emerging from the barrier where fog transformed into snow, the first Barekusu crossed into Titanshade.

They moved slowly, majestic shapes solidifying in the swirl of ice fog. For all the size of the crowd, not a single person made a sound. No shouts, no cheering, not even the inevitable heckler in the crowd. Only respectful silence. The Barekusu's wide rear legs kept time with their thick three-fingered front hands, ambulating on all fours. Barely visible, a second set of narrow, thin-fingered hands grew from the inner side of those massive wrists. With each stride these delicate "sly hands" stroked the coats of shaggy fur, pulling loose strands to be woven into valuable kusuma wool.

As the caravan drew closer, I could see their breath streaming out of nostrils the size of my fist, and the Barekusu's thick outer coats, covered by frost, each ice crystal standing out as if meticulously drawn by an artist. It reinforced their mysterious nature, even more because their outer clothing was entirely kusuma, blending into their own pelt colors and giving them the appearance of wild creatures who now strode the streets of the city, creatures born long before cobblestone wound meandering paths around the Mount, and who would be here long after Titanshade and all its citizens had sunk beneath the snow.

Jax sighed. It was a quiet, musical tinkle, the sound of countless curved teeth clicking in his speaking mouth accompanied by a low, wistful note. "You think they're going to help patch things up with the AFS?"

"Maybe. Or maybe they're here to lay their own claim on the manna." I looked back at the building where Donna Raun had beaten a friend to death for no discernible reason. "Either way they're slowing down my investigation." The Barekusu were traders, priests, guides, and teachers. And like anyone on a pedestal, they weren't to be trusted. I pulled my coat tighter, warding off the creeping chill of Borderlands air. "Let's get back to work, Jax."

But Ajax was lost in thought, watching the slowly swaying backs of the nomad priests. So I waited beside him.

For their part, the Barekusu seemed to take no notice of the crowd beyond the occasional twitch of one of the half-dozen pointed ear flaps circling their heads and cresting through their fur like the ornaments of a crown. Their eyes were hidden from our sight by layers of horn. Growing in half circles, like a series of broken dinner plates, each overlapping horn protected the Barekusu's face, while also providing privacy. The horn slats were also covered in rime from the journey across the ice plains, and occasionally a Barekusu would flex them open and shut, shedding the accumulated ice onto the cobblestones beneath their feet.

Something brushed across the top of my head, light, feathery, and sticky. I ducked, shouting a curse. The Barekusu nearest us took no notice, but one on the far side of the caravan slowed his pace. His eye horns hinged open like a set of slat blinds, revealing an eyeball the size of my fist, bisected both horizontally and vertically. There were four separate irises pointing in four separate directions, wary of any possible predators. In a blink they snapped together, converging into a single dark and wriggling shape, staring at me from behind horn plates whose irregular, saw-toothed ends could rend flesh from bone. As he passed me, his gaze returned to the path before him, but I couldn't look away from the gray and green stripes along his back ridge.

All around, people craned their heads, trying to guess who had shouted and caught the Barekusu's attention. I tugged my scarf higher around my collar. It was time to return to something I could understand: a dead body six floors up who needed me to unravel his murder.

I pushed my way through one of several camera crews. As I did, the sound engineer swore and snatched off her headphones. I could hear the squeal of feedback from the headset, a sound undercut by a low, angry buzzing. The other crews seemed to be having the same issue, and my heartbeat picked up its tempo. I turned in place, searching for anything out of the ordinary. The crowd had begun to murmur, and I turned to find the caravan abruptly halted. The Barekusu stretched out their necks, nostrils flaring, sniffing the breeze like a dog enjoying a summer day. A long moment passed, and around me the sound engineers gingerly put their headphones back on. I looked down the street and saw the distinctive gray and green stripes of the Barekusu who'd looked at me. He began to move, and all around the caravan followed suit. But my attention wasn't on the newcomers to our city. I was thinking about that buzzing, the same sound I'd been hearing since the manna strike, the same sound we'd all heard at the concert site when Bobby Kearn's body transformed. And just like that time, people other than me had heard it as well. And that meant . . .

I twisted my hips, turning to stare at the building where Saul's corpse lay, and where a woman and a patrol cop were sitting in the next room.

"Jax, come on!" I shouted. And began to run.

RUSHING BACK TO THE CRIME scene, I took the stairs two at a time. At least for the first few flights. Maybe the first flight. In any case, by the time I hit the sixth floor, I was approaching the scene at a measured pace.

We entered the floor to find the hallway crammed with spectators watching the procession from the single window affording a view. One of them held a transistor radio, tuned in to news coverage of the event. Deep-voiced, serious news anchors described each step of the Barekusu, as if the angle of any given frost-covered hair would hold untold secrets of the Path. *Coming toward us now is a young Barekusu with markings similar to the early arrival, Guide Serrow. It's an extraordinary sight, and one that—*

The announcer cut off abruptly, as a rushing, swirling noise drowned his voice in static and a not-quite-melodic whine. Yanking his head away from the radio, the teenager swore and cranked the dial, but the howl was present on all stations. "What the Hells . . ." he muttered, before giving up and switching it off.

"You okay, Carter?"

I realized I'd frozen in the hall as the scene played out, Ajax at my back.

"Yeah." I stared at the kid by the window. Maybe his radio was broken. And maybe I'd win the lottery that week.

"Let's go," I said, and began jogging down the hall.

We entered the crime scene fast enough to make Dixon jump out of his chair and his hand drop to his sidearm. Ignoring him, I pointed at Donna.

"Is she doing anything weird?"

Ordinarily we'd have a murder suspect contained in the back of a cruiser. Having her sit in the apartment where she'd murdered her roommate wasn't a good idea no matter how you sliced it, but that wasn't an option right now.

Dixon took his hand off his sidearm and blinked. He covered his confusion by pointing at the suspect. "No! She's sitting there. Not moving or anything."

The TV wasn't on, nor was the radio. Apparently Dixon didn't have much interest in current affairs. But still, I heard voices. I took two long strides to the wall, and placed it—the neighbors' television. I swallowed, a sense of relief settling over me. Then other sound got louder.

I turned. The bedroom door was still closed, and the new sound came from behind it. A kind of blind thumping, the sound of someone stumbling to a dark bathroom after waking from a deep sleep. I pointed at the door, knowing the answer, but asking anyway. "Techs managed to get through the procession traffic?"

Dixon blinked and pursed his lips. "No. Haven't seen 'em yet."

A breath caught in my throat as the voices next door were lost in a roar of static. I rushed into the bedroom, followed by Jax, shouting at Dixon: "Keep her away!"

We burst into the bedroom, only to find it exactly as we'd left it. I narrowed my eyes, studying the scene. Saulie was still a mess. The dead man was mostly covered by the linens that had tumbled from the bed. His head was wedged beneath one bed, his feet stretching across the narrow gap between to touch the flannel sheets of the other. No matter what Donna and Saulie had cooked up, their plan hadn't gone well.

"Did you hear thumping?" I asked.

"No thumping," he said. "I heard that buzz, though, right after you asked about the techs."

So maybe it was my imagination. I shook the thoughts out of my head, clearing the mental dust and distractions. We had a confessed killer, and a victim, and stack of to-be-filed paperwork waiting for us back at the bunker. What more could an aging cop want?

Jax muttered something about checking on Donna, then the door latch clicked shut behind me. I crouched, eyeing the dead man, and wondering what he'd seen in his last moments. I had no intention of letting this crime scene get the rushed treatment Bobby Kearn had gotten. I didn't know Saulie, but he deserved better. Everyone deserved better.

I pulled the edge of the already-stiffening bed linens and got a long look at the dead man's face. I'd seen plenty of deaths, from auto wrecks on the hairpin turns winding the Mount to picking apart pieces of gangsters who'd been trapped in alleyway brawls. I could tell cold-blooded, calculating murders from heat-of-the-moment rage killings. Whatever had sparked Donna's anger, it had consumed her. She'd beaten her friend's body long after he was dead. She'd hit him so hard that much of the skin on his face had either pulled inward with the blows or sloughed off completely, and one strike had almost snapped his jaw. In fact . . . I leaned closer. That was weird, to see a break at the chin cleft, since a blow on the side of the jaw was more common, and tended to align with a weaker joint. I pulled my pencil out and wrapped the end of the bed linen around the tip. Using it as a probe, I moved the flesh on that section of his face. It was a strange wound, and I felt the blood roar in my ears, pulsing with the rhythm of my heartbeat. I pulled back—and realized that the roaring wasn't coming from within me.

The body twitched, then jerked. It spasmed, inching closer to me. The jaw opened, but not at the hinges. It opened at the fracture, the cleft widening until the remaining flesh fell away with a sick tearing sound. The body lunged, the new opening in its jaw mimicking a Mollenkampi's biting mouth snapping at my fingers. Saulie's mouth stretched and grew wider still, a jagged screech rising from his chest as the remnants of his jaw split apart, opening and snapping back together with a wet slap. His body twisted, then threw itself to the floor once again.

I rolled to my left, twisting around to face the body. I rose to my knees and reached for my weapon, calling out loud and clear: "I need backup!"

Whatever controlled the body, it wasn't done yet. It writhed and spasmed, jerking violently to the left, hard enough that I thought I heard bones cracking as it smashed into the bed frame. It flattened to the floor as Jax and Dixon burst into the room, and I thought it might be done. Then it shot straight upward, actually lifting the bed into the air, before crashing down again.

Jax flanked me on one side, sidearm in hand as I scrambled to my feet. I barked a quick, "Get back out!" and pushed the slack-jawed Dixon ahead of me. Jax kept his head and didn't open fire as the thing that had been Saul Petrevisch flopped and twisted like an unmanned fire hose. Instead he kicked the door shut and kept his weapon drawn.

Donna screamed at us from the chair, "Was that Saulie? Is he alive?" From the ragged timbre of her voice, she'd begun to scream as soon as Saul's body had transformed.

Dixon had fallen back halfway between us and the handcuffed Donna. Jax's weapon was pointed at the bedroom door, but he flashed his eyes my way. "What happened? Did you," his voiced dropped, "do something?"

"What could I do that would cause that?" I demanded, though I knew it was a fair question.

"Saulie!" Donna was still screaming. "You have to help him, he's not dead!"

There was silence from the bedroom, and that made me more nervous. What if whatever had happened only occurred when I was in the vicinity?

I pointed at Dixon. "Get to the street. Find the nearest patrol with a radio. I don't care if it's your car or you flag another officer down. Just get hold of Dispatch. We're gonna need an ARC team out here."

"Oh, you *think*?" Dixon was a smartass, but he didn't argue the point. And he wasn't smart enough to ask why, if it was so urgent, weren't we using Donna's phone? A moment later he was gone, and that left Jax, me, and the confessed killer. But I was already beginning to believe that although she may have been the hand that swung the weapon, she wasn't the intellect behind the attack. I motioned Jax over closer, and spoke in a whisper.

"The body moved as soon as I poked it."

"You what?"

"I was looking at the wounds."

"Is poking a body with a stick *ever* part of official procedure?"

"Fine." My words grew sharper. "I examined the victim's wound with an instrument to determine the relative depth of impact. Now are you going to shut up or do you want me to give you a written report?"

He waved me on, and I supposed that permission to continue was as close to an apology as someone whose life had just been threatened by a spasming corpse is likely to get.

"He's not alive," I said.

"I got that much."

"Did you ever do that thing in junior high, when they stick electrodes in a dead frog and zap it, to see the muscles contract?"

He nodded. "You think it was some kind of reflex?"

"Like having electricity pumped through it. Or magic."

"No one's gone in there with manna," he said.

"The snake oil—"

"Has a fraction of a drop. It's not enough to actually do any sorcery, especially not by untrained users. Unless," his speech slowed as he thought through the scenario, "someone in that room was a battery for magic."

"Not you, too? Guyer's bad enough." I wiped a hand across my mouth, one lip swollen where I'd bitten it during our fast retreat. "I wasn't even in the room when we first heard noises, remember? And I'd have known if I'd done something to the body. Trust me, I've had every variation of this conversation already." And I had, mostly with Gellica, the woman who'd been my support beam as I realized I'd had some kind of connection with the next gen manna. Or she had been, until she trusted me and I let her down so hard that it'd shattered the relationship. My people skills have never been what you'd call polished.

"Get comfortable," I told Jax, "we're gonna be here a while. Because Sheena may have killed Bobby Kearn and Donna may have killed Saulie, but something or someone drove them to it. And it might not be done."

THE ARC TEAM ARRIVED IN nice cars and taxis. Like the Special Response Teams, they were always on call. But instead of responding to hostage situations or barricades, the ARC teams dealt with manna, magic, and madness. Their clear mandate was "do whatever you need to, just get there fast."

Two divination officers walked in, one black-cloaked human, one Mollenkampi in a red and black fishbone suit, the shimmering iridescence of the weave indicating his importance and potential power. All sorcerers kept manna close to them in some way or another, the exact style depending on their preference and bankroll.

"Is Guyer here?" I asked.

The Mollenkampi didn't slow down, but the human paused long enough to shake his head and adjust his thick-rimmed glasses. That was a relief—I wasn't sure I could handle seeing her at another of these crime scenes.

"You're Callahan, right?" I'd crossed paths with most of the DOs at one time or another, even if those meetings usually degenerated into a screaming match over the use of manna and whether a given death warranted the expense.

"Yes, thank you." His attention was off me already and he walked down the hall humming an off-kilter tune, before vanishing into the apartment where Saul Petrevisch had lost his life.

"Guyer's not here, Carter." I turned to face the new voice and found a third DO in the hallway. Tall and with a buck-toothed, boyish grin, Harris approached with his hand extended. A repeat of the first time I'd met him. "But she had a message for you. She asked you to call her when you get a chance."

I frowned, but nodded.

"Actually," he continued. "She didn't so much ask as insist. And she didn't use the words, 'when he gets a chance.'" He paused. "I think it was much more of a do-it-now insistence. If you get my meaning."

"I do. And I'll call her." Hands in my pockets, I looked down the hall at the other DOs. "Three of you, huh? I'd almost think you didn't trust me."

"Trust but verify." He flashed his buck teeth in a quick grin. "Yeah, it's my first call with three DOs, too. We live in interesting times, hey?"

I turned to Harris, wondering at the dodge. "How long have you lived in Titanshade?"

"Little less than a year."

"Why'd you come?" I squinted, looking him over. Most of his clothing was concealed by his cloak, except for the cuffs and collars of dress clothes. But he also wore thick-soled boots, the kind I associated with bikers. "You moved up here before the manna strike, when the smart money said the oil wells were drying out, and the city was about to contract."

"Because the other city-states weren't hiring at the time. Plus, the cold never bothered me too much." He smiled again. "I didn't realize that it was quite so warm in the ritzy parts of town."

That sounded like a polite generalization. Something he was hoping we'd skip over. I did, but pushed back into another topic he didn't seem excited to talk about. "Why are there three of you?"

His smile faded, and he whistled through his teeth. "Because this isn't the only one today."

"What?" I pointed at the apartment door. "Like this? Coming back to life?"

"No. I meant people are attacking each other for no reason. And Carter," he dropped his voice, "they're hearing the buzz, like we did at the festival." He glanced down the hall, in the direction the other DOs had gone, his eyes wide and serious. "It's all I can say right now. Believe me, you'll hear more soon enough."

He patted me on the back and walked away, leaving me to wonder what could be causing other events, and whether I had anything to do with them. In something of a daze, I headed down to the street. There I found Jax seated on the building's front stoop, notepad and pencil in hand as he traced the day's events.

"You find anything enlightening in there?" I sat next to him, the rough stone steps cold to the touch in the Borderlands air.

"Not yet," he said. At some point his head bandage had come loose, and he'd unwound the gauze and tucked it into his breast pocket, like a blood-stained pocket square.

The crowd had mostly dispersed, the awe and excitement surrounding the caravan's arrival fading away like early morning window frost. By now, the Barekusu were probably entering the city's center, where the rich and influential crowd would be doing their best to appear richer and more influential than they actually were.

"Guyer wants me to call her," I said. "Probably wants to accuse me of warping magic, or doing mind control, or something else asinine."

"So call her," he said. "You're not going to find out what she wants by speculating."

I took a breath and chewed my lip, then plunged ahead. "You know I didn't do anything to that body up there, right?"

"No. I don't know," he said. "No one does. That's the problem."

We locked eyes, and I looked away first.

"But I doubt you had anything to do with it," he said. "I saw the people interacting with their radios, and I heard the buzzing on the televisions. I don't think that was all from a single cop with an inexplicable manna connection."

"Either way," I said. "We've got a murder to solve."

"Do we?" He ran a careful hand over sore head plates. "Because I'm pretty sure I heard Donna confess."

"She can confess all she wants. But whatever happened to Saul's body, to Bobby Kearn . . ." I sighed, my breath creating a fleeting, misty cloud. "Whatever's going on, it's much stranger than a fight between roommates."

"Saul Petrevisch was a small-time user and an even smaller-time dealer. Whatever magic is happening, it's expensive. People's lives are worth less than magic in this town. You taught me that."

I wanted to insist he was wrong, that everyone's life is worth an infinite amount of manna. I also wanted to tell him that the good guys always win and the guilty parties go to jail. But I could only tell so many laughable lies in a given day. Instead, I moved on to a more pressing issue.

"It's important that you not talk to Talena about this," I said. "Not more than you have to." There was no point in dragging someone I cared about even further into the strange quagmire of my life.

He blinked. "Is there anyone less qualified than you to give me relationship advice when it comes to Talena?" He laughed, then shook his head. "I can handle it just fine."

"Nobody can handle anything about Talena, and you know it." I huffed hot breath into my hands, and rubbed the stumps of my missing fingers. The chill air was starting to make them ache.

Jax clacked his biting jaws. "We're not having this conversation here."

"If you're pissed because I kept the other thing to myself—"

He interrupted me. "You *thought* you were keeping it to yourself. That's the problem. You think you're a closed book, but everyone around you knows you're going through something. I don't know where you get off acting like it doesn't affect us."

"Us?"

"Yes. Me, Talena, everyone else on Homicide. Everyone who has to guess what your mood's going to be like on any given day before we ask for something outrageous like, 'Can you pass the vinegar?'" He shoved the notepad and pencil back in his jacket pocket. "You're brilliant at what you do," he said. "And that's a damn lucky thing, because otherwise no one would put up with your BS." He stood and brushed off the back of his pants, shedding the dirt of the Borderlands stoop. "You make your phone call. I'll be in the car."

He walked away, cutting through the pedestrian traffic and jaywalking across the street.

I grunted a note of disagreement, but he was already too far to hear it. Regardless, I still owed Guyer a call. I stood, strolled to the nearest pay phone, and dropped in my coin. I dialed her pager number and left the number off the pay phone dial. I stood by the phone, waiting on her call-back.

A human man walked up, apparently intent on using the phone. I flashed my badge and said, "Sorry pal, police business."

"What does that mean, police business?"

"It means I'm using the phone."

"You clearly are not. You're standing there preventing anyone else from using it."

The phone rang, and I spread my hands in my best public-servant-what-can-I-do way, then lifted the receiver. "Yeah?"

The guy crossed his arms and glared as Guyer's voice spoke in my ear. "Oh. It's you."

"You sound less than excited," I said. "I heard you wanted to talk to me."

"That was before everything went to Hells."

"What are you talking about?"

"We've had fourteen 187s so far today."

That was far above the normal number of homicides for a single day, but it wasn't completely unheard of. The man beside me looked at his watch.

"You wanted me to call in to tell me that?"

"I wanted to tell you that we're seeing a shocking number of homicides, and that many of them are accompanied by confessions."

I dragged in a breath. "Let me guess," I said. "Confessions from people who are confused and terrified, who were overcome with anger and lashed out at anyone nearby."

"How did you know that?"

The guy leaned into my space. "Are you going to be much longer?"

I covered the mouthpiece of the phone. "You in a hurry?"

"Yes! Obviously!" He tightened his grip on his briefcase. "My tax dollars don't pay for you to stand around talking to your friends."

"Okay." I spoke into the phone once more. "Hey, I need you to do something for me."

Guyer paused. "Did you not hear what I said?"

"Put in a report with the nearest patrol car. Suspicious individual at the corner of Bryer and Jenis."

The man frowned. I made a show of looking him over, then continued.

"Aged about fifty, wearing white button-up shirt, tan trousers, light green sweater under a black overcoat and hat."

The man shook his head. "You can't intimidate me—"

Guyer said, "What the Hells are you talking about?" But the man couldn't hear that.

"I just need them to detain him while I confirm he's not the murder victim's missing roommate. I should be able to do that in a few hours."

"You can't arrest me for no reason!"

I covered the mouthpiece again. "No one's arresting you. But you might be detained until we have control of the situation. Like I said, shouldn't take more than a few hours." His faced reddened. "Sorry about you being in such a hurry and all. But I have to follow up every possible lead. We don't want to waste those tax dollars."

He tucked his newspaper under his arm and marched away as fast as his tan trousers would allow, glancing down the street as if a patrol car might come bounding around the corner, lights blazing, at any moment.

"Okay, Guyer. I'm back."

The DO was chuckling. "Did he fall for it?"

"They always do."

"Good for you," she said. "But listen, we need to talk, and the sooner the better. You have time tonight?"

"No."

"Make time. I'll be at Hammer Head's for dinner. Meet me there." She hung up before I could tell her no.

It was another hour or so, but when the last of the caravan congestion cleared, we handed Donna off to a pair of patrol cops.

So Donna disappeared into the back of a patrol car, and we drove the Hasam back to the Bunker in silence.

As we parked, I asked Jax if he was still fuming about what I'd said about Talena.

"Well, yes, as a matter of fact, I am. But I'm even more concerned about this killing. It's too similar to Bobby Kearn's murder. If there's some common cause, does that mean it's going to happen again?"

"Harris said there's more bodies acting like electrocuted frogs." I turned to face him. "But that's not what you're thinking of, is it? You're thinking of what happened right before Sheena attacked Bobby."

"Bobby Kearn and Saul Petrevisch. Both victims and their killers had access to the same batch of snake oil. What if the supply is tainted in some way?" He unfastened his seat belt. "We ought to notify Guyer. At the very least we need to fill out a CS report."

I winced. Controlled substance reports were a pain. "I already told Guyer."

"We still have to fill out the report," he said. Then asked, "How did she react?"

"She's buying me dinner."

He paused. "Well, that sounds nice."

"She's suspicious," I said. "Of me, and what happens around me. And that means she's suspicious of you." I looked at him, waiting for his objections, but they didn't come. "That's what I was getting at when I said you oughta keep this to yourself."

He got out of the car, but leaned into the open door to answer me. "Talena's more resourceful than you give her credit for."

"When I said no one can handle her, I meant her included." I exited the car and he slammed his door shut.

I spun the keys around my finger. "I'm just saying—"

"We should be careful," he said. "I heard you the first time."

"Yeah." I stretched my back and wondered about the guy at the pay phone, if throwing a scare into him was the equivalent of demanding free coffee from a store owner. And I wondered what that said about me. I scrubbed a hand down my face, trying to shake loose the thoughts. "This was a pretty shit day, partner. I'll be glad when it's over."

BACK AT OUR DESKS, JAX and I began to build the flotilla of forms and reports that would ferry Donna Raun through Titanshade's justice system. After we were done she'd be in the hands of the City Attorney's Office. Maybe they'd let her plead down to lesser charges, or maybe she'd spend the rest of her life behind bars. Honestly, I did my best not to dwell on it. That's part of the job, as much as anything else: compartmentalize, rationalize, forget about the living and focus on the next dead body demanding justice.

I stood, stretched, and announced, "I gotta go to the can. I'll be right back."

When I returned I saw Ajax staring at the ceiling, his fingers idly drumming on a file folder.

"What's up?" I asked.

"Nothing." He pushed yet another carbon-paper sandwich across the desk, a blue arrow indicating where I was to sign. With his other hand he pulled the folder to the far side of the desk. An attempted distraction.

I pretended to fall for it, and asked, "You stressed about the badge?"

He raised a brow. "You deduce that all on your own? I really do have so much to learn from you."

"Glad you're coming around." I signed the form where he'd indicated. "Listen, I've gotta do this thing with Guyer. But after that, let's talk. We can get this badge thing taken care of one way or another."

I creased the signed form down the middle, raised it to eye height, and gave it a push. The crease caused it to act as a crude paper airplane, fluttering across the desk and tilting up at an unexpected angle. Jax reached for it, and while his hands were in the air I grabbed the file folder he'd slid aside, nearly toppling his neat towers of paper as I did. Ignoring his trill of protest, I flipped it open and found a report from Children's Services.

Clipped to the report was a photo of a scared and angry teenager named Ronald, taken into the system when his mother died during a raid on an angel's roost. I had a brief flash of the room where she'd died, the smell of sweat and heat in the air as her body began to consume itself. Maybe she'd have still been alive if I'd understood how my manna bond worked. Seeing the kid's photo made something in my chest go cold. I closed the folder and tossed it back to Jax.

"You can't take in strays," I said. "Bad enough you adopted that cat from the angel's roost." The cat had been one of the few residents to come out of the raid alive. "You name him yet?"

Jax tapped the folder on his desk, knocking the papers into perfect alignment before setting it neatly aside. "I gave him to Ronald."

Of course he had.

"I know you mean well," I said. "But what are you hoping to achieve?"

Jax tilted his head. "Worst case, the cat gets ignored and takes off for a new home. Best case? Maybe the kid has someone to care for, and to care about him in return. You spend so much time caring about homicide victims. Try giving a little thought to the people they left behind."

I made a show of checking the time. "I was serious about meeting up after Guyer. Will you be here when I get back?"

"No. I have dinner plans of my own."

"And that's more important than your badge?" I kept my voice low, to avoid being overheard.

He answered with an irritated hum. "I called the Camden Terrace substation and asked them to search the snow-runner we used. Nothing. I also radioed the festival—"

I winced. "Not a good idea."

"I was going to go in person, but I got a little sidetracked by your quick errand out to visit Saul Petrevisch. So I radioed the festival site and left a message for your pal CaDell. He's searching Sheena's room looking for dropped police equipment. If it's found, he'll hold it for me. In the meantime," he took a deep breath, "tomorrow morning I'll go to Captain Bryyh and report it lost."

I didn't say anything. I'd already told Ajax he was principled, and repeating it wouldn't mean anything, especially if he was about to eat a ten-day suspension and fine.

I met Guyer at Hammer Head's, a popular watering hole with the men and women of the Titanshade PD. As such, my order of a soda didn't raise any eyebrows at the bar. There were enough cops who needed to step away from alcohol, and the bartenders always served soda in a tumbler with a twist of lime, the better to fend off any social awkwardness.

I found Guyer in a back booth, picking at a salad while flipping through a paperback. Compared to my wrinkled brown suit or the patrol cops who'd traded their patrol scarlet for blue jeans and light sweaters, Guyer was out of place. She wore a black leather jacket with a thick maroon band and a white racing stripe running parallel up one arm, over the chest, and down the opposite arm. A bright green T-shirt with a motorbike logo peeked out from behind the jacket. Her fingers sparkled with an assortment of rings, and her hair was done up in several tightly interwoven braids. Guyer looked as if she were about to be in a street race or go on a date. Either way, it indicated that she had other plans for the evening, and that gave me hope that I might be set free relatively quickly.

She dog-eared a page as I approached, setting the book on a pair of gloves with checkered lines representing stylized finger bones. "About time," she said.

"I like to keep my audience in suspense." That was a lie. My failure to be on time was entirely accidental. "What're you dressed for?"

She scowled. "I had plans to go for a ride up on the hills. But the Barekusu camp means all kinds of access is shut off."

I considered that. The hills at the foot of the Mount weren't great for cars, and she wasn't dressed for bicycling.

"You off-road?" I asked.

"What do you think?" She wiggled her arms, causing the leather of her outfit to creak. "I have a scrambler." Scramblers were dirt bikes that were also street legal. Guyer used the term with the forced confidence of someone who'd only recently learned a new phrase. Her jacket had a new leather shine to it, and I thought of Harris's biker-style boots.

"How recently did you pick up that hobby?"

Guyer pushed the half-finished salad to the side. "Let's talk about why you're here."

"Fine," I said. "So talk."

"I asked you to be open with me in the snow-runner. And you were. Now I'm returning the favor."

The booth's vinyl seat wheezed in protest as I sat back, arms folded.

"Yesterday you told me that you only affect magic if you hit these invisible threads."

"That's right."

"The first report of this buzzing was yesterday. I already told you how many 187s we've had since then. All over the city today, people are turning up beaten, stabbed, throttled, and otherwise homicided into an early grave. And every one of them had some kind of connection to either snake oil or pure next gen manna. Do you know what that means?"

I knew exactly what it meant. Next gen manna had rained down from the strike, soaking me to the bone as I stood over Harlan Cedrow's corpse. The iridescent liquid had stemmed the bleeding from my missing fingers and damned me to some kind of connection with magic that no one understood. Least of all me.

Guyer steepled her fingers. "It means you weren't involved."

I blinked. "Come again?"

"The buzzing sound, the thing that all these killers are talking about. It's not related to you. It can't be. Not if what you told me in the snow-runner is true."

I chewed my lip. If it was something happening across Titanshade, whether I was present or not, what did that mean? Hesitant, I talked my way through it. "Bobby Kearn was killed because the buzzing drove Sheena to madness. And that happened while I was hours away."

"Exactly," she said. "Whatever the buzzing is, it's got nothing to do with you."

I sighed, relieved I wasn't going to have to fight Guyer on this one.

She inched forward. "The transformations, though, that's got you written all over it."

I pulled back. "What?"

"The wings that came out of the drummer. And today, the snake oil dealer."

"His name was Saul Petrevisch."

"That's the one. Point is, over a dozen buzz-related homicides since yesterday, but only two where the bodies transformed after death. You were there for both of them." She took a breath, one hand resting on the table, the other on the book. "I don't know what's causing the reaction. But whatever you're doing—and I don't think you mean to—it's tied to death, and to the echoes of the dead."

I rolled the bottom of the tumbler across my palm, wishing I'd ordered something stronger. "I don't know what that means."

She spun the paperback so I could read the title. *Your Death and You.*

I squinted. "Is that a self-help book?"

She frowned. "You say that like it's a bad thing. Dr. Henning's helped countless people. If you were a little more open, you could accept help from other people. Maybe even from yourself."

"If you want to help, let's talk about Vandie Cedrow. She was at the rig, and we know her family is dirty as all the Hells. And," I hesitated slightly before opening up with more information, "I felt threads connecting her to Bobby Kearn's body."

Guyer blinked. "Why didn't you tell me this in the snow-runner?"

"I don't know. There was a lot to tell, and not a lot of time to tell it."

She drummed her fingers on the book. "As far as I know, Vandie Cedrow wasn't any closer to today's murders than you were."

"Correct me if I'm wrong, but isn't the whole point of magic to connect items across a distance?"

She hesitated, mouth slightly open. "That's true. But that also applies to you, doesn't it?"

I shook my head, lowering my voice and hunkering down a little further. "But there wasn't anything tying me to the body. I'd have felt it if there was."

Guyer pinched her lips. "That's the problem with you having this unique ability. No one can fact check it. You say there's threads, you say there aren't. All we have is your word."

"You think I'd lie about this?"

"No. And I believe you. But I also believe in evidence and probable cause. And right now you've got neither."

She stared at me. I stared at the wall. After a few deep breaths, just like the department shrinks taught me, I spoke again.

"What about the victims? You already tried to contact Bobby Kearn. Harris was at the Saul Petrevisch murder site, when the ARC team snatched it away. Have you talked to him?"

"I did." She spoke slowly, selecting words like a man buying fruit at a grocer, carefully inspecting each one for signs of worms. "The echoes are . . . I suppose 'off' is the best description. It's like listening to someone screaming from the bottom of a well. We don't have any useful information from them about the transformations."

I grunted, tugging at my lower lip while I thought. There had to be some way to show there was no connection between me and the transformations.

"Look," Guyer's voice was softer now, "I'd like you to meet someone."

My head snapped back, eyes widening. "Who have you told about this?"

"No one. I want you to talk someone who I think could help you."

She flipped the book over. The back had a photo of the author, his face blurred by a smear of salad dressing.

"Who the Hells is that?"

"His name," she said, "is Dr. Henning."

The professor was a study in browns. Brown hair, brown bushy beard, brown eyes slightly enlarged by the round lenses of his glasses. All of it brought home by a brown cardigan over a blue shirt and white tie. Guyer slid the book across the table.

"This is for you," she said.

I groaned, but she cut me off with a wave of her hand.

"You're always going on about seeing things from the victim's eyes. Always worried about protecting the dead. Imp's blade, Carter, my job's to talk to the dead, and even I think you need to worry about the living. This book will help you get through the death, and see the light in the living."

Worrying about the living brought nothing but heartache. But even as isolated as I was, I still had people I cared for. Shared suffering can create bonds, and we all take solace in those nearest us. Maybe that's what had drawn Gellica and me together, our bond of mutual risk and connection to magic. Of course, whatever we might have had crashed before it even got started. One more entry in my ongoing list of bridges burned and friends disappointed.

"I'm sure a book will help out immensely," I said. "I really need to be going, though. I'll catch you later."

I rose, but halted when Guyer said, "I don't want to end up doing this the hard way."

Half crouched over the table, my tie threatened to swing into the sorcerer's salad. I pressed it to my chest with one hand. "What's that supposed to mean?"

"I mean you can't go out on the streets if you pose a danger."

"Is that a threat?"

"It doesn't need to be. But if you force me to, I'll bring in Dr. Baelen."

Baelen was the observer sent by the AFS to watch for health risks posed by next gen manna. In reality, she was plucking anyone who had a negative reaction out of the public eye and holding them for observation. As always the wheels of progress were greased with the blood of inconvenient bystanders.

Guyer was the TPD liaison for the medical exams. I knew there was no love lost between her and Baelen, so I decided to call her bluff.

"You'd never just hand me over to Baelen. Hells, you've blocked her from coming after me in the past." As I spoke Guyer's eyes flashed and my mistake became very clear.

"I would turn you over in a heartbeat if it saves lives." Guyer's nostrils flared. "If one of your buddies from Homicide stumbled out of here after slamming down drinks, and headed straight to the Bunker, would you let them start their day? Or would you get involved?"

"There's only one way I'd get involved," I said. "And it wouldn't be crawling to internal affairs or tattling to an outsider."

"Good for you," she said. "The point is, you wouldn't let them hurt someone else, or sabotage their own career. You'd do it because if you didn't, whatever happened next would be on your head. So if you think my earlier statement was a threat, that's on you. Now sit down."

I locked eyes with Guyer, and I knew that she was serious. Defeated, I dropped back into my seat.

"Who else knows?" she asked.

"Jax."

"I figured. No one else?"

I did my best not to think of the astonishment on Gellica's face when I demonstrated my ability to impact manna-linked items. The mixture of excitement and relief, as we both realized we weren't solitary freaks. And, days later, the look on her face when she'd walked away in disappointment.

"No," I said. "No one at all."

"Good. Keep it that way." Guyer crossed her arms, leather crunching with the motion. "In the meantime, read the book. You'll save us all a lot of heartache if you accept what's happening."

Grudgingly, I reached down and plucked it off of the table, where I'd planned to accidentally leave it behind.

"You tried to show me what you could do once before," she said. "If I requisitioned some next gen manna, think you could try again?"

"Sure," I said. "You get the glittery stuff from underground, and I'll put on a show. Then you can leave me alone."

She seemed to consider that. "I don't think the problem is people leaving you alone or not."

I opened my mouth to tell her how full of it she was, but she talked over me.

"I know you don't believe me," she said. "But I think you'll be far better off if you can find a little forgiveness for others. Do that, and maybe you'll find it for yourself, as well."

I thought of Ronald, the kid Jax had followed up on. I could still see the kid's mom as vividly as if I were still in the room, holding her hand as her body crumbled away, devoured by the manna threads wrapped around her. Threads that had grown strong because of my unknowing involvement. I didn't kill her, but I'd shortened her time on the Path. If not for me, she'd have lived longer. Maybe long enough to say goodbye to her son. Maybe long enough to find help.

I didn't think I'd be forgiving myself anytime soon.

With a shake of my head to clear away the past, I said, "So can I go?"

Guyer sat back. "I tried. When it all burns up for you, remember that I tried." We stared at each other for several seconds, before she dismissed me with a wave. "Yes, you can go."

I gave my most noncommittal grunt, and headed for the door. I wasn't a sorcerer. I was something else entirely. And no self-help book was going to hold the answers. I paused for only the briefest of prayers, my hand over the entry vent as the shouts of welcome and good cheer echoed behind me. And then I was gone, emerging once more into that city, teeming with crime and greed, betrayal and glory. I dragged in a breath and walked the streets of Titanshade.

I LEFT HAMMER HEAD'S IRRITATED AND hungry. I didn't like being reminded of the moral price we all paid to simply exist in the city. Even worse, none of the nearby restaurants or noodle stands caught my eye. I wanted something fast and portable, and most of the street vendors were on break, not willing to compete with sit-down restaurants for the dinner rush. Farther down the block, the squeal of ill-maintained brakes and the asthmatic wheeze of hydraulic doors announced the arrival of a city bus. That sealed it. I'd head to the Bunker, where I could make a couple calls and get batter-dipped something or other at one of the street vendors sure to be catering to the night shift.

I managed to find an open seat on the bus, mostly because no one else was willing to sit next to the guy with foam-specked lips proclaiming that the end of the world was coming. He was working himself up into a righteous froth about how we'd all end up plunged into a hole, deposited into one of the many Hells below. I supposed we'd all spend eternity beside the Titan, whose screams warmed the city with every new torment the imps inflicted on him. I turned to the window. At least the guy's ravings and rancid breath guaranteed no one else would try and talk to me.

The Bunker was a few blocks up, and I got off there, holding my breath against the inevitable cloud of road dirt and exhaust as the bus pulled away. I turned the corner onto Lestrange Avenue, where a long row of food trucks jockeyed for the attention of hungry pedestrians. I found one that looked promising and got in line. While I waited, I perused the small rack of magazines the vendor had strapped to the side of her vehicle. Mostly newsprint rags with sensational headlines, along with one or two glossies. One cover caught my eye, a photo of a petite older woman, clothes stretched taut in an unnatural wind, her face a snarl of rage and determination. It was Ambassador Paulus in the heat of the sorcerous duel from two weeks ago. To her right, I could just make out the silhouette of a Mollenkampi. Broadcast live on television, the duel had taken the lifetime politician and schemer and made her a pop-culture icon. But that moment's fame would fade, and she'd remain what she was at heart: a callous and cruel power monger, interested in an agenda that only she understood.

I tapped the paperback against my thigh and looked back at the menu. The selection promised mouth-scalding heat, and at the moment, that sounded perfect.

"What are you reading?"

I turned. Talena Michaels stood a few paces away, hands stuffed in her jeans pockets, a mild smirk on her lips. Noticeably, she wasn't in her typical outfit of layered shirts, opting instead for a lightweight blouse topped by a linen half-jacket. Her hair was up, revealing a pair of teardrop earrings. *Imps below*, I thought, *she's on a date.*

"Don't normally see you in this part of town," I said.

"I've had a lot of bad experiences with cops."

"I know," I said. She'd been arrested, falsely accused, and restrained in her hospital bed. It'd broken my heart to see someone I'd helped raise be put through that.

Talena shrugged. "It mostly started in my childhood."

She always had been a smartass.

"I seem to recall a cop bailing you out of a bad spot on more than one occasion." I moved to the front of the line and nodded a greeting to the woman working the grill. "Two proiler pitas, extra sauce." I looked over my shoulder and asked Talena, "You want one? My treat."

"Nah, I'm waiting on someone."

"Make 'em spicy," I told the vendor. Talena joined me as I stepped to the side to wait on my order. I pointed at the glossy magazine featuring Paulus. "That who you're meeting?"

The silhouette beside Paulus was barely identifiable—a cop didn't have the dramatic appeal of a sorcerer at the height of her powers—but Talena and I knew it was Jax.

She smiled. "The man in the shadows."

"You guys have big plans?"

"Not really," she said, giving me no information at all. "I'm meeting him across the street." She indicated the Bunker's front doors.

The vendor called out an exaggerated, "Pita u-u-u-pp!" and I collected my dinner.

"I'll walk with you," I said. We strolled to the front of the Bunker, near the large glass double doors of the public entrance. I did my best to be intelligible between bites.

"I haven't seen you much lately."

She gave me an exaggerated frown. "You haven't seen me much since I've been an adult."

"Probably for the best," I said. "You cramp my style." That at least got a laugh, and I relaxed a little. Talena and I had a way of getting under each other's skin, and our typical conversations were strolls through a minefield of misunderstanding and stubbornness. "Last I heard you were looking for office space."

"Community space," she said. "Someplace for people on the street to share information. Reliable facts, with no agenda."

"Facts, huh? I figured they could use a sandwich."

"Sometimes that's part of it," she said. "What guideposts are giving out food, what buildings are safe to squat in. The kind of thing that people in power don't want to acknowledge. Most people want to pretend no one's forced to sleep on the street, that no one ever had the world pulled out from underneath them and is left wondering where their next meal is coming from." She pursed her lips and glanced up at the halls of power around us. "Most people want to pretend it couldn't happen to them."

"And you can fix that?"

Her hands dropped to her hips, and we slowed our pace. "No one can *fix* that. Firefighters can't unlight a burning house, but they can put water on the flame. I can spread information about safety and basic rights because that's what I can do to help." Talena's lips curled, a verbal brawler starting to enjoy herself. "Better than your usual strategy of complaining about the heat as you watch the house burn down."

"Let's wait inside," I said, hoping to find a topic that would get us less fired up. "Jax is gonna come through the lobby anyway."

We passed through the double doors and found a pair of empty seats among the rows of interconnected hard plastic chairs that served as the Bunker's waiting area. The desk sergeant acknowledged me with a nod, and overhead a television blared the dramatic music and prerecorded typing that signaled the start of the nightly news.

"So where is this new office?" I said, then corrected myself. "Community center, I mean."

She chuckled. "It's in Sylvan, near Arlington Ave." I winced, and immediately regretted it as her jaw set and shoulders pulled back. "What? You don't approve of my neighborhood?"

"Nah," I said. "It's just, you know, a little rough that far leeward. I'll talk to some guys on the patrol, ask them to swing by and keep an eye on the place."

She made a disgusted noise in the back of her throat. "Number one, having redbacks around would scare off my clients. And I don't need you or anyone else calling in favors for me."

"Why would they be scared if they're not doing anything wrong?" It was a stupid thing to say. There's an old saying that there's always a foul being committed on the carabella pitch, but no referee worth a damn would call them all. It's the same with policing. There's always a reason to pull someone over, to question their right to be in that neighborhood or in the city as a whole. And it's the easiest thing in the world to abuse that power. I raised my hands. "I didn't mean it like—"

"Oh, I know what you meant." Her cheeks were flushed. "But maybe if people in the 'nice' neighborhoods didn't call the cops anytime they spotted someone in a lower tax bracket, it wouldn't be such a heavy burden on the folks in scarlet."

"Believe it or not, patrol cops don't particularly enjoy playing nanny to the wealthy." Social paranoia calls usually required a patrol car to crawl through the neighborhood, trying hard to be seen by whoever put in the call, verifying that a given pedestrian wasn't intoxicated or violent, and then driving away. "It's a waste of resources, but it's still better to get three false calls than know that someone didn't pick up the phone when it could have made a difference."

"The problem is when your crews in scarlet get sick of the calls and decide to eliminate the source."

I swallowed my last mouthful of pita, feeling the flush of anger along my own cheeks. "No one's *eliminating* anything. And I don't like the implication."

She snorted. "Tell that to the people who get picked up and driven to a neighborhood where they 'belong.'" The girl I'd helped raise looked around the waiting area, unhappy with the nervous and scared faces of people waiting on friends or family being held, or desperate to find an advocate to set things right. "In this town a patrol car drops someone in the wrong neighborhood and it's a good chance they'll get a beating. That's assuming they didn't get one in the squad car." She jerked her chin at the TV news playing over our heads. "And with CaCuri getting elected to alderman, it's only getting worse."

On the news, the city's newest member of City Council walked past a scrum of reporters, sunglasses on and head held high, center of attention, just as she'd always wanted. Katie CaCuri should have been convicted of trafficking, extortion, and racketeering years ago. Instead, she'd simply made the transition to big-time corruption: she'd got herself elected alderman. Her rise to power had tipped the delicate balance of power toward the Titanshade isolationists, who wanted less interaction with the other city-states of the AFS.

"So does that mean you're all aboard the federal train these days?" It wasn't pleasant to see CaCuri doing well, and I was glad when the news feed switched out. The newscaster was back, closing the broadcast with a sappy feel-good story about rescued animals.

She coughed out her amusement. "Hardly. Paulus and the AFS have had their hands on the city's throat for decades. It's time to shake things up in this town. The people are calling for it. They want to see change. Real change."

"Real change? What does that even mean?" I'd had a long day, I was irritated, and I couldn't keep the irritation from showing in my voice. "You sound like Vandie Cedrow, preaching about the geo-vents and redirecting warmth."

Talena clucked her tongue. "Vandie Cedrow's a rich kid who spent most of her life out of the city. She talks a good game, but she wants a big fix. That's easy to wish for, but it skips over the actual work that needs to be done on a one-to-one level. Cedrow's a wanna-be revolutionary with something to prove."

"Not to mention having to live down her uncle," I said.

"I can relate." She meant it as a joke, but it still rankled me.

"Don't get me wrong. The warmth distribution is a real issue. People are freezing out on the Borderlands, crammed into buildings that haven't seen a code enforcement officer since they were built. The working poor, full-time employed, but can't afford to pay deposit or rent and are squatting or living on top floors in the Borderlands, sleeping in mummy bags and praying for a piece of the manna boom. If it ever comes." She shook her head, frustration mounting. "Cedrow's right about one thing. We need hope. If you tell everyone that life sucks and they need to buck up and bear it, they'll give up."

"Hope? You mean crap like that?" I pointed at the television, where the anchor still prattled on about a Titanshader who'd rescued a litter of puppies from a burning building. "Because that right there is sleight-of-hand. A feel-good distraction from real problems."

The studio anchor pursed his lips, looking smug and sympathetic and oh-so punchable. Anger crept into my voice, the words rising in volume before I could stop it. "They want us to see the one person in a million who shows an ounce of decency, as if a single stake in the ground is going to stop a landslide of deceit, cruelty, and selfishness."

"Every time I think you've hit the limit of stupidity you manage to raise the bar yet again." She clasped one hand to her forehead, hand-woven friendship bracelets and a steel ba symbol covering her wrist, silent testimony to her faith and the many people she'd helped. "What the Hells do you think I do all day? Do you seriously think I just hand out pamphlets and yell at pimps? I'm out there getting people the resources they need to survive. Every day there are new people on the street, and they've got zero safety net. One mistake, one single misstep, and they're gonna end up as a file on your desk. So yeah, I think every one of those tiny little acts of kindness matters. Because all of them add up to something worth fighting for."

"So fight for it," I said. "Stop complaining about pushing the boulder uphill, and organize a bunch of fuckers with shovels to come over and level the landscape. You want to make change, that's how you do it." I walked past the television, hopped on one of the plastic chairs beneath it, and slapped the power button off. Someone in the crowd hissed, a critique on my parenting skills that I immediately ignored. "You do that and we'll both sleep better at night."

"Oh, I am changing it. I'm actually making a difference, instead of locking up kids for minor infractions, leaving them with records that'll keep them chained to low-wage jobs the rest of their lives. I organize voter registration drives, get ballot measures put together—"

"Politics? You think I meant politics?" I forced a loud, obviously fake laugh. "Hells, politics makes your neighborhood look like a playground. If you actually started to change things, you think CaCuri or the other dirt-bags in City Hall would leave you alive long enough to see the law passed? Politics, please."

"Uh, am I interrupting?" At some point Jax had arrived. I reared on him, noticing the fresh clothes and still-damp head plates. He must've showered in the Bunker's locker room.

Talena turned to Jax and snapped a terse, "We're going."

She stormed past me, her shoulder bumping mine with enough force that I could tell it was intentional, just like Vandie Cedrow had done at the festival site. But unlike the wealthy socialite's ineffective shove, Talena kept her center of gravity low, just like I'd taught her, and I fell back a step. It was the closest we'd come to a hug since her mother died.

Jax glared at me and raised his hands in silent, bewildered accusation, *What did you do to my date?*, then turned on one heel to follow her. I didn't call after them. It wasn't the worst fight Talena and

I'd ever had, and if history was any indicator, I figured we'd probably be on talking terms again within a few months.

When I got home I dumped my coat on the couch and walked to the record player. I dropped the needle on some vinyl I'd picked up earlier that week and gave myself a slow, bluesy soundtrack as I looked for something to eat—even the pitas hadn't satisfied the growl in my stomach. I poked through my fridge and immediately heard a mew as I became Rumple's focus of attention. I identified several boxes of takeout that hadn't aged beyond reasonable consumption. I mixed them all into a glass dish and stuck them in the oven. While I waited for my casserole surprise to heat up, I poured a bowl of cat food and set it down just in time for the orange and white fur ball to start chewing on that instead of my ankles.

Rumple noisily crunched his way through the kibble, so focused on the food in his bowl that he was barely aware of my presence. I thought of that focus, and how someone like Bobby Kearn could have been so intent on a task as simple as tying his shoes before a knife plunged into his back. Was it simply because he'd sampled the angel tears, or was it something else? It felt like a thread worth holding on to. Sometimes that's how it works—some image or idea triggers a thought that leads to another thought, that leads to a breakthrough. Ninety percent of detective work is quiet, methodical and boring, punctuated by insight and violence and the sorrow of those left behind.

I left Rumple to his meal and dragged a kitchen chair to the window. I cracked open my beer, followed by the window. The window's ballast rope had snapped, and I propped it open with the book Guyer had forced on me. I sat back and took a long swig of beer as the sound of traffic merged with music from my stereo, the city's underscore drowning out the noise of my neighbors' latest screaming match.

Titanshade was a city of teeming millions, every one of whom wanted more—more space, more money, more sex, more power, more time to themselves. No matter what someone's *more* was, there never seemed to be enough to go around. I'd defended those people when I wore patrol reds, and I'd tried to throttle the supply of street drugs when I worked Vice. But catching killers had been my true calling. Rumple snaked through the legs of my chair, then reared up, shoving his muzzle into my free hand. I scratched his head and asked myself if I'd go into a burning building to save him. He let out a high-pitched mew, and gently nibbled my finger. I sighed.

I'd go through a dozen burning buildings, if that's what it took. Or more.

Working in Homicide I wasn't defending against future crimes or playing counselor without the training. I was trying to balance out the scales for those irrevocably wronged. It was a good chore for a guy who never quite learned to connect with the living. The kind of man who spent his evenings alone, balancing his chair on its back legs and staring at the cover of *Your Death and You* while he thought about his life.

So I drank all my beers and watched my city, and eventually I fell asleep to the sound of the music and the traffic and Rumple's purr. Or maybe it was the growl of my stomach.

OF ALL THE CHANGES CAUSED by the discovery of next gen manna, perhaps my least favorite was that I had to report for regular physicals. All the first responders who'd been present at the manna strike were monitored for any sign of unusual activity. We were regularly told this was to catch any ill effects as early as possible. By now, we all knew that was a lie. Both the AFS and the city leaders had no intention of walking away from a source of wealth and power like next gen manna. If we showed signs of illness or ill effect, we stood in the way of that great financial machine. We were under a microscope on a weekly basis, and our examiner was Dr. Baelen.

And that was why I'd come in with a plan.

"Have you experienced anything unusual in the last week? And look up at the ceiling, please." Baelen adjusted her headlamp across the green expanse of her forehead, tilting the reflecting disk so it wouldn't interfere with the prominent fin running across her head.

"Not really." I kept my voice neutral and focused on the ceiling tiles as a set of cold fingers dug into the flesh under my jaw, the hooked barbs of her nails almost penetrating the skin. An AFS-funded researcher, Baelen had arrived in Titanshade hoping to make a name for herself with her research. Unlike other newcomers, she had the authority to hold me hostage if she could show any unusual activity on my part.

"You've put on weight," she said.

"Maybe a little." I prepared a litany of defenses and deflections, but she inquired no further. It seemed the good doctor was distracted.

The other members of the weekly group sat in a loose circle. Baelen's assistants moved among them, collecting samples and probing uncomfortably. Most of her team were genuine medical professionals, but a few stood to the side, ill-concealed sidearms creating conspicuous lumps at their waists. Soldiers in scrubs, a not-so-subtle reminder that federal troops controlled the manna site, and thus the future of Titanshade.

And there's nothing that those in power enjoy more than treating others like children.

"Open up and say ahhh." Baelen's fin perked up slightly as she peered into my mouth. "You should floss more," she said with a distinct note of disapproval. "You were on the ice plains recently, correct?"

No point in my playing dumb, since all she had to do was read a newspaper to learn the truth.

"Muh-huh," I said, mouth still open.

"And did you encounter anything peculiar while you were out there?"

"Eh." I did my best to imply indifference.

"Because the news is full of stories about unusual behavior," she said. "All kinds of rumors." She snapped off the light. "You can close your mouth."

The door to the makeshift exam room opened, admitting a latecomer to our little gathering.

"Sorry, Doc." Andrews was a broad-chested Mollenkampi patrol cop, a simple man who liked to keep his head down and collect his paycheck, while doing a little good along the way. His shoulders slumped, he was pallid, and sweat dribbled down his temples.

The rest of us tensed, but Baelen returned her attention to me, dismissing Andrews with a curt, "Have a seat, Officer Andrews. Johnson will take your bloodwork."

I sat in silence, as she pretended to jot a note in her ever-present clipboard while she shot glances at Andrews. "No unusual occurrences, nothing of note?"

"You already asked that."

Her fin rose and fell, and she pulled back. "Because you didn't answer the first time." She crossed her arms, voice stronger. "In fact, it's my impression that you don't answer any of my questions the first time they're asked."

I didn't say anything. To Baelen, I was a lab rat with a peculiar tumor, one that might be valuable to her career if she could just split me open and poke around inside. She couldn't, not yet. To do that, she'd have to find a way to show that my imprisonment would be for the greater good. I had a momentary flutter of discomfort, wondering about the various people I'd arrested for that very reason. But there was a need to lock away wolves from the sheep, even if the system wasn't perfect about identifying which was which.

"Well, Detective?"

But then again, that was why I had a plan. I had to leave Baelen some crumbs.

"I do have a ringing in my ears," I said. "Kind of like a buzzing."

"Hmm." Baelen leaned in, giving me a blast of her moist and peaty breath. I blinked rapidly. "Say more."

"Well," I said, "I've been hearing about this buzzing going on. Everyone's talking about it in the Bunker. You know how cops are."

She jotted a note, and I continued.

"Anyway, after I read the papers I'm kind of worried about it, the buzz I'm hearing."

"How loud is it?"

I shrugged. "Pretty faint. If I'm in a quiet room, and don't say anything, it's in the background."

"And it sounds like static?"

"More like a high-pitched ringing."

"Any mood swings?"

I frowned. "Well, no . . ."

"Sounds like tinnitus, a ringing in the ears that sounds like an air raid siren. Several varieties. It's common among Mollenkampi, though humans can get it, too."

"You sure?" I did my best to put a note of concern in my voice. "The buzzing is all over the papers."

She looked unimpressed, as I'd hoped she would. The media had run with the mysterious sound that was apparently linked to a rash of homicides. "The Buzz Kill Murders," the headlines had declared. Accompanied by gory photos of the crime scene and old photos of the killers in the worst possible light. It was the editorial choices inherent in media. Pick a photo of the suspect standing with friends and family and they look innocent; pick a photo where they have one eye closed and their mouth half open, and they look unhinged. In any case, it was sensationalist panic-mongering, and the fact that I was citing it made Baelen take what I was saying less seriously.

And that made her note the buzzing in my file, and dismiss it in a single motion.

"I'll ask again," she peered into my eyes, "have you seen something unusual?"

I had an array of choice answers. But I settled on a simple, "Nope."

Baelen frowned, but didn't push me further. My plan had worked better than expected.

The good doctor stood and made a show of turning to stare at the wall clock. Then she addressed the group.

"Today is a short session. As always, with regard to these studies the AFS thanks you for your cooperation, your compliance, and your silence. You are free to go."

Along with the other lab rats I stood and gathered my things. Meanwhile, the nurses who'd done bloodwork consulted with Baelen. The slender Gillmyn raised her voice one more time.

"If you'll stay behind, Officer Andrews. Since you arrived late, we'll need a little longer to finish your process."

The rest of the room froze. Andrews looked at her with baggy, bloodshot eyes. "Doc?"

"You arrived late. We need a little longer to complete your examination." Back ramrod-straight, Baelen forced a chipper tone. "No reason to hold the whole group."

Andrews slumped back into his chair. The rest of the lab rats exchanged looks, but there was nothing to be done. One by one, we filed out of the room.

In the hallway I lingered rather than head for the elevator. "I'm going to hit the vending machines," I said. "You want anything?"

"I'm good." Jax paused. "There're vending machines on the third floor, you know."

"Yeah, well." I stared at the door to Baelen's makeshift lab. "I'm curious to see the options up here."

Suddenly Jax was standing next to me. "Me, too."

I retreated down the hall to the vending machines and fed them my offering of coins, receiving a plastic-wrapped square of stale brownie in return. It wasn't more than a few minutes before Andrews emerged, flanked by two of the pseudo-nurses.

"What's going on?" I asked. The soldiers didn't break stride.

Andrews looked at us. "I'm . . ." He started coughing.

"Where are you taking him?" I managed to not quite shout the question as I blocked their path. "He's got the flu or something. Let him go home and rest."

"He's been enrolled in the advanced research program." It was Baelen, standing in the exam room doorway, clipboard clutched to her chest and her head angled like a lizard studying a fly.

"For what?" I asked. We'd seen other cops end up with that designation, for bad dreams or weight loss or anxiety. None of them had come back, and their few visitors reported seeing them as overly medicated husks of themselves. Potential witnesses drugged into silence.

"For observation," she said. "Until he's well."

Jax shook his head. "You can't do that unilaterally. We'll contact the TPD liaison."

"Be my guest, gentlemen. Though she's already been apprised."

Baelen indicated the far end of the hall, where DO Guyer was approaching rapidly.

"What's the meaning of this?" she demanded.

In response, Baelen extended the clipboard. Guyer snatched it away and scanned the top sheet. Her face darkened.

"This is—"

"Properly documented? Yes, it is." Baelen held out a webbed hand.

Guyer stared at her with narrowed eyes. But eventually she thrust the clipboard into the researcher's grasp.

"Carry on, then," Baelen said, and retreated back into the examination room.

I turned to Guyer, but she waved me off. "I'll see what I can do," she said, then headed for the elevators. Only Jax and I stood in front of Andrews and his escort.

The soldiers didn't force Andrews. In truth, I'm not sure what would have happened if they had. He went along willingly, too tired to fight, and too wise to think it would have mattered. Jax and I could only stand by as they passed, leaving us alone in the hallway.

"You still advocating that I tell the world about my trick with the threads?" I asked.

Jax watched Andrews and his captors disappear into the elevator, the doors sliding shut behind them like a pair of vertical jaws.

"No."

We started the walk back to Homicide in silence.

The Bunker's corridors seemed endless, all of them lined with vinyl tiles and humming fluorescent lights. Sometimes it felt like we worked in the intestines of a great beast, swallowing both criminals and those who chased them, digesting and depositing us all on the other side.

As we walked, conversations buzzed in the air around us, a cocktail of jokes, insults, and of course, stories. Stories were the social lubricant of the Bunker. The kind of stories that cops tell each other to get a laugh or sympathetic slap on the back, stories that highlight the absurdity and tragedy of daily life. We tell stories to learn what not to do and to purge bad memories from our minds. Stories are to cops what a hot shower is to a construction worker: a cleansing pain that washes away the filth, leaving you ready for another day of suffering.

The latest batch of stories were both puzzling and disturbingly familiar. Family gatherings erupting into violence; strangers jostling for space on a bus ending up at each other's throat; a carabella team's practice turning into a homicide scene. In every instance the perpetrator was easily identified, usually confessed, and expressed bewilderment about why any of it had even occurred. It was a kind of seasonal burst of craziness that made old-timers talk of moon phases, and made newer cops suspect designer drugs. They were both wrong, of course. To learn the truth, all they had to do was listen to the song of anger ringing in their ears.

The patrol had their hands full, and the assaults that had become murders were beginning to make an impact on the caseload in the Bullpen. If things continued as they were, the holding cells in the Bunker would run out of space before long. When I'd seen others hear the buzzing at the festival scene, I'd been relieved. It was proof that it wasn't in my head. Now I'd come to fear what that change meant, and just how widespread this madness would become.

Standing near the blackboard, a particularly well-dressed Mollenkampi and his gangly, muscled human partner held the department's rapt attention. I walked past, but Jax slowed to listen to Angus and Bangles tell their story. No one else called me over to join the group. That was fine with me and I only halfheartedly listened in as I completed some additional paperwork on the Donna Raun case.

"I shit you not," Bangles was saying, a loose grin barely masking the weariness on her face. "This guy ran out of his apartment, naked as the day he was born, and attacked the street musician like he'd heard one too many flat notes and couldn't take it anymore!" The assembled group of detectives chuckled along with her, and she continued. "By the time Angus and I were on scene, the guy had snapped out of it and was standing there with the bloody squeezebox hiding his junk."

Angus wore one of his trademark suits, though I'd noticed in recent months he'd moved toward a slightly more modern cut. He must have gotten advice about how best to appeal to some demographic or city influencer. He was a born social climber, and was the likely pick to succeed Bryyh as department captain. Angus was a master of the game; I hadn't even managed to learn how the pieces moved.

Jax spoke up. "I don't know what's going on out there," he said, "but it's not normal. It can't be normal."

One of the other detectives gave Ajax a good-natured shove and declared him to be soft. When I didn't live up to social standards, I was given the cold shoulder and labeled bad luck. I never quite figured out the difference between Ajax and myself.

Ajax must've spotted me, because he made his way to our desks. "Bangles was just telling—"

"I heard. Sounds like whatever got Bobby Kearn and Saul Petrevisch killed is going around."

"You heard?" He took a seat. "You listened to her story while you sulked at your desk. And yet you wonder why you don't have more friends."

"I was forced to listen because she was announcing it to the world while I was trying to get some work done."

"And what work is that?" His eyes crinkled, amused. "Can you name what form you are filling out?"

"That's fine. You're the pretty face of our team, and I'm the brains."

Jax swiveled in his chair, the spring mechanism creaking slightly. "In other words, I'll be friendly and you'll pout in the corner."

I sneered, not liking how much that sounded like Talena's comments from the night before.

He leaned back. "You're older, but that doesn't mean I haven't done my time in the academy and on the streets. I've worked my rear end off to be a detective and I'm not going to let you belittle me, Carter. I've earned my right to be here." Jax swung his arms, showing that the Bullpen was the "here" he'd earned. It would've been touching if it weren't so naive.

"I know you have, kid." But I didn't have the heart to tell him how much pain and sorrow he'd signed up for. Proving himself as a cop meant he'd be first in line to be sacrificed when a politician decided it was for the greater good, or simply meant a few more votes come election day. He'd seen what happened to Andrews, and sooner or later he'd figure it out for himself.

"I'm still hungry," I said. He ignored me, so I tried again. "How about grabbing food?"

"You buying?"

"Sure," I said. That got him to look up, and I added, "If you loan me some cash."

He rolled his eyes, but said, "Fine. But I can't handle the cafeteria. Let's find something healthier."

TO APPEASE JAX WE AVOIDED the unhealthy and bland cafeteria food, opting instead for the unhealthy but palatable street vendors who gathered on the side of the Bunker and catered to the poor diets and limited budgets of the Titanshade PD.

I grabbed a sausage roll and Jax ordered a cup of soup. I liked it when he got soup. A Mollenkampi's dual mouths also divided up the labor of eating, and a cup of soup meant that I wouldn't have to suffer through seeing him shuffle his chewed food from his oversized biting mouth to the more discreet speaking mouth in his throat.

Our respective meals in hand, we took a short stroll to one of the nearby picnic tables set aside for our use. We weren't far from the stream of pedestrians, but they passed by quickly, and in classic Titanshader fashion were indifferent to even the most scandalous conversations.

"Do any of these homicides make sense to you?" I asked.

"Do they ever?"

I rolled my eyes and shifted my feet on the dirt-streaked table leg.

"No, I mean it," he said. "Have you ever walked onto a murder scene and said to yourself, 'You know, these people are making really good decisions!'"

"Point taken. But there's a difference between dumb choices and not making a choice at all. These murders where the killers barely know what happened, just that they were angry or felt so betrayed about dirty dishes that they had to beat a man to death . . ." I shook my head. "There's always some like that, sure. But not this many."

Jax popped the lid off his soup container and fanned a hand over it. Mollenkampi might have a fearsome set of long-toothed jaws and an ability to self-harmonize, but their inability to blow cool air over their food made it a net loss in my books.

He asked, "You think it's the noise?"

I nodded. "Don't you?"

"You hear it when you do your thing with the threads. I'm guessing it doesn't make you want to kill people?"

"No. But it doesn't let me think like myself, either."

"What does it feel like?"

"Being underwater," I said. "Cold. Muffled. And pressure all over."

"Like you're at the bottom of the ocean."

"I guess. And I get hungry. No matter what I do, I want more." I wiped my hands on the napkin. "Dr. Baelen's going to make me disappear."

He blinked, either at the claim or the sudden shift in topic. "I didn't like seeing Andrews taken away either. But you saw Guyer's face. If she can do anything, she will."

"He's headed to a secure ward, locked away with the other patrol cops and medics who've been taken since the manna strike. And they're the lucky ones. What do you think Baelen would do with me?"

Jax didn't answer, staring instead into his soup like a divination officer reading tea leaves. Sometimes I forgot how young he was. I took a deep breath and prepared to tell him the truth in the gentlest terms possible.

"Everyone in power is corrupt and out to exploit us," I said. "Unless we're too much of a headache. Then they'll just kill us and use our deaths as an excuse to crack down on civil liberties."

He started coughing, and I half stood, afraid he was choking. Then I realized he was laughing though a mouthful of soup. "You listen to your DJ buddy too much."

"Handsome Hanford is all about conspiracies. I'm talking about millions of people, all of them trying to look out for themselves. No conspiracy, no plan, just the cold, lonely truth that we're alone, and no one cares about us."

"You really are a little bit of sunshine, aren't you?" He wiped his speaking mouth with a napkin. "People are capable of as much kindness as cruelty."

"Yeah," I said. "That's the worst part."

For a moment we sat in silence.

"You've got more years on the job," he said, "but I saw my fair share of corruption before I ever came to Titanshade, and I think you're oversimplifying. Besides, you have as much integrity as anyone else, even if you like to pretend you don't."

"If you say so." I closed my eyes, wallowing in the sounds of the city. Car horns and a million conversations, constant jackhammering at construction sites and panhandlers and street performers, all of us living in an improbable oasis of warmth on the ice plains. Jax was right, all of us were capable of kindness and cruelty in equal measure. Sometimes I wondered how someplace so filthy, self-absorbed, and callously indifferent to the sufferings of others could still be the source of so much good. I wonder if normal people think the same thing about cops.

"So what do you recommend?" I sat up straighter and changed the tone of my voice. Nonverbal cues that it was time for what people like us had to do in order to survive: compartmentalize and move on.

"We could interview Sheena and Donna. Talk to Sheena's brother Michael and see what he thought about her behavior before and after she attacked Kearn. We could track down Vandie Cedrow and find out the story behind Saul Petrevisch getting fired. Or maybe track down Murphy CaDell and get it from him."

I grunted. That property management company address still nagged at me. Expensive real estate didn't make sense for an operation like that.

"Let's step back," I said. "Look at the bigger questions. For the sake of argument, let's say it's the buzzing causing the murders."

Jax shrugged. "Okay."

"So what's causing the buzzing?"

A deep breath. "Well, it could be an unknown natural phenomenon. Windstorms, magnetic fields, that kind of thing. There's intentional interference, like a pirate radio station or, I don't know, some kind of jamming frequency. Then unintentional interference, bleed-over from a too-powerful radio tower."

"Okay," I said, knowing full well what was coming. "None of that causes people to fly into violent rages, though, does it?"

"No." His biting mouth clacked rhythmically as he talked his way through it. "So next we're into the realm of the unnatural. Magic or related effects. I wouldn't say that's a possibility at all, except for . . ." He glanced at me, then looked away.

"Except for me, I got it."

"Right. So." He stretched both mandibles and stared at the sky for a long moment. "You first felt the buzz after you came into contact with snake oil."

"Sort of. It's the next gen manna that does it. Whether it's diluted in snake oil or pure."

"The point is," he said, "that the effects could be coming from snake oil labs or dealers. Or it could be coming from the massive reservoir of manna on the ice plains."

I scratched my neck. He had a point. "Could it be caused by someone? A sorcerer, maybe. Someone with the political pull to have access to next gen manna and the complete lack of any moral guidance."

"Ambassador Paulus."

"Maybe. She's doesn't care who gets crushed in her campaign for more power. And she's experimented with manna before."

He perked up. "She has?"

I winced. She had indeed, and the result of that experiment was named Gellica, a woman who moved through the upper crust of society with the same ease that she padded through the hills in the shape of a feline. But I couldn't tell Jax about that—I'd already betrayed Gellica once, and her secrets weren't mine to reveal.

"She has," I said, quickly adding, "but she's not the only one. Harlan Cedrow found the manna reservoir that way. Hells, he even imported his own tech support. Heidelbrecht slipped away from me once, and he deserves to be dragged into the light as much as anyone else."

"And now Cedrow's niece Vandie is right at the center of everything. She was nearby when Bobby Kearn was killed, and when his body transformed."

"There's no ignoring the Barekusu, either."

"What do you mean?" He drew back.

"I mean it's amazing timing, them arriving right when all this breaks out into the open. Plus, at least one of them had a next gen manna connection. I felt the thread at the parade. They claim they're here to meditate on the manna discovery. I don't know what they're really doing here. The one that came early, the sorcerer—what's her name?"

"Serrow." He sounded apprehensive. "But she wasn't anywhere near Shelter in the Bend. None of the Barekusu were."

"But they *were* near Saul Petrevisch's apartment. They were right outside."

"The problem is," said Jax, "that we don't really know if distance has anything to do with it at all."

"That's the trouble with magic. We almost have to write it off as a possibility in order to get anywhere."

Jax took a long sip of soup. "Magic has rules, too."

I stared at the fog-shrouded shape of the Mount. "No. Guyer told us about that once. She said magic doesn't have rules, it has, whatchacallit . . ."

"Probabilities."

"Right. The more manna, the more likely it is to get a reliable outcome. A skilled sorcerer can make a little manna perform in an expected fashion. An unskilled user could—"

"—have anything happen at all."

"Look." I set my half-eaten lunch on the tabletop, careful to tuck a napkin underneath it first. "We are not going to start finishing—"

"—each others' sentences?" His eyes crinkled.

I snatched my sausage roll off the table with a growl. "I do not know what I did to be saddled with you as a partner."

"If I recall, it had something to do with a couple decades of erratic and undisciplined behavior."

I snorted. "I got disciplined plenty." I took a bite and spoke through a mouthful of dough and spiced meat. "You want to make yourself useful? Let's focus on the people who might have the ability and motive to do this."

"Motive for what?" Jax's voice trilled, exasperated. "For the murders? You talked to Sheena and Donna. Even *they* didn't think they had a motive." He waved a hand in the direction of the Bunker's higher floors. "You heard the stories coming in to the Bullpen. Everyone's going on 187 runs, and wrapping them up in record time. So is someone masterminding a wave of unintended homicides?"

"What if that's exactly what they are—unintended? What if the killings aren't the crime, but just a side effect?"

"A side effect of the buzzing? Or is the buzzing the side effect of something bigger?"

"I don't know."

"Because maybe all of it is a side effect of the manna strike. Or maybe it's a side effect of something we haven't even learned about yet."

I dragged a hand over my head as Ajax pressed on.

"How do we run an investigation if we don't even know what the crime was?"

"We start the only place we can," I said. "With what we do know. We examine all the recent cases, and search for commonalities. We search for patterns and make theories and test them. We follow where the evidence leads and ask questions. But we sure as Hells don't give up before we even try." I leaned forward. "We can't get to Vandie today, and the Barekusu are going to be tough to talk to at all. So whatdya say we stop by Ambassador Paulus's place and ask a few questions?"

Jax looked up at the Bunker. "I need to talk to Captain Bryyh about my badge."

"Yeah. But here's the thing—you already skipped a day after losing it, right?"

He glared at me.

"Exactly," I said. "So you're gonna get hit with the penalty one way or another. Let's go visit the esteemed ambassador now, while I've still got you with me."

Jax stood. "Okay, but we need to be open with each other. You sit on something like your threads again, and you put us both in danger. We clear on that?"

"Clear as cold ice." I held his gaze, refusing to let myself think about Gellica's true nature, and all the reasons that keeping that secret might come back to haunt us.

He grunted a two-toned note of skepticism. "Alright. Let's go talk to the ambassador." He headed toward the garage.

I followed behind, shoving our lunch waste in the already over-flowing trash bin.

16

THERE WAS AN ESTABLISHED POWER structure in Titanshade, like every city-state, town, or neighborhood. During the oil boom the major financial players had been executives and rig owners, while the mayor and City Council were the centers of local political power. But Titanshade didn't exist in a vacuum. It was also a member of the Assembly of Free States, a coalition of independent city-states that spent as much time feuding among themselves as cooperating. Like every city-state, Titanshade sent a representative to sit on the AFS Council, and in turn the AFS sent an ambassador to convey the wishes of the council to our fair city. In theory these ambassadors held advisory positions but in fact they held as much sway as the local governments. For all their influence, ambassadors were vulnerable to the changing political winds in both their assigned city-state and in the AFS capital, and most were discarded as quickly as tissues.

As was so often the case, Titanshade was the exception that proved the rule. Our city had enjoyed the presence of Ambassador Paulus for decades.

Paulus was a sorcerer, a politician, and a master manipulator. And that was her friendly, public-facing persona. She was much less pleasant once you got to know her. But no one wanted to tinker with success, and as long as Titanshade's oil rigs kept the world's economic engines turning, people like her were safe and secure. But with the discovery of manna and the government-ordered halt on oil drilling, the rules of the game had changed. So the question was, could Paulus be scared enough that she would try and tamper with snake oil? And if so, what did she possibly have to gain?

One way to find out was by paying a surprise visit to our federal government's esteemed representative.

Paulus lived in a sprawling home perched on the Hills, a short distance from the steep vertical walls that marked the place where the Mount had risen, or been cast down on top of the Titan, depending on how much romanticism and faith you had. This close to the Mount the air was so sulfur-tinged that even a Titanshade native like myself noticed. It was the rotten-egg smell of wealth and power.

The wrought-iron gate at the front of the drive was manned by two humans in tan slacks, black shirts, and mirrored sunglasses. It was the kind of outfit favored by those who wanted to be identifiable as security personnel without the hassle of wearing badges. When we pulled up they flanked the Hasam. One approached the driver's side window, the other stepped to the side, disappearing from our line of sight.

The guard at the window spoke loudly, asking our business. We told him we just wanted a word, and he stepped away, speaking softly into a walkie-talkie. A moment later he returned with a clipboard.

"Badges and IDs," he said.

I brought mine out, fumbling slightly to cover Jax's hesitation at handing over his store-bought badge. The guard jotted down the names and numbers and his partner reappeared to roll back the gate and grant access.

"That's new," I said, pulling the Hasam up the brick drive.

"The guards?" said Jax. He hadn't been with me on my single previous visit to Paulus's home.

"The type of guard. There was a rent-a-thug at the gate last time. But those two moved like pros. Maybe former military."

The house itself was a multistory building with ornate finishes, ringed by exotic plants imported from the south and maintained at great expense. We parked in front of the home, behind a lengthy black sedan with tinted windows. Near the front door a small group of well-dressed people scurried around a petite woman in her early sixties.

Paulus.

Jax and I approached. The crowd parted when the ambassador turned her attention to us.

"Officers," she adjusted her own pair of mirrored sunglasses, designer logo glinting in the afternoon sun, "I'm surprised to see you on my personal property. This must be an emergency."

I shrugged. "A word in private, Ambassador?"

"No time for privacy, officers. I'm sure that whatever you have to say can't be too salacious, after all." Despite her protestations, she issued a terse set of directions to each of the flunkies surrounding her, and they melted away, leaving us alone with Paulus.

She crossed her arms. It was a move that created a sharp triangle out of her gray suit, from the knife-sharp line of her shoulder pads down to the large belt used as an accessory. "Talk fast and don't waste my time."

Jax started to speak, but I placed a hand on his arm.

"What's with the enhanced security?" I asked.

One corner of her mouth crept up. "Death threats. The AFS is still conducting tests on the areas around the manna strike, and the freeze on new drilling has caused some of the furloughed rig workers to tell me how they'd like to right the scales."

"You think they're serious?"

"Never underestimate the hard-handed men of Titanshade." She smiled, and I knew from experience that there would be no trace of humor in her eyes, even if they weren't hidden behind the tiny, curved reflections of Jax and myself. "Ask your questions, gentlemen. And then depart. My time is as short as my patience."

"Fine," I said. "I wouldn't want to waste the time of someone important like you."

She didn't respond. Just beyond earshot, the lackeys glanced at their watches and shuffled papers, acting uninterested. It was probably the same routine they went through anytime their boss was about to eviscerate someone. Possibly literally.

"I was wondering," I said, "how much access you have to the next gen manna. I know you buy traditional manna on the open market, but with the manna from underground coming available only in small batches, are you able to access any before?"

"Before what?"

"Oh, you know." I shuffled my feet. "Before the government takes its final measure. Do you get to play with the new stuff?"

"Absolutely not," she said. "It's processed and brought to market just like any other precious material. I have no special access. Now do you have more of these questions, or do you want to tell me why you're really here?"

"What do you mean?"

"Please. Your dumb schlub routine worked on me the first time we met," she said. "It hasn't since, so I don't know why you're still trying. Now him?" She pointed at Ajax. "That's no act. He's a small-town hick, swinging above his pay grade. I've seen him in action." She gave Jax a look of stark appraisal. "If you ever want to earn an adult pay-check, Ajax, we can talk."

Jax nodded, not taking the bait. I cleared my throat and she turned her attention back to me.

"Ah. But you, Carter, understand more about the city and its residents than you let on. And it's still significantly less than you think you do. You'll never be a real power in this town." She took off her sunglasses and stared me in the eyes. "No matter what kind of strings you can pull."

My chest tightened. Paulus had witnessed me manipulate manna on Titan's Day. She may have been able to piece together what I could do, but I doubted it. No, it was far more likely that she'd gotten that information from the first person I'd confided in about my manna connection. Her daughter, Gellica. The thought of her manipulating Gellica was enough to push me forward once more.

"Funny thing about pulling on threads. The entire sweater tends to unravel." I waved a hand when I said it, as if I were feeling for threads around us. It was her turn to take a step back. Wind swirled a few pieces of trash along the ground, and the air along her arms shimmered, as though Paulus had an invisible python draped across her neck. Down the drive, Paulus's lackeys changed from affected disinterest to concern, and several of them backed even farther away, fidgeting nervously. My skin prickled. I'd encountered the strength of that invisible creature firsthand.

We were interrupted by a rumble that made the bricks tremble beneath our feet. Up the drive rolled a wide-based car, engine growling like an angry lion awakening with a hangover. It was a brand-new Longinus Lancer, built for power and painted a purple so deep that it almost looked like you could dive into it. The car rolled past us to the far side of the drive's turnaround. The engine cut and a woman got out, keys spinning around her index finger.

Her face was a younger version of Paulus's, the same chestnut complexion, the same dimpled chin. But she didn't have Paulus's unemotional shark's eyes. Gellica truly cared about the people around her, and was working to make the city a more livable place. But she'd had the bad luck to be born a product of Paulus's ego, and to be raised under the wing of her mother and employer. Gellica carried as many secrets as I did.

She stood across from us, and I thought that maybe, just maybe, she was about to approach. Then she turned on a heel and walked into the house.

"Carter?" Jax's voice was raised, as if he'd called to me more than once.

"Don't bother, young man. He's only seeing something he can't have." Paulus's sunglasses were back on, and she straightened her suit. "I do need to be going. My security will see you out." She nodded to one of her aides, who scampered off, no doubt to fetch guards to shadow us as we departed.

We climbed into the Hasam and rolled out to the street, where I pulled over and glared at the wrought-iron gate as it drew shut.

"Okay," said Jax. "So what did we learn from that?"

I couldn't stop seeing Gellica disappear through the front door. She was a creature of science and magic, created by Paulus in a lab with the help of an amoral researcher. Gellica was as much of a freak as I was. She needed manna to stay alive, and I needed her to remind me we weren't alone. Maybe the only person in the world who could relate to my secret, and I'd ruined the relationship like I ruined all the others I'd ever had.

"Not much," I said.

Jax hummed, fingers drumming a rhythm on his knee. "There was one thing. For all the extra security she'd picked up, Paulus didn't seem terribly concerned by the death threats. But when you moved forward, Paulus's reaction was to back up."

I didn't answer right away, replaying the scene in my head. He was right.

"She's more frightened of you than of desperate roughnecks," he said. "What does that tell us?"

He stared at me, and I stared at the drive leading to Paulus's plush mansion, my fists clenched on the steering wheel.

"That I'm dangerous," I said. "Even if I don't want to be."

We sat in silence until Jax's pager buzzed, followed a moment later by my own. We both fished them out and read the tiny green screens. Code 187.

"Well," he said. "Looks like we have another homicide victim to meet." He lifted the mic and radioed Dispatch for the address. I put the Hasam in gear and started down another winding road.

WE CHECKED IN WITH DISPATCH, and were given an address in the kind of new-money neighborhood that was mostly occupied by engineers and junior execs who had enough income to move to a warmer zone, but the good sense to not overspend and live beyond their means. It wasn't a normal area for us to get a call; the crimes here tended to be committed behind closed doors and were less likely to be fatal, though just as likely to stay with the victims forever.

Our call brought us to a hardware store, and the cluster of lookie-loos fighting for the right to peer into the shop's front window confirmed we were at the right place. In front of the store a TPD patrol car sat double-parked, an elderly Mollenkampi man in the backseat, with the rounded shoulders and forward lean that came with having his hands cuffed behind him. We cut through the crowd by displaying our badges and barking orders to clear the way.

When we reached the storefront I came to an abrupt halt, causing Ajax to collide with me briefly.

"Hells below," I muttered.

The reason for the crowd's interest was obvious. In the large display window a young Mollenkampi man wearing an apron and a name tag was draped across a half-built display of sale items. Around him white price tags had turned red, the result of dozens of nails that penetrated his skin and fastened him to the display. Some had gone clean through his flesh, while the heads of others were clearly visible, transforming the dead man into a giant pincushion.

"Let's get inside," Jax said, pulling me along into the store.

Past the door we found more confusion. The employees were gathered around, some weeping, some shell-shocked and terrified. A pair of patrol cops, looking equally shocked, were attempting to take down statements from multiple people at once. It was total chaos. Someone had to step up and fix it. I forced myself to rally.

"Alright!" I gestured to one of the patrol. "You. Get a tarp and cover that front window. That'll disperse the crowd."

"With what?"

"It's a hardware store," I said. I pointed at one of the employees, a freckle-faced human girl. "You have tarps here, right?" She nodded, her nose wrinkled, looking confused. "Then give one to officer dumbass here, and help him tarp over that window. Do it from the outside, so you don't touch anything."

"And you," I wheeled on the patrol taking statements, "have these people separated into who saw something and who didn't. And who do you have detained in your vehicle?"

"That's the killer," the patrol said, a little pride creeping back into his voice. "He admitted to doing the handiwork out front."

The other patrol had finally started moving, accompanying the freckled employee through the front door, tarp in hand. Outside, a Mollenkampi woman pressed a well-used camera to the window, one hand cupped around the lens to prevent glare. I recognized her and the human who was grinning over her shoulder. That grotesque front window display was definitely front-page fodder, and Klare and Taran Glouchester would kill for the chance at this byline.

I signaled to Jax. "Help get this shit-show sorted out. I'm gonna chase off those vultures."

I caught up to the patrol and employee as they attempted to hang the tarp. The reporter, Glouchester, lifted it immediately, giving his photographer partner another angle.

"I've got coverage," Klare said.

"Take another one anyway," he said, "you never know which one'll be the money shot."

I brushed against him, knocking my knee into the side of his leg and making him stumble forward, dropping the tarp. The contact was invisible in the press of onlookers.

"You touch that tarp, and Officer Stevens here is going to arrest you for tampering with evidence." I had no idea what the kid's name was, but it sounded more official with a title.

A few onlookers faded away, not wanting to get caught up in a legal issue, but most stuck around, whispering to each other and hoping to see a sudden escalation.

"Evidence?" Glouchester snarled. "It's on the other side of plate glass."

"The killer may have touched the window. If any prints are obscured, we'll know who was all over this thing."

"You're a bigger asshole every time I see you, you know that, Carter?"

When Glouchester dropped my name, the whispering intensified. I glanced at the patrol cop. He and the freckle-cheeked employee were making quick work of the tarp. I turned my back on the representatives of the media and walked to the patrol car. I slid into the front seat and faced the old man in handcuffs.

"I'm a Homicide detective," I said, and waved my badge in his direction. "You want to tell me what happened in there?"

The old man was in tears, and mucus dripped from his biting mouth's yellowed tusks. His head plate color had started to fade, and it looked like he'd applied a lacquer to them, in an attempt to restore the vibrancy he'd enjoyed in his youth. His story was familiar—he'd been working alongside the younger employee when he'd been consumed by an irrational anger. "I don't know why I did it," he said. "I don't know. It was like Brandon had stabbed me in the back, like he'd done something so bad that I wanted to erase him, bring him back to life, and do it again. And I took the nail gun and I—" He broke off, catching his breath. "I did what you saw in there. But the worst part . . ."

"Go ahead," I urged, as gently as I could.

"It felt good. Like I was scratching an itch that'd been bothering me forever." His eyes were wide, as though shocked at his own confession. "Oh, Hells. What did I do?"

He sniffled futilely as mucus drained from his nostrils and biting mouth, and lowered his head, terrified, confused, and ashamed. I sighed.

"I didn't get your name," I said.

"Alto."

"Okay, listen, Alto. If I undo those handcuffs so you can wipe your face, are you going to do anything stupid?"

He shook his head.

"Alright, I'm going to get the key. I'll be back shortly."

"Yeah. Thank you."

I left the car, ignoring Glouchester's shouted questions and the *click-click* of Klare's camera as she circled me. I reentered the store and found Jax talking to the manager, who was walking him through what he'd done after he'd seen the attack.

"I was over here," he said, "and I turned off the motorized display and soundtrack, and went running."

I waved at the other patrol cop, who'd returned to the store and was standing next to the freckled human woman.

"You get it all done?" I indicated the tarp. It looked secure, but I wanted to verify.

"Oh, yeah. Um, the name's not Stevens, though, it's—"

"Trust me, if that vulture gets your name wrong, it's only going to help you out. And as it stands, you've got someone to blame if your name isn't reported correctly in the paper." I watched understanding creep into his eyes. He'd learn one way or another. The job teaches us all how to survive.

"Giving you a heads-up," I said. "I'm getting good info from the suspect, and I want to give him a reward. I'm going to unlock his cuffs." He nodded his acknowledgment and turned back to Freckles, who hadn't left his side. Maybe she liked a guy in uniform, maybe she was in shock.

I returned to the car, happy to see that the crowd was dispersing now that the grotesque imagery was hidden. Even Glouchester and Klare had retreated across the street, reclining against the side of a dinged-up sedan.

I opened the back door, peering down at the old man. "You make me regret doing this and the cuffs go back on, you got that?"

He nodded, and I squatted down to uncuff him. "You have a hanky, Alto?" I asked.

He shook his head. "They took it." On the dash of the patrol car was an unlabeled bag with his personal items. I closed the back door and climbed into the front passenger seat. I dropped the cuffs in the center console, then opened the evidence bag and glanced into it. It held a wallet, key ring, and handkerchief. A Mollenkampi's hanky takes a great deal of abuse. Used to mop the excess mucus that drains from their nose through their biting mouth, they're unpleasant to touch at the best of times. So I shook the bag, making sure nothing was attached to or hidden in the hanky, then let the end of the fabric hang out of the opening. I held it up to the narrow slit in the backseat cage used to pass paperwork to and from anyone seated in the back.

"Thank you." The old man drew the hanky through the access slot, and wiped down his tusks.

"So what were you and he talking about, before . . ." I shrugged, "whatever happened, happened."

"Brandon was telling me that he had a cure-all ointment," he said. "Supposed to fix anything. He said it was going to clear up his skin. He had a real crush on Kacie, the lady with the freckles."

"Brandon? Was that the name of . . ." I gestured toward the now-obscured display window.

"Yes," he nodded.

"And this ointment. Was it snake oil?" I said. I hadn't noticed any manna threads in the store, but I hadn't examined the body yet.

"No! Nothing like that. It was manna infused in an ointment, see? You rub it on whatever hurts. He even offered some for me to try on my arthritis."

With an ear-popping crackle, the store radio began to blare music, yet another Dinah McIntire track. At the same time, a dissonant grinding noise came from inside the store. I snarled a quick "Stay here!" and slammed the patrol door shut.

I sprinted back into the store, looking at the tarp and assuming that Glouchester or Klare had come back for another peek. The thought of them interfering brewed a strange rage inside me. As if they'd betrayed us somehow, and I had an impulse to give them exactly what they deserved. But the tarp material was untouched, and I shook the thoughts from my head. The crowd of lookie-loos was milling about, many of them with furrowed brows, as if struggling through their own thoughts of betrayal.

I dashed through the store entrance and found the manager frantically slapping at the control panel I'd seen earlier. He was panicked, shouting, "It won't stop! I don't know why it won't stop!"

Across the store not-Stevens and Jax were searching for a way to unplug the display as the corpse of the teen stock clerk was dragged from one side of the window display to the other. Finally Jax pulled a bundle of wires from under the elevated stand, and the nightmarish thing ground to a halt as Dinah McIntire's wail dropped an octave and trailed off. My heart was still thumping, but I had time to let out a breath. Then the body wrenched backward and shoved, prying itself off of the display in a series of wet pops as it came free from the nails still embedded in the backing material.

The teenager's face was bisected by a vertical slit, like the one Saul Petrevisch had grown. But the dead teen's mark continued down his throat. As he lurched forward, discarding the torn and nail-perforated apron, it was clear that the slit traced a line down his narrow chest. I braced myself, sure that I knew what was coming next. And sure enough, Brandon's body rushed at me, just as Bobby Kearn and Saul had done. Ignoring the screams and shouts around us, I drew my revolver, focused on the transformed center of mass . . . and froze.

As Brandon galloped toward me, his shirt fell open and the line down his chest was revealed to be a mouth. The skin of his chest and belly pulled back, revealing layers of thin triangular blades, like rows of shark's teeth, and beyond them were the pinks, purples, and whites of his muscles, organs, and ribcage. I had enough time to process what I was seeing, and then he was next to me . . . and then past me, leaving me untouched.

The dead teenager ran straight through the entrance, plunging into the crowd trying to peer past the tarp to get a glimpse of gore. That was when the screaming began in earnest.

The crowd fled into the street. There was a screeching of tires followed by a metallic crunch, the unmistakable sound of a collision. That was what snapped me out of my shocked stare. I turned to not-Stevens and pointed at the door. "Control the crowd, and radio in for help!" Not bothering to look, I shouted, "Jax, with me!"

I turned and ran, revolver held at a high ready. I exited the front of the store to find the crowd fleeing. To my right, an utterly ordinary traffic accident: a beetle-driven Therreau wagon had collided with a sports car. The tibron beetle, like all of its species, never stopped moving. Almost as large as the sport coupe it had run into, it had crawled halfway onto the vehicle's hood. I glanced at the Therreau driver, but he was in the back of the wagon, cowering in terror as his supplies rolled out of the rear, bouncing across the uneven street. I followed his gaze, and my mouth fell open.

Brandon had dropped to all fours, traveling in great bounds, vaulting across the sidewalk and onto the cobblestone street. Then he abruptly slowed, as something dangled below him.

With no flesh holding them inside, Brandon's intestines had fallen through the jaws in his stomach, striking the pavement in a wet pile. The mouth stretched forward, shark's teeth pressing past the shell, scraping across the cobblestones and closing on the intestines. The sound of chewing was wet and horrible, the boy's organs pulled back into his body only to fall out again in clumps. He moved forward again in a sudden dash of speed, loose innards dragging across the ground as he leapt ahead, the maw in his stomach crunching wetly.

The teenager slammed into the side of the patrol car with immense force, enough to throw open the trunk and shatter the near window. The old man scrambled across the seat. He slapped his hands against the far window, muffled pleas barely audible over the noise and chaos around us. He was trapped in there, unable to open the door or roll down the window to escape. And I was the last one to close that door.

I lowered my weapon and fired. To save our murder suspect. To end the danger. But more than anything, to destroy the waking nightmare before me. The handgun slugs ripped through Brandon's torso, but weren't enough to halt his progress. Brandon threw himself at the patrol car once more, jamming one arm through the broken window and seizing Alto by the throat. I scrambled to reload my revolver. The older man's screams grew high-pitched; his struggles intensified, then stopped altogether. I raised my weapon once again, uncertain what good it would do.

Then a thunderclap over my shoulder left my ears ringing, and Brandon's head snapped back and froze, as if suspended in amber. My eyes focused, and I saw that much of his face was missing. I turned. Jax stood by the rear of the patrol car. The broken trunk was open, and he'd retrieved the shotgun from its rack. His eyes were wide and his mandibles hung limply. Behind me came a sickly thump, as the dead teenager lost whatever unnatural animation had motivated him, and toppled over. Jax racked the slide, ejected the round, and set the shotgun back into the trunk of the patrol car. Then he leaned against the rear bumper and stared at the boy's corpse.

I didn't drop my weapon. We'd already witnessed corpses striking out at the living, and I wasn't going to take any chances. I was still standing at the ready when wailing sirens drew closer and flashing lights bathed our profiles in alternating shades of red and blue as Klare circled the scene, her camera *click-click*ing like beetle legs on cobblestone streets.

THE FRESHLY ARRIVED PATROL OFFICERS cordoned off the scene, and before long an ARC team was circling Brandon's transformed body, waving their hands and muttering to themselves. Across the street, Klare was working the crowd, getting more snapshots. Her partner was nowhere to be found. That made me worry that Glouchester was skulking around my crime scene.

I chewed my lip and scanned the crowd. A slim Mollenkampi man in slacks and a dress shirt stood near the kid's corpse. He looked familiar, and the way the ARC teams deferred to him made it clear that he was someone important. I realized that I didn't see Ajax, either. I started for the hardware store entrance, hoping to find him inside, when someone called my name.

Harris, the DO from the Bobby Kearn case, waved an arm in my direction. The black fabric of his cloak rippled, its glyphs shimmering in and out of sight and making him seem more mirage than man. I considered ignoring him and going about my business, but he called again.

"Captain wants to see you." And he beckoned for me to follow.

I sighed and followed Harris past other black-robed figures. Some of them acknowledged me, others turned frosty shoulders my way. It was hard to say what I'd done to piss them off. Not for a lack of reasons, but for the wide variety to choose from.

"This is quite the mess," Harris said, indicating the now-motionless jaws exposed in the belly of the teenager. Brandon had been as unnaturally transformed as Saul Petrevisch's and Bobby Kearn's bodies had been. I squinted, wondering at the similarity between the newly emerged jaws and the vertical separation that had appeared on Saul's head. Why had Saul attacked me, but Brandon chased down Alto in the patrol car?

"This way." Harris guided me to the far side of the beetle, where another tech team crawled through the crunched panels of the patrol car, documenting the death of the man who'd killed the teen inside, before being killed by the same teen outside. I paused, leaning past a tech to swing a hand near Alto's body. My fingers caught in the air near his face, threads of manna acting like an invisible fly strip. I swallowed with some difficulty. The old man said Brandon had some kind of ointment cure-all. It must've been cut with a little black-market manna to give the liquid a bite and boost the price. It must've been on his handkerchief, the one I hadn't wanted to touch. If I'd only gotten over myself and touched the thing, I'd have sensed the threads and kept it from him. If I had, maybe he'd still be alive.

"Don't let's dawdle, now," said Harris. "Shouldn't keep the big man waiting."

I eyed Harris's cloak, and the black biker boots peeking out beneath the hem. "You've got a strong accent, from pretty far south. How'd you end up here?"

His grin flashed wide. "Romance! It's the edge of the world, hey? Besides, if you grow up where I did, you can head to one of the coastal cities, or north. And nothing's more north than Titanshade."

"You didn't opt for the coast?"

"Scared of sharks." Harris's toothy grin widened, then he let loose with a full-throated howl of amusement, a disturbing sound at a murder scene.

We came to a stop in front of the small Mollenkampi in civilian dress. Up close, I spotted the badge riding on his belt. His slacks were strangely bunched around the hips, and his shirt was slightly puffed out. I also realized why he was familiar—he was the plainclothes sorcerer who'd shown up at the Saul Petrevisch crime scene.

"Detective Carter," said Harris, "meet Captain Auberjois." The smaller Mollenkampi nodded a greeting, fingers tapping a staccato rhythm on his lower tusks. We stood there for a moment, Harris and I staring at the captain, the captain staring at the corpse.

The Arcane Regulation and Containment teams were a new creation, which meant Auberjois had unexpectedly shot to the rank of captain. I wondered if he'd obtained the position by brownnosing, hard work, or having an influential relative. Whatever the secret of his success, I had better things to do than stand around in silence.

"Okay then," I said. "I'm going back to work. There's a cop named Stevens around here somewhere. If you need me, just let him know."

Auberjois finally turned his attention to me.

"You seem to show up at the most interesting events," he said.

"Comes with the town," I said. "Titanshade's the kind of place where interesting things get you killed."

His eyes crinkled. "My job is to examine exceptionally interesting events in order to identify patterns. And you are a pattern." He regarded me with careful consideration, the kind of look he'd probably give a puzzle piece that didn't quite match the shapes or sizes of the gaps he was trying to fill. "Some people say you're in tight with Paulus."

"Is that a fact?"

"They say you fought with her at that Titan's Day fiasco. They say you took down her political enemies." He spoke leisurely, watching my body language like a card player. "And take her employees out to dinner."

My gut clenched like I'd just been sucker-punched. Someone must have seen Gellica and me out together. That put both of us at risk.

I forced a grin and shoved my balled fists into my pockets. "Sounds like *they* have a grudge."

"Wouldn't be the first time Paulus managed to get her claws into the force. And she's done it through blackmail, cash, and pretty faces before. Anyone who doesn't see that is either a fool or already in her pocket." He tilted his head, eyes narrowed. "Which are you?"

I admired a person who didn't like Paulus, but I didn't have time to provide an education about my relationship with her.

"You interrupted your workout to be here. So are you going to insult me, or did you want to view a crime scene?" I asked. "What was it, anyway—a quick jog around the block?"

Auberjois straightened and stepped back. Eyes on Harris, he asked me, "Do my teams talk about my habits?"

I rocked onto my heels. "There're lumps around your hips, shoulders, and waist." He glanced down at his outfit as I continued. "They move, indicating cloth. But not on your knees, so shorts. And since you're not wearing a tie," I pointed at his unbuttoned collar, "we can all see the green collar of your T-shirt. Most undershirts don't have splashes of color, so I'm guessing you threw on clothes over your workout outfit. Looks like you have something on your arms as well. I figure sweat bands."

His eyes crinkled and one mandible quivered. "Not quite," he said, bringing his forearms together with a jarring metallic clank. "And I always run in the evenings. I don't suppose it said anything before you shot him?"

The sudden shift in topic took me by surprise. "I didn't kill anyone. That was my partner."

"I didn't say kill, I said *shot*. You shot him first, correct?"

I sucked at my teeth. "What are you getting at?"

"The big mouth growing out of his stomach. Did it say anything? Did it growl or yip or howl?"

I thought about it. "No. It just bit into anything that came within range."

"Like it was angry."

I considered that. "Like it was hungry." I didn't say, *Like Sheena had been hungry. Like I'd been hungry so often lately.*

"Hm." He blinked, then nodded, a single sharp movement that felt like he'd filed something away. "Very good, Detective. If I need you again, I'll let you know."

I didn't care for his attitude toward me, but I liked the way he thought. He seemed like the kind of cop who could follow breadcrumbs.

"I think the music had something to do with it."

Auberjois blinked rapidly, as if disturbed from a slumber. "The what?"

"The music. The store's speakers started playing a new Dinah

McIntire track right before—" I broke off, not sure what to call the thing on the streets before us. "Before this happened. Put that together with what happened at Shelter in the Bend, and you know there's some kind of connection."

"When the body of Bobby McIntire—"

"Bobby Kearn," I corrected.

"Yes. That's right. When his body transformed, was this song playing?"

"No," I said. "But the feedback on the radio, the buzzing, that's all started since McIntire's been in town." My volume edged up slightly. "You said you watch for patterns. The music's a pattern. I think McIntire and Vandra Cedrow are tied into this, somehow."

He looked at the sky, eyes moving, pondering that. "That song has been on at least one radio in this town every second for the last month. Hells, my daughter wore out the 8-track we bought her for Titan's Day, and that's only been a couple weeks. The fact that there was a song or some kind of noise at each event? You might as well point out there was oxygen in the room at all the crime scenes. And as for the Cedrow family," Auberjois gave a polite cough, "it's not surprising that they're still top of mind for you."

I shook my head, angry that yet another person was ignoring the obvious. I started to speak but Auberjois interrupted.

"It's a reasonable thought," he said. "And you're right, it is a pattern. But seeing patterns is only the first step. Patterns are everywhere, and an equal part of my job is sorting out the truly relevant. You and your partner were at the Bobby Kearn and Saul Petrevisch events, and now you're here. That's a painfully obvious pattern. Were you responsible for the transformations?"

My throat constricted. I made a sound, but it was far from a fully formed word.

"No," he said. "You're here because it's your job. Whatever the real cause, it's got something to do with magic and those who wield it without concern." As he spoke, his eyes drifted mountwise, toward the city center and the seat of the government, where Paulus kept her offices. There was no mystery about who he saw as the connecting fiber of this mystery.

Another black-cloaked DO approached, and Auberjois's voice took on the tones of someone ending a conversation. "Thank you for the input, Detective. We'll take it under consideration." He turned away, and I opened my mouth to protest, but Harris touched my back, warning me to bite my tongue. I stalked away from them, walking blind until I almost ran into a Mollenkampi woman standing slightly to the side of the major activity. She had her back to me, and I began to mutter an insincere apology when I got a look at her face.

"Hello, Klare," I said. She wore her camera on a leather strap, slung over one shoulder with the easy grace of a soldier whose relaxed posture betrayed a weapon always at the ready. I held my hand at an angle, preventing her from raising the camera to attack position. I signaled a patrol officer and pointed at Klare. He walked our way, and I turned to the photographer. "Where's your partner? He sneaking into the store?"

"He's back at the *Union Record*, developing the film from earlier. Trying to beat the rush," she said. Then she quietly added, "This wasn't your fault."

I started. "What?"

"We mostly work the crime beat," she said. "It's our job to watch cops and killers. I've seen that you get blamed for all kinds of things that go wrong. It's usually your fault, at least partially, but not this time. Whatever that thing is," she jerked her biting jaws at Brandon's transformed corpse, "it had no interest in you. It was plain bad luck you were here."

I almost laughed. For once, the press didn't want to make me a central figure. And for once, they were wrong. Guyer wouldn't listen to me, Auberjois wouldn't listen, not even the press would hear me out—not that I was going to give them a formal try.

"Does this mean the press has lost your weird fascination with me?"

"It's not us that's fascinated," she said. "It's the public. They're fascinated with anything related to the manna strike." She laughed, a sound like wind chimes. "But you're not the hot item anymore. These days we're all jockeying to be part of the press pool to talk to the Barekusu."

"You always want to talk to the stars, don't you?"

She whistled her derision. "It's not like that. Glouchester's working on something big."

"What?"

"You'll just have to read the papers, Carter." Her eyes crinkled, and she shot a photo of me from hip height.

The patrol cop walked up, a strapping Gillmyn I didn't recognize. I released Klare into his care. "Please guide our esteemed member of the press off our crime scene." I hesitated before adding, "She's fine to stand to the side of the tape, though. Someplace with a good field of view."

Klare nodded her thanks and walked away, ignoring the Gillmyn's attempt to make small talk.

Once again I headed toward the hardware store's front entrance. Inside the store was where my job led, less sensational than the transformation, but still essential. Two more senseless deaths meant hours of work ahead of us. And just like the other killings, it felt like we were missing something.

Inside the store I caught sight of Jax standing in one corner, absently wiping his tusks. I strolled up and pointed in the direction of the destruction outside.

"I was wondering, are you going to write your memoir someday?" I asked. "Because this'd make a great chapter. You could put that college education to use and—"

"Not now, Carter."

My attempt at empathy rebuffed, I moved on. "You want to try to get all this entered in tonight? I'd like to get a bite to eat first. We could get back to the rest of the caseload tomorrow."

He paused. "No. I'm off tomorrow."

"You are?"

"I'm going to the music festival."

I winced. He'd told Dinah McIntire that he was excited to be going. "That's a bad idea," I said.

"We already have tickets," he said.

"We?"

He shrugged, looking sheepish, if that's possible for a guy whose teeth could tear through my thigh. "Talena bought them as a gift."

I pressed the heels of my hands against my temples and held in a cry of frustration. "You saw what happened up there. Why would you go back?"

He whistled, layering a bit of sarcasm into his words. "Right. Because there's all kinds of places you can think of that haven't been the scene of a violent crime."

I closed my eyes, imagining Bobby Kearn's transformation, and wondering how that could possibly be seen as grim but not terrifying. Ajax kept talking.

"At least the concert will take people's minds off of what's happening."

"Unless that's where it all started. Until we know what causes this," I pointed at the blood-streaked window display, "that crowd could be fifteen thousand potential killers, waiting to be driven into a frenzy."

Jax shook his head. "It happened at the rig. It happened at Saul and Donna's apartment. It happened at a hardware store. And those are just the events we personally witnessed. Whatever's going on, there's nothing to indicate it's more or less dangerous at the concert."

He shoved his hands into his pockets and leaned closer. "Besides, I got word from Murphy CaDell. He says he found something for me. You got me to delay talking to Captain Bryyh so long, it looks like I might actually get out of this mess with my badge."

I frowned and turned away, looking at the sorcerers gathered around the bodies of Brandon and Alto.

"The kid, Brandon. His body didn't care about me. Didn't even slow down. But the others, Saul and Bobby, they charged straight at me."

"I've been thinking about that," said Jax. "Yes, they charged at you, but try to remember where you were standing. At the festival, we were in the dressing room, and your back was to the door. And when we were with Saul Petrevisch you were—"

"Between him and the door." I fell back a step as the real pattern became clear. "They were trying to get past me. Toward what?"

Jax looked at the dented door and shattered window of the police cruiser. "Toward revenge."

The transformed bodies had been trying to get to their killers. I'd simply been in their way.

19

JAX MAY HAVE BEEN GOING to a concert, but I had a full day of mind-numbing paperwork staring me down. We worked together to move the hardware store mess off our plates, but the next day was dedicated to working through follow-up reports on our open and recently cleared cases. Normal, run-of-the-mill homicides deserved our attention as well. The incidentals of piecing together murders never stops. Every victim needs to be served, even in the midst of madness and uncertainty. Maybe that's when it's most important.

By early evening I was sitting at my desk in the Bullpen, filling out forms and thinking about the things we'd seen and heard. I pressed a finger on the photo of the young victim from the hardware store. I slid his photo back and replaced it with the one of Saul, the man beaten to death by his roommate. Saul had provided snake oil to Sheena, who'd in turn killed Bobby Kearn, the murder that had sucked us into this whole elaborate scenario. The snake oil was a connection between them, but Sheena and Bobby's link to Vandie Cedrow was tenuous at best. And as for the buzzing incidents across the city? A few had shown some level of connection to the drug trade, but Hells, if you grabbed a dozen people off the street, chances were good that two or three of them had either used an illicit substance or knew someone who did.

I twisted my shoulders until there was a satisfying crack in my lower back. Still stretching, I glanced around. The Bullpen had a scant half-dozen occupants that night. Police worked around the clock, the Bunker was always open, and there were always Homicide detectives on duty, though the night shift was more lightly staffed than day shift. Not that there was less violence, but there was a better chance of locating witnesses or reaching a judge when you needed one during the day.

One of the other detectives on duty was a middle-aged woman with yellow head plates. Crenoline had pulled a television on a rolling AV cart beside her desk, the antenna extended as far as possible and pointed toward the window. She waited through commercial after commercial for the concert coverage to begin. I dropped my hands onto my desktop and snarled over my shoulder. "Do we really need to listen to this garbage?"

Crenoline glared at me. "I'm trying to figure out who killed a pimp in the back bathroom of a bar that's so filthy I have to shower just from thinking about it. And for that privilege, I gave away my chance to see the performance of a lifetime. And on top of that, I have to sit here with you?" She snorted. "The dial stays where it is, understand?"

Like most Mollenkampi, she put a layer of tonality on her words, but her sarcasm was far less musical than Jax's eloquent notes of skeptical disdain. Even Ajax was at the show, probably screaming himself hoarse. He was also there with Talena. I knew better than to obsess about the risk they carried being there, so instead I obsessed about what Auberjois had said about Gellica.

How many people knew she and I had gone out for dinner? Did those same rumors cover my awkward departure that night, leaving her on the front stoop of her home? Were there whispers about our connection to each other, and to magic?

Or was she really, as Auberjois had implied, simply another attempt of Paulus's to infiltrate the Bunker and solidify her control of the city's power structure? If Gellica had shown interest only on Paulus's orders, then I was better off staying away from her. But if Gellica had been genuine, then it was possible that our almost-relationship put her in danger. And if she was hurt because I failed to warn her . . .

The Hells with it.

I grabbed my jacket and headed out.

I drove with one hand, the other spinning the radio dial. The airwaves were wall-to-wall with chatter about the concert's premiere night. Radio stations had been dribbling out a new Dinah McIntire single every day or so in the lead-up to the concert, but the music industry buzz was all about the unreleased track—"Titan's Song," embargoed until she performed it live for the first time that night, at the precise moment when the moon topped the Mount. I had to admit, the lady knew how to work her fans into a frenzy.

A feeding frenzy is exactly what I was afraid was going to happen.

I parked the Hasam and studied Gellica's home. Two stories and nicely maintained, it was high-end without being ostentatious. No lights in the windows, no movement along the curtains. It was early enough that she likely wasn't asleep, so she probably wasn't home. I grabbed the keys, but didn't turn them in the ignition. *I should wait for her.*

I made it a ten count before turning over the engine. I could always come back. I'd try Paulus's home, then Gellica's office to see if I could find her.

Sick of the endless array of McIntire tracks, I killed the radio, leaving the chirp of Dispatch to keep me company. There was an armed robbery in Old Orchard, a drive-by shooting in Guilder's Glen, and some kind of traffic jam in Eden Prairie, a neighborhood in the Hills, near the Barekusu camp. Overall, a quiet night for Titanshade.

I pulled up to Paulus's gate. Since we'd been there last, Paulus had provided her security with a lean-to shed. One more sign that she was taking the threats from the roughnecks seriously. There was electric service in the shed, evidenced by the flickering glow of a television dancing on the mandibled face of one guard. The other strolled up to my window, squinted at my badge, and consulted a clipboard. The resulting frown told me I'd be having trouble.

"Can't do it," he said.

I hesitated for a heartbeat, to make my indignation clear. "You understand this is official business, right?"

He shook the clipboard. "Sorry, pal. I got two badge numbers on here that are no-gos, and yours is one of them."

I started to argue more, but paused as a rumble filled the air. A deep purple Longinus Lancer prowled along the street, heading in our direction.

"Ah, Hells." The guard shifted his feet. "Look, you gotta go. Come back with a warrant. Otherwise, you're out of luck."

The Lancer slowed, then moved forward, blocking my retreat and idling angrily. I craned my neck to watch Gellica get out of her vehicle as her radio bleated out a breathless description of the concert.

The guard straightened his back. "Sorry, ma'am. This gentleman is leaving."

Gellica tilted her head toward the shed. "It's fine. Watch your show. He'll be gone in a moment."

She waited for the guard to retreat into the shed, her fingers tugging at the laced cuffs of her shirtsleeves. She didn't speak until he was inside.

"What do you want, Carter?"

"To talk."

I got out of the Hasam and crossed the few steps in her direction. The Lancer's door stood open, a barrier of steel and glass between us. Heat radiated from the hood. She'd been putting it through its paces, and judging from the direction of her arrival, she'd taken it on the narrow, winding roads along the Mount.

"Doing a little joy riding?"

"Some. Had to take a detour near the Barekusu camp. There's some kind of traffic thing."

"Huh. I know someone who off-roads. She said the same thing about—"

"You came here to talk about traffic?"

I sucked in a breath.

"Look," I said. "I know you don't want to talk to me."

"Did you get my note?"

"Oh, I got your message." It had been big, plush, and delivered by two furniture movers straight into my living room. The couch where we'd once bared our secrets had been turned into the largest kiss-off note in history. "But I need to tell you about a conversation with a divination officer."

"Oh? Did they get some entrails on your shoes?"

"No, he pressed me about my social life."

She crossed her arms. "And?"

"And he knew you and I had spent time together." She didn't seem put out, so I pressed on. "If he knows that, then what else does he know?" I glanced over my shoulder. Both guards were hunched around the television, oblivious to our conversation. "He might know about me and manna or about your, you know . . ." I didn't exactly know how to say that she was a magic-infused clone who could transform into a shadowy panther. Sometimes it's best just to trail off meaningfully.

She shifted her weight and laughed. "So you suddenly grew concerned and wanted to scamper over and make sure I was safe."

"Okay, fine. I apologize for warning you about a potential threat. If you've got somewhere to be, I'll leave you to it."

She rolled her eyes. "I came here to watch the concert on a big-screen TV. And you're holding me up because you want me to know you're worried about me?"

"I'm worried about both of us."

"Oh, well that makes me feel much better."

"Look, I do worry about you," I said. "You can believe it or not, but it's a fact. And I'm worried about who knows about us."

"There's not an *us* anymore."

"Yeah, that's abundantly clear." I kept my back angled to the guard shed, to be safe. "I mean someone might know about us and our connection to manna."

Gellica frowned, looking an awful lot like Paulus.

On her car radio the announcer cut into a commercial to breathlessly announce, *"She's on! She's on!"*

Gellica's lips pulled back. "Great. The most exciting thing that will happen all week, and I'm missing it."

"I don't know how widespread this rumor is," I said. "And I'm worried that someone will piece our connection together."

"Hold that thought."

She pushed away from the Lancer and walked toward the guard shack. The two guards barely noticed us standing by the window. They huddled near the television, their expressions ranging from mild interest to fascination. I stood next to Gellica, rounding out the group with my utter disdain.

We watched the televised display through the window, Gellica's car radio providing a slightly out-of-sync soundtrack. The screen showed a misty, fog-filled main tent. The cameras were fixed, filming from a distance. No music swelled, only the screams and shouts of adoration from the crowd. Then the smoke and fog lifted rapidly, sucked up and away, I guessed by large fans.

The lifting curtains of smoke revealed the tent's clear rear panel. Through it, the moon was a swirling blue and white orb perched directly above the jagged peaks of the Mount, a precious gem mounted on a ring. Even I had to admit that it was the perfect backdrop for a festival called Ice on Her Fingers. And there, center stage, was Dinah McIntire. One of the guards whistle-clicked her admiration. "Look at her!"

McIntire wore a bright red halter-top dress with a plunging neckline and fringe on fringe on fringe. Her hair was loose and luxurious, shockingly out of fashion. Scandalously long, it flowed over her neck, shoulders, and back. Her head was held at an angle, chin in the air, accentuating the fall of her gloriously unkempt natural curls. Raising the microphone to her lips, she announced, "We gather to celebrate life."

The drums started. A machine or perhaps an imported drummer replacing the lamented Bobby Kearn.

"We celebrate renewal," she said, "discovery."

Strings swelled beneath her words. "And a city that has never known how to quit." Horns raised their voices, pulsing brass notes. Dinah began to bounce one hip, and the layers of fringe moved as well.

"Tonight we celebrate . . . the 'Titan's Song'!"

Spotlights swung like searchlights in a prison yard as pyrotechnics ignited a horizontal slash across the stage. McIntire gave in to the music, bouncing, swaying, and with each beat the layers of fringe rose and fell, teasing the sight of her body, amplifying every movement. But always under total control.

There was no denying the blend of showmanship, sex appeal, and raw star power that McIntire brought to the stage. She was a diva, and all eyes were on her. Even I had to admit that she was amazing—a total transformation from the person I'd met backstage.

But as she raised her voice the static on the radio swelled, and the audio skittered beneath it, a series of screeches and muted creaks, like fresh snow under rubber boots. The security guard frantically adjusted the tuner with one hand, the antenna with the other.

The radio in my car squealed, a burst of static and rage, then Dispatch called for any available units to respond to a code 1888 in Eden Prairie, near the Barekusu camp. I wondered if I'd heard wrong. Code 1888 signaled a natural disaster.

I faced Gellica. "We'll finish this later."

"We're already finished." She walked toward her car, to unblock my Hasam. She looked mountwise, down the road she'd come from. "Not sure if it matters, but the camp is where traffic had been bad."

I grunted and climbed into the Hasam. The conversation hadn't exactly gone as planned, but it also hadn't gone as badly as it might have. Maybe the night was looking up. I hit the gas and rode on to whatever disturbance awaited.

The Barekusu caravan had set up camp on one of the hills at the foot of the Mount. A sheer-faced mound of stone that towered over the street below, it was the kind of place that had a great view but had defied even the most creative real-estate developer. By the time I arrived, scarlet-clad patrol cops flooded the streets, torn from their patrols by the same Dispatch call that I'd responded to. Beyond them was a cluster of stopped cars, the drivers standing to the side and staring at what looked like a wide black puddle on the cobblestone street.

I swore under my breath, irritated that I'd been pulled away from an important conversation because some tanker had a liquid cargo spill. I parked the Hasam and stuck the pill-box light on the dash to keep from being towed away. At the top of the hill were the shaggy outlines of Barekusu, a line of adults and children staring down at us.

As I got nearer, I saw a pair of bikers on scramblers pull to the side of the road. I recognized the leather jacket with a maroon band and white piping that Guyer had worn at Hammer Head's. I guessed that she and Harris must have been listening in on the police band. I headed in their direction, then stopped and squinted at the puddle. I could've sworn it had grown. Even stranger, the crowd of drivers abandoned their vehicles to run away from it. I squinted, trying to see what exactly it was, as the shape continued to expand. When it reached the cars' front tires they tipped forward with a grinding metallic sound, teetering on the edge of the puddle before upending completely and disappearing into it.

The shape in the street was no puddle. It was a hole.

I jumped on the hood of the nearest car and waved my arms in the air, badge in hand, hoping that somehow the tiny metal shield would give my words more authority.

"Get out! Get everyone the Hells out of here!" I looked at the hill, and the Barekusu staring down at the scene. "It's not safe! Get away from the edge!"

There was simply no way I could get them to listen, to get to safety fast enough. Then a voice far louder than my own barked a command. "Evacuate the area! If you can hear the sound of my voice, evacuate now!"

Standing on the far side of the hole, DO Guyer was speaking into a megaphone, pulled from the hands of one of the patrol cops. But her voice rang out from all sides. As she spoke she scattered a handful of coins, pebbles, and small debris into the air and at both sides of the street. She'd connected the megaphone with the items and they acted as remote speakers, broadcasting and amplifying her voice further. The faces along the streets and on the hill began to disappear, responding to her volume and authority. I took advantage of the moment to rush forward and clear additional pedestrians from the hole's edge.

Drawing closer, I realized the depth of the hole that had opened up the street, exposing the honeycombing of geo-vents, sewer lines, and utility cables that kept the city livable. The cobblestone streets and vehicles had tumbled downward into a shockingly large cavern.

Everything I knew about the city told me that the geo-vents shouldn't have been that big. Even the deepest tunnels were suspected to only be human-size.

I turned my attention to the lookie-loos and barked orders at them, flashing my badge to the few who balked at compliance. Slowly, we pushed the crowds away. I was beginning to feel better when the hill collapsed.

The tremendous roar of the dirt and stone wave was terrible, accompanied by shouts from the crowd and the officers fighting to maintain sanity in the chaos. The entire front of the hill tumbled into the devouring hole, a landslide of rock that swept brush and vehicles ahead, sweeping it into the gaping maw of the sinkhole.

I'd seen at least one body in that initial collapse, and I knew there would be more before the night was through. Before I had time to obsess on that thought, a burst of wind shot past me, so fast and powerful that I almost lost my balance.

Down the street Ambassador Paulus emerged through the crowd, pushing bystanders aside and striding into the chaos, eyes blazing and tattoos alight with an iridescent glow as beasts scribed in manna-laced ink writhed across her arms. Slowing slightly, Paulus's fingers wove through the air as if plucking an imaginary flower from the sky. The invisible thing that had passed me emerged from the smoke, carrying an elderly woman, her arms clasped around an appendage made visible only by the dusting of dirt and ash. I caught a glimpse of the thing's form, and my bowels twisted at the unnatural and illogical structure of it. But if that thing did Paulus's bidding, and she had sent it to save a life, I'd swallow all the disgust and revulsion in the world to let it happen.

The thing dropped the woman near the edge of the hole, then it pulsed, shedding the dust and eradicating even the hint of its form from my vision. Shoving aside my apprehension, I ran to her, glad I didn't sense Paulus's creature as I helped the woman to her feet and guided her to one of the ambulances. Medics and firefighters swarmed around us, shouting commands over the sirens and chaos as the hills and street below gave way and were swallowed.

Nearby, Guyer chanted and gesticulated, focusing her thoughts as she tied the piece of rebar she held to one of the trucks that teetered on the edge of the hole. Even at this distance I could see the sheen of sweat on her brow.

I dashed in her direction, not knowing what I'd do to help, but desperate to do so. Chunks of the hill were falling away, smashing onto the sidewalk, pelting me with shards of rock and showers of dirt. I leapt over debris and dodged a particularly large piece as it fell, sending me skidding to a halt as I slammed into the side of an abandoned scooter. The handlebar dug into my gut, and I pushed away, opposite hand windmilling to keep my balance. That was when the manna tendrils wrapped around my hand.

I pulled back without thought, and they tugged me in the opposite direction. I caught my breath, struggling not to panic, then realized I was standing above a scattering of the manna-linked coins and pebbles Guyer had used for amplification.

I gripped them, feeling the sticky spider's thread connection between them and Guyer's discarded megaphone. She'd used next gen manna. *Why?* Fighting a grin, I realized she'd been true to her word of getting next gen manna to test my ability to manipulate manna. Now it was about to pay off.

I twisted my fists, gripping the threads in my hands, and let the energy flow into me, draining it like a man wandering the salt plains drains a canteen, like a self-loathing drunk drains a tumbler of whiskey. And just like a drunk, all I wanted was more, to fill myself with magic and manna and power and—

Maybe I'd have given into that instinct if it weren't for the surrounding chaos cutting through my mental haze. So I fought to ignore the bracing cold bands that tightened around my chest, a combination of pressure and chill, as if I'd fallen through the icy surface of a lake and plunged into freezing waters. As if I lay at the bottom of the ocean, a whale whose song would never be heard by the others of my species. I knew what I had to do to relieve the pressure.

Sprinting to Guyer's side, I grabbed her hand, my fingers sliding over her knuckles until I touched the metal rebar and felt the faint thread that connected it to the truck. She jumped, eyes wide, and I gave her a smile that even I realized stretched too wide on my face. But I couldn't help it. I was so cold, so excited, so hungry, and I could taste the manna that bound the rebar to the truck, even as Guyer struggled to lift it.

I resisted the urge to feed. Instead I channeled all the energy I'd taken into it. Guyer went suddenly still as I fed the connecting threads, magnifying their power. I let go, and she swung the rebar in an arc. The truck leapt away from the hole's gaping maw and slammed into the collapsing hill with incredible force, a single stake holding the crumbling rock at bay and giving the Barekusu time to escape.

But the accelerated rate of manna use proved too much. The truck began to warp and crumble as the magical bond consumed the manna that Guyer had applied, and then the truck itself. As they always were, the magical connection was too hungry to simply stop after running out of fuel.

With a ground-shaking rumble, the rest of the hill collapsed. Huge chunks dropped away, plunging toward the ground. Guyer dropped her hand and took a step away, staring at me and holding the rebar, and for a moment I thought she'd strike me like I'd struck down Harlan Cedrow and stopped his mad rampage across the ice plains. An act of desperation that made Vandie Cedrow see me as a killer, and total strangers see me as a savior.

Guyer's mouth hung open, and she stared at me as she screamed over the roar of the hill's collapse. "What the Hells did you do?"

Now she understood the impact I had on magic, not just as a mental abstract. She had felt it firsthand, and realized what it meant to directly impact the ability of sorcerers like her.

We locked eyes, until I turned back to the chaos. I shouted, getting the attention of some bystanders and directing them to move back to safety. Behind me Guyer spoke again.

"Carter, that wasn't—"

I yelled to a nearby patrol, and they waved me off as they moved to the next person who needed help.

"Carter . . ."

I ignored her, and the next thing she said was a scream. "Carter!"

I spun to face her, eyes shielded against the fires that were breaking out in the surrounding buildings, in time to hear the roar and groan of the street giving way as the cobblestones drained from beneath my feet like beans from a bag. And I tumbled into the sinkhole that was devouring my city.

20

THE FALL ITSELF WAS A blur of shapes and murky colors. I landed on my back, remembering nothing from the training I'd received as far back as the academy about how to fall without getting hurt. Instead I simply lay there, desperate to draw a breath as pain shot across my chest and throbbed around my kidneys. When the air rushed back into my lungs I sat up, barely in time to roll to my side and avoid another pile of falling debris.

Cobblestones clattered onto the spot where I'd been lying a moment before, pelting me with splinters of stone and dust. Once the deadly rain stopped I gingerly climbed to my feet, wondering if I'd managed to break anything serious. The rotten-egg scent of sulfur was overwhelming, and that, combined with the dust in the air, made both breathing and seeing difficult. My head spun, and I felt a million years from the heady mix of power and consuming hunger when I'd drawn in manna minutes earlier.

Gathering myself, I looked around. I'd landed on a ledge, in a section of the sinkhole near the center of the street. That meant I didn't have to worry about an entire building toppling onto me, but cobblestones and vehicles were a real threat.

The ledge I occupied was two paces wide and a half-dozen long. Beyond its lip the sinkhole stretched down into the darkness, a black wall that echoed with the impacting metal and shattering glass as the buildings and cars landed in an invisible heap.

All around, the walls were pocked with holes ranging in size from fist-width to large enough to crawl through. I stared at them, then realized that they must surely have been branches of the geo-vents that heated the city and made life in Titanshade possible. The societal proscription against tampering with vents ran deep, and I felt an unexpected twinge of guilt for even seeing them laid bare, like walking in on a parent changing clothes, seeing their once-strong body grown feeble with age. I averted my eyes and looked upward to the street.

Between me and the surface was a maze of torn electrical lines and jagged rims from shattered sewer pipes, buried since the days when the whole city had been raised to provide proper sanitation, the city's waste being shuffled off to processing plants in the deep-freeze of the ice plains. I stepped onto the loose cobblestones beside me, using them as a boost as I tried to climb out. I was still relatively close to the surface, and could almost jump up to grab it, but it was just beyond my reach. I tried to decide if making a grab for those utilities was worth the risk of the shock or infection that they might bring. Luckily, before I could decide, Guyer's face appeared over the edge.

"Carter?"

I waved, and the concern eased on her face. "Shortcuts," she muttered, before gesturing to someone I couldn't see. "Over here!"

There were muffled shouts and instructions being passed around overhead, and even though my head was ringing I knew enough to wait and see what my rescuers had planned. Maybe that's why I noticed the body on the ledge below me.

As I waited for the patrol officers to return, I perched on the edge of the ledge I was on, straining my eyes in the dim light and calling out on the off chance that the person below me was still alive.

"Police officer! Can you hear me?"

No motion, no response. No way to reach them. But when a rope came down from above I noticed there was enough slack for me to reach the ledge below.

I cupped my hands around my mouth and shouted. "Hold on! I'm going to reach someone else!"

With the rope wrapped around my waist I was able to slow my descent. At the second ledge I carefully added my weight, keeping a tight grip on the rope and fearing that the whole thing would slide away at any moment. But it didn't, and eventually I reached out to touch the dust-covered figure. As soon as I made contact, I knew they weren't alive.

I rolled the figure over, but instead of a fresh corpse, killed by the fall, or with a bashed-in skull from falling debris, I found a desiccated, almost mummified human male. Whoever he was, he hadn't died in the fallout of the sinkhole. He'd been there already.

I stared at the body for a long moment. Because beyond the impossibility of finding a body that far beneath the city, beyond the sheer insanity of there being a cavern this large in the heart of the city, something else had caught my eye—beneath the body was the glint of clean metal. A Titanshade detective badge, still shiny and new.

My shock must have immobilized me for too long, because a new round of shouts greeted me from above. However long this brief respite from the hole's expansion would last, I simply didn't have time to sit there and ponder the mystery before me. So I did the first thing that came to mind: I scooped up the badge, threw the body over my shoulder, and began climbing the rope.

With several patrol cops pulling from the top and making minimal progress on my own, it wasn't long before I was up to and over the lip of the sinkhole. Hands scrabbled at my shirt to help pull me over and jerked away as they discovered the corpse I carried with me. I stood cradling the body as if it were a newborn child, just seeing the light of the world. I spotted Guyer rushing past and stepped in her direction. She either didn't see me or chose to keep running. I slowed to a stop and called to her, but one of the patrol cops gave me a rough shove and a command to clear the area.

My rescuers began sprinting away from the hole. I followed, doing my best to hold the mummified body together, a bundle of sticks wrapped in tissue paper. Even a quick glance told me that I had lost a good portion of it in my desperate climb to safety.

Farther down the street, I searched for Guyer once again. I approached her and she eyed me and the body with equal parts concern and distrust.

"Listen," I said. "I found this man's body in the hole. But look at him." I raised the body slightly. "There is no way that he died just now. He's . . ."

"He's been down there for years." Guyer bit her lip, understanding what that meant. She hesitated, her eyes flicking at my hand, wrapped around the body's shoulder, missing fingers on display. For a moment she wore a look of uncertainty, maybe even distrust. A scream from the distance drew her attention, and she shook her head. "Get him someplace secure. We'll deal with it later."

I did as she instructed, turning my back on the madness of collapsing buildings and an all-consuming gaping maw in the ground. People fled past me as I walked, mummified corpse in my arms, the badge that had lain beneath it safely tucked away in my pocket. I slowed, watching them pass. Guyer, Harris, even Paulus worked to save the living. And me? I was slipping into the shadows with a corpse. I forced myself to turn away from the fires and closed my ears to the screams. The sinkhole might have been a natural disaster or it might have been an intentional act. If it was intentional, then the body in my arms could be the key to unraveling what had caused this nightmare. I started forward again, leaving others to continue the immediate process of saving lives.

I stumbled against the side of the Hasam, dust sticking to my sweat-soaked shirt turning into mud and dripping down in thin rivulets. I managed to shoulder the door open, tip the seat forward, and slide the body into the back seat. It was far from an ideal way to handle potential evidence, but there wasn't much choice, given the situation.

Chest heaving, I stared down at the body in the back seat. The corpse was clad in a nondescript dark suit, and quality shirt and tie. Classic styling that made it hard to say whether it had lain underground for months or years. Digging in my pocket, I pulled out the PD shield that had been beneath the body. I didn't know Jax's badge number, but to see a badge that clean, with the numbers and shield crisp and unworn, I had no doubt it was his.

We had to learn what happened, because whoever had put it there had tried to implicate us in the body's presence. But now wasn't the time, not with a sinkhole claiming an unmeasured cost in lives and property. I drew a ragged breath and glanced around. It was the best I could do, and I hoped it would take. Another screech of metal on metal pulled me to the streets. Outside, the fires spread in the buildings alongside the sinkhole, lighting their silhouettes against the night. I pushed closer, my lungs filling with dust and the candy-sweet smell of fire foam. All around heroes rushed to help those in need, a mix of first responders and regular people coming together to save lives. There was determination in their eyes, but also fear.

We couldn't even trust the ground we walked on, and every shiver, every tremor made us stare at our feet, silently praying we wouldn't see it tumble away, opening up to blackness below. But the everyday heroes worked on, and I did my best to keep up with them.

It was into the early morning hours when I made it back to the Hasam. I was happy to see that the car and body were as I left them. I had borrowed water from the medics to wash the ash and dust from my face, and picked up a fresh coffee. I figured that was all I really needed before I got started.

I sat in the front seat and stared past the headrest, studying the corpse. I tried to remember exactly how he had been positioned in the sinkhole. He must have been moved to plant the badge, but the sinkhole had poured so much debris into the whole area that it was all covered with a uniform layer of dust.

I didn't see an immediate cause of death, and he'd been damaged when I carried him out. One leg and chunks of his torso had fallen off, left behind in my abrupt and violent exit from the sinkhole. Still, he had coat and pants, and that meant there was a chance I'd find identification. I flipped open his coat, noticing that the collar was open and tie loosened. Not unlike the way that Mollenkampi dress to provide more room for their speaking mouths. But the skeleton was clearly human, which meant that he had likely been warm at one point. The fact that he still wore a jacket made me question how warm or cold he could've gotten. I found a few old pens and scraps of paper with meaningless notes jotted on them, and I found a necklace with a ba, the symbol of the Infinite Path, around his neck. Finally in his pants pocket I found a wallet that held a few dozen bills of various denominations, and a pair of IDs. One a driver's license, expired de-cades ago, and the other a laminated identification emblazoned with interlocking circles of the AFS. That card gave his name as Tanis Klein, along with the title Assistant to Ambassadorial Sector.

A sudden rap on the windshield startled me, and I spun to face the intruder. DO Auberjois stood outside the Hasam, eyes fixed on the mummified corpse in the back seat. Eventually he motioned for me to roll down the window.

I did, and handed over the ID and driver's license. "He had these on him."

Auberjois studied the ID for far longer than it would've taken to simply read it. He was a smart man, and I suspected he was doing the political calculations of whether it was worth the risk to confront the ambassador about this corpse. The decedent was clearly part of the AFS delegation, and the date on the license placed him in the time frame of Paulus's ascent to power. Add in the TPD badge, and it was a perfectly gift-wrapped present for someone like Auberjois, who harbored a deep dislike of Paulus and distrusted me. The question was, how would he react?

Auberjois placed one hand on the roof of the Hasam and bent low, head almost sticking through the open window. "Why the Hells didn't you hand him over to a tech team?"

"They're occupied. Plus, I opted to skip the scene documentation, since there were cars falling on it at the time." That was true as far as it went, though the real reason I was studying the body alone was that I wanted to make sure there weren't any other surprises like Ajax's badge hidden away. Someone was planting evidence in order to implicate me or my partner, and it had been pure luck that I'd found it first.

He raised a hand to his head plates, tracing the shapes absently as he spoke. "We need to get this body someplace secure, and open a proper investigation."

"You don't need to tell me how to investigate a homicide," I said.

"Then act like it." He glared at me. "As far as we know this man got himself lost in the geo-vents on his own, and left a shriveled-up corpse for us to find and puzzle over."

We both knew that was nonsense. Nobody got lost in the geovents, any more than they got lost in a bank vault after hours. But I swallowed my bile and nodded. "I'll get him to the Medical Examiner's office," I said. "We can store him there, and he'll be secure until we can come back at it with a full investigation." Because if the trail did lead to Paulus, we'd need a lot more evidence to back us up.

"How many people have seen this?" He waved the ID in my face.

"Just you."

"How many saw you carry the body to your car?"

I shook my head. "A half dozen? Maybe more. Maybe much more if the news crews were rolling. But with the hillside collapsing and the Barekusu running for their lives—"

"They probably didn't notice you," he finished. "Good." He seemed to consider all of this, and then nodded to himself. "Move the body like you suggested. If anyone asks, it's just another corpse you pulled out of the rubble. Tell your captain about this, and no one else. Is that clear?"

"Clear," I agreed, still a little shaken by how seriously Auberjois was taking this situation. If he'd been any more gung-ho, I'd have felt some suspicion about his motivation. But he seemed more concerned about the headache and logistics involved in sorting out what had just happened. Whoever had planted the body and badge, it didn't seem like Auberjois was in on it.

I secured the remains in the back seat, and started the engine as Auberjois walked away. I'd get Klein to the medical examiner's office as soon as possible. We'd find this poor bastard a spot in the body stacks, and start to unravel the mystery of his death from there.

I spent most of the night in the ME's office, but didn't get much further. The pathologists had their hands full with the influx of other, more recent victims. In the early morning hours I headed back to the Bullpen, where I found Ajax sitting at his desk, head in hands, eyes closed. He wore white slacks and a blue silk shirt decorated with a silver mountain scene.

I sat down and slapped my hands on the desk. He jerked awake.

"Guess you heard the news on your way back from the concert, huh?"

Eyes blinking, he said, "Yes. I dropped off Talena and came straight here."

"Did you talk to CaDell about your badge?"

"Yeah." Jax shrugged. "He said they didn't find anything. He'll keep looking, but . . ." He glanced at my dirt-streaked clothes. "What happened?"

"First, some good news." I pulled out his badge, cupping it in my hand as I reached across the desk. He stared at it as if he couldn't quite wrap his head around its sudden appearance. Finally, he reached out and took it with tentative fingers.

"Where'd you find this? Was it in the Hasam the whole time?"

"Yeah, well," I leaned forward, "that's the bad news . . ."

Over the next half hour I filled him in on everything, the buzzing howl, the sinkhole, Auberjois's involvement, the body, and his badge. He was quieter than usual, only asking a few questions. The whole time, his eyes were on his badge, watching as he traced the embossed shield and badge number. When I was done, he held it up.

"Someone at the festival found this," he said.

"Most likely."

"I could have lost it in the snow-runner," he said. "Or someplace else."

"Could have," I said. "But if it was the snow-runner, it would've been found by another cop, or a service crew. And what's more likely, that it fell off in the snow-runner or while you wrestled with Dinah McIntire's dancers?"

"Someone found it," he repeated. I could practically hear the mental footsteps as he walked himself through it.

"Someone," I agreed. "But there are only two people who are really running that festival."

"Vandie Cedrow and Dinah McIntire."

"So the question is, do either of them have a reason to try and tie you to a dead body and a natural disaster? Because I sure as Hells can't think of one."

"You said the body was old."

"Right. Looks like it's been down there for decades."

"So whoever planted the badge wasn't trying to hang a murder on me."

"No. They were trying to make it look like you'd been in the vents. In Titanshade, that's a far more serious offense."

Jax rotated the badge so it faced me. "When you saw this, did you know who it belonged to?"

"I had a pretty damn good guess."

His eyes crinkled. "But you didn't know. You don't have my badge number memorized. And whoever found this would only know that it belonged to one of us. Which means they may have wanted to target anyone, to throw confusion into the mix. Or they could have been targeting you."

"Same problem. They wouldn't know it belonged to me, either," I said.

"If someone had to guess whether it was you or me that lost a badge, who's the more likely suspect?"

"You're lucky I even gave that thing back to you." But I couldn't deny his point. Stretching my back, I sighed and said, "Between Dinah and Vandie, only one of them dislikes me enough to do something like this."

"And how is Vandie Cedrow getting into the geo-vents? How did she know when the sinkhole would happen?" Ajax was chasing the next question. "Was the body planted along with the badge, or did Vandie plant the badge on a body that was already there?"

"I don't know."

"You said—"

"Jax, I don't know!"

He sat back, absently tugging the sleeve of his nice silk shirt. "It doesn't matter."

"What doesn't?"

"The badge." His voice grew crisper, a jangling anger sounding in the counter tones as he spoke. "You talked me into not reporting it missing. So there's no record of it being gone, and no proof that it was ever on the body."

"No," I admitted, "nothing that would stand up in court. But that doesn't mean we can't tell anyone." I turned and looked at Captain Bryyh's office.

"We could have avoided this by just talking to her in the first place," he said.

"We live in the world created by our mistakes, kid."

"It'd be nice to live in a world where the mistakes are my own." He looked at his watch. "She ought to be here within the hour."

But she wasn't there within an hour, or two hours. It wasn't like her, and it sent a tickle of concern down the back of my neck. After three hours we admitted that we each had to go home and sleep. We'd have to pick the case back up that afternoon.

RUMPLE GLOWERED AT ME WHEN I got home, and he stalked back and forth while I crawled out of my clothes and into the shower. It wasn't until food fell into his bowl that he seemed to forgive me for my absence. Watching him eat, I dropped into a kitchen chair and lost myself in thought.

I thought of a teenager with an unnatural mouth in his stomach, devouring his own entrails as he took vengeance on an old man who'd killed an hour earlier, all of it driven by the invisible maddening buzz. I thought of the sinkhole and the screams of the crowd, of the people I'd saved and the many more I hadn't. I thought of burned bridges, of Gellica and what we could have had. I thought of burned lives, of Ronald, and his mother holding my hand as she died. I thought of all of them, and I wondered how I could face one more day while I was running on little food and no sleep. I stalked over to the tall cabinet that served as a pantry, and rummaged for a bottle of rum that I occasionally used for cooking. *Just a little drop,* I thought. *Just for today. Just to get through the madness.*

I found the bottle and hefted it, peering inside. If there had been anything in it, I don't know what I'd have done. Instead, I decided I'd stop on the way home and buy rum. Or maybe whiskey. Something cheap and potent.

I tossed the empty bottle into the trash, slipped on another cheap suit, and managed to make my exit without looking at myself in the mirror.

Bryyh's office was still vacant as noon approached, an absence that was fairly out of character. Rather than wait around, Jax and I decided to visit the site where I'd found Klein's body. The entire area was suspect and off-limits except to those workers deemed essential. We, of course, were essential. Along with everyone else who kept the wheels of the city turning so that the wealthy could feel safe as they cashed their paychecks. As for the furloughed rig workers and the employees sitting at home and worrying about their rent? No one seemed to care too much about them either way. It was almost enough to make me think Vandie Cedrow was on to something.

The hole had stabilized when it reached the edges of the cavern below, spreading little farther than when I'd seen it last. The area immediately around it was cordoned off, and dozens of construction workers and firefighters worked the site. The frantic rescue of the previous night had given way to a slower, more methodical retrieval operation.

We slipped past the caution tape barrier and approached the edge of the sinkhole, close to where I'd found the body. The ground was like walking on cake sponge, pocked with holes and giving slightly under our weight.

"Maybe we should go around the front," Jax said.

I crouched, looking into the nearest hole in the pavement. The spring sun was behind us, shining deep into the irregularly shaped hole. At the bottom, or perhaps on a ledge, a truck's side-view mirror had come to rest. Its miraculously intact surface reflected the surrounding skyline and our faces. I saw myself, arm propped on one knee, unshaven and disheveled; Jax stood behind me, always organized and prepared. Both of us were so deep in the hole that we might never come out.

"Hey!" A shouted warning from a supervisor. "Area's unstable.

Clear out!" She wore a hard hat and neon vest, and sweat beaded down her temples and neck, a combination of the normal warmth of the Mount's proximity and the relentless heat and sulfur fumes that rose from the sinkhole.

We stepped away, abandoning our reflection, and approached the work crews. The teams had found a path of stable footing, and they spiraled down the edges of the main opening, a living chain of human, Mollenkampi, and Gillmyn hands lifting debris and passing it up and away. Occasionally they came to a stop as they uncovered a body, and the entire chain fell silent, hoping for word of a survivor. Every time, the hope was shattered. Every time, the work began again.

Jax and I watched the work progress.

"You want to get in there?" he asked.

"Yeah," I said. "Yeah, I do."

The supervisor who'd chided us earlier at first turned us away, but relented when we identified ourselves as TPD. She handed us each a vest, gloves, and hard hat, and we joined the chain of workers. For hours we lost ourselves in the work. Moving one rock, one steel beam at a time, searching for a clue that would lead to a life clinging to a fragile thread. Finding only death.

It wasn't difficult work, not where we were placed. Just passing rocks from one set of hands to another. But the heat of the vents and the intensity of the sulfur smell made it feel like we were working in the tropics. Worse, the stink of fire and destruction still saturated the air. Every breath grated the nose and throat, watering our eyes and making us all spit constantly, as we tried to exorcise the lingering taste of smoke and singed plastic from the back of our tongues. During a pause, as jugs of water were passed up and down the line for relief, the worker to our right turned to face me. He breathed heavily, hands on his knees as he eyed us carefully.

"You're the manna strike guy, ain't you? Parker."

"That's him," said Jax. "Detective Parker."

I glared, but didn't correct my partner.

"You oughta be more careful," the breathless guy said. "The ground seems to open up when you're around, don't it?" He guffawed, pleased with his joke.

"I'll be sure to keep that in mind." I slipped off my hard hat and wiped sweat from my brow. "You know what caused it?"

"Nah," he said. "Sinkholes aren't normally caused by anything. A cavity in the planet's tooth, you know?"

"So it just collapsed. Nothing unnatural, no . . . I don't know, explosives or anything?"

"No evidence of it, least not that I've heard." He accepted the water jug from the woman behind him, and took a long swig before passing it to me. "Your bomb squad people were all over the place, and eventually they just sulked away. If they'd found something, they'd be making a stink, right?"

He was right. Though why the Hells would anyone plant a badge on a corpse unless they knew it was going to be found? I took a drink of water, relishing the feel even if it was lukewarm and tasted of whatever plastic the jug was made of. I passed the communal water on to Jax, who drank and passed it on in turn.

I looked up, the spring sun playing across my brow. We were two weeks past Titan's Day, and the nights had loosened their grip, growing shorter and heading toward summer days of almost ceaseless light. I shaded my eyes, and saw hairy figures on the hill, standing where the caravan had camped. I pointed them out to Jax.

"Are they watching us work?" I asked, panting slightly.

Jax looked from the hill to the sidewalk overhead. "No. They're watching them."

I crawled up the ledge, and managed to see a small parade of legs. It looked like a gaggle of reporters following a group of Barekusu walking beside humans in fatigues. I described the scene to Jax.

"Probably Serrow, the sorcerer who arrived before the caravan, and maybe Weylan himself. I don't know about the soldiers."

"AFS engineering corps," grumbled the man to our right. "They've been swarming the place. Showing no respect for the vents."

He didn't need to explain. The ground held the warmth that kept us alive and the oil that fueled our economy. It had even provided the next gen manna so many hoped would bring new jobs. In Titanshade, underground was a source of life and wealth. No one from outside would understand the way we did.

The group drew closer, almost directly above us, and we could hear the low, resonant voice of the Barekusu.

"The Titan is an old faith, something that existed outside the Path, and was embraced by our ancestors' teachings."

Jax stared upward. "I think that's Weylan," he whispered.

Like most people in the city, I grew up celebrating the Titan. Observing Titan's Day and reciting the prayer of thanks when I left the warmth of the geo-vents. Schoolbooks depicted him as a bound, muscular human—or Mollenkampi, depending on the edition. But always he was shown tormented by the Imps, his screams generating the heat that kept us alive in this frigid climate. I suppose it's important to let kids know what life has in store for them.

I pulled myself up a little higher, but still couldn't see more than the legs. Boots and shoes, camouflaged trouser cuffs, and hairy padded paws. One in a notable black and green pattern. The one who'd stared at me during the parade into town.

"I believe we can be of assistance," one of the Barekusu said, voice deep and resonant. "We can work with Titanshade's institutions of learning. To explore and document what lies beneath the city. Perhaps to learn more about local customs and beliefs that predate the Path."

The voices faded as they moved away.

"Joke's on him," I said. "We don't have much in the way of learning around here."

"Yeah." Jax seemed thoughtful. "That was a very . . . different take on folk tradition than we were taught at Trelaheda."

"So your college didn't teach the Path the same way that guy does. There's no one way to walk the Path, right?"

"No. But it's . . ." He whistled under his breath. "That Barekusu is showing much more interest in older beliefs than is normal. It was nice, is all."

Ajax was delighted. And that was good. Personally, I was confused. In his speech, Weylan showed less concern about wounded Barekusu, and more interest in using the sinkhole to make diplomatic gains. Had the caravan truly come for altruistic reasons, or were they here to snatch a piece of the manna strike for themselves?

The Barekusu departed, the foreman blew the whistle, signaling it was time for us to begin again. We put our backs to it, and the hours fell away.

Rock by rock, one bucket at a time, the debris was being removed. It was far too big a project to get done in one day, and the cars and larger pieces of rubble would need to be craned out. It felt simultaneously awful and good to work that hard, like I was doing penance through physical labor. Away from our line, there were engineers working ahead, checking the debris for stability, working to reconnect the intricate honeycombing of vents that provided the city with warmth. It was one of those teams that let out a shout, and the three shrill whistles that called a halt to the operation.

But instead of calling for a rescue squad, the engineers called, "Get some redbacks down here!"

Everyone in our group craned their necks, looking up to the voice. Another worker scampered off to find patrol cops. The red-faced man pointed to us. "Sounds like they're playing your song, Parker."

I exhaled and looked at Ajax. He shrugged. The labor was far less taxing for someone in his physical condition. "Let's go see what they need."

We picked our way through the debris field and badged the engineers. They stepped away, revealing another ledge like the one I'd fallen onto the previous night. They'd pulled aside a layer of rocks and jagged chunks of demolished steel, revealing a slight depression in the wall, almost a protective alcove. Beneath a pile of shattered windshield glass was another mummified body.

I stepped closer and crouched down for a better view.

The body was weathered and misshapen from mummification but still recognizable as that of a young girl. Maybe fourteen years of age, she was human, with wispy dark hair clinging to the desiccated scalp. She wore a maroon jumpsuit, cinched with a dark gray belt. It looked like the kind of thing that might be assigned to a prisoner at a juvenile detention facility. The face was leathered and taut, dehydrated, with just the hint of the dimpled chin that I knew so well. The mummified girl was a younger version of Gellica, and of Ambassador Paulus.

For a moment I wasn't clinging to the side of a sinkhole at the foot of the Mount. Instead, I was in my kitchen, listening as Gellica told me her greatest secret, that she hadn't been born, she'd been grown. Paulus had made a dozen attempts to obtain immortality, and the closest she'd come was a half-human, half-magical clone: Gellica, who'd grown up knowing that her sisters had died and been disposed of. I was looking at proof that even that insanity had been a lie. The body before us was simply a teenage girl to the others; I knew it was far more. Jax's badge may have been planted, but the mummified body of Paulus's clone meant the intrusion in the geo-vents had more secrets than we'd believed.

I pressed a hand to my hip, peering at the body and doing my best to not let any of those thoughts show.

"Carter?" Jax pointed toward the body. "Around her neck."

The brittle fabric of a lanyard held an ID. I brushed away glass shards and flipped the ID. Paulus's photo stared back at me. Below the photo was her name and title of Ambassadorial Envoy. That dated it to Paulus's ascent to power, when she was simply an old-money aristocrat beginning to flex her political muscle. Had the girl stolen Paulus's ID? Was it given to her? Only she and Paulus knew, and one of them wasn't talking.

Around us, the engineers were muttering. One of them, a young Mollenkampi woman whose mandibles trembled excitedly, said, "She must have been in here for years. There were people in here for *years*!"

I winced. As word got out about this, rumors and speculation would grow. We'd quickly become yet another high-profile case.

Crouching beside me, Jax spoke in a whisper. "She was curled up in a small alcove in that cavern. She wasn't with the other body; she wasn't stretched out searching for rescue. You know what I think she was doing?"

I stared into her eye sockets, dry voids begging for help, for justice. "Yeah," I said. "You think she was hiding."

"So," Jax tapped a tusk as he peered at the body of the victim, "why would a child be hiding in a cavern that shouldn't exist, from an adult who worked for the AFS?"

"I don't know." I let the ID fall back to the dead girl's chest. "But I know who we can ask."

We needed to talk to Paulus. We needed to do it immediately. And that meant we needed help from Captain Bryyh.

I wheeled my desk chair across the Bullpen and settled outside Bryyh's office, to be sure I didn't miss her. I'd just started to doze off when she arrived. She paused in front of me, took one look at my filthy clothes, and simply sighed. Her exhaustion was as obvious in her slumped posture as it was in her bloodshot eyes.

"Wake up, Carter."

"Hey, Cap." I waved to Jax, and he headed over to meet us.

Bryyh pulled back a lip, and looked at Jax's outfit dubiously, but didn't upbraid me further. "What do you want?" she said as we followed her into her office. "And don't you sit down in here. You'll dirty up my furniture." That was mildly laughable, as the dust still hung in the air, even indoors, clinging to her braids, making them look even grayer than usual.

Regardless, we stayed on our feet as Bryyh dropped her purse behind the desk and took a seat. I briefed her on the body I'd found during the sinkhole collapse, and additional ones we'd just uncovered, and the IDs that tied them to the AFS. I didn't mention the detective badge I'd found beneath the body.

"The AFS." Bryyh closed her eyes. "What would anyone be doing in the vents, let alone the federal government?"

"It's not like it's without precedent," I said. "There was that pawnbroker who tunneled into the bank on the far side of his block. I don't remember his name."

Her hands were folded in her lap, her ever-present frown more thoughtful than fierce. "Jabez. I still think he was set up."

"But the tunnel was real. And there are cases of stashes burrowed to hide drugs, weapons, even people."

"Small-time hoods and bank robbers. You're talking about government employees. What would white-collar workers want with that kind of crime?"

"Titanshaders don't mess with geo-vents," I said. "Too much social conditioning. But the feds? They don't give a damn about what we think, or what their games might do to our city."

"Paulus was born in Titanshade."

"She's the exception," I said. "She doesn't care about anything but her own power, and she'd have a staff of federal workers to coerce into doing whatever she said."

Bryyh steepled her fingers. "You think she had something to do with the sinkhole?"

I hesitated. "No. I think that she had something to do with the bodies in the cavern." I set a missing person's report on her desk, the tattered tractor-feed holes on the sides frayed by my nervous plucking while I waited. "Tanis Klein was reported missing by his wife almost thirty-four years ago. And I bet we'll find something similar with the new bodies found today. Paulus wouldn't leave them lying around if she knew where they were. I think someone is using those bodies to throw suspicion on Paulus."

Bryyh tilted her head, a motion that caused the beads decorating her graying braids to sway, ticking a brief rhythm. "But he'd been down there untouched for decades."

Jax cleared his throat. "Well, that's the other thing . . ." In a rush of words, he confessed to losing his badge, waiting to report it, and discovering that it had been found beneath a decades-old body. By the time he was done, Bryyh's frown had etched itself in place.

"Detective Ajax, I was under the impression that you were a dependable and clear-headed officer. I see that I was mistaken in that belief."

I attempted to steer the conversation. "But what it tells us—"

"I don't need you to connect the dots for me," she said. "If someone planted Ajax's badge, then they not only knew about the bodies, they knew the bodies would be found."

"Which means they knew the sinkhole was going to open up," I said. "And if they had Ajax's badge, then they're connected to the McIntire festival somehow. I don't want to see them skate away from this untouched."

"I spent the last twelve hours with a friend and her children, waiting to see if her husband was coming out of that hole. The looks on those babies' faces . . ." Bryyh's lips pressed together, drawn into a line too tight for words of sorrow to penetrate. She looked to the photos that lined her desk, the smiling faces of her family, captured in time. "No, whoever opened up that hole isn't going to get away with it."

"Auberjois might fight us," Jax said. "He clearly hates Paulus, and he thinks Carter is in the ambassador's pocket. I expect he doesn't like me simply by association. He'll want to chase Paulus, and he'll think we're defending her if we look at something else."

"And we can't really tell him about the badge," I said. "Because he'd see that as proof that we're working for Paulus."

"He's still green when it comes to handling the administration of the job," she said. "If he gives you grief, he'll be days trying to cut through the red tape I'll spin."

I felt my shoulders relax slightly.

Jax shifted his feet. "So about the badge . . ."

"Oh, I'll have your ass for that," she said. "Not today, but soon. In the meantime, just know that it's coming and quake in fear." She stared at him until he dropped his eyes.

"I'd like to talk to Paulus," I said. "And soon. Before she learns about it through the grapevine."

Bryyh frowned. "That's risky."

"I can't get to her on my own. But if a police captain pulled some strings? That would help."

"You are a glutton for punishment." Her frown didn't budge, but her eyes carried a bit of sparkle. "Fine. I'll see what I can do. Now go clean up. You look a mess, even for the two of you."

22

WE WERE ABLE TO INTERVIEW Paulus the next day. Although it took Bryyh's string-pulling to get it done, the pretense was simple enough: People had died at the sinkhole, and Paulus had been present to witness it. She was told that the sinkhole deaths were being treated as a murder investigation so anyone responsible could be charged with negligent homicide. She was also told that detectives would be out to take her statement as a witness. She wasn't told that it would be me and Ajax.

I drove, winding through the streets in our Hasam. And I took the opportunity to quiz him about the concert. The timing of the sinkhole opening was too tidy to ignore.

"So there was nothing out of the ordinary?"

"No."

"Nothing at all? Not the slightest buzz from the speakers or hitch in the production?"

"You're starting to sound like Dr. Baelen," he said. "It was a great show, that was it." He shifted in his seat. "Really, you should have seen Dinah. She came out in this incredible outfit and she said—"

"Yeah, I saw it." I cut off a minibus, ignoring the driver's honks of protest. "What's the appeal, anyway?"

He whistled his amusement. "You have to ask what the appeal of music is? I've seen where you live. You have a cat, a couch, and a stereo system."

"It's not only about the music for you, though, is it? You're a fan. That's different."

He chewed on that as we slowed at an intersection.

"The music's great," he said. "But you're right, it is more than that. Maybe it's the attitude. Dinah's true to herself. I like that she puts her heart on her sleeve."

"Because that's what you do?"

"No . . ." He fiddled with his tie and stared out the window. "But it's how I'd *like* to live. When I find music or books or movies that put their emotions out there, it makes me feel like I'm taking a step in that direction."

I bit my lip. I had a half dozen comebacks, and not a one of them would've pierced his veil of sincerity. I liked Jax. He was a good person, and I trusted him. It broke my heart to know the city eventually grinds every ounce of decency out of people like that.

"Whatever," I said. "We're here. Try not to emote all over the place when we talk to Paulus, okay?"

We parked, and walked the rest of the way to Wayfinder's Hospital. Inside, Paulus was glad-handing hospital donors and having her picture taken with dying children. We found her wrapping up a bedside visit with one of the young victims of the sinkhole. The press tossed out softball questions, and even got the boy to give a thumbs-up. Paulus was sporting a well-tailored business suit and her blouse was a shimmering brown a shade lighter than her skin tone. The sleeves were long, hiding the manna-ink tattoos that encircled her biceps, pulsing with a life of their own.

She tousled the kid's hair and walked away. Once she was clear of the room, an aide handed her a towel. She didn't break stride as she scrubbed her hands clean and addressed us. "What would you like to know?"

"Did you notice any unusual activity before the sinkhole opened?" I said.

"No." She tossed the towel back into the aide's arms. "I heard the noise, realized what was going on, and did what I had to. Like everyone else."

We turned the corner. A team of nurses and surgeons stood in the hall, being directed by a human with a banker's fashion sense. A quick photo op, and at a sign from the suit, everyone dispersed.

"Does it bother you?" I asked.

"The sinkhole was a tragedy," she said, rattling off the words as though reciting them for a quiz. "Every life lost is felt by the leadership of the city and the AFS. We all mourn as one."

"Not that. I meant them." I pointed at the departing hospital workers. "Compare that to the attention that Dinah McIntire is getting. Adoration for a singer, and manufactured scenes for the woman who wields real power. Hardly seems fair, does it?"

"These health-care heroes are busy saving lives," she said, without a drop of enthusiasm. "They're not honored to meet me. I'm honored to meet them. You have it backward as usual, Carter."

Jax interrupted. "So that's a no to anything unusual *before* the sinkhole. What about during? You were in the thick of things, and you have a trained sorcerer's eye. Did you observe anything noteworthy?"

"I did not." Paulus walked down another hall, as directed by her aide, a woman who I thought might have been among the group I'd seen at Paulus's home. I wondered if she was the kind of person who'd follow an order to stumble into someplace like the geo-vents, someplace she might die, forgotten and alone.

Paulus's eyes swept the hall, taking in the press and well-dressed administrative staff, all of them likely potential political donors. Not once did she look into the rooms themselves. I doubted it was out of excess courtesy for the occupants' privacy.

"What I did notice," she said, "was entirely expected. Titanshade's public servants working with myself and others, joining together to save lives and mitigate property damage. An inspirational example of the city's strength when we work with the power of the AFS." She sighed, almost contentedly. "It's nice to find value in a tragic event."

Jax's biting jaw flexed and he made a sound of protest. She shot a glance at my partner.

"Don't play innocent, Detective. It's unbecoming." We slowed outside a room to let a nurse emerge, one hand full of cotton swabs, the other holding a hypodermic needle. Paulus turned her attention to me. "Of course, your partner is talented and young. He'll always be useful. You, Carter? You're like a used syringe."

"Am I?"

"Yes." Paulus watched the nurse deposit her cargo into a wall-mounted waste receptacle. "You are sharp and potentially infectious. Best to seal you off and bury you in a landfill." She paused, a ghost of a smile dancing along her lips. "Metaphorically speaking."

"Of course."

She resumed her walk toward the next cluster of hospital employees. I kept pace, watching her face. She was focusing on the next group of glad-handers, probably recalling names and previous interactions. Distracted, in other words.

I asked, "What can you tell us about Tanis Klein?"

Paulus blinked, tilted her head, then stopped. She raised a finger, as if trying to place the name. "He worked in the same office as me, years ago. Why?"

"Because he's one of the victims of the sinkhole."

"That's too bad. I didn't even know he was back in town." She flashed a smile. "Funny how life sneaks up on you like that."

"There's a buzz in the air," I said. "One that gets into people's heads. You wouldn't know about that, would you?"

"No. And I quite wish that someone would take care of it, whatever it is."

We stood in silence, Jax and the aide observing our showdown. Finally she said, "Was there anything else?"

I flipped my notebook shut. "Enjoy your photo session. Maybe they'll ask for your autograph."

The ambassador stalked away, the aide trailing in her wake.

"This isn't like her," I said.

Jax straightened his tie. "Why, because she didn't drop a building on your head?"

"Because she's here." I took my eyes off the ambassador and looked at Jax. "Paulus doesn't do photo ops with sick kids. She's got an agenda."

"She's *always* got an agenda."

I chuckled. "Yeah, but this feels different. Reactionary. And she didn't even blink when I mentioned Klein."

"You think she already knew?"

"Maybe. She might know we've found him, or she might simply know his body was down there."

"Either way, she knows now. And she'll do something about it. People like her attack on instinct, like sharks."

"She's not a shark," I said. "She's a kraken, hiding in deep water and waiting to pull down entire ships."

"You know, for a guy who's never been in water deeper than his bathtub, you're showing a sudden interest in sea creatures."

I opened my mouth, meaning to tell him how wrong he was. But he was right. Where *had* that imagery come from? I couldn't explain it, so I closed my mouth, and thought of something else. What was in those vents that made Klein wander into them decades earlier, and what did Paulus know about it?

Instead I simply said, "Let's see what we can turn up on Tanis Klein."

The Titanshade Medical Examiner's Office was strained to capacity with the sudden influx of bodies. Dozens had died in the sinkhole, and several more were skating the line between life and death.

We entered to the sound of raised voices, human and Mollenkampi. That wasn't unusual in the Bunker, but the ME's office was normally more reserved. There was no one running the entry desk. Exchanging a glance, Jax and I made our way toward the source of the argument.

We followed the sound to one of the examination rooms, where a small group of public servants were trading insults over the mummified body of Gellica's . . . sister? What *was* the proper name for a magical clone derived from the same source material?

The senior staff pathologist was Doc Mumphrey, a large man wearing bright red suspenders, who spoke in a rumbling, off-kilter baritone. When we arrived he was deep in conversation with DO Harris and Captain Auberjois. Mumphrey's admin Susan stood to the side, hands flying as she translated Auberjois's rant into sign language. I knew from experience that Mumphrey was able to get along in many conversations, but the Mollenkampi DO had a distinct lack of lips for him to read.

Auberjois had reached that point in an argument where persuasion had given over to simply repeating one's point at a louder volume. "The autopsy needs to be done immediately," he said. "This is my case, and I'm telling you it needs to be done!"

Susan finished the translation a heartbeat behind the outraged Mollenkampi sorcerer, and Mumphrey shrugged. "It's not your case," he said, with the weary tone of someone who'd said the same thing more than once. "The paperwork says different."

"It'll be treated as a homicide, until the ME rules otherwise." I spoke up loud, startling the DO.

"And with the backlog from the sinkhole," I sighed, puffing out my cheeks, "who knows when they'll have a chance to review them?"

"We need to learn what happened to her."

"Isn't that what divination officers do?" I asked. "Talk to the dead?"

Auberjois glared. "We tried. It's been far too long since the moment of death. The echo has faded."

Mumphrey harrumphed, and Susan frowned while she translated. "They also didn't ask before making an attempt."

The pathologist found the methods of divination to be unpalatable, perhaps even unethical. Personally, it was something I did my best not to consider. There was already so much gray in the world, why stick your toe into another ethical whirlpool?

"It's just as well," said Harris. "With as old as that echo would have been, it's more than likely it would've been faint and confused. I doubt we'd have gotten anything useful from the young lady."

"As soon as we have something concrete, we'll let you know." Jax's voice was calming, even lyrical. But it didn't placate Auberjois.

"So you can go reporting to Paulus? Or have you already?"

I stiffened. He didn't know where we'd come from, and we hadn't told her anything. Or had we? Had I played into Paulus's hands by trying to shake a reaction out of her? I kept my face neutral and looked instead at the body of the mummified teenager.

Auberjois stormed out, frustrated by the situation, or perhaps by my failure to take the bait. Harris followed, shrugging and smiling an apology before he left.

"Carter." Mumphrey's voice drew me back, away from the door. He stood closer to the body stacks, attempting to appear nonchalant. "I want you to see something."

He led me back into the body stacks, where a sheet-draped form lay on a steel gurney.

"I got a little curious about your snake oil salesman who attacked you after death." Mumphrey rested a hand on the edge of the privacy sheet. "I'll have to tell Auberjois, but I didn't want him to see this before you did."

"Petrevisch?"

"The same. But when I did, I got a little shock." He pulled back the sheet. I tensed, prepared to face the transformed figure of Saul Petrevisch for the first time since his corpse had attacked me. Instead, the gurney slab held a shriveled raisin the size of a man. Even as I watched, a little more of it crumbled to ash.

"Bobby Kearn?"

"Same condition."

Whatever the source of their magic, the manna threads hadn't been severed. Magic was a hungry force. It fueled the workings between bound objects by consuming manna. If the objects were drained of manna before the connection was broken, then the material itself would wither away, like Guyer's manna-bound truck at the sinkhole.

I crouched, eyeing the crumbled and consumed body. Was this what awaited Gellica, if she didn't have a supply of manna? Was it the ultimate end for me? What would happen if Paulus was taken down, if the flow of manna was squelched before it even began? Paulus was corrupt, but the same was true of every political machine. There were dirty cops, and that didn't mean we were all equally culpable. Or at least, not cops like Jax, who cared more about their heart and helping people than benefits and pensions.

The corrupt head of the beast, people like Paulus, they had to be stopped. But there had to be ways to do it without injuring the many innocents around her. The trick was, how could we tell them apart?

THE SINKHOLE HAD DAMAGED THE geo-vents and disrupted the natural flow of warm air. That made it high profile, a transgression of the city's most valuable asset, the lifeline we all clung to every time we walked past a vent. Since the neighborhoods impacted were the residences of the wealthy and elite, fixing it was a higher priority than if it had only affected the already cold Borderlands neighborhoods.

So maybe that gave Auberjois wiggle room with the City Attorney's Office. Or maybe they could read the political tea leaves, or they figured that Auberjois would take the fall if things went sideways. Whatever the reason, as the evidence of tampering with the vents mounted and rumors of mummified bodies with ties to Paulus began to swirl, I feared the ambassador's days of freedom were numbered. I feared it not for her sake, but because of what that meant to Gellica. No one in Titanshade was innocent, and Gellica had her share of questionable acts. But she worked for Paulus out of a mixture of fear and aspiration: fear of what Paulus could do to her, and aspiration that their work might actually make the city a safer, better place. She was almost as delusional as those of us who wore badges.

From painful experience, I knew that the problem with investigating Paulus was that she had almost as much pull as the entire police force. I'd have been glad to share that insight with Captain Auberjois, but he was still convinced I was in the ambassador's pocket, and had no interest in anything I might have to say. It took an intervention from Captain Bryyh to arrange a sit-down between the

DO captain and me and Jax. Bryyh was along to play referee. There was also a surprise guest: Assistant City Attorney Flifex, a narrow-faced man willing to dirty his hands so that his boss would have some distance in case things went wrong. The prosecutor showed little interest in the meeting, perched on the arm of an office chair, absently cleaning his fingernails with a business card plucked from Auberjois's desk.

The newly minted captain stood in front of a murder board, a smaller-scale version of the one we had in the Bullpen. He stood with his feet wide, hands clasped behind his back, and his mandibles at rest. It looked like he had a speech prepared, and when he spoke, it sounded like, it, too.

"We are still at the early stages of this investigation," he said. "But we have found evidence of tampering with the geo-vents, and we believe that the sinkhole event is tied to the mind-altering buzz being reported. If Paulus continues to have freedom of movement, and potential access to the sinkhole, there's no telling what kind of evidence she could destroy."

"Skip the prepared notes," Bryyh said.

"We have a strong indication that Paulus was behind the opening of the sinkhole. It's time to place her under arrest, even if it's on a lesser charge."

"Why?" I said.

Auberjois looked annoyed. "So that she doesn't have the opportunity—"

"No. I mean, why open the sinkhole? It's not like she'd gain anything from it. She already has money, she already has power. How would a sinkhole on the edge of the city help her? And if she is behind it, why would she send a child down there?" On the wall, the girl who looked so much like Gellica stared down from her photo. I wondered if Gellica had lied to me about having no siblings, or if she'd simply repeated lies that Paulus had told to her. I cleared my throat and asked, "Any luck on an ID?"

"Not yet," said Auberjois. "No match for her prints in the system."

That surprised me, though it shouldn't have. Identical twins don't have matching fingerprints. I suppose a clone wouldn't, either.

"How is that possible? She's got to have a record," Jax said. "Look at that jumpsuit. It certainly looks like a government-issued prison uniform."

"Juvenile detention," Flifex chimed in. "It's different now, but thirty years ago . . ." He punctuated the sentence with a shrug. "It's possible they kept poor records. Or someone arranged for them to be permanently misfiled."

"Here's the thing." Auberjois leaned forward, hands intertwined, trying his best to convey the image of the thoughtful detective. "Who has the juice to make detention center records disappear?"

Flifex nodded once. Slowly, thoughtfully. But I knew it was a false path. There weren't any fingerprints on file because the mummified girl almost certainly didn't have a birth certificate, or legal residence. Paulus hadn't made her disappear, she'd *made her*, full stop. And I couldn't tell anyone that particular secret without endangering Gellica and myself. I pinched the waddle of flesh beneath my jaw. *It really is so much easier when people dislike you for simple, honest reasons*, I thought.

"We need to use the low-hanging fruit to bring her in now," Auberjois was saying, "before she gets wind of what we're up to. It's no secret that she's got ears in the Bunker."

He didn't need to look at me when he said it. We all knew he thought I was on Paulus's payroll. Of course, I was withholding information. But I was doing so only to protect Gellica, not to help Paulus, or even myself. I kept telling myself that made a difference.

"We heard you the first time, Captain." Flifex barely looked up from his nails. "Bring her in on what evidence?"

"There is evidence she had an employee in the vents," Auberjois said.

Jax spoke up. "When we were at the sinkhole site we were told there was no evidence of sabotage, or even that the cavern or sinkhole is anything but a natural phenomenon. Is that accurate?"

"Yes." Bryyh spoke before Auberjois could answer. "There's still debris to remove, but no signs of intentional destruction or that the cavern was made by any of the eight Families."

Jax stepped away from the wall. "So whoever was in the cavern wasn't mining, or intending to create a structural weakness a few decades down the line."

"The problem is that they were there at all," said Auberjois. "Someone breaks into your home, it's illegal. Doesn't matter if they steal anything or not."

"It matters what we charge them with," said Flifex. "And it can matter quite a bit when it comes time for sentencing. If you want to put Paulus in prison, I suggest we make sure that she stays there for a very, very long time." He smiled faintly, the expression of someone who understood the risks we were dealing with.

"The press is running with the mummy story," said Auberjois. "The public's in an uproar, because the mummies mean someone is tampering with the one thing that keeps us all warm and toasty at night. People are cold and scared, and if the sentiment has ever turned against Paulus enough that we can get a fair shake in a trial, this is the moment."

Flifex made a noise that could only be described as a 'scoff.'

"This is preposterous," he said. "Any fool would be able to see that this arrest is politically motivated."

"I agree," I said.

Bryyh side-eyed me. "Since when do you care about public perception?"

"Since it threatens to prevent a conviction and distracts us from the real issues at hand."

"We'll take an ARC team," said Auberjois, doing his best to ignore us. "And we should have an SRT squad on-site in case it gets ugly."

Flifex's bowler threatened to slide off the chair back where he'd laid it. He moved its perch to a safer location. "Really, Captain, that seems excessive."

Special Response Teams were used when large-scale force was expected to be needed, or at least threatened. Barricades, hostage situations, high-profile arrests.

"Auberjois's right about that much," I said. "They can sit in a carrier down the street unless needed. We can leave our big guns holstered, but we still gotta bring 'em to the fight."

Flifex folded the used business card into tidy thirds, then dropped it into the trash bin. "That's nice, but it'll take weeks to establish the groundwork and push this through."

Auberjois's eyes crinkled with amusement. Up until that moment, I hadn't realized what a showman he was.

"He doesn't need you to obtain an arrest warrant," I told Flifex. "That's between a detective and a judge. You're here as a courtesy. A sign of the enormous regard with which we all hold your office."

Bryyh cleared her throat, pulling me back into step. "Carter . . ."

Flifex seemed unfazed. "You don't need me for the warrant, that's true. But you certainly need our office if you want to see charges filed, and the good ambassador prosecuted." He crossed his legs and tightened the pleat in his pant leg between finger and thumb. "Otherwise, you'll simply be pissing on the leg of one of the most powerful figures in the AFS, who also happens to be a sorcerer. I have crossed paths with the ambassador, and oh, I assure you, when she is angry, she is keen and shrewd."

I grinned. "It ain't just when she's angry, pal."

"Precisely," Flifex said. "So by all means leave me out of this disaster in the making. I for one can live with not being on the ambassador's hit list." The double meaning caught him as he said it, and he tittered silently at his own wordplay.

I started to respond, but Auberjois interrupted me. "Here's the thing," he said. "Your boss is an elected official. And next year he's up for reelection. When the papers get wind of how much info we have on her, he'll have a full-time job defending his decision to sit on his hands."

"You wouldn't dare," said Flifex.

"We wouldn't," agreed Auberjois. "But we don't have to. Look at this," he pointed at the photos of the mummified corpses, "and think about all the homes and businesses without heat. You really think we can keep this bottled up?"

Flifex chewed his lip. Jax pressed on. "Paulus is on more than a few hit lists herself. A political rival like Katie CaCuri only needs to hear from one patrol cop or administrative personnel, one person in the whole of the Bunker's thousands, who's heard rumors that Paulus is tied to the sinkhole. It'll be all over the news the next morning."

Auberjois was about to answer but I cut in, stealing his thunder, and hoping to demonstrate that I wasn't Paulus's man.

"The captain here wants to use the low-hanging fruit. There is evidence that she had operatives in the vents. You charge her with damage to public property and ask for no bail because of the shocking nature of the crimes and her obvious flight risk. Then she'll sit in jail long enough for us to uncover the details on the negligent homicide, and possibly some of her countless other crimes we're assuming she's guilty of."

"That's a fishing expedition."

"No," said Auberjois. "It's a focused investigation of the vent tampering. But if other facts turn up along the way . . ." He shrugged.

"Then," I said, "the dead find justice, and the CA is a hero."

Flifex stroked his goatee, pondering the angles. Then he stood, gathering his bowler hat and paper-thin overcoat in his hands. "Very well. When are you dragging this mess before a judge?"

"Like the detective mentioned, you're here as a courtesy." Auberjois drew a sealed envelope out of the folder, the closing notes of our dance number. "I already have the warrant. Now we just need to go get our bad guy."

"I see." Flifex put on his hat and carefully adjusted its angle to the proper amount of jaunt. "Good luck to you, then." He tipped his head to the rest of us and departed.

"So much for our sit-down and make-friendly," I said.

"Stow it, Carter." Bryyh's eyes were on Auberjois. "Why did you play it that way? Why wait for us to be here, too?"

"Your celebrity detective already figured that out." Auberjois clacked his jaws. "Courtesy, of course. A sign of the *enormous* regard with which I hold your department. Paulus has a public appearance scheduled for tomorrow. We'll take her then. She'll go quietly, if only to not cause a scene. Let's hope she doesn't change her plans in the meantime."

"I think you've said enough." Bryyh abruptly stood and headed for the door, and Jax and I walked behind. Once in the hall, we held a discussion, our voices low.

"Is it just me," Jax said, "or did Auberjois tell us the details of when he's going after Paulus, but not Flifex?"

"That was intentional," I said. "If Paulus changes her plans at the last minute, he can accuse me of tipping her off."

"It's like feeding info to an informant to test their reliability," Bryyh agreed. "But there's a thousand reasons Paulus might reschedule an event. This is a definite attempt to get Carter over a barrel."

Jax thought that over. "What an asshole."

Bryyh's eyes bulged, and she barely kept a smile in check.

Jax continued, his voice rising. "So what do we do?"

"Nothing," said Bryyh. "He wants to take her down, let him try. I won't shed any tears for her."

"Me either." I glared back at the closed door of Auberjois's office. "But why's he so hung up on Paulus? She kill his puppy or something?"

Bryyh grimaced. "He's trying to prove his value. Auberjois is the new head of a new department. The need for ARC teams didn't exist until a month ago, and for all he knows it'll disappear just as fast. If that happens, he'll be the first to be relegated to some unpleasant, dead-end assignment."

"I meant, what do we do about Paulus?" Jax said.

"Right," I said. "There's a city full of corruption, but he's focused on Paulus. Auberjois has to know that she's dangerous as all the Hells."

Bryyh gripped her shoulder, stretching muscles undoubtedly tensed from stress and desk work. "Politically, she's vulnerable right now. The scandals around the manna strike mean she's got less cover than she used to. If Auberjois does bring her down he'll be able to coast on that single collar for the rest of his career." She breathed deep. "And it's not like he's defenseless. He's a sorcerer with a badge, and he's got a whole department of sorcerers reporting to him. I'm not even sure the administration realizes what they've created in him."

"What I'm *asking*," Jax said, before returning to a whisper, "is what do we do if Paulus catches a cold, or someone cancels, and her public event doesn't happen?"

Bryyh slowed her pace as we reached the elevators. "Then a police captain will be convinced that one of us is feeding info to Paulus."

"I should have told him about my badge," Jax said, voice small.

"No," said Bryyh. "That train left the station long ago. Whatever he's found, he thinks it's solid enough to take to a judge. We were in there just for theater, and to put us on notice."

I massaged the stumps on my mangled hand. "To put me on notice."

She frowned. "In the meantime, let's hope the ambassador's schedule doesn't get disrupted."

24

SO WE KNEW THE TIME of Paulus's arrest, but were unable to do anything about it. Jax and I parked our Hasam down the street from the social club where Paulus was due to make a public appearance alongside Weylan, the celebrity Barekusu guide. We thought we might at least see the event when it happened. Ragweed Road was in a posh neighborhood, and we might have been out of place if not for the crowds and reporters who'd already gathered for the joint hand-pressing session. So we were able to sit and eat our take-out noodles and chug caffeine in peace, as we waited to see it all descend into chaos.

Jax had a napkin tucked in his collar, pulled down far enough that he could eat and talk without worrying about adding a few extra dots to the pattern on his tie.

"Tell me if I'm wrong," he said, "but I don't see any way Paulus's people being in the vents decades ago would cause the sinkhole to collapse now."

"No." I caught myself. "We don't know for sure. They may have planted the seeds, somehow weakened the ground. But I doubt it."

"Because the timing is too tight, isn't it?" He bounced his head, as if counting days on a calendar. "I lost my badge on Firstday and the sinkhole opened up Quaddro night. So someone was in the hole during that three-day gap. And whoever it was, they knew the bodies would be found shortly, or else why plant the badge at all?"

"It's a mess," I agreed. "The sinkhole uncovered an old crime—the intruders in the vents. But because of the badge we know it's actually a recent crime. Someone entered the vents, left the badge, and did nothing about the bodies. And I don't think we're the only people being set up."

"Paulus." He slid a forkful of noodles down his mouth.

I nodded. "She's arrogant, and arrogant people can be sloppy. But planting a badge on her own crime scene? No, she's the one person we know didn't try to take us down."

"The fact that Paulus is implicated means that she's not involved in the newest interference."

"Yes."

"But we can't say so, because the other bit of evidence was my badge, and we sat on that piece of information until it was too late."

I glared into the side-view mirror, watching the pedestrians going by. The other missing piece was the identity of Gellica's sister. But I couldn't say anything about that, either, without exposing Gellica's secret. And I couldn't watch her hauled away like poor Andrews.

I sighed. "Would it make you feel better if I said you were right about the badge?"

"Yes."

"Too bad."

My pager buzzed. I dug around in my coat pocket and fished it out. Code 187. Jax picked up the radio and thumbed the push-to-talk. He reported in to Dispatch, but instead of a prompt reply with an address, the dispatcher hesitated. "One moment, Detective . . ."

I gave Jax a shrug. There was a burst of static, then the dispatcher was back. "Please check your pager for a call-in number."

Jax's pager buzzed, followed by mine. The same phone number appeared on each of the tiny green screens.

I looked at my partner. "Guess we go find a pay phone."

We fired up the Hasam and cruised a bit until we found one near a gas station. We called in and the extension picked up.

"Carter?" A dual-toned Mollenkampi voice chirped in my ear. "This is Auberjois. I need you to approach the following address with great care." Guyer's boss articulated each word, adding resonant bass notes and making the request seem like the most important thing in the world.

He read me the address. 1800 Ragweed Road. It was down the road from the spot in which we'd just been parked.

"What's this about?"

"Murder," he said. "That's what you do. Now get to that address and investigate. And when the newspaper and TV cameras show up, I want you to be sure you're seen."

"Make sure I'm . . ." I paused. "Say that again?"

"I already have an ARC team on-site, but they need a Homicide detective, and I want you to be the first on scene, and to smile for the cameras. Is that clear?"

"Captain Bryyh—"

"Is one hundred percent behind this move. This isn't a request, Detective."

"I'll get there when I get there," I snarled, and disconnected the line. My anger was real but my delaying tactic was a bluff. I wouldn't leave a murder victim waiting for justice.

1800 Ragweed Road was, of all things, a guidepost. St. Azzec's catered to the wealthy and well-kept. Ironic, since its patron, Azzec the Lost, was a Mollenkampi philosopher famous for questioning the nature of the One True Path, only coming to embrace its philosophies at the end of his life. In other settings, a St. Azzec's Guidepost would be welcoming of all those who sought insight. In Titanshade, it was pre-emptively protected against intrusion by anyone below a minimum income level. Official department policy for such high-profile locations is to enter quietly through the back. Unofficial department policy would never have me within a thousand paces of the place. But the DO had insisted our job was to be seen. So I decided to take him up on it.

The scrum of reporters around the front door snapped our photo and shouted questions as Jax and I strode to the guidepost. The nature of those questions took me by surprise—they were all about Barekusu. I exchanged a quick glance with Ajax. His brow was furrowed, and he looked as confused as I felt. Still, we paused by the entrance and let the press go mad, as Auberjois had instructed. I spotted Klare in the scrum, and I felt sure my photo would be running in *The Titanshade Union Record* that night.

We were ushered past the ornate iron detailing on heavy wooden doors by a foursome of patrol officers. No scarlet crime scene tape hung on the doors, but the patrol's presence spoke volumes: the department brass wanted to make a very public statement about how they were responding to whatever had happened behind those doors.

Inside, the layout was simple, like most guideposts. A series of benches in the main chamber, a raised dais for the guides to speak from, a series of candle-lined alcoves for meditation, and curtains hiding the side passages intended for those seeking the inspiration and other-worldly visions of Dream Sight. The wealth showed in the details. Expensive candles, gold leaf and intricate carving on benches that would be far out of place on an actual trail. All this bore witness to the wealth of the guidepost members. This despite the fact that guideposts technically don't have members. Like any waystation on the trail, they are open to all comers. And just like anything that is open to all, they are susceptible to being monopolized by the powerful.

Jax turned to me, his badge shiny and clean hanging on his jacket breast pocket. "What do you think is going on?" He seemed more anxious than normal, almost eager. He'd trained in a seminary, and maybe the thought of violence being done in a guidepost was enough to get his back up.

"How would I know? I haven't been here any longer than you. Let's go ask someone who has." I moved down the center aisle toward the small crowd of patrol cops. I recognized a few of them and exchanged nods. One of them indicated the hallway at her back.

"They're in the dream chamber. That one," she said, pointing. "The other, that's where the mess is. You'll want to brace yourself before going in there."

"Thank you." Jax pushed aside the curtain and led the way to the dream chamber.

The hall was slightly less ornate than the main chamber of the guidepost, likely because it was seen less often, and maybe the donors weren't the type to chase deep dreaming. In any case, we heard voices from one of the three chambers off of the hallway, and we pushed our way inside.

There we found one divination officer and two plainclothes personnel I didn't recognize huddled around a Barekusu I did. It was one of the Barekusu who'd preceded the caravan's arrival, Serrow, the sorcerer. Her voice and photo had become pictures on the evening news in the last week or so, but in those instances she had never looked so downtrodden.

Serrow crouched on her back legs, head bowed so low the light brown hair along her neck almost touched the stone-tiled floor. The crown of pointed ears circling her head drooped, and her horn slats were lowered, hiding her eyes. Her arms were pulled in tight, elbows close to her ribcage and her show hands clenched. Barekusu hands were complex things; their arms terminated with a thick three-fingered hand, heavily callused from walking on all fours. Each finger was the width of my wrist, and the two front-facing fingers had a gap perfectly sized for the back-facing finger to fold into. This was the Barekusu show hand, and it could take the near-continuous walking of the caravan in stride. Serrow's sly hands were hidden.

My badge was on display on my breast pocket, though neither as shiny nor as clean as my partner's. I announced our arrival. "Detectives Carter and Ajax. What's the situation?"

The DO was an aging Mollenkampi woman who seemed enormously happy to see us. She started to respond, but one of the plainclothes humans interrupted.

"Thank you for coming," he said, thin blond mustache quivering slightly, "but we have this under control. Please wait outside, and we'll brief you in a few moments."

I gave him an *aw-shucks* grin and scratched my head. "Well, here's the thing. Is there a body? Because that's usually why you call Homicide detectives." I looked at Jax. "Don't you find that's the case? That there's usually a dead body somewhere around if we show up?"

The DO shuffled her feet and peered at the plainclothes guys, as if deflecting the conflict. I figured both men to be younger than me.

Better dressed and better groomed as well. One wore a suit, the other a sweater pulled over a shirt and tie. Fairly thin fabrics, even on the sweater. These were people accustomed to staying in the warmth of the city's center, and their fine watches and recently shined shoes made it unlikely they were police.

The one with the pencil-thin mustache inhaled, then said in a rush, "Yes, there is a deceased individual, but as I say—"

"Then it's hardly under control, is it?" I said. "In fact, judging from the press scrum going on outside it's not going to get under control anytime soon. And since I don't see another Homicide detective crew anywhere around here, that means we're first on scene, so this is our case. And *that* means that you'll do as we say, or you'll be squeezed into the back seat of our Hasam and hauled downtown."

The tiny mustache guy blinked, his mouth slightly open. The one with the shaved head and flushed face threw in his own thoughts. "There's no call for rudeness—"

"This is my polite voice," I said. "But I'll escalate this shit faster than you can blink, and you'll be explaining to the owner of whatever boots you lick how the Hells you ended up needing to be bailed out of the Bunker."

I turned to the DO. "What's the story?"

Before they could speak, the Barekusu let out a rumbling sigh, a sound both soothing and unnerving. "I killed a man, Detective. That is why you are here. To hold me accountable."

The Barekusu reared back slightly, and the horn plates over her eyes raised far enough for me to see more of her bisected eyes. She looked mournful and serious, but I didn't have enough firsthand experience with Barekusu to say for certain.

The mustache guy started to speak up but I cut him off. "Save it, Pencil-thin."

His lips twitched, as he tried to parse that out. "Excuse me?"

"Are you her lawyer?"

"Ah. No. I'm from the mayor's office, and I'm here to help." The man put extra emphasis on "mayor's" and "help," letting me know he really meant "someone more powerful than you" and "tell you what to do."

I jerked my chin at the bald guy. "What about you? You the mayor's man as well?"

Baldy was a little more subtle. "I serve with the Assembly of Free States delegation. I'm simply here to provide assistance and support at the request of Ambassador Paulus." He was sophisticated enough to realize that was all he had to say. He wasn't smart enough to realize that it made him a threat in my eyes. Although knowing that his boss was going to end the day in handcuffs, I almost felt sorry for him. Almost.

"Great! So the two of you can provide help and assistance by getting the Hells out of this room. Wait in the outer chamber until we're ready for you."

Baldy retreated a step, but Pencil-thin didn't quite understand the lay of the land. "We were here, and can verify that this situation—"

I shouted over my shoulder: "Patrol!"

Pencil-thin shook his head. "Detective, I don't think—"

One of the patrol cops poked her head in the chamber, and I said, "These two men are material witnesses. Escort them to the outer chamber. Do not let them leave. Do not let them use the phone. Do not let them use the restroom. Understood?"

The patrol nodded. That wasn't good enough. The task I was assigning her was essential.

"What's that?" I demanded.

"Understood." She glowered, probably thinking I was an authoritarian SOB, but it was crucial that those two men not contact their superiors.

"Good," I said. "I'll let you know when I'm ready for them."

Pencil-thin and the AFS man stared.

"I'd go, if I were you," said Jax. "He wasn't joking about the back of the Hasam being uncomfortable."

The two political hacks shuffled out of the room with wide eyes and muttered protestations. They'd probably forgotten what it felt like to butt heads with someone who didn't care about their job titles.

The DO looked like she needed to lie down. "I should go, too. I'm not even supposed to be here. I'm not a field operative." Her mandibles twitched faster and faster, and her voice was starting to sound constricted. "I was here to see Serrow speak. I don't know what I'm doing." That explained why I hadn't recognized her, and why the political flacks had been able to push her around.

Serrow said something then, but she said it in the DO's own language. Her deep lowing, plus snaps from all four hands, made a shockingly accurate replication of Kampi. The DO's eyes lit up, and both she and Ajax stood a little straighter. A compliment from a Barekusu had that effect, even if she was a murder suspect.

"You should stay," I told the DO. "I'll need to talk to you in a little bit. First, we're going through this whole thing step by step." To the Barekusu, I said, "Why don't you start from the beginning."

THE BAREKUSU AND I STUDIED each other.

Barekusu had the reputation of having a herd's natural de-fenses and mind-sets. Typically peaceful and orderly, they were quick to protect each other when threatened, closing ranks against outsid-ers. In that way, they weren't unlike cops. I wondered if they had high rates of divorce and alcoholism, as well.

"How would you like me to begin?" Serrow shifted on her hind legs, giving me a glimpse of one eye, the quartered pupil darting in four separate directions at once. The horn slats let them survey their surroundings, shading their eyes and making it hard to see where they were looking. An innate sense of direction combined with their peripheral vision gave them an uncanny knack for situational aware-ness. It was difficult, almost impossible, to sneak up on a Barekusu. Which is why I chose to tackle her head-on.

"Start with why you came here, end with why you killed someone. We'll see where we go from there." I positioned myself directly across from her.

Her three-fingered hands rose in the air, then tilted back, like a waiter holding a tray overhead. The motion revealed her delicate sly hands. More slender than my own, and with more fingers than her show hands. Five on her right, four on the left, indicating that she was right handed. I filed that away.

I don't know which came first, the way we describe Barekusu hands or the way we talk about those sleight-of-hand experts who can mimic sorcery through mundane methods. The stage trickster distracts the audience with flourishes of one hand—the show hand—while manipulating or palming an object with their sly hand. Similarly, Barekusu sly hands worked behind the scenes, raking their fine undercoat and coarse outer hairs, collecting loose strands to weave into kusuma textiles. Combining the strength and durability of the outercoat and the undercoat's silky feel, kusuma fabrics were treasured across the continent. The Barekusu were equal parts scholars, diplomats, and merchant kings.

"I came to the guidepost to lead a meditation." Serrow spoke in a low singsong voice, the sound of a plastic tube being swung overhead. A *whoosh whoosh* that sent a slight chill up the back of my neck. "I never thought I'd be chosen to commit such an act . . ."

"Chosen? What do you mean?"

She took a long breath, and nostrils the size of my fist flared. She had two or three times my mass and could have crushed me with her sheer bulk, if nothing else. The bone eye plates rose and lowered, jagged and irregular as a series of overlapping slate roofing tiles. I wasn't used to reading Barekusu expressions, but I took it to mean she wasn't quite able to look me in the eye.

"Only that I felt my actions weren't mine. That something overtook me."

The buzzing. I steeled myself, afraid we'd be encountering yet another transformed body.

"How many people were here?" Jax's pencil hung over his notebook.

"I don't believe I counted, a few dozen perhaps? Most of them, though, were in the larger chamber. Out there, everything was fine." Her grammar was impeccable. Like most Barekusu, Serrow seemed to have a natural inclination for languages, which meant communication shouldn't be an issue.

"When did things start to be not fine?" I asked.

"While I was in the dream chamber," she said.

"Had you taken any sedatives?"

Her head rotated like a doorknob in mid-turn, swinging her fur and flapping her ear tips. I guessed it to be the equivalent of shaking one's head. Still, I asked for clarity, "Is that a no?"

"It is a no, Detective. It was thought best that I not enter a true trance, out of consideration for the waiting crowd."

"Who was in the room with you?"

"Myself, one reporter, and one assistant from the city."

"Only one reporter?"

The DO spoke up. "They were doing a press pool," she said, mandibles stretching. "One reporter, no photographer. Not unusual for an event like this."

I acknowledged that with a nod, keeping my focus on the Barekusu guide. "The assistant from the city, was that one of the men in here earlier?"

"No," she said. "That person is, I believe, sedated."

"Sedated?" I glanced at the DO, but Serrow answered first.

"I believe they were injured in the events. Or perhaps they were traumatized by what happened."

"She wasn't injured," the DO said. "She'd stepped out of the room to get refreshments. She's lying down, now. She needed to after she came in and saw, well . . . the aftermath."

"And what was that, exactly?" asked Jax.

Sly hand fingers stretched toward the Barekusu's chest, stroking and adjusting her fur. Although the physiology may have been different, the drive was clearly recognizable: I'd seen countless witnesses and suspects fiddle with their clothes or hair in the same way.

"You may not believe me when I say this, but it's true: I don't entirely know."

"Just do the best you can."

She huffed, composing herself, and I felt her breath against my cheeks. It smelled of honey and fresh-cut grass.

"I was relaxing, in a light meditation. But what I heard was not something I've encountered before. Have you read of whale song?"

"Whales sang?"

"I've read of it in books, and older Barekusu have confirmed it to me. Before they were extinct, whales sang long, low songs that reverberated through the ocean. What I heard today was similar. Deep and low, and sounding like it came from far, far below, a wail swelling into a chorus of rage. And I believe the more I listened, the more it resonated in my chest, in my head, in—" Serrow's arms twitched, and her sly hands worked through her fine-haired coat even faster.

"I embraced it," she said. "I gave myself to the song and I swayed, and I danced, and I clenched my hands . . ." With a snap, the sly hands disappeared, and the powerful show hands were back, folded into massive fists. I wondered what that grip would do to human bones. "When the song faded, I looked down at the reporter's . . ." The horn plates rose, and she stared at me, the split pupils dancing around like minnows in a fishbowl.

I took a breath. "Those men before, they weren't your lawyers."

"I believe not."

"I suggest you get some."

The Mollenkampi DO walked us down the short hall to the chamber where the attack had taken place. The tech crew waited at the opposite end of the hall, shuffling their feet and looking anxious. I didn't know if that was caused by the press attention, the idea of such a crime happening in a guidepost, or something else.

We crossed the threshold into the crime scene, and I immediately felt an itching need to get out of there myself. The reporter's body was exactly as Serrow had described. Everything about the crime scene indicated that she was telling the truth, to the best of her abilities. The victim was in a pile, twisted and broken in more places than I could count. It was what I'd expected to see. What I hadn't expected was that I'd know him.

Taran Glouchester, the reporter for *The Titanshade Union Record*, was dead. I remembered his partner Klare telling me they wanted in on the press pool. That had been shortly before the sinkhole, though it felt like years ago.

There was shockingly little blood, a detail that made the limp rag-doll positioning of the body all the more surreal. His legs jutted out at unnatural angles, his head turned almost all the way around, crushed ribs and deflated lungs making his torso appear far too narrow. His arms splayed outward, forming a lazy pinwheel. The open, glassy eyes stared at the sputtering candles set in the walls, and I wondered if that had been the last thing he'd seen.

Walking the perimeter of the room as discreetly as possible, I didn't perceive any strands of next gen manna. I turned to the Mollenkampi DO with the drooping face.

"Are you gonna do your thing?" I asked.

"My thing?"

"Divination."

"What for? There's a confession, witnesses. There's no mystery!" She shook her head. "I'd get my caboose chewed if I spent manna on this case."

I grunted a note of discontent, but she was right. Everyone in City Hall was going to want this to drop off the radar as soon as possible.

Jax and I exchanged a glance, the unspoken advice, *Watch for a transformation.* Jax called the techs from down the hall while I edged in closer, starting my examination of the room. I was anxious to at least close the poor bastard's eyes. I'd never liked Glouchester, but I wasn't happy to see him end up in that state, either.

Ultimately, the entire day was devoted to the crime scene. Processing a murder can be slow, shockingly so to those who aren't used to it. The two political flacks got angrier as the day wore on, and I let them dangle out in the common area. Eventually they raised a fuss as I strolled by for the thirtieth time. I acted surprised that they were still there, then directed them to leave statements with the patrol who'd been sitting beside them the whole time. I walked away, ignoring the cursing and complaining behind my back.

Jax didn't look up from his notepad. "Did you do that just to aggravate them?"

"No," I said. "Though that's a nice bonus. We can't let Baldy give Paulus a panicked phone call. If she pulls out of her public appearance, then Auberjois's plan falls to pieces, and he blames us for tipping Paulus."

While Baldy and Pencil-thin gave their statements, I peered outside and found that the press was surprisingly absent. I took it as a clear sign that the arrest of Paulus had occurred, and the media hounds had chased after the story of the disgraced politician, probably assuming that whatever was happening with Serrow couldn't be as salacious as a disgraced politician falling from glory.

I turned and shouted across the room to the patrol officer taking the statements. "They're free to go when you're done!"

The two lackeys stormed out of St. Azzec's. Pencil-thin shot me a look full of daggers on his way out the door. I smiled and waved goodbye.

But not all the press was gone. Klare prowled back and forth along the far sidewalk, brow furrowed. She spotted me and turned, standing still for a heartbeat, then striding directly through traffic, heedless of the honks and curses in her wake.

She yelled at me as she approached. "Where's Glouchester?"

I tightened my grip on the door, and glanced into the overcast fog, and the silhouette of the Mount. "I can't say."

"What the Hells does that mean, you 'can't say'?" She closed in, and I could smell perfume and the acid hint of used flash bulbs. "Are you holding him for questioning? Is this how you deal with a free press?"

"Klare . . ." Still not looking at her, still not certain how to proceed. I took a breath and looked her in the eye. I knew what it was like to have a partner.

"I can't speak to the details of this case until the victim's family is notified."

She blinked, shaking her head as she processed what I was saying. Her mandibles twitched helplessly. "The victim's . . . Are—are you—"

"I can't comment further," I said, bowing my head and lowering my voice. "I'm sorry."

I stepped back and dropped my hands, letting the guidepost doors swing shut on Klare's sorrow.

High-profile crimes are tricky things. The brass at the Bunker always wants to show that they care about the headline-making news, without seeming like they're trying to make political gains out of it. Having two such events in a single day made it even more complicated. I was expecting the usual influx of VIPs eager to get camera time while letting the citizenry know that the men and women in scarlet would be on the case. Instead, we were almost left entirely alone.

The tech team left as soon as they could, and Serrow sat in the back meditation room, door guarded by a pair of patrol cops. The administrative DO—I'd never quite gotten her name—had disappeared, as well. As for me and Jax, we retreated to the crime scene. Glouchester's body hadn't been moved yet, and we figured it was a good spot to talk without being overheard.

I took a knee, studying the layout of Glouchester's limbs. I'd already felt around the body, but I did so again.

Jax paused the intricate tune he'd been humming. "What are the odds that they'll leave this case with us?"

"A little south of zero. It's not like they'd have left it with us anyway, considering the location. But with this suspect?" I swung my hands over Glouchester, from twisted neck to broken toe. "All we can do is do our best to make sure it's started on the right foot, and steered in the direction of a righteous conviction."

Jax began humming again. "Any of your invisible threads on him?"

"No." I was still searching. I even patted the body down as if searching for a weapon. Not so much as a twinge of manna.

"What's that mean?"

"I don't know. Bobby Kearn, Saul, both hardware store victims, everyone who's been killed because of the buzz has used snake oil of some kind. Maybe Glouchester used traditional manna, and that can be affected, too. Or maybe he didn't." I looked up at Jax. He'd stopped humming. "And that means Serrow lied."

Footsteps in the hallway brought me to my feet. The door opened, and Captain Bryyh entered the room. I gave her a sheepish shrug. For most of my career she had helped me fly under the radar, letting me do what I was good at with a minimum of fuss and public examination. She had tried to guide me down that path since the manna strike, but Jax and I had a consistent knack for receiving unwanted media attention. For once, I felt I owed her an apology about breaking that rule.

"Hey, Cap. Listen, we were told to come down here and be seen."

She bobbed her head. "I signed off on it."

"Really?" Auberjois had insisted that was the case, but I still hadn't quite believed it. "What happened to keeping our heads down?"

Bryyh stared at me with a deeply lined face, lines etched from years of too little sleep and too much responsibility. "Carter, that snow's long since melted. We are way past the point of keeping a low profile for you. At this point, all the players have realized that you are a tool to pull out and use to further their PR plans. You might as well get used to it, because when the politicians find a tool, they keep using it until it either breaks or stops working."

"And then?"

"Then they blame their shitty craftsmanship on the tool, and throw it away." She looked at the scrum of political flacks jockeying for position. "Let's just hope you've got a sharp enough edge that you might still cut one of those bastards if they're sloppy."

"I don't understand."

She looked at Glouchester's broken body. "As important as this crime scene is, why do you think no one else showed up?"

I shrugged. Jax kept his mouth shut.

"Because," she said, "you two are recognizable. You'll get your photo in the paper, and the city knows the Bunker is taking this seriously. But if the Barekusu start complaining, or the public thinks the killer's getting a free pass, who's the face of the investigation?"

Jax whistled. "We are."

She nodded. "The two of you are like the pillow a hired killer shoves over a victim's face before pulling the trigger. You make things a little quieter and catch the blowback."

"I just want to do my job."

"Sometimes, being a distraction is the job." Bryyh squared her shoulders. "I'll be back shortly." She left in the opposite direction from the room holding Serrow. Alone again, Jax and I stared at the reporter's body.

"You think Serrow's gonna do time for this?" I squatted, and waved a hand over Glouchester's ruined limbs. No threads, no transformation.

"How can she not?" he said. "Weylan usually gets what he wants, but even he can only do so much. It's rare to see a Barekusu convicted of a crime, but Serrow won't be the first."

"Most people see them as peaceful. Almost like embodiments of the Path." I stood and rubbed my hands together. "I suppose we all have our assumptions."

"Sure. Lots of people think humans are techies and breed like rabbits. Gillmyn have cannibalistic children."

"And Mollenkampi?"

"We harmonize really well."

"Uh-huh."

"You want me to sing a little something?"

"No."

"You sure? A little lullaby might make you feel better."

I shot him a sideways look. The deep creases around his eyes made it clear just how delighted he was with his own joke.

Bryyh returned, entering the room, closing the door quietly behind her. She rolled her neck and said, "The two of you ought to get the Hells out of here."

"Are we booking Serrow?"

She exhaled slowly. I knew her well enough to recognize frustration. "Yes and no. We're doing this remotely."

"Remotely? What's that mean?"

"It means she's being arrested, then a judge is going to get on the phone to release her into her own custody. She'll turn herself in later. There's a lot of unofficial debate over having two high-profile political figures arrested in a single day."

"We don't make arrests based on PR," I said, voice rising. "I don't care what you say about us. It's about—"

"Don't you dare lecture me!" said Bryyh. "I've been running this department since you were busting candies and roughnecks on the streets. I'm well aware that homicide investigations shouldn't be about public perception." She blinked, as if turning something over in her head. "And it doesn't need to be, not really. But for right now, we've got to play their game."

"How?"

"Serrow will be confined to the Barekusu camp. You two get out of here, like I said. Go to the courthouse and get the case filed."

I grunted. "We can send a couple patrol down to do that."

"Not on this one," she said. "On *this* one I want to make sure everything is done to the letter. That's why I want you there."

I realized she was talking to Jax.

"What about me?" I said.

"Tag along with Ajax. Pay attention and maybe you'll learn a little something about process. Now I need to go finish acting out my part in this little show."

Bryyh exited, and I rolled my eyes at Jax, hoping to commiserate.

"Come on," he said, but paused at the door. "Did you bring your notepad and pencil? You might want to take notes on my process."

I had a snappy comeback, but by the time I thought of it he was out the door and disappearing down the hall.

26

THE MUSIC IN THE CLERK of Court's office was loud enough that I couldn't ignore it, and muffled enough that I couldn't catch the not-quite-present melody. It was like trying to savor a mouth full of cotton candy, dissolving on your tongue so fast it was almost never there. I leaned against the counter and stared at the wall calendar, which hadn't yet been flipped over to the new month. The calendar featured a frizzy-haired kitten in oversized sunglasses perched over the slogan "Dangerously cute." Two paces away a patrol cop stood with blood on his sleeve and blossoming bruises along his jaw. Shoulders sloped, his elbows rested on his service belt, using it as a portable shelf. I remembered that stance well, a brief respite from carrying the weight of a four-year-old child draped over my back. I gave him a nod, and he responded in kind.

"Tough night?" I asked.

"Table of drunk-and-disorderlies. Wouldn't leave, and didn't take kindly to being asked twice."

That was the life of a patrol cop. Any given run could result in a fight for your life, and a half hour later you're waiting for a civil servant to process pages while you stand at a counter listening to slow jams. I'd liked and hated working a patrol beat all at the same time. The best and worst of the city was on display and in your face every night. I was madly proud of the things that I and other cops had done to help people in need, and I never stopped beating myself up over the times we'd fallen short.

The clerk walked back to the counter and timestamped the patrol cop's case paperwork. He thanked the clerk and headed back out just as the music segued into Dinah McIntire's "Titan's Song" single. It was clearly going to be an inescapable soundtrack to all of our lives as we moved toward the long days of summer. A glance over my shoulder confirmed what I suspected: Jax was at the rear of the waiting area, bobbing his head and tapping his foot in slightly off-time accompaniment to the beat. And there was something familiar about the bass line, though I couldn't place it. I was about to comment on Jax's poor dance skills when the music died, interrupted by the DJ making an announcement.

"Breaking news in the Barekusu assault case," she said. *"Weylan has given a press conference at the foothills of the Mount, near the Barekusu encampment."* There was a brief pause before the hiss of prerecorded tape began to roll. The low-pitched, sonorous voice of the Barekusu leader came through the speaker, accompanied by the squeak of his horn plates adjusting as he spoke.

"I believe I can only apologize," he said. *"On behalf of this caravan and all Barekusu across Eyjan, I can only state how wrong our sister was, and that she shall make restitution. Her actions are like the sinkhole, leaving a gaping wound in our lives and our beliefs. It shall not heal until is it fully explored."*

Jax angled his head, listening closely.

"What's up?" I said, but he raised a hand to shush me.

"But even in difficult times," the Barekusu said, *"the citizens of this proud city have an opportunity to explore something more—I believe the sinkhole has given us an opportunity to study the very foundation on which Titanshade was built."*

Bored, I looked back to the kitten calendar and tuned out the rhetoric. A moment later the DJ returned, informing us that *The Titanshade Union Record*, the late Taran Glouchester's employer, had issued a statement lamenting the death and announcing that they had scheduled a series of exclusive sit-down interviews with the caravan leader. When everything was said and done, their circulation numbers would skyrocket.

I turned to Jax. "What got your attention all of a sudden?"

He stared at the ceiling, eyes narrowed, clearly still processing what he'd just heard. "Strange how Weylan immediately pivoted to the importance of excavation. His caravan is in the spotlight in a bad way, and instead of making amends for Serrow's attack, he's burning a lot of political capital on urging an investigation of the tunnels."

"He got what he wanted. Serrow's not in jail, and this paperwork we're filing is pointless."

"That's my point," he said. "Listening to Weylan, it sounds like Serrow isn't his priority. The same thing when we heard him at the sinkhole. He's more interested in the history of the city, which . . . Well, he is a scholar. Maybe it's just how he thinks."

The DJ moved on to address the other massive news of the day—the arrest of Ambassador Paulus. *"Speculation abounds over what the vent intrusion was for. Is this part of a larger criminal enterprise? Stay tuned for more breaking news on WELZ, the station for smooth hits all day and all of the night!"*

I expected we'd hear much more speculation abounding in the coming days. My concerns were more immediate than leftover theories from Ajax's poli-sci classes.

"You believe that Serrow doesn't know why she attacked Glouchester?" I said. "Or was she playing us?"

Jax rubbed the tortoiseshell marking that trailed down the back of his neck. "I don't know. Glouchester's body was at peace. No transformation. And no . . ." He waved a hand in the air, a bad mime of being caught in spiderwebs.

"No," I said. "None of that."

Our conversation paused as the clerk returned and slipped the approved documents into the timestamp machine. Its metallic *da-chunk* marked the moment that the case had opened. The clerk plopped our documents on the counter with a perfunctory, "Have a good night."

We collected the paperwork and made our way to the elevators, neither one of us happy with how the evening was progressing. I punched the call button and the door sprang open with a startlingly loud *ding*. We stepped into the cab and the doors slid closed. Jax said, "Okay, it's time we talk about this a little bit more."

"You know, I was with Jenny for ten *years* and I don't think we had half as many 'we need to talk about this' conversations as you and I have had in three months."

Jax seemed thoughtful. "Well, how often did the two of you find corpses that transformed into nightmare creatures?"

Fair enough. I glanced at the floor indicator and saw we were almost to the garage. "Say your piece."

"Something is causing these transformations, something is causing the buzzing sound in speakers and microphones, and something is generating whatever it is that you're sensing when you're around manna."

"Next gen manna," I corrected. "Older stuff I can't pick up on at all."

"Right. So if it came from a whale, you can't interact with it. But if it's from the ground, you can."

The elevator doors opened into the parking garage. "I suppose so. I hadn't really thought of it that way."

The courthouse garage sat on the top floor of the building. The heat from the geo-vents was too precious to waste on parking space and vehicles, so the majority of dedicated parking lots were situated at the top of buildings, usually accessed by tight-radius spiral ramps on one or more corners.

"The whales connection is interesting." He glanced around as we walked toward the Hasam. "I mean, Serrow described the sound as something like a whale song."

"Yeah, well, she also described it as a chorus of angry spirits."

"That's true . . ." He snapped his fingers. "Donna Raun talked about hades, and angry spirits."

I slowed my pace. "Are you about to tell me that I'm being haunted by ghost whales?"

"No. Definitely not." We reached the Hasam and he walked around to the passenger side while I slid behind the wheel and reached over to unlock his door. He got in and kept talking. "But to be fair, on the list of crazy things we've seen, ghost whales aren't exactly tipping the scales. You know what I'm saying?"

I didn't answer, just fired up the Hasam and pulled into the throughway.

"I mean," he said, "if humans were hunted to extinction because you had something valuable in your bellies, you'd probably be upset too, right?"

"Kid," I said, clenching my mutilated hand on the steering wheel, "I'm not entirely sure something isn't doing that exact thing."

I slowed at the toll booth and flashed my badge. The guard nodded, the crossbar rose, and we began our descent.

"Want me to drop you at your place?" I glanced over at Jax, who was staring out the passenger window. "I can take the car back to the Bunker and taxi home."

"No thanks. I want to grab a couple things from my desk anyway."

We rode the blocks between the courthouse and the Bunker in silence. Not until we entered the Bunker's first-floor garage, built to accommodate vehicles too heavy to sit on a roof parking lot, did he bring up what was on his mind.

"Do you think the Barekusu know what's going on with the buzzing? Is it why they're here?"

"The buzzing and transformations time perfectly with their arrival," I said. "And the fact that Serrow is going to walk away from all this with a slap on the wrist is suspicious."

"Everything's suspicious to us. That's our job."

I dropped off the keys with the service team, and signed the Hasam into inventory. "But it doesn't time perfectly. The first transformation was well before the caravan arrived."

Ajax nodded, but I slowed, reconsidering that statement.

"When exactly did the first Barekusu representatives get into town?" I asked. "The ones who arrived ahead of the caravan?"

"Three weeks ago," he said.

"Anything could have happened in those three weeks."

"I wasn't done talking." He glared at me. "The Barekusu stand out in a crowd. So they'd have to find some way to get around unnoticed through one of the most densely populated cities on the planet."

"They can fit on a truck," I said.

"Uh-huh." He wiped down a tusk. "A box truck, maybe. I'm not saying it couldn't happen, I'm just saying—"

"Yeah, yeah. I got it."

"Something like that requires too many people, keeping too many secrets." He shook his head. "You've been listening to too much Handsome Hanford conspiracy hour."

"I didn't say it was a conspiracy."

"In addition, there's already a sorcerer in this town who uses bribes and coercion to control the wheels of government. Someone who's got everything to gain by influencing the use of next gen manna. Someone who was arrested earlier today."

"Look," I said, "I'm happy to see Paulus get busted as much as any-one." We paused at the elevator lobby. "But Paulus is the status quo. I don't see how she benefits from the chaos of these murders."

I didn't tell him that I knew for a fact she'd experimented with manna in illegal and deeply immoral fashion before, experiments that had resulted in Gellica's birth. I trusted Jax, but that secret wasn't mine to share.

The elevator opened, and we waited as a pair of patrol entered behind us. Jax and I paused our conversation, unwilling to let our brash speculation be overheard. As the doors were sliding shut, a well-manicured hand snaked between them and pushed them open. DO Guyer walked into the elevator, wearing a gray skirt and matching blouse, her manna-laced cloak carefully folded over one arm.

She jabbed the button for the fifth floor with her elbow, then faced me and Ajax.

"Surprised to run into you boys here," she said. "I saw the two of you in the background of all that coverage of the Serrow arrest. Funny how that works."

The two patrol held their tongues but watched out of the corner of their eyes as the DO pursed her lips and angled her head, making a show of pondering the odds. "It's almost as though . . ." She paused, letting the implication linger in the air. "No, it couldn't be. No one would ever want the two of you around for political points, right?"

"We go where we're told," I said. "I happen to know you're not above taking orders. Especially from outsiders like Baelen."

Guyer's lips pulled tight. "I'm doing what I can," she said. "And considering how I've helped you with her in the past, I'm surprised I have to say that."

It was a short ride to the second floor, and the patrol stepped out slowly, as if they would have preferred to stay and watch the entertainment. I hoped that Guyer would at least have the decency to wait until the doors closed before continuing. But decency has always been in short supply at the Bunker.

"Did you at least read the book?" she said.

I almost asked, *What book?* Then I remembered *Your Death and You*, which was currently sitting next to my window, waiting for its next turn as a prop. The doors closed, and we began to rise.

"Of course I did."

"What did you think about the chapter on postmortem subcutaneous runic apparition?"

I didn't answer, but looked at the floor numbers, as if that'd get us there faster.

"I heard from Harris," she said, free hand resting on her hip. "The divination on the victims at the hardware store is complete. Just more of the same. Confusion and anger from the old man, and incoherent screaming from the kid."

"What about Glouchester?"

"No ritual scheduled," she said. "Going straight to the ME, and then his family can have him."

"What? Why not?" But I already knew the answer. The DO at the guidepost had told us: no manna would be allocated for speaking to a victim if there was a confession and City Hall wanted it to disappear from the headlines.

Guyer shook her head, lips pulling down into a frown that practically screamed her frustration as she added one more rationale.

"There was no transformation," she said. "First priority goes to the ones like your victims at the hardware store."

The elevator stopped, giving us all a slight bounce upward. The doors opened onto the third floor.

"This is where we get off," I said, but Guyer blocked our path, her free hand holding the doors open, resulting in a ding from the elevator.

"We need to know what's causing this buzzing, and who or what is behind it. More than that—" She glanced over her shoulder, making sure that no one was within earshot. "There is clearly a link between the transformed bodies and you. Maybe both of you." She turned to Ajax. "I'd feel a lot better about that if I hadn't seen you clinging to Paulus on top of the CaCuris' building as everything went to shit a few weeks ago."

She closed her eyes, scrunching up her nose as if trying to wish away the memories of Titan's Day. The elevator bell tolled once more in helpless protest.

"I've been doing a lot of reading," she said, voice dropping in volume. "It's possible this is some kind of reaction to the way you two were exposed at the manna strike."

Jax shifted, interest showing both in body language and intonation. "Oh?"

Guyer nodded. "Back in the golden age of magic, when whaling ships covered the oceans, there were all kinds of stories about manna-linked objects not working around whales. Maybe it was because there was so much manna in one spot. Hells, after the next gen strike we don't even know if the whales actually produced manna, like we always believed. It feels like we don't know anything anymore." She pushed the doors open once more. "We need facts. We need to get you in front of someone who can figure out if we can at least identify what's going on."

And that was the reason that we couldn't confide in her.

"You can't expect us to trust that psychopath Baelen," I said. "After what happened to Andrews?"

"I'm not talking about Baelen." Guyer still held the door open. The chiding ding turned into a strident ringing. "I'm talking about Dr. Jennings. We need to know what's causing the transformations. We'll figure out the buzzing later."

"They're the same thing," I said. "Whatever the transformations are, it's got nothing to do with me. The kid at the hardware store blew past me like I wasn't even there. And Saul and Bobby were both trying to get to the doors. The question isn't what this has to do with us, it's why would someone want these people killed, and what connection do they have with the sinkhole."

The DO took a breath, and started over. "Okay. You don't believe me? Fine. Baelen is supposed to smooth over minor issues, I've no doubt about that. But she's not going to do that for corpse-animating magic. What do you think all the people who see next gen manna as the future will do if it turns out they're investing in something that drives people insane and transforms their dead loved ones into monsters?"

I frowned and looked away, maybe because even I knew it was mostly just wishful thinking. "The transformation is tied to the buzzing. It's gotta be."

Guyer's lips curled back, and she turned toward Jax. "Is he always this stubborn?"

Jax spread his hands. "As far as I can tell, yeah."

"Don't fight me on this, Carter. It's something you can't win and neither one of us wants to go through."

We all stood there, not speaking as the doors rang in protest. Finally, Guyer stepped aside and allowed Jax and me access to our department. We walked into the hall and the doors whisked shut, carrying her off to whatever grim rituals occupied a sorcerer late at night.

Jax inclined his head toward the elevator. "And that right there is why we need to figure out what's going on."

"Why, to satiate her curiosity?"

"No, to make sure one of the few friends that you actually have, who was willing to go to the mat for us over and over again, stays on our side." He stressed the *our*, which was a nice gesture, even if we both knew that if things really went to Hells he'd be walking on to another assignment, while I'd be finding my spot in the unemployment line.

We arrived at our desks and I gathered up my newspapers and notes. Jax slid open his top drawer, grabbing a small package and covering it with a file folder he seemed to pluck up at random. He clearly wanted a little privacy.

"What's that?" I demanded.

"Work stuff." He headed for the elevator.

"No, what's in the box?" I dogged his steps.

At the elevator lobby he pressed the down button and took a breath. "It's a gift."

"For who?"

He shifted the box and file to his other arm, keeping his body between me and it. "Talena."

"What is it? That's too small for candy. Is it a book? She likes books."

"I know she likes books, Carter."

"So what is it?"

He stepped into the elevator, and I moved to follow.

"Carter?"

"Yeah?"

"You forgot your keys."

My hands flew to my pockets, patting them down as I swore and stepped back toward our shared desks. Then I froze. "Wait. Didn't I give them to the garage attendant?"

I turned back and caught the briefest glimpse of Jax's face, all big eyes and innocence as the elevator doors closed between us.

Really, he wasn't a bad match for Talena.

Suddenly finding myself alone, I pressed the call button once more. I was tired of reacting. Getting to root causes sometimes requires shaking the tree. That was why I had a visit to make. And I never keep an ambassador waiting.

PAULUS HAD PREDATOR'S EYES.

Half-shut and seemingly indifferent, she was in fact watching my every move. She reminded me of nature shows where big cats circled their prey, searching for ways to separate the weak and weary from the herd. Paulus was the kind of predator who took great delight in the kill. I'd seen firsthand how her eyes stretched wide to take in every agonizing moment of her victim's final struggles when she thought she'd won.

Standing in front of her cell, I couldn't help but doubt whether the bars could hold her, if the manna in her tattoos would allow her to bend steel like butter, and walk through the halls as her own personal ice storm: cold, deadly, and howling with rage.

But the ambassador seemed content to stay where she was.

"Detective," she said, angling her head, a caged hawk curious about her visitor. "Forgive me if I don't stand." She remained seated on the bunk, its simple mattress and thin blanket a far cry from the luxury of her mansion in the hills.

I settled into a cross-armed stance, feet wide, directly in front of the door to her cell. It was a path she'd soon have to cross one way or another, whether it led to freedom or a trip to the high walls of Sequendin prison.

"That shade suits you," I said. Paulus wore a light blue jumpsuit, the color given to prisoners classified as special confinement, typically a mix of celebrities and snitches at risk of assault.

I pursed my lips and tapped my chin, the way I'd seen some of my more pompous teachers do, right before I slept through their lectures. "What's interesting is the way the AFS supports the—"

"Honestly, Detective, I doubt you've ever said an interesting thing in your life." She crossed her ankles and traced a finger over the rough fabric of her jail-house blanket. Paulus regularly wore her hair cut short, and she'd apparently been allowed to shower since her incarceration, leaving it flat and damp across her scalp. "Have you merely come to gloat, or . . ." She tilted her head once more, looking at me from a different angle. "No. You have something to say, don't you? Take your time. I know it can be awfully difficult for you to process your thoughts."

In the different times I'd tangled with Paulus, one of the most effective ways I'd found to get under her skin was to drag out the conversation, to take too long and drift onto too many tangents. The busy political operative with a high opinion of herself would always grate at the sense that her time was being wasted. Now, the script had been flipped. She had more time than she knew what to do with, and she was dedicating her full attention to me.

"Not much time to chat," I said. "I'm on my way to visit another prisoner. I've simply slowed in the middle of my walk."

Her eyes narrowed, and flicked down the hall. No guards were visible. Just like the special-treatment blue pajamas she was wearing, the cell she sat in was special as well. Set aside from the general population, close enough for the guards to observe, but far enough that it was out of earshot; they didn't have to listen to the occupants complain. She wouldn't be kept there long. Not long at all. But there was time enough for a chat.

Paulus tugged on her lower lip, eyes on the vacant space beside me, where an escort would normally be standing.

"So this isn't an official visit?" she said.

"We're not in a visitation room," I pointed out. "No lawyers, no supervisor watching from another room. No tape recorder." I paused, letting that sink in. There would be no record of whatever we said here.

I scratched my chin, hand muffling my words and obscuring my lips from anyone who happened to be watching. "I was wondering if you're going to fight this thing or just do the jail time."

"Do I strike you as someone who wouldn't put up a fight?"

"You didn't resist arrest."

"There's a difference between surrender and knowing when to strike."

I thought that over. "Do you know what you're charged with?"

"Something asinine about the sinkhole, a natural disaster that I neither caused nor profit from. You already made your clumsy inquiry about Tanis Klein, and I've heard rumors about a dead body with no name. As if the streets weren't full of them."

"What you don't know could fill that sinkhole back up. The girl with no name is the real threat."

"Oh?"

"Because I recognized her," I said. "She looks like you. And Gellica."

Paulus was silent, but the blanket under her hand bunched together as she squeezed it. Rage or fear, it didn't matter. The reaction told me I was right.

"Sooner or later," I said, "someone is going to put it together, and search your home. Far more thoroughly than if they're just looking for embarrassing documents or illegal substances. If they know you have . . . Well, I don't know what you have down there. But I know what it produced. *Who* it produced. And I somehow don't think that'll sit well with the public, or the AFS Council." I shrugged. I'd made my accusation. The rest of my standard operating procedure was a combination of threats and cajoling, neither of which would be effective against Paulus.

"You're done, Ambassador. Your career, your money, your manna. Everything that you base your power on, it's all wrapped up and flushed away. The only question is, are you going to let it destroy everything around you as well?"

She swallowed. Her eyes weren't narrowed, weren't wide. They simply sagged, the softening eyes of someone realizing that they can't avoid the trap, because the trap has already been sprung. She took two long breaths. Then a spark came back to those predator's eyes as they locked on mine. "Tell her."

I didn't nod, didn't give the least sign of acknowledgment. I'd give

Gellica fair warning of what was coming. But I finally had the upper hand with Paulus, and I wasn't going to let anything change that.

I left her there, staring out through bars more immutable than the laws of physics. Because even if she ran, her life was over. Everything she'd built was tumbling down. Unless I helped clear her name. And I wouldn't do that, not for anything.

Not even justice.

The next morning I grabbed the stack of papers shoved into my department mailbox and flipped through them as I waited for Jax to arrive. I had a handful of phone messages, most from Klare, the photographer from the *Union Record*. There was also the background file on Bobby Kearn, from Cloudswar. I skimmed the report, but my mind was elsewhere. Klare bothered me. She was tenacious, and would keep coming after me until she felt justice had been done. The trouble was, I didn't know if that would happen. I pushed the messages and report aside when Jax arrived.

"Don't bother getting comfortable," I said. "We need to make a social call."

I gave him enough time to grab a coffee and we headed out for the short walk to 1 Government Center. There, I asked Jax to sign in at the front desk while I waited in reception. I hadn't been in the building since I'd visited Gellica to take her into my confidence and plead for her forgiveness. It seemed like I did a lot of that whenever she and I talked.

"You sure we shouldn't have made an appointment?" Jax said, voice low as he sat next to me.

"No," I said. "But Gellica will see us. She can't get out of it. There's an ongoing investigation into her boss."

"Oh? We can't force our way in. She may be willing to see someone from the Bunker. But I doubt that someone is you."

"Fair enough," I said. "Especially considering Paulus got our badge numbers when we visited her at home. I'm guessing her personal security shared that info with the security here."

Ajax swiveled to face the security desk. But he relaxed just as fast, understanding creeping into his voice.

"When they took our badge numbers," he said, "I had that duplicate we got from the pawnshop."

"Never waste a bit of luck," I said.

Jax shook his head and looked out the glass doors to the street, leaving me to retreat into my own thoughts. Mostly, that consisted of Paulus's voice: *Tell her.* I didn't like the idea of taking advice from a sorcerer who'd been glad to see me suffer before, but Gellica deserved to know what was going on. And if Gellica and I were going to stay civil long enough for me to give that warning, then I needed another adult in the room. Hence, Detective Ajax.

The guard at the desk waved us to the elevator bank. "This way, please."

I glanced at my partner. "See?"

Gellica's office was far busier than I'd ever seen it. We paused at the door, and received a brief, chilly glare from her assistant, but he stood and escorted us past the doors that separated the sanctum from the space outside. "Ambassador?" he said, and I thought for a moment he'd made a mistake. But Gellica raised her head, brows furrowing as she saw me, and I remembered that she was, in fact, the acting ambassador until the AFS Council stripped Paulus of her rank and appointed a replacement. Gellica was overseeing a smooth transition to the end of her career.

She stood. Hair held back in a no-nonsense ponytail, she wore a gray silk blouse and a blue suit, a decorative necktie loosened in the Mollenkampi fashion. But while Jax wore his tie slightly undone to allow him to speak more freely, Gellica was making a statement. She was dressed professionally, but hadn't bothered to embrace the full clout of her new position. She understood as much as anyone that her role was temporary, and all the political will of Paulus's enemies—and most of her fair-weather friends—would be arrayed against her.

"Detective," she said to me, then to my partner, "Ajax, it's good to see you. Sit down. I'll be with you in a minute." Then she turned her attention back to the three assistants in suits who sat around her desk.

While she finished up her business, I tried to get comfortable on one of the chairs in her formal sitting space. She'd had a couch the last time I'd been in her office. A couch that she'd ultimately given to me rather than put up with having to speak to me again. I glanced in her direction. Gellica was a creation of magic and science, a clone who required a regular intake of manna to survive. Her eyes were so similar to Paulus's, but Gellica wasn't a predator. She was a competitor. She'd beat you but she'd do it by the rules. And after her skill and head games wore you into the ground, she'd help you up and say, "Good game."

The other AFS employees filed out and Gellica took a seat opposite me, to Jax's right. Having Jax was a mixed blessing. His was a calming presence; with him there we couldn't speak as bluntly as I might like, but we also couldn't devolve into a screaming match, either.

Tell her, Paulus had said, and I knew that I'd find a way.

"Why are you here?" Hands clasped over her knee, Gellica stared at me. There was iron under her voice, and I fought back an impulse to snarl.

"The same reason you're suddenly working above your pay grade."

She glanced at the door. "My attorney should be present for this. She'll be here shortly."

"Well, we're not your lawyers . . ."

"On that, at least, we're agreed."

"But we don't want Paulus imprisoned for something she didn't do."

"Are you implying that I can't trust the police department to seek justice?"

"I'm saying that you should consult with your attorney, and then do everything to help us." I shrugged. "And be a little hesitant about trusting anyone else asking about the case."

Gellica's smile was faint. "Don't worry. I've put more than enough trust in the police before this. It won't happen again." She straightened in her chair. "I don't know what caused that sinkhole, but I know the ambassador didn't have anything to gain from it."

"We don't see how she'd benefit, either," I said. "But the sinkhole isn't her primary concern."

"No? Because by arresting her you've made it our primary concern, when we should be focusing on helping the citizens regain their heat and get back to a normal life." Gellica crossed her legs. "As you said, you're not my lawyer. But she's on her way."

"Paulus isn't being charged with creating a sinkhole," I said. "You know that. You also know the charges are about tampering with the vents." I reached into my coat pocket and drew out a set of glossy photos of the mummified bodies. "There was another body in the sinkhole," I said. "A teenage girl. We haven't been able to identify her yet. I'm sure her parent is very worried about her."

"I'm sure they are." She'd missed my use of the singular parent.

"I think you should see this one, and maybe ponder it. Look into a mirror, if that's what it takes."

She squinted, staring me down. I shook the photos again, and she accepted them. The dead AFS man was on top, and she flipped past it with only a downward tug at her lips. But her jaw dropped when she saw the mummified girl. I knew that she recognized proof of Paulus's experiments blending manna and science. Gellica had been born of that illegal research, aided by a morally bankrupt researcher. The same Dr. Heidelbrecht who ultimately went to work for Vandie Cedrow's uncle, producing a gas that drove innocents to kill, and led to the discovery of the manna strike.

"Is this . . ."

"They were found inside the geo-vents." I shifted my weight. It was an awkward dance of a conversation. I wanted to say, *Pack your things and run.* I wanted to tell her that being a magical clone put as much of a target on her back as the manna threads did on mine. There were limits to what I could say, because Jax was there. But then again, having Jax there was what prevented it from devolving into a shouting match.

She handed the photos back face down, as if they would be that easy to erase. "I can't help you."

"Keep them," I said. "See if they jog any memories." She'd told me that she was the only one of Paulus's experiments to be viable. *Of a dozen brood mates,* she'd said, *I was the only one to survive.* That photo proved otherwise. There had been others before Gellica.

"If there's anything you know about Ambassador Paulus's past, this would be a good time to tell us," said Jax.

I nodded. "It'll all come out in the end, but we don't have time to fight this out in court."

She coughed out a laugh. "That's what courts are for."

"People are going to die," I said.

Jax hummed a somber note. "There might be more weaknesses in the vent system. If more sinkholes are on the way, it could be catastrophic."

"You've spent your entire life protecting the dead, and now you're so interested in saving the living. Why now?" She didn't say, *Why did you wait until we weren't speaking?*

"I always cared about the living," I said.

"You have a funny way of showing it." Gellica broke eye contact, and glanced at the door again. The attorney would be showing up shortly. "Some people talk a big game, Carter."

"Like Vandie Cedrow?" Jax's question surprised me, but it was a smart ask. I'd raised questions about Vandie enough that it was worth establishing any connection between the Cedrow and Paulus threads.

Gellica raised an eyebrow. "I suppose so."

"You know her?"

"I know of her. Bright, had a good reputation until her family situation . . ." She punctuated the sentence with a *what-can-you-do* wave of her hand. If anyone understood odd family, it was Gellica. "But she's a socialite, not a power player. She wants to make change, but doesn't quite know how to do it."

Jax looked thoughtful as he cleaned off a tusk with a handkerchief. "Not like grassroots organizations. I've seen the difference those make firsthand." I knew he meant Talena's work.

Gellica nodded, as if awarding him a point. "Street-level organizers are important, and it feels good to look people in the eye as you're helping them. I respect that, I do. But it's not what's truly effective."

I crossed my arms. "I suppose you're about to tell us what is?"

Jax clacked his teeth at me and I stopped talking.

"Real change," she said, "change on the kind of scale that matters?

It's made not in gossip magazines, not on the streets, and not even in the halls of power."

"No?"

"No. It's made over dinner. In box seats at an opera or carabella match."

My lips pulled back, and I fought to minimize the sneer in my voice. "The rich making decisions for the rest of us."

"There are a limited number of people who have the ability to create waves," she said. "Drop a pebble in a lake, and it creates a blip. Even the most well-intentioned pebble, and no offense to your friend, Ajax, simply can't make a big enough impression. But the wealthy, the influential, the politicians and business owners? They're boulders. And when they drop, they make *waves*."

"Waves aren't any more permanent than ripples."

"No, but they're bigger." Gellica rubbed her hands together, warming to the topic. "There's nothing that we can do, for good or ill, that can't be undone by the next generation of fools and sages. But we can affect the right now. And for the people out there," she pointed at the window, the view of the city, "on the streets and huddled in their homes, wondering how they're going to make ends meet? For them, *right now* is good enough."

I wanted to believe in her. I wanted to trust her, this woman who cared about the right now, who'd trusted me with secrets of her magical creation and shape-shifting strangeness. But as much as she'd wanted to embrace our shared connection to the supernatural, I wanted to turn away. And that meant our every interaction was destined to disappointment.

"The problem is that the people you admire, all those wave makers? They only do enough work to keep people satisfied, to buy time to enjoy their warm condos and nice cars."

Gellica's shoulders pulled back. She had a weakness for fast cars. "Better to enjoy life and help others, than to wallow in self-pity as the world burns around you."

"Okay, enough!" We both jumped, and found Jax glaring at us. "You two have something to work out. I get it. But if you think I'm going to waste my time playing nanny—"

"Hold on," I said, but he talked over me.

"—then you're mistaken. There are people who lost their lives in the sinkhole. There are people who are scared about it happening again. And until we've gotten that situation resolved, the two of you are going to play nice. You got me?"

I frowned, but kept my mouth shut. Gellica nodded, all business.

"Fair enough." She stood. "Thank you for the photos." Her eyes met mine. "But if you have anything else to discuss with me, contact my attorney."

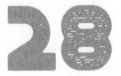

JAX PAUSED WHEN WE GOT to the street.

"Are you going to tell me what that was about?"

There was nothing to tell him. I couldn't spill Gellica's secret, but even if I could, would I lead with the magical homunculus clone or the shape-changing into a big shadow cat?

"Don't worry about it, kid."

"I know you two were getting close, but there's obviously something else going on. Something involving Paulus and the bodies in the sinkhole."

I kept walking.

Ajax whistle-clicked his displeasure, but jogged to catch up. "I thought we were finally getting to the point of you trusting me."

"Don't take it personally," I said. "I trusted someone once. It's not a mistake I'll be making again."

He stopped chasing me, and I slowed.

"Oh yeah," he said. "Every now and then I remember why you're single and popular."

I favored him with my most unpleasant scowl, then pushed forward, disappearing into the jostling crowd, blending in with all the other throngs of lonely people, every one of us isolated in the huddled masses. I needed time to think, time to put together a plan. And more than that, I needed a drink.

I stopped home first. I needed to feed Rumple and drop off my revolver. I can't claim I've never carried while in a bar, but there's a difference between grabbing a quick drink and needing to crawl into a bottle and ponder the world.

I managed to get the corner spot at the bar of Mickey the Finn's. It was my favorite seat, down near the bar-back's access. Lots of coming and going of the busy staff meant that I could flag down someone to order another round, and it was out of the way enough that I'd be left alone to read the sports page by pretty much anyone with common decency. That's why I knew I was out of luck when the spots on either side of me were claimed.

"What'll it be?" the bartender asked. The young, well-dressed Mollenkampi who'd sat to my right ordered a low-alcohol beer from a company that spent more on its advertising campaigns than its brewing process. The human woman to my left opted for an unpretentious house wine.

"That's a mistake," I told her, as the bartender walked away. "This isn't a wine kind of joint."

Smiling, and looking a whole Hells of a lot like her mother, Talena said, "I'll risk it." To my right, Jax said, "You couldn't have gotten here too long ago—you're still mostly upright."

I had, though. I'd been there for quite a while.

"Sometimes I think about buying my own bar stool," I said. "Something ornate, maybe even regal. I'd bring it with me to all my favorite bars."

"Why's that?"

"I'd be able to claim a seat by myself, and no one could elbow in next to me." I folded the paper and set it on the bar top.

Jax chuckled, and thanked the bartender as he was handed a beer on a cardboard coaster. "That seems like way more heavy lifting than you'd be interested in."

I considered that, then lifted my glass to concede the point. Plus, I supposed an ornate bar stool was a bad idea for someone who generally preferred not to be noticed.

A multitoned snarl from behind caused me to turn, in time for a pair of powerful biting jaws to clamp shut inches from my face. I jerked back reflexively, heart pounding. The pain of a Mollenkampi bite was deeply ingrained in my mind, and the ache in my finger stumps was always present when I moved in the colder reaches of the city.

It was Klare, the reporter from the *Union Record*. Jax had a hand on her shoulder faster than I could follow, and she snarled at him. I peeled myself off of the bar, back muscle twinging where I'd pressed into the curved metal trim of the bar edge.

I patted Jax on the back. "Let her be." We didn't need to be seen getting into a literal shoving match with the press.

I turned toward the bar, trying to put my back to her, but Klare pressed closer.

"Are you happy to let the overgrown muskrat loose on the city? Do you get off thinking that you can catch her again? Or are you only making an exception because Serrow killed a reporter?"

I was doing my best to ignore her, and Jax was more level-headed than me. But he'd brought Talena along, and she wasn't the sort to back down from a fight.

"What the Hells is your issue?" She'd turned, one hand gripping the paper, the other on the bar stool seat. Her feet were on the floor, where she'd have better leverage. She was ready to use her fists, the stool, probably my bottle if need be. My little girl, all grown up and ready to beat up a reporter.

Klare's jaws snapped shut. "My problem is corrupt cops not doing their job."

A Gillmyn floated behind Klare, and tugged on her shoulder. "Um, maybe we should let them be?" His head was stooped, and he wasn't looking me in the eye. I squinted at him. He looked familiar. Klare shrugged off his hand.

"Glouchester was on to that fraud, and she killed him for it. And you let her skate."

"You don't know your ass from a hole in the ground," said Talena. She hadn't moved, but she was like a coiled spring.

Jax cleared his throat. "She lost a friend, Talena. Let her slide." He kept his voice calm. The Gillmyn nodded, agreeing silently.

Now Klare looked at Jax.

"That's right, I lost someone. A man you all disrespected because he told the truth." Her biting jaw trembled slightly, and I wondered if she'd been drinking to her partner's memory. "I told you Glouchester was on to something big. He knew the Barekusu were funneling cash to radical groups. That's why Serrow killed him."

"She killed him because she heard the buzzing," I said. "The Buzz Kills, like your reporter friends call them. A little sizzle to sell some papers."

She angled her shoulders, addressing me once more. "You know why we add in the sizzle?"

"To sell papers?" I thought I'd already said that, and briefly wondered if I'd had too much to drink.

"Because we give a shit about getting killers off the street. Headlines like that," she pointed at the paper clenched in Talena's fist, "bring readers. And readers turn into witnesses. So you keep sitting around passing judgment. If that's the price I have to pay to see a killer behind bars, I'll make it any day of the week. Morning and evening editions."

"I respect that." I struggled to keep my balance on the stool. "But that doesn't apply to Serrow."

"Of course it doesn't." She half turned, as if ready to leave.

"You know why the city attorney files charges, and not cops?"

She didn't answer.

"It's because they're the ones who have to prove it in court. We almost always know who did the dirt." I licked my lips. "I got a double homicide sitting on my desk right now, twin brothers killed in front of a dozen witnesses. The witnesses know who did it, I know who did it, and you know what? No one will testify. If it were up to me, we'd go arrest those bastards today, put them in Sequendin prison and let them rot. But I can't do that. The CA's office won't let me because here's not a chance in Hells that we'll get a conviction."

"And that's good?"

"It's *necessary*. Because sometimes those bad guys we're so sure are guilty? Turns out they weren't. Not all the time, but enough. And if we got to drop people in jail just because we *think* they're guilty . . ." I stared at a neon sign behind the bar, thinking of Paulus.

"But Serrow's guilty as all Hells. She even confessed, and you handed her back over to Weylan and his caravan."

"You don't know what she confessed to."

"Get off it. I'm a reporter, you really think you can keep something like that under your hat?"

"I suppose not." I studied her Gillmyn companion. He looked away, and I placed him. He was the patrol cop I'd asked to escort her from the hardware store crime scene. So now I was a matchmaker, too? At least I knew her source.

I drained my beer and displayed the empty glass to the bartender. "Just one more," I called, and thought to myself, *The drinker's greatest lie.*

I managed to return my focus to Klare as I waited for my next round. "If it were up to me, I'd have stuck Serrow in a wagon and hauled her hairy ass to the Bunker. The CA decided not to, because they saw something else they had to serve."

"Politics."

"Could be. Could be they want to be sure that the Barekusu won't get their hump-shaped backs up and claim some kind of immunity." I nodded my thanks as a new round magically appeared on the bar. I couldn't remember ordering one. I took a long draw, letting the hops bite my tongue. "They're playing a political game. But if that's the trade they have to make?" I threw her words back at her. "They'll do it any day of the week."

Klare clacked her biting jaws, and Jax said something in Kampi, words and clicks that had a rhythm and melody and sounded like a sorrowful litany.

"Save your sympathies," said Klare. "Just put that bitch behind bars, before someone else settles the score."

"Hey," I said, mostly not slurring my words, "you can do it better? Enroll in the academy, we'll see if you can do it better!"

She stormed away, tailed by the Gillmyn. I sighed. My beer was almost gone, and I wondered if I should order another.

"That was surprising," said Talena.

"What?" I shrugged. "She's mourning a friend. We get that sometimes."

"I suppose you do." Her eyes darted to Ajax, then back to me. "But I meant your defense of the CA's office. Did you mean it?"

"Kinda." I drained the beer and held the glass up to the light. The bartender said, "Coming up!" and I decided the next round was meant to be. *Just one more*, I told myself.

"Kinda?" Talena sipped her wine. She was still on her first drink. How did people do that? There were nights I drank people's leftovers, since it seemed like such a shame to let it go to waste. "What do you mean, kinda?"

"I mean *kinda*. You know—sort of, but not really? The city attorney makes decisions for all kinds of reasons. Doesn't mean they're always the right reasons. They're just reasons. That's why they're the shitty attorney." I pushed my empty glass farther down the bar. "Hey!" I called at the bartender. "Can I get something with some kick?"

"You've had about all the kick you can take," Jax said. I stared at his talking mouth, the tiny, needle-sharp teeth that tinkled with every syllable.

"There are a lot of mistakes we make," I said. "I make more than most. But I always pay my tab when the bill comes due."

"That's true," the bartender said, dropping off two fingers of amber liquid. Something with a little more kick.

I gripped the tumbler, marveling at the precision of the pour. The liquid perfectly matched the height of my left ring and pinky fingers, the ones I was missing. "Maybe I'm trying to fill them back up," I said.

"Fill what?"

"My fingers," I said.

I looked around, realized Talena was to my left, and felt a rush of happiness. She was so like her mom, stubborn and funny and generous. I was damn proud of her, and wished I could think of the words to say so. Instead I gave her a smile and said, "Hey. I'm really sorry I made fun of your shitty neighborhood."

Her jaw clenched, and she pushed the half-empty glass of wine across the bar. "I've had enough." I tracked her movements in the bar mirror as she stood and crossed behind me to squeeze Ajax's arm. "You coming?"

He hesitated. "I better make sure everyone gets home okay. Can you wait a while?"

Lips tight, she shook her head. "Not tonight. Catch you next time."

Then she was gone, and I had a different glass in my hand. I turned, and found a heavy-set Gillmyn in her seat, arguing with someone about a local carabella team. It took me a minute to figure out that someone was me. Jax was still to my right, thumbing through his notebook.

"I don't know," I proclaimed.

He looked up. "Don't know what?"

I smacked my lips, marveling slightly at their distant, numb feeling. "What I'm trying to fill."

I ordered just one more shot, threw it back, and disappeared into darkness.

29

SAT UP, BELCHED, AND IMMEDIATELY regretted both those actions. I shook my head into a semblance of clarity and looked around. Then I froze. I wasn't home.

I was tangled up in a red-striped sheet, my shoes off, lying on a couch. The walls were covered with bookshelves. There were rows of bland black and gray hardcovers with titles like *Logic: A Textbook* or *Manna and the Path During Warfare*. Two shorter shelves packed with a rainbow of colorful paperbacks, their spines cracked into vertical stripes from multiple readings. These had more evocative titles. *The Robber Prince's Conquest, The Concubine of Cloudswar, The Heart is a Battleprize, A Dalliance or Two.*

There was a noise, and I spun in that direction. I regretted it immediately. Jax strolled in, carrying a mug of coffee and bottle of pain relievers.

"Oh, you're awake. Good. I was afraid I'd have to call the coroner's office this morning."

"What happened?" I gripped the couch, hoping the room would stabilize.

"What do you remember?" He handed me the coffee.

"We were having a couple drinks," I said. "Then . . ."

"You woke up on someone's couch. Does that happen to you frequently?"

It happened most every night, since I tended to pass out on the couch at home. But I didn't tell him that. I washed two pills down with a swig of coffee. I sloshed a little on myself in the process, unaccustomed to drinking from a cup tapered to fit a Mollenkampi mouth.

"You remember the big guy sitting to your left?" he asked.

"Sorta."

"Well, you and he really disagreed about carabella."

I ran a hand over my head, probing sore spots and wondering how badly I was bruised. "You didn't take me to a doctor?"

"Didn't seem like a good idea, considering you'd picked a fight."

"I must've lost."

"No, you won."

"Feels like I lost."

"It probably feels like you took him to the floor then threw up on him. Since that's what happened."

That would explain the breath, at least. I did my best to drown it with more coffee. The details of the previous night were fuzzy. What had Klare said about people working together? She'd do it better than me? My head ached, and I could barely focus.

"You in shape to head for the Bunker?" He held out a blue washcloth.

I accepted the cold washcloth and pressed it to my face. "I do need to swing by my place and feed Rumple."

"That cat's got to be hungry."

"He's used to unusual hours." I took a breath and braced myself. "Last night. Was Talena . . . ?"

"She was gone by then," he said, shaking the last drops of vinegar into his coffee. "Luckily for both of us."

"Both of us?"

"I don't think she's crazy about me hanging out with you socially. She thinks it encourages bad behavior." He was already dressed for work, in a tidy suit and tie. He sat in a velvet chair with a low-slung back, his legs crossed, holding a steaming mug emblazoned with the Trelaheda University seal.

"You'd think she'd hope you'd rub off on me."

"You'd think, but when I brought that up to her, she told me a story about a mechanic who washed his hands every night. She said the towels never got any cleaner."

I sat up, pausing to let the room catch up with me. I plucked one of the paperbacks from the smaller shelf.

"*The Ravenmaster's Daughter*," I said. "This from a literature class you had in college?"

Jax sipped his coffee. "You watch a lot of carabella. I know this, since you were so vocal about it last night. Why do you think that is?"

"I enjoy sports."

"You also know that the game will last for a set amount of time, and one team or the other will end up the winner. It's about as far afield from a murder investigation as you can get."

"You like to know how a story's going to end?"

"I like to know it's *going* to end." He set his mug down. "The fact that the ending is happy, at least for the moment, is a bonus."

I stared at the bright colors and windswept landscape on the cover. "There are no happily ever afters."

"There are in these." He sighed, and shook his head. "Maybe none of us are guaranteed one in real life. But that's no reason to close yourself off from it, either."

I picked up another book, this one titled *A Dalliance of Duchesses*. "I don't know . . ."

"Okay, fine. How about this: consider that the guy who reads romance pried a drunk Gillmyn off you, convinced the bartender not to press charges, and dragged you home to safety. So maybe keep your literary criticisms to yourself?"

"I thought you said I won?"

"I was protecting your fragile sense of self-worth."

"Fine." I tossed the books on the couch. "Let's get out of here."

It was slow moving as I got up. Jax waited, patient as a parent, which only darkened my mood further. He'd been assigned to me as a babysitter, back when we first met. Back then, it'd angered me that Bryyh thought I needed that kind of oversight. Now, sitting hungover in Jax's apartment, it made me sick to my stomach to admit she might have been right. I wanted to address it, to say something that would let Jax know how much I appreciated his help. But when I opened my mouth, all that came out was a belch. Which is when I realized that self-loathing wasn't the only thing making me nauseous.

"Bathroom," I said.

"What?"

"Bathroom!" I pressed the back of one wrist to my mouth, and bolted in the direction Jax was pointing.

A half hour later, I'd splashed water on my face, rinsed out my mouth, and announced I was ready to face the morning.

"It's almost noon."

"Are we late?" I didn't need Bryyh breathing down my neck.

"No, we're on second shift today," he said. "Regular rotation." Not that the distinction meant much to detectives. Being off-duty mostly meant that the expected turnaround time for answering a page went from immediate to almost immediate.

"Then we'll face what's left of the morning, and conquer the afternoon," I said. "But first I need to stop home, pick up my weapon, and feed my cat."

"And maybe take an actual shower?"

I raised the coffee cup. "And maybe that, too."

30

INSISTED WE CATCH A CAB from Jax's apartment. Previous experience had taught me that hangovers and bus rides don't mix well.

Traffic crept at a glacial pace. Titanshade is a crowded town, millions of us piling into the relatively small footprint of geo-vents southwest of the Mount. The sinkhole had only made things worse. The cabbie's radio chirped with a litany of streets closed to allow crews to reconnect severed vent lines with metal ductwork. It seemed like no one knew how to get anywhere anymore, and things were going to get worse before they got better.

During a particularly stagnant lull, I tapped Jax on the shoulder and pointed out the window.

"See that crane? The one loading ice into the water tower."

Ice suppliers cut large blocks on the plains and trucked them into the city, stocking them in rooftop towers to melt and provide supplemental water to the residents. Getting the ice into the towers was tricky, and many suppliers used a crane with two sets of three-pronged pincers. One pincer lifted the tower's access panel while the other deposited the ice.

"It's called a kusu crane," I said.

Jax whistled his understanding. The similarity to the Barekusu's hand anatomy was clear.

"The Barekusu are everywhere," I said. "Their influence, at least. They're the oldest child, and all the other Families grew up in their shadow."

"Where are you going with this, Carter?"

"Having influence is one thing. Knowing you have it is another." It was like Klare and the other reporters intentionally calling attention to a crime with a flashy headline. "Do they realize it? The Barekusu, I mean."

Jax hesitated. "I suppose they do."

I closed my eyes and hoped the headache would dissipate, but thoughts about what a Barekusu could do if they were willing to flex that influence only made it worse. Or maybe it was the horns and exhaust of traffic.

Finally we reached my place. As I climbed out, Jax's pager buzzed. He glanced at it and hesitated, then leaned forward as if he were planning to come up with me.

"I'm fine," I said. "You don't need to momma bird me."

He eyed me doubtfully, still seated in the cab. "You're barely standing."

I displayed my own pager, which showed no message. "Was that a personal page?"

He nodded.

"Talena?"

He answered with a quick melody of clicks, and added, "She's angry. And worried."

"About you or me?"

He didn't answer.

The driver turned in his seat. "You guys waiting or going or what?"

"Go on ahead and call her back," I told Jax. "Take a sick day or something, and make it up to her. I'll cover for you at the office." I handed a few bills to the driver, enough for my fare and at least part of Jax's trip downtown. "Call if you need me."

Jax nodded and sat back, glancing at the pager.

"If Bryyh asks, I'll tell her you got a bad case of wine poisoning." I slapped the roof of the cab and stepped away, raising my voice. "And thanks for watching my back."

Ignoring the pounding in my head, I made my way up the stairs to my apartment. I fed Rumple. I changed my clothes. I drank a tall glass of water, then another. I poured myself a third and turned on the radio, dialing down the palm-sized volume control and spinning the tuner until I found some news. My headache hadn't receded enough for music, but background talk would be a nice distraction. The top story covered the latest sinkhole developments.

With the geo-vents disturbed, wealthy households suddenly found themselves underdressed, their tropical plants wilting, their property values plummeting. That caused them to tighten their purse strings, and politicians found themselves threatened by the loss of the one thing more valuable than votes: campaign donations. So politicians wanted repairs to move faster, while academics and guides led by Weylan encouraged a slower, more exploratory approach. And activists like Vandie Cedrow called for the repairs to channel more warmth to the city's edges, a suggestion that the rich and powerful found laughable.

I took another long swig of water, and reminded myself I didn't have to fix the vents. I only had to decide if I was going to let Paulus take the fall for damaging them. If I did, I'd have to swallow the fact that she hadn't caused the sinkhole. And I'd have to accept that the truth would remain buried. I slammed the empty glass on the counter, and my head paid the price.

Paulus didn't need to be rescued, let alone by me. But still . . . I wouldn't be able to let go until I knew what had caused the sinkhole and the buzzing. And I feared that the answer would hit close to home. Queasy at the idea, I steadied myself on the countertop, then stumbled toward the bathroom.

The scalding heat of the shower felt good, but it also drew the stench of the sinkhole and resulting fires out of my pores. By the time I emerged the bathroom smelled like a campfire, but my hangover had abated slightly. I slipped into clean clothes and headed to the kitchen to fry myself some lunch.

The radio coverage had moved on to the scandalous accusations against Ambassador Paulus, as well as the buzzing/singing that had begun to appear on speakers ranging from police radios to telephone handsets, interrupting the nightly news and invading movie theaters. This latest twist had bumped the profile of the violence the press had dubbed the Buzz Kill Murders. It even had its own bumper music on the news.

With the headlines completed, the next DJ came on as I was dumping my dirty dishes on top of the existing stack in the sink. I was happy to hear Handsome Hanford's voice. His show mixed music and conspiracy theories ranging from the paranoid to the surreal. Hanford hyped his daily favorites from his throne on the radio dial, and the callers lit up the phone lines trying to advance their own idiotic agendas for Hanford to ponder, reject, or promote.

I figured he'd be a good person to talk to.

The broadcast booth for WYOT was located in a humble building in the northern Borderlands, where the real estate was cheap and the buildings tall enough to host a strong radio transmitter. I liked to stop in on occasion because the receptionist gave me free coffee. And I always enjoyed talking to Handsome Hanford.

There were over a dozen radio stations local to Titanshade, but none laid down tracks like WYOT. Hanford was their best DJ, and a kid from the old neighborhood. We'd met in middle school, sitting in the hallway after we'd both been kicked out of our respective fourth-period classes. His history lesson had covered the order the Families had awoken on Eyjan, and the teacher had taught them a phrase to help keep the order straight: *Believe Me, Young Eagles Have Such Great Holidays.* Hanford had volunteered an easier-to-remember phrase that was easily the foulest sentence I'd ever heard. That weekend we got drunk on beers liberated from his parents' fridge and had been thick as thieves ever since. When I'd gone in for lawman, he'd drifted to the much more practical ambition of rock star. I'd ended up a detective, him a DJ.

I slipped into the broadcast booth near the end of a music track, pulling up a chair and slipping on a pair of battered headphones, the NOYS logo faded almost to illegibility. I left one ear uncovered, so we could talk between on-air moments. The music ended and I froze,

242 • DAN STOUT

careful not to make a sound while the red Live light was on. The city's favorite DJ leaned forward, bushy mustache practically touching the mic while he spoke in his trademark husky baritone.

"Alright sugars, this is Handsome Hanford, spinning the hits that shake your hips." He thumbed a button and a recorded coyote howl pierced the airwaves. "Keep that dial locked in, 'cause it's Dinah McIntire week and we've got a power block of festival tunes to lose the blues. I'm talking tracks from the lady herself, as well as Mulberry Wine and Steve and the Machines, all headed your way after these brief messages."

Another swift button-punch queued up a car dealership commercial, cajoling Hanford's loyal listeners to trade in their junker for a new model with the potential for conversion from gasoline to a manna-fueled engine with the tagline, *The future . . . is magic!*

Hanford lowered the volume and swiveled his chair to face me. I raised a paper bag containing a pair of number-three combos from one of my favorite food trucks. Buying a friend lunch was the least I could do.

"Righteous! Put it over on that table." His natural speaking voice was a half octave higher and crackled with sarcasm. "Should I even ask if you read the latest issue?"

Ignoring him, I pointed at the turntables. "Dinah McIntire week?" I didn't bother to keep the indignation out of my voice. "Are you a complete sellout?"

"This time of day, yeah. It's why I do my best work at night. Besides, you might as well accept the fact that she's the hottest thing to hit town in the last decade." He adjusted the red-shaded sunglasses he wore at all times. "Is that a 'no' about the magazine?"

"I've been a little busy lately. Fighting crime, righting wrongs, things like that."

Hanford let out an exaggerated sigh as he leaned over to pick through a satchel by the side of his desk. He pulled out a saddle-stapled magazine and handed it to me.

"You should read it," he said. "There's powerful truths in there."

The cover featured a blurry photo of a disc against a cloudy sky, beneath the title, *The UFObserver*. I knew Hanford's name would be on the masthead somewhere. When not spinning albums, he was the leading cataloger of conspiracy theories, unusual sightings, and mysterious contacts in the city. Much of his show was a diatribe against unknowable, amorphous entities controlling our destiny. I liked him because he made me feel sane by comparison.

He consulted a wall of record sleeves and 8-tracks, his fingers riffling through them like the pages of a phone book. "What's on your mind?"

"There's a mysterious buzz turning people into killers and an enormous hole that opened up in the middle of town and I'm pretty sure that they're going to hang it on the wrong person. Or did you mean something besides the obvious?"

"Well, you didn't show up earlier, so I figured you had it handled. The student doesn't arrive until they're prepared to internalize the master's lesson." He pointed to the magazine. "There's an article in there about a snow cat that's seen on the fringes of the ice plains when catastrophe's on the way. I think of it whenever I hear your name on the news."

That sounded disturbingly like someone I knew. "So in this metaphor am I the cat or the catastrophe?"

"You're the student, dipshit. And since when do you know what a metaphor is?"

I laughed, and immediately regretted it. The hangover hadn't fully retreated. A little quieter, I said, "I've been hanging around a college crowd."

I laid out our lunch as Hanford flipped two albums out of the wall, leaving their sleeves sitting at an angle to make it easy to replace them. The records went onto two turntables. He positioned the needles so that they'd be ready to drop, then turned back to me.

"I can tell you're stressed. You deal with dead people and disasters all day, every day. What's different now?"

"There's a lot of lives on the line. Maybe the whole city." I forced a shrug. "And maybe my freedom, but that's nothing new."

"Then why are you . . . Hold on."

He rolled back to the console and punched a button while also dropping the needle on one of the records. The commercials gave way to a slinky guitar riff that threaded through a walking bass line. I recognized the dual-toned vocalization of Mulberry Wine, a Mollenkampi girl group that had hit it big the previous summer. Hanford spun back and grabbed his pita, being careful to tuck a napkin into his widespread shirt collar. He always dressed nice, even in his booth. Where some people wore classic lines and expensive labels, Hanford went for bleeding edge of fashion. A quest for eternal youth, sadly undercut by the ponytail tacked on the back of his balding head.

Hanford peeked into his pita sandwich. "You remembered banana peppers! You're a champ." He took a bite and gave a loud grunt of approval. "Oh, that's good."

I took a breath. "You saw that Paulus is going to take the fall for the sinkhole appearing in the middle of town."

"But the first thing outta your mouth was that you don't think she did it," he said. "And you can't pass up the opportunity to defend an innocent woman."

I almost choked on my soda. "There's nothing innocent about her."

"There's nothing innocent about anyone." He wiped his lips on the back of his hand. "Okay, so you're trying to buck an entire system to prevent a miscarriage of justice. And you know for sure that's what this is? Paulus didn't do it?"

"Almost certainly not." I paused. "Not this, anyway. But she's done a lot of shit. I mean, a *lot* of bad shit."

"So you'll let her hang for this, hoping that the scales balance out?"

I shrugged.

"Ah!" Hanford raised a finger. "This is a dilemma."

"It is?"

"You say she did not do this specific misdeed," he dropped back into his DJ big announcement voice, "that she did not create this gaping hole in the heart of our city. Yet someone did. Which means that if she takes the blame, then the person who is guilty goes unpunished. And then you have created the very thing which you sought to destroy."

"You are a total pain in the ass."

Hanford took another bite, and spoke in his normal tones, albeit with a full mouth. "If you had doubts, then why'd they charge her?" He looked thoughtful. "Was it Flifex? He was the one with his picture in the paper."

"No. Someone in the Bunker gave the order." I trusted Hanford, but still knew better than to drop Auberjois's name. "Flifex was just the one who made a speech. I think the city attorney is leaving him out as the face in case things go sideways on the Paulus prosecution."

"You feel bad for him?"

"Yes and no. He's a prick, but I don't think he'd be doing this if it were up to him. It's a losing position for him all the way around."

Hanford peered at me over the lenses of his glasses. "There's something else on your mind," he said. "I can tell these things."

"I'm worried about fallout from this investigation."

"What do you care? Long as the guilty get punished, the innocent go free . . . your usual shtick. Unless it's the people around you?" He stroked his mustache ends. "Tell me about your partner."

I paused. "Ajax?"

"You got another partner?"

"Fair enough," I said through a mouthful of sandwich. "Not much to tell. He's young, smart. Comes from a messed-up family, but he did a stint in a seminary. I'll probably end up trashing that poor kid's career."

"I seriously doubt it. If anything gets trashed, it won't be done by you. He wants to work big cases?" Hanford shrugged. "Bad press comes with the territory."

"It's not the tabloids I'm worried about." I set my pita down. "We're brushing up against powerful people. The kind of influence that goes past stopping a promotion. The kind that can get you locked away in a psych ward."

Hanford whistled, his inner conspiracy nut awakened. "Now you're talking my language! That sounds like big government. But then, Paulus is AFS. And she's the princess in the tower who you're trying to rescue."

"That is absolutely not what is happening," I said. "And fairytale princesses generally aren't amoral powermongers."

"I see you haven't met many princesses," he said.

"Fair point." But there was one thing I'd never forgive Paulus for. I cleared my throat and said, "She went after Talena."

"Jenny's kid?"

I nodded. "Paulus framed her. Not out of spite, but because it was more convenient. The truth would have rocked the boat."

He was quieter. "I can see why you'd like to let her hang."

I didn't respond.

"Anyway, you might not be able to do anything, right? You got any friends in those rarefied political circles?"

"No." I crumpled my napkin, thought of Gellica, and flattened it again. "Maybe. There's one person. She might care about the truth. She's . . ." Visions of Gellica blending into her shadow, the cat shape emerging. "She's special."

"Oh yeah? Is she single?"

I gave him a sour face. "It's not like that."

"Yeah? Let me guess, she's out of your league and not interested in a cop? Hate to break it to you, man, but that's the kind of woman you like. It's safer to love from a distance when you know there's no chance it'll be returned."

That was the trouble. There was nothing even remotely safe about Gellica.

"Save the pop psychology for one of your call-in shows," I said.

"Okay. Go ahead and tell me all about your inaccessible crush and how she might care about the truth."

I chewed my pita, searching for the right way to tell him as much as possible, without telling him everything. Before I could answer, he held up a hand.

"Hold on." He went back to the mic, unleashing the distinctive WYOT coyote sound cue before informing his listeners what tracks they'd been listening to, and what to expect coming up. His on-air voice practically thrummed with excitement about the next songs, hooking his listeners and pulling them along with him. In his own way, Hanford lived in a different city than I did. He looked out the window and saw things improving, science and technology helping people. For him, it was a world of wonder and magic, and mysterious objects in the sky. I suppose that's what comes from spending your days isolated in a glass booth. He still lived as though he were that same kid in high school, open and accepting and always dependable. By the time he turned back around, I had a new question for him.

"You're a confident guy," I said. "How do you know when you're on the right track?"

Hanford blinked, and cracked his neck. "I listen to my inner song."

An innocent comment, but still, my blood ran cold. "What do you mean?"

"I'm forty-two. I'm not the same person I was at thirty-two, twenty-two, or twelve. I'm an echo of who those people were, and they all sing in a different key. And when I'm doing the right thing, they harmonize in me."

"Ah." My heart slowed. "A moral compass isn't enough. Compasses don't win battles."

"No, but they get you to the battlefield."

I chuckled. "Problem is most battlefields are a losing scenario for the people in the trenches. Like Flifex and his Paulus dilemma. If he wins, he's made an enemy of the AFS. If he loses, Paulus will be back in power and looking for revenge. Same thing with this rash of murders—" I cut off, not wanting to wade into details.

"You mean the buzz killers?"

I winced, not liking to use press nicknames for tragedy. "Yeah."

"Oh, man, that's dangerous business," he said, tapping the magazine cover. "You'll *definitely* want to read this issue. It sheds light on the cabals behind all kinds of weird phenomena." I must have made a face, because he hurried on, adding, "Look, the manna strike changed everything, baby. People are outright desperate to be part of it. One way or another."

I thought about the size of the potential manna revenue. "Big money makes people do stupid things," I admitted.

"Carter, Carter, Carter . . ." Hanford gave an exaggerated shake of his head. "The money isn't the key, man. Haven't you learned anything after talking with me all these years?"

"I learned to never say I'm paying before you order at a restaurant."

"Cute." He ran a hand over his forehead, pushing back curls that hadn't existed for the better part of a decade. "This is what they warned us about way back in high school economics. Manna was all but gone, the oil wells were running dry, then boom!" He snapped his fingers. "It's all coming back."

"Discovering a massive resource is a bad thing? I may have missed that class."

"You were there, you just were asleep." He smiled. "If things that are precious become commonplace, everyone who matters will be upended. The rich will be terrified, the powerful desperate. When you're messing with the fundamentals of supply and demand, it's the powerful who have the most to lose. That's a lot of pressure to make those resources precious once again." He leaned forward. "The powerful need the status quo, man. It's the desperate and disadvantaged who are willing to rock the boat."

I considered that for a while, popping my elbows over the back of the chair as I stared up at the ceiling, the only part of the room not plastered over by autographed posters of pop stars. The station must have sent away for them. No major names ever played a concert in Titanshade. Not until Dinah McIntire and her festival came to the ice plains. That had rocked the boat, for sure.

"Why do you think people look to the skies for flying saucers?" I asked.

"Probably because 'flying' implies the sky is the best place to look."

"No. I mean, why do people want mysteries at all? Isn't there enough crap right in front of them to keep their minds busy?"

"Oh, that." He rolled back across the room and switched album tracks again. "The real world is a drag. It's boring. We all know what to expect. Is it so wrong to want a sense of wonder again? Like when we were young and innocent?"

"We were never innocent."

"You said the same thing about Paulus."

I grimaced. "What I mean is, don't you have enough to wonder about in the real world?"

Hanford flicked his ponytail. "They're not mutually exclusive, man! I can watch the skies and still appreciate the everyday life. People might see miracles, but they like flowers and puppy dogs, too." He stopped short, as if something had just occurred to him. "Hey, do you believe in miracles?"

"No."

"You've never seen anything that defies the natural order?"

Now that was a loaded question. I thought of the web of manna connections, and the way I'd seen corpses inexplicably transform. But that was magic, and as strange as it was, it was still natural. Then, maybe because we'd been talking about Talena, I thought of her and her work with people in need. I figured there were some things that went beyond even magic.

"Anytime I see an act of kindness it's a miracle," I said. "It surprises me every time. Like seeing a candle being lit in the middle of a blizzard. It's a miracle that it happens, and it's a miracle that it isn't snuffed out or exploited the moment it occurs." I wadded up my pita wrapper and threw it in the trash.

"And the people who perform acts of kindness, are they miracles, too?"

"I suppose." I flashed back to my argument with Talena, when I'd mocked the news for celebrating an act of simple kindness. Not for the first time, it occurred to me that I could be a real prick.

"Is that what you do?" he asked. "Spend all your time finding killers and saving lives. Are you lighting candles in the dark?"

"Hells no," I snorted, then reconsidered the question. "I protect the people who do the lighting."

"Right on," he said. "Thing is, once your eyes are adjusted to the light, you can't see a thing when you step away from it. The best protectors are the ones who dwell in the dark."

Lunch was over. I stood up. "Thanks, Hanford. Have a good one."

"Same to you." He waved a farewell. "And maybe set aside one of them candles for yourself every now and then, huh? And next time bring some fries!"

I left the WYOT studios and walked to the bus stop, the chill Borderlands air clearing my head. As I walked, I thought about Hanford's comment that those who stood to lose the most were most desperate to maintain the status quo. Paulus was at risk of losing everything, but Vandie Cedrow already had. And of the two of them, the younger Cedrow seemed the more likely to try something dramatic.

I remembered Klare's insistence that Glouchester knew the Barekusu were funneling cash to radical groups. Was that why Serrow killed him? Or had she truly been driven mad by the buzzing like she claimed?

I thought of Ajax's badge, hidden beneath a long-abandoned body in the vents. Vandie Cedrow had already lost everything and needed a revolution in order to get it back. I'd let myself get distracted by Paulus and Gellica. I needed to interview Vandie Cedrow and those who knew her. I needed to know why the Barekusu were giving her money. I needed to go back to the festival, and I needed to do it now.

THE ONE THING THAT I knew for sure was that there wasn't any chance in all the Hells that someone was going to let me back into the festival site. The Bobby Kearn murder was closed out, and Dinah McIntire and Vandie Cedrow both had lawyers whose hourly billable rate was higher than my weekly paycheck. Plus, I'd have to figure out how to get a vehicle to get out there in the first place.

The Titanshade PD doesn't let just anyone take out expensive vehicles and play on the ice plains. I could always rent a snow-runner or ice-plains-ready vehicle, but that meant spending a healthy chunk of the fore-mentioned meager paycheck. On top of that, I'd have a far harder time getting into the grounds if I showed up with a civilian vehicle. But if I wanted to take a department snow-runner, I'd need to fill out the appropriate requisition forms, then wait until they were processed and I was notified of their approval. Without a pressing case need, it could take weeks. Basically, it was a no-win situation.

Or I could cheat.

I dropped into a precinct substation near Camden Terrace and asked for Franklin DiLeno. Franklin was a nice enough guy, and a horrible poker player. He was into me for more than a hundred taels and I was betting that if I could offer him a way to lighten that load, he'd be interested.

As a sergeant at a substation on the Borderlands, Franklin had both a fair amount of pull and access to ice-plains vehicles. If anyone could wrangle a snow-runner on short notice, it was him.

"I dunno, Carter. What if we need it?" Franklin rubbed at his hairline like he was searching for imperfections. The same tell as when he had a garbage hand of cards.

"Then you use the other one. That's the whole point of having more than one."

It took a fair amount of wrangling, and a discount on the money he owed me, but I managed to convince him that it was in everyone's best interests if I could be put in a snow-runner and be allowed to wander off for a day.

The next problem was that the rig was private property, existing outside of the city's jurisdiction. I had no reason to make an appearance and no authority if I did. Unless someone called and asked for it. I had one more stop to make.

"Hey, Trevor," I said, standing in the doorway of the NICI training center. "I was wondering if you could do me a quick favor?"

I'd spent several painful days in that windowless room of flickering monitors, while Trevor tried to teach me the basics of the National Index of Criminal Investigations. I'd never achieved even borderline competence, but Trevor and I had come to an uneasy truce—he stopped trying to teach me, and in exchange I didn't remind him that there were, in fact, people who didn't relish the coming digital revolution.

"Depends what it is." Trevor leaned back in his seat. He had a protein shake on his desk, and his left hand compulsively worked a grip strength squeezer. The Gillmyn's obsession with personal fitness even extended to his hand muscles.

"Well, I wanted to see if any complaints had been filed with the TPD about activity at the Dinah McIntire concert."

"Wouldn't you already know?" The grip strengthener's spring added a rhythmic mechanical squeak to our conversation.

I'd been working on the assumption that there'd been no complaints called in to the TPD, simply because I hadn't heard anything about it. But the Bullpen would only get involved with someone getting stabbed in the crowd, or intentionally run over in the parking lot. There were a lot more reasons to complain to the cops that stopped short of homicide.

"I want to see what all the different departments have gotten," I said.

His eyes lit up. "Now that," he said, "definitely calls for NICI. I'm glad you came to me, little man!"

I hadn't been called 'little man' since—well, since the last time I'd seen Trevor.

He stood, white muscle shirt showing underneath his open collar. "Not to worry. T-Bone's got you covered!"

"That is great," I said. "Really great."

We went through a listing of calls, cross-referencing the ones made to the various departments and searching for key words McIntire, Shelter in the Bend, and music festival. It wasn't perfect, but it did what I needed. Before long, I had a litany of complaints from callers who'd been offended by everything from public exposure to drug use to littering. There was even one call reporting too many people in one spot, and that it was sure to bring the ice plain crashing down around them. I wondered if the caller had thought of the massive city to the south, Titanshade's teeming millions and countless tons of building materials. Then I wondered if they'd been justified when the city collapsed in on itself with the sinkhole. I tried not to think about it after that.

Eventually I had everything I needed, and thanked Trevor.

"You got it, little dude!"

As grateful as I was, I kind of hated him right then. But I kept my mouth shut and took the printouts of the various complaints. I contacted Dispatch to notate the fact that I'd be going out on runs for them, and headed north on a complete fishing expedition. It probably wasn't the kind of thing I'd get fired for. But it sure as Hells wouldn't make it less likely, either.

I rode out in the snow-runner, the heat going full blast and the radio turned off. I had hours to think about what I'd do when I got there. I still ended up arriving without anything even remotely approaching a plan.

The ice road was far more worn down than the last time I'd made the trip, with private vehicles and chartered buses creating ruts that now jostled and jolted me. When I arrived at the Shelter in the Bend rig site, I found that the whole place looked more battered than I remembered. Sections of snow and ice were discolored, and trash and debris whipped around in lazy circles, trapped by the wind or frozen to the ice plains surface. Icicles hung from temporary shelters, and snowdrifts settled in the curves of the tent, pulling the fabric dangerously taut. I wondered how long it would be before the icy desert surrounding Titanshade reclaimed the festival site for its own.

I idled the snow-runner at the gate as the security guard leaned out from the small shelter toward my window, his breath lining his beard with ice crystals even in that brief exposure.

"Tickets or pass, please."

I badged him and pointed at the rig. "Need to get in and do a sweep of the area."

"Were you . . . I haven't heard about this. Were you called in?"

"I go where I'm sent, pal."

"I don't know. Wait here. I need to radio about this."

He looked for the radio and I halted him with a quick, "Hey! You can call anyone you want, but there have been multiple requests for police involvement from Titanshade citizens. I don't want to be out here, and the quicker I get in, the quicker I go home. So you call whoever you want, but I'm not waiting around for you to do it."

"It's my job."

"It's your temporary job. You don't look like you rolled up here with McIntire's crew. So you'll be here when they're gone. Unless you want to deal with an ongoing headache of impeding a criminal investigation, I suggest you let me pass."

"Imp's blades," the guy hissed through gritted teeth. "Fine, go on in. Someone'll meet you at the gate and escort you inside."

I pulled past him, heading for the parking lot around the side, where I hoped to be out of sight of anyone waiting on me at the front gates. The grounds were packed, and it took me some time to find a parking spot. I scanned the tent lines and the few outbuildings that existed outside the billowing fabric of the tents, searching for telltale signs of a closed-circuit camera system. I didn't see any, but I had to assume that I was being monitored. Just in case, I made sure to keep my movements calm and measured as I exited the vehicle. I wanted to ensure any potential record of my behavior didn't come back to haunt me.

Searching for the side door Guyer and I had found during the Bobby Kearn investigation, I passed the array of rental housing, seeing only a few bleary-eyed festivalgoers moving around in heavy coats. I guessed that most of the other rentals were occupied with revelers sleeping off the night before. It took a little while to locate the entrance, mostly because the bulky box trucks were no longer scattered around the festival site. They must have been hidden away during the show, as if the fact that all the performers and equipment had been delivered would spoil the magic for the concertgoers.

Securing my coat, I entered the bitter cold and dashed for the employee entrance. I pushed into the side door unhindered and moved down the hallway with a purposeful amble. I reached the end of the outbuilding and entered the maze of tented hallways, looking for the doghouse headquarters of the rig. I confirmed my earlier suspicion that the tent maze was intended at least in part as a security feature, as I repeatedly wandered down a wrong branch of the path. I grew more and more confused, and the green and tan fabric rippled and swayed around me, giving the impression that I was wandering the bloodstream of a great, angry beast.

My anxiety rose with every wrong turn. I only had a limited time on the property, and if it was going to be effective, I needed to find and confront Vandie Cedrow as soon as possible.

"Detective Carter."

I turned, and found Dinah McIntire and a pair of attendants striding down the tented corridor. Beneath a thick calf-length fur coat, she wore a yellow leotard, cut high at the hips, and dark brown nude-look leggings. The aqua sweat bands on her wrists and ankles color-matched the leotard's decorative belt and the laces on her sneakers. Her forehead was beaded with sweat.

"There you are," she said. "CaDell told me you were here, and I said to leave you be. No need for you to put up with his tedious questions when I wanted to see you myself. I even cut short my morning training to find you."

"You always wear furs to exercise?"

"I do when the temperature outside could kill me." She passed me, adding, "Walk with me a moment." She was accompanied by two assistants, a man in a bulky sweater and a woman in a conservatively cut suit. Each holding a clipboard, each remaining a few steps behind, like attendants following their queen. Which was, I guess, accurate enough.

I kept pace at her side. "I'm surprised you've got in a workout already. Most of your audience isn't even awake yet."

"Good," she said. "This festival is for them to enjoy themselves. For my team and me, this is business." She glanced at me. "When we play, we play. But when we work, we *work*."

"I've never had a particularly good balance between work and life, myself." I unbuttoned my coat, already sweating in the heated environment.

"It's a hectic schedule, and things can slip between the cracks. For example, I never got the chance to thank you for coming when you did. It was a difficult time, and Bobby's death was—" She winced. "It was horrible. And I wasn't in the mindset to deal with it properly."

"You had a lot on your plate." She'd tracked me down to fish for validation. We get that sometimes, a survivor or someone on the periphery of a crime, who wants reassurance they're not at fault.

"Exactly. And now that the shows are almost over, I can catch my breath a little."

"You certainly made an impact on the city," I said. "Between the crowds and the hair . . ."

She smiled, and it was like standing in a sunbeam. Her face practically blazed with pleasure. "I'm so glad to hear that. The whole point of performance is to bring something to the people." The woman had a reservoir of charisma. I might even have bought her depiction of herself as a self-sacrificing angel if I hadn't overhead the ruthlessness with which she drove her crew.

"If you don't mind me asking," I said, "why Titanshade? You could draw a crowd anywhere. To drive across the continent and set up a concert venue here?"

"Haven't you ever done something simply because it's hard to do?"

I considered that. "I don't think so. I've done some difficult things. I've done lots of stupid things. But I don't think I've ever done anything simply to prove I can. But it's no harder or easier to set up a concert out here now than a year ago. But you weren't here a year ago, were you?"

She laughed. "Fair enough." We came to a fork in the path, and she guided me with a gesture. We moved into a slightly brighter tent corridor, one that I hadn't discovered yet. "I came out here for two reasons. The first is that the eyes of the world are on your fair city. All of Eyjan is watching to see what will happen with the manna well. And most of those people buy albums."

I nodded. "Smart. And the second reason?"

"Vandie asked me to."

"You're friends?" I was surprised. "How do you know her?"

"From social events, I suppose. Parties, fundraisers, maybe a getaway or two on Edgar Banterro's yacht. Vandie's quite a likable person, and when she had her . . . family tragedy," McIntire's phrasing was the most distancing description of having an uncle go on a killing spree that I could imagine, "and her financial situation changed, some of the social circle turned on her."

"Because of her uncle, or because of her lack of funds?"

"Depends on which one of our friends you ask. But Vandie's always been resourceful. And when she found herself managing an oil rig the government won't allow to operate, she pitched me on the concept of a concert. I was already working on PR for the new album, so it was perfect timing. Vandie makes a little money to live on, I get great visibility right when I need it, and her crew and mine get plenty of work. Everything you see around you is my responsibility. When I'm in an arena, it's like the stage is my beating heart. It's what we do for those that depend on us, and for the fans." She smiled. "Are you a fan, Detective?"

"I'm more into the Daisey Chainz, stuff like that."

"*Credible Witness* or *The Water Album*?"

"Oh, *Witness* for sure," I said, surprised. "You know the Chainz?"

"Of course. The bass line in 'Titan's Song' is inspired by 'Favorite Monsters.'"

Suddenly, the elements that had seemed familiar about 'Titan's Song' made sense. It must have shown, because McIntire laughed.

"You should open up and live a little, Detective Carter of the Titanshade Police Corps."

"Police Department," I corrected.

She rolled her head against the thick speckled fur along her collar. The perspiration on her forehead glittered in the tent lights. "And why are you back here?"

"To talk with Ms. Cedrow," I said. "Routine follow-ups, that sort of thing."

"Of course." She raised one hand, gesturing without checking to see if her assistants were there. She simply assumed it was so, like I assumed that my heart would beat or that my blood would flow. "Cavanaugh? Please show our guest to Vandie's residence."

The small-framed man scampered forward. "This way, Detective."

"Her residence?" I said, still speaking to Dinah. "Is Vandie living here?"

Dinah frowned. "It's . . . Her family was majority stakeholder in some company—"

"Rediron Drilling?"

"I think so. Whatever it was, it was seized." She shook her head. "It doesn't matter."

"It matters to me. How long has she been living here?"

Dinah didn't respond. She slipped her hands into her pockets and pulled the fur tighter, though no draft had whispered along the tented corridor.

"I can't make you answer my tedious questions," I said. "But I can make things difficult until you do."

"Fine!" She shrugged, throwing the coat open again. "You think Vandie had a bit of cash after her uncle died. That's not it. She lost everything that generated income, along with her connections to those inclined to help her. Most of her personal wealth was tied up in her family's stock, which plummeted to almost nothing. She was left with only a few things that were in a preexisting trust."

"How do you know all this?"

"Because she told me when she pitched me on the concert."

"That's when she convinced you to cross the continent to perform in an empty oil field," I said, "that she owns."

"You're not listening." Dinah crinkled her nose. "I said she's managing the oil rig. She doesn't own it."

"Rediron—"

"Did own it, yes, but many assets were seized when her uncle was arrested. And none of that was released. We're not paying Vandie rent. We're not even paying Rediron. We're paying a court-appointed trustee, who was delighted to capture a percentage of the rent before he passed it on into the bankruptcy trust account."

Vandie's situation mirrored the AFS control of the manna strike. Maybe the city would be able to drill, but the feds would be taking most of the profit off the top.

"Then why did Vandie want you here?" I asked. "Not just the city, but here, at a rig she doesn't own?"

"Because what she has left is her own savings, an office warehouse, and the facility management company that worked out of it."

I thought of Murphy CaDell's business card. "Tremby Property Management?"

"Now you're getting it. Vandie wanted us here because she had the maintenance contract on the facility. Well, the non-rig parts of the facility. It was probably a bit of nepotism a year ago, but it's saving her life now. Vandie should own the entire place, and instead she's scrubbing the toilets." Dinah rubbed her hands together. "Now do you see why we're out here? It's smart PR, and I'm helping a good person in the process."

I nodded my thanks and Dinah McIntire smiled. "It was interesting to meet you, Carter. I'll be sure to let everyone in Fracinica know that I met the famous detective." She spun, sending the tail of her coat whirling out like a cape, and strode down the tented corridor like she'd strode across so many stages.

Cavanaugh moved along quietly, and deposited me at the front of one of the rig buildings that had been subsumed by the tent structures. I recognized it as the doghouse, the brain center for the rig. I turned to thank my guide but he was already hustling away, no doubt ready for his next assignment from Dinah McIntire.

I rapped on the door and twisted the handle. Locked. "Oh, Cavanaugh?"

Down the hall, the man hesitated. "Yes?"

"Do you have keys to this section?"

"I do, but . . ."

"Great! I'll just wait inside, then." I stepped back, and swung a hand toward the door.

He still hesitated.

"Or, if you're not comfortable doing that, we could walk around until we found Miss Cedrow herself?"

The idea of a prolonged absence from Dinah seemed to tip the balance. Cavanaugh hustled forward, pushing through an array of keys. "There's only a few keys for the whole place," he muttered, trying one after the other. I began to wonder if Vandie had thought ahead to change the lock on her private quarters, but then it turned with a click, and Cavanaugh swung open the door. "There you are." He departed without waiting for further banter.

I stepped through the door and closed it softly, listening to see if anyone stirred inside. I locked the door behind me, and moved through the building. I'd been in a handful of similar locations, most often as a kid on field trips or visiting my old man. Most recently when I'd chased Vandie's uncle out onto the ice plains. The layout here was similar, though it had been converted from an administrative building into an office and residence.

I'd come to confront Vandie Cedrow, but the opportunity to get a glimpse at her private stash was too good to pass up. I didn't know what I was looking for, but I figured that whatever Vandie had stored under lock and key might be of interest. If I saw something worth the bother, I could come back later with a warrant.

The back office of the doghouse had once belonged to the site supervisor, but had been converted to living quarters. Vandie's quarters would've had an amazing view if it hadn't been swallowed whole by the festival tent. Windows facing north and south instead looked out on nothing but billowing fabric.

Signs of life were scattered around the place. There were expensive suitcases stacked along one wall, each filled with expensively fashionable bohemian chic clothing. Clothes and notebooks scattered over the bed, and the barely rumpled sheets. The kind of signs left behind by someone who was rarely present, or who was sleeping as infrequently as her body would allow. The only other furniture in the room was the site super's desk, pushed back against a wall to make room for the bed. The desktop was covered with blueprints and schematics, apparently for the rig site and the newly fabricated tent system. All of them were stamped with TPM—Tremby Property Management. I assumed that was the name of Vandie's company. But all of that was background noise. Of more interest was the reel-to-reel player and notebooks.

The tape machine and notebooks sat in a stack. She'd been transcribing? There was no attempt to hide them, likely the arrogance of someone young and wealthy enough to always have their private space respected. I flipped through the top notebook. The second page had a name that caught my eye. Heidelbrecht.

The out-of-control researcher who had helped Harlan Cedrow in his mad quest for oil. The man who'd weaponized madness and ignored anything approaching morality or empathy along the way. The scientist who'd aided Paulus in her self-absorbed pursuit of immortality, and had accidentally created the blend of magic and cloned life that would eventually be named Gellica.

I grabbed the top notebook, and one of the tapes, and shoved them into my coat pockets. Any more than that and it would be noticeable. And I suddenly very much wanted to leave the rig site without being searched.

Glancing around the office one last time, I moved back through the hall, and toward the front door. Hand outstretched, I froze.

Footsteps in the hall. I'd been seen by multiple people, and Dinah had said she'd been told I was on-site. I had to assume that Vandie knew I was there, and that Dinah had mentioned that I was headed to her barracks. I had precious few moments.

I retreated, heading for one of the back rooms. With no time to plan, I grabbed a magazine off the table, and stood near one of the chairs. If I was spotted, I'd claim that I was waiting on Vandie. Of course, I'd have to sell that to Vandie's crew of roughnecks working security. And if I failed? It wouldn't be the first time a dispute was settled by leaving a body to freeze on the ice plains.

STOOD IN THE DARKENED LIVING room, as the door unlocked, then opened. Light from the passageway spilled inside, disappearing when the door closed. Footsteps, light and quick. No hesitation or subterfuge. It was either Vandie, or someone familiar with the layout. The steps moved down the hall, toward the kitchenette and converted living area.

I was still pressed against the wall, magazine in hand. I considered making a break for it, but the clattering sound from the bedroom froze me in my tracks. It was the sound of items being desperately thrown into boxes. It wasn't the behavior of a property manager coming home after a long day's work, even if they used to own the place.

Listening to the intruder move around, I was barely aware of cobwebs drifting across my face. I reached to brush them away, but they stuck to my hand, entwining around the flesh of my palm and thumb, hooking on the air where my missing two fingers should have been. The buzzing roar of a distant crowd screaming itself hoarse began to build, filling my ears. The threads were fat with power, connections of next gen manna that drifted through the air. There was an overwhelming urge to reach out and pluck the string, a spider inviting a fly into the parlor. My stomach gurgled. I wondered when I'd eaten last. I forced my hands to still, to leave the threads intact, untouched and uneaten. Focusing on my breathing, I stood rooted to the ground.

A dozen heartbeats was all it took, then footsteps returned, coming back down the hall from the office. I remained motionless, back pressed into the bookshelf, knickknacks and old photos and industrial safety manuals digging into my spine. The footsteps once again passed by quickly, now accompanied by the sound of bulky items shifting in a container. The rhythm interrupted, jumbled, as if someone were transferring a burdensome load to another arm. The doorknob turned. Light spilled across the entryway, and then it was dark again. Whoever had been there was now gone.

I emerged and headed down the hall to the back bedroom. One of the suitcases had been overturned, and its clothes dumped on the bed. I didn't see the suitcase itself. But something else was missing. The reel-to-reel player, tapes, and notebooks were gone. I let out a string of quiet curses. The missing items clearly weren't going to go unnoticed, and as far as anyone knew, I was the last person who had been let inside.

Had that been Vandie coming to her own apartment? Had she sent someone else? Or had it been a theft? I didn't know if I had to sprint out of there or not. I scratched my chin, contemplating. I'd taken some of the notes and tapes. If Vandie accused me of taking all of them, it wasn't that much different. But if she thought a third party had taken them, then it was a stroke of luck—my borrowed notes and tapes would likely go unnoticed. Either way, I was almost undoubtedly best served by a hasty exit.

My entire reason for coming so far had been to find and confront Vandie. But my already thin rationale for being here was crumbling underneath my feet. The guard on the road knew I was there, and surely he'd called in and announced my presence to Vandie's man Murphy CaDell by now. The security team of ex-rig workers was loyal to Vandie, and would view a lone cop as a headache at best, and at worst an opportunity to vent some frustration in a location where they'd likely never face consequences. Dinah McIntire and her assistant knew I was there, but if I disappeared they'd assume I left safely. Maybe this wasn't going to go bad on me, but if it was, I'd much rather not be surrounded by Vandie's friends and employees.

I went back to the desk, and rummaged until I found one of the tent schematics I'd seen earlier. I studied it, then folded it down to be inconspicuous. I turned, but a round shape caught my attention.

Whoever the interloper was, they'd missed two of the tapes. I didn't hesitate, just grabbed them and headed for the door.

With the schematic as my guide, I made my way out of the tents in the most direct path possible, stopping or sidestepping anytime I heard footsteps approaching. Once outside, I made a beeline for the snow-runner. On the way out, I threw a mock salute to the guard.

It took a few hours of driving across the ice plains, but I finally stopped peering into the snow-runner's side mirrors to watch the road unspool behind me. Already the traffic out to Shelter in the Bend was starting to appear. The final concertgoers for the final concert, hurtling like flies to the web.

RETURNED THE SNOW-RUNNER TO THE Camden Terrace substation and headed home. I fed Rumple and started my own dinner heating up while I rummaged in the bedroom closet. I'd managed to collect enough crap over the years to fill up my apartment, and my closet was a refuge of things that had broken and I intended to mend, things I'd mended and then immediately rebroken, and things that I couldn't quite bring myself to throw out. There, beneath dust-covered photo albums and a box of Talena's old school projects, I found what I was looking for: a beaten-up reel-to-reel player.

I popped on the first of the three tapes I'd taken from the rig and took a breath. I had a fleeting premonition that hitting play would give voice to some sorcerer's pre-recorded spell that ended the world. Instead, there was simply the click of the lever and the whir of the tape moving across the head. A moment later, a voice broke the silence, slightly distorted by the recording, but unmistakable. It was Dr. Heidelbrecht, the insane and viciously egotistical scientist who'd aided Harlan Cedrow in his mad search for oil.

The madman's clipped syllables pronounced the date, then rattled an introduction. "My dearest employer," he said, "it is with great enthusiasm that I tackle the tasks with which you have presented me." Heidelbrecht's sentences were as convoluted as his thinking. "You have made an excellent investment by bringing me on board at this most critical of junctures. As you know, I have a tremendous amount of experience, both theoretical and practical, in matters of manna manipulation, elevation, and exploration. If you'll pardon the digression, I would like to review some of the accomplishments and accolades with which I have been laureled."

I dragged over a chair. I'd had a conversation with Heidelbrecht once before, and I knew this would take a while. His voice summoned unpleasant memories, of experiments on animals and sentient Families, of callous disregard for the innocents consumed in his quest for renown and a quick profit. In his brief time here, there was no disputing his importance to the city and to the lives of countless people. Without Heidelbrecht and his twisted experiments, there would be no manna strike, and neither Gellica, Vandie, nor I would have been in the predicament we were in. The last time I'd seen Heidelbrecht I'd missed the opportunity to drag him in front of a judge and jury, and I desperately wanted to correct that mistake.

On the recording, Heidelbrecht had finally gotten past his bona fides and moved on to the proposal for Cedrow. "By combining manna and a given substance, there can be created a bond of sympathetic magic. Even without the strategies of the so-called sorcerers, this sense of connection can persist over great distances—a homing beacon, in a sense." I shivered, knowing full well what that meant. Harlan Cedrow had sponsored illegal research under the guise of a charitable organization. Research that had impacted people I cared about. Heidelbrecht built on Cedrow's work and pushed it into even darker, more twisted waters.

"Interestingly," the recording hissed, "there may also be connections between manna and the source of the geo-vent heating system. I looked into it once before, and while the project itself ended prematurely due to regrettable moral timidity, it held great promise."

I jabbed the pause button, needing a moment to process that. I rewound and listened again, confirming that he really was talking about the geo-vents. This changed everything. Heidelbrecht was actually laying out a connection between manna and the source of the city's warmth. Was he talking about the Titan? Something else?

I took a breath and hit play, eager to hear more. Instead I sat and listened to him slather more praise on his own accomplishments. I glanced at the amount of tape remaining, and the notebook's many pages. It was filled with cramped writing, a mixture of notes, transcriptions, nonsense rhymes, and flower doodles. I had hours of work ahead of me. I dragged a hand over my face, and allowed myself a fleeting moment of regret for not stopping for caffeine. Rumple strolled over, sliding against my leg and letting out his normal afterdinner purr of thanks. I ruffled the fur along his back, then I got to work on the tapes.

Heidelbrecht eventually mentioned that the geo-vents could be an escape route, especially closer to the Mount, where the main vent trunks are larger. I thought back to his sudden disappearance when I'd confronted him previously. Was that how he'd escaped me? The man was a worm who always managed to wiggle free of the hook at the last minute.

I kept flipping through the notes as I listened along. Vandie had seemed equally bored with the bulk of the recordings, as all sorts of abstract scribbles filled the margins. Flowers and lightning bolts and long series of Ls and Us, Ds and Rs forming a decorative border. On one page she'd even broken into a bad poem. *Laughing Larry Doesn't Rightly Realize Doing Little* . . . it went on. But for all the nonsense, the transcriptions were carefully picked over, often with notes in multiple colors of ink, indicating she'd returned to it over and over.

On the third reel, I found the information I needed.

"It is my esteemed opinion," Heidelbrecht spouted off, "that the heating system of Titanshade could effectively be turned on or off, or readjusted as one saw fit, by controlling three key locales. It would be possible to form a corporate business entity that could serve as the central heating energy conduit for the entire city. Millions would pay monthly fees for access to the heat source, and if they were late," a muffled finger snap was audible, "they'd experience the true nature of this horrendous climate. Should you be interested in such a project, I would be delighted to write up a proposal at my usual rate . . ." I clamped a hand over my mouth as he went into another sales pitch. The thought of abusing the geo-vents that way was sickening, both taboo socially and morally repugnant.

Something warm and furry pushed across my calf. Rumple, either sensing my discomfort or hoping for a snack. I felt along the floor, and turned up a green and white sparkly cat toy to distract him.

I put myself in Vandie's place, tried to imagine what she'd thought when she realized that her dream of revolutionizing the warmth distribution system already had an answer, discovered by the same madman who'd aided her uncle. But he wanted to use it to bleed the city's poor. I made myself feel the pulse of adrenaline she'd have experienced. I imagined her thrilling to the sheer audacity of Heidelbrecht's vision, and a tingle as she pondered the bleak evilness that made it forbidden fruit.

I dangled the toy in front of Rumple. "No interest, huh?" I tossed it into the shoebox where the rest of Rumple's rejected toys lived. He strolled to the box, tail raised in a lazy S-curve, and sniffed.

Sitting back, I considered what I was learning. Was it the idea of a central heating system that had reeled Vandie in? For someone who conceived of herself as a righteous crusader for a new generation, greed seemed like an awfully pedestrian motive. I pulled off one of my shoes to get at an itch, half-listening to Heidelbrecht go on about various rock formations and how they might amplify or dampen the reach of manna bonds, and tried to picture Vandie Cedrow sitting at her desk, furiously copying notes, rewinding, copying more. *What did you want, Vandie?*

Rumple emerged from the box with a plastic ring I'd popped off a milk container. He trotted over, and dropped it at my feet. I remembered one of Vandie's bumper stickers plastered on the side of the desk: *Spread the Wealth, Spread the Warmth, Spread the LOVE!*

Love was ambiguous, and Vandie didn't seem to have much in the way of personal wealth to spread. But the warmth? I scratched my foot and thought on it. What if Vandie literally wanted to spread the warmth of the geo-vents? What if she believed that Heidelbrecht's research could allow her to bring the warmth of the Titan's suffering to everyone in equal measure? It was a chance to create change on a massive scale.

I jumped up and began pacing, kicking off the other shoe as I went. "You'd need money to do that," I muttered. "Lots of money. And enough knowhow to access the vents." I paused, then ran back to the notes, flipping through them again. She had the clues from Heidel-brecht, and she had connections with people like Murphy CaDell who knew drilling and logistics. She was, without a doubt, in a position to start digging in the precious ground beneath our feet.

I winced at the thought. The one thing you couldn't do in Titan-shade was damage the geo-vents. Still . . .

Vandie must have been overcome with excitement as she listened to the tapes. Heidelbrecht was making the case that not only was it possible to follow the geo-vents to their source, he was claiming that he'd actually done so. Or almost. He would have if it weren't for that meddling previous employer and their conservative stance. I imagined Vandie's rage at that unknown employer, who had snuffed out the very equality of warmth Vandie believed in so much. Of course, I had a good guess as to who that person was. The only other person I knew of in Titanshade who'd employed Heidelbrecht. Ambassador Paulus.

And that would explain the bodies in the vents. They were clearly tied to Paulus, and they were clearly related to the experiments that created Gellica. Rumple chirped, irritated that I'd lost track of our game.

"Let's assume," I told him, "that Vandie planted the badge. She saw the bodies, and Paulus's ID. She'd have realized Paulus was Heidel-brecht's previous employer." I rotated the milk ring across the backs of my knuckles, walking it from right hand to left and back again. All that physical therapy hadn't been for nothing.

"Vandie blames me for her uncle's death, and now knows Paulus once held the keys to redistribute the city's warmth but chose to do nothing. She arranged the sinkhole in hope of punishing both of us. But how did she do it?" Rumple watched the dance, legs gathered under him, eyes as focused on me as Paulus's had been at the jail. I flicked the ring and he dove for it, chasing the bait with the entirety of his heart and soul. I grinned.

All this was conjecture. I needed proof. The one person who knew the full story of the bodies was Paulus. And maybe—just maybe—I had the leverage to make her talk.

SINCE OUR LAST CONVERSATION, PAULUS had been moved from the special observation cell. That meant it wouldn't be easy to speak to her without being overheard. After a flurry of early morning phone calls, I'd put together a plan.

First, I booked time in a jailhouse examination room. Then I stopped by a newsstand to pick up a copy of that week's *Sporting Digest*. The cover photo was Larkin Hall, the big Gillmyn enforcer for the Old Orchard Carabella Club.

At the jailhouse entrance I signed in and surrendered my weapon. Copy of the *Digest* in hand, I made my way to interview room 18. Waiting on my arrival were a pair of guards. One I didn't know, but the other was a red-faced human named Mitchell. I held up the magazine. The headline screamed THE ALL NEW O2C2! and promised an extensive write-up on page thirty-two.

"I know you're a fan," I said. "Story starts on page forty." I handed the magazine to Mitchell, who flipped to page forty and found the envelope with a stack of eight-tael bills. He nodded, then disappeared.

The other guard stepped aside, and I entered the interview room, where Paulus and her lawyer were waiting.

I took my seat and faced Paulus. "I want to talk about the bodies in the vents," I said. "Your lawyer is welcome to be present."

"You're lucky I was available on short notice," Jankowski said. She wore an expensive suit of gray on gray.

"I think your client will want to be fully forthcoming in this interview." I stared at Paulus. She held my gaze and said nothing.

The far wall was dominated by a mirror. Contrary to popular belief, that wasn't so that observers could watch the interview. It was there so that the detainee would spend time wondering if there were. Feeling watched made some people less likely to act out, and made others more likely to talk. Either way, this sit-down had been arranged quickly enough that Auberjois and any other interested parties in the Bunker didn't know what I was up to. And part of the payment to Mitchell was to ensure no one wandered in during the next quarter hour. The rest of the payment would pay off shortly.

In the mirror, I saw the red light on the camera blink off. I stood, walked to the camera, and unplugged the feed. In a few seconds, Mitchell would flip the power back on, but there would be no video evidence of me disconnecting the camera.

Jankowski jumped up. "What in the Hells do you think you're doing?"

I answered the lawyer, but kept my eyes on Paulus. "I'm clearing the board. And I'm waiting to see if you follow suit."

The lawyer grabbed her bag. "We are done here." She turned. "Guard!"

Paulus raised a hand as Jankowski strode to the door. "Leave us be."

"Absolutely not." The lawyer slammed a hand against the door. No one answered. "This is an attempt to intimidate you."

That actually pulled a genuine smile from somewhere deep in Paulus's withered soul. "Do I look intimidated?"

Jankowski frowned. "You look overconfident."

"Two weeks ago I skewered a man on live television, then went home and ate cookies." She paused, and Jankowski showed a sudden interest in her briefcase. "Wait outside, counselor. If you hear screaming," she leaned forward, "delay the guards so I'll have more time to play."

I knocked on the door. "Guard!" It swung open a crack, and I made eye contact with Mitchell's friend. It opened wider. Shooting me a glance that made it clear I could expect some kind of written protest, Jankowski hustled past me.

Once the door closed, Paulus said, "I assume that whatever strings you pulled are limited, so I suggest you make this quick."

"I want to talk openly," I said. "And if you talk openly with me, I'll see about getting you a deal."

"A deal?" she said. "I doubt that. Otherwise that charming little beetle of a man Flifex would be here."

I shifted in my chair, but didn't deny it. Just like charges, decisions about deals belonged to the city attorney. I moved on to my next point.

"If someone else is arrested for tampering with the vents, you'll go free. And if you're honest with me, I think I can find the person who's guilty."

"To call these charges weak would be generous," she said. "I'll walk out of here no matter what you do."

I reached into my coat pocket. My fingers brushed against the empty shoulder holster and I wished I'd hidden away a backup. Instead, I fished out copies of the notebook pages I'd taken from Vandie's office. I slid them over to Paulus.

"Second paragraph in," I said, and focused on Paulus's face as she read.

The ambassador's eyes darted across the page, then slowed, stopped, and started from the top, reading every line. With each shift of her pupils, her lips grew tighter and her cheeks darkened.

"Your buddy Heidelbrecht apparently didn't keep secrets that well," I said. Paulus didn't respond. "He doesn't name our mutual friend," even with no camera, I wasn't about to mention Gellica directly, "and he doesn't even specify what exactly he was up to, poking around in the geo-vents, but he sure doesn't mind bragging about going down there."

She shook the paper. "This could be anything. The handwriting—"

"It's a transcription," I said. "And we have the original recordings." That wasn't exactly true. I had three tapes, and the transcription didn't match up. But someone had the rest, and that meant the threat to Paulus—and Gellica—was genuine.

Paulus stared at me, then at the dead camera. "Why are you here?"

"Because two weeks ago you skewered a man on live television," I said. "And then went home for cookies. You're cold and unshakable. But this transcript? That's got you shook." I popped an arm over the chair back, the picture of nonchalance. "I know the sinkhole isn't your fault. And it'd be fun to watch you try and deal with that and this transcription at the same time. But I need to stop whoever is actually messing with the vents before more people die."

"You'll destroy this?" She held the letter.

"No," I said. "But if I find the real culprit behind the vent tampering, it'll fade away and be forgotten."

She stared at the transcript, lip curling, and I could sense the rage build inside her.

"This is turning into a murder investigation," I said. "And it will drag down everything you've created. Every*one* you've created."

"Nothing created lasts forever."

"And yet, you did dream of it." I turned, holding her gaze. "Didn't you?"

She didn't drop her eyes in shame, didn't pull back her lips and snarl in anger. She merely said, "No, Officer, I did not." And then she smiled, ever so faintly and ever so briefly.

That brief echo of a smile chilled me more than a million screamed words ever could. Because Paulus, for all her concerns about peace and stability, was a monster. Any kindness she showed the world was balanced by her reasoning: she only cared about winning, about achieving her goals, even if those were as arbitrary and self-contradictory as helping the poor and suppressing the vote. Paulus's morality was formless and fluid, like whiskey poured into an improvised container. Like her daughter's ability to shape-shift into a shadow creature.

"How many of your children died down there?" I asked.

"Really, Carter, I don't know how many times I need to deny your overactive imagination."

"Were they canaries in the mine? Warning you where not to send your more valuable assets."

Her face hardened. "A child is a parent's most valuable asset. They are the future."

"And a chance at immortality?"

"The closest any of us will ever come," she said. "So no, I did not send my imaginary children into your imaginary pit of doom, to talk to your imaginary Titan." She smoothed a wrinkle in her jumpsuit. "Is there anything else you'd like me to clarify for you? I have quite a bit of free time. We might even make inroads on ignorance that runs as deep as yours."

"Yeah, actually. Just one thing. After you were arrested, your house was searched."

"Yes."

"They didn't find anything there, despite Gellica telling me that she'd been raised in your home."

Paulus rolled her eyes. "Well, first of all there was nothing to find, because I didn't do anything wrong. Secondly, Gellica may say she was raised in the most severe circumstances, but you've seen my home. Would it bother you to grow up there?"

Paulus came from old oil money, and owned a mansion at the foot of the Mount. There was only one honest answer to that question.

"Not in the house, no."

"And if I were going to do something to the vents, which I did not, I certainly wouldn't have done it in my own home."

"Then where?"

She didn't answer, and I leaned into the table. Paulus flinched. I realized that when Jankowski left, some of Paulus's bluster had gone with her. Paulus was certainly still dangerous, but she had the same hesitation she'd shown when I confronted her in front of her home. She'd at least guessed some of what I could do, and it made her nervous. *Good.*

I pressed her again. "I can fix this. Tell me what you were up to, tell me all of it, and I might be able to fix this."

"And let me out of here? You'd never do that."

"I'd do it for her."

She studied my face. "Yes, you might." Paulus blinked, and seemed to come to a decision. "Tanis Klein was a trusted associate. My right hand, in those days. He was intensely loyal." I must have made a face, because she added, "Loyalty is simple. Pay your people extremely well and keep track of their secrets. It works wonders."

"Sure."

She tsk-tsked, but continued. "As you already guessed, if I were to conduct legally questionable research, I'd have used a secure facility and hired an expert in these things."

"Heidelbrecht?"

"I wouldn't know. This is purely speculative."

"Speculate faster," I said.

"If an experimental subject had gotten loose, she would have gone in the direction where there was the least security."

"The vents." I pressed my palms into the table surface, to keep from forming fists.

"And a motivated employee such as Tanis," Paulus continued, "would have gone after her. Hypothetically."

"But the vents are a maze," I said.

"Yes."

"They'd get lost."

"Indeed."

A moment's silence. I couldn't bring myself to ask what happened next. She told me anyway.

"After that," she said, "the experiment would come to a halt. Any access would be sealed over, anyone involved would be given motivation to leave the city."

"You left them to die."

"What else could I do?"

"Call for help."

"And throw myself on the mercy of the hardhanded men of Titanshade? No, I think you know better than that. Look how you're treated, and you're one of their own." She hesitated, her dimpled chin clenching and relaxing. "You asked where a facility like that might be located. It would be a building with its ground level used for storage, or left vacant."

"This is Titanshade," I said. "Nothing's vacant for very long."

"Even in Titanshade, there are vacancies. Full occupancy means your rents are too low. In any case," she cut off further objection, "I would have used a separate company to buy and hold anything like that."

"A warehouse or a vacant building," I said.

"A vacant first floor, in an occupied building. The rents pay for expenses, and it could be held indefinitely."

"Address?"

She looked away. "I wouldn't know, since it doesn't exist."

We'd hit the limits of her concern for Gellica. I leaned forward and lifted Vandie's transcription. "Do you know what this will do to your daughter?"

Someone knocked on the door. I sat back, slipping the transcription back into my coat as the door swung open. A technician stuck his head in.

"Sorry, Detective," he said. "There's some kind of issue with the recording. We can move you to another room, or you can wait while I fix it."

Over his shoulder, I spotted Mitchell, looking embarrassed at how quickly his plan had collapsed.

"No," I said. "We're done anyway. I was just getting a lesson in real estate." I turned back to Paulus. "In a situation like we discussed, the owner would still need to tend to the building. Keep the exterior up to code, that sort of thing."

She pursed her lips, silent.

"They'd need a facility management company. I hear excellent things about TPM."

"Yes." She drew out the single syllable, studying my face. "They recently bought out another company. One I'd used in the past. You know them?"

"Not exactly."

I'd seen the TPM logo before. On the blueprints and schematics in Vandie's office. The management company had been the one gift Vandie Cedrow retained from her uncle. In my years on the street, I'd seen some bizarre coincidences. This wasn't one of them.

I T WAS AN AFTERNOON'S WORK to turn up a former TPM employee with a criminal record. I paid the guy a visit and asked nicely for a list of the company's clients. He coughed it up without a fuss—anything to get a cop off his front stoop. He also confirmed that Vandie's first act after landing the festival contract had been to leverage the buyout of a smaller boutique management company. From there I eliminated the properties that didn't meet the criteria: too far from the Mount or fully occupied. Finally, I was left with the perfect candidate.

I paged Jax and an hour later we met in the Estante shopping district. The vertical signs along the corner indicated that the building held a handbag shop, a men's clothing store, and a stationery store. The other upper floors, unlabeled, likely held offices, where men and women in suits dropped their expensive handbags on desktops while exchanging overpriced business cards—the whole ecosystem of consumer culture. But we only cared about the first floor. Vacant, with papered-over glass. In this neighborhood, the paper couldn't be scrap newspaper or fish wrap. It had to be decorative and charming, making promises of exciting retail spaces to come, though records showed that floor had stood empty for decades. Until TPM took over management.

We parked by a posh sit-down restaurant, two cops in a division car eating takeout five paces away from diners who probably spent more on pet grooming than my annual salary. I brought Jax up to speed, telling him that I'd paid a visit to the festival grounds, been let into Vandie's office by staff, and seen documents pertaining to the geo-vents in plain sight. My only lie was one of omission. I neglected to mention I'd taken the tapes and notebooks. Just like I failed to mention the source of the technical glitch during my interview with Paulus, or how I'd gotten a snow-runner off the books. I figured that would provide him a little cover if my career came crashing down around us.

I did tell him that someone mysterious had swept the rest of the tapes away, and that I suspected we were about to run into the heart of Vandie's operation.

He took it all in silently, nodding to himself and stirring more vinegar into his coffee. "So we've got no warrant, and not the thinnest echo of a chance to get one from even the most lenient judges on the bench."

"We'll have to sweet talk our way in, or spot something that provides justification for letting ourselves inside."

"And you've been working on this all day, without consulting me?"

I shrugged. "I had to get it done."

"Hold my coffee." He handed me his sour-smelling cup while he dug out his wallet. Opening it, he produced Murphy CaDell's business card. "See the address on here?"

I did, and immediately remembered standing at the festival site, holding CaDell's card and wondering what a property management company was doing with such a posh address in the Estante district. "She probably wanted an office near the geo-vent access," I said.

"Right," he agreed. "You probably could've saved a couple hours by checking in with me, but that's okay. I was making progress on the actual murder cases we've been assigned."

"This *is* a case. The deaths of Tanis Klein and the mystery teenager, along with anyone else who died in that sinkhole." I handed him the card and his coffee. "Now are you ready to check out this building, or do you have some more complaining to do?"

We strolled along the opposite side of the road, acting as though we were talking about something else, but actually covering the visual reconnaissance.

"The thing that I'm curious about," Jax said, "isn't why you went to the festival. CaDell lied to me about the badge, then it showed up in the sinkhole. I get that. What I want to know is, why did you go alone?"

"You were taking the day off. I was working to forget about my hangover. I didn't want to bother you."

"Is that why you talked to Paulus alone? That was this morning, Carter."

I wasn't going to talk about my methods or motivations in that meeting. Instead, I nodded toward the building. "Front door looks completely papered over." The paper covered not only the glass of the door, but the frame itself. "No one's getting in or out that way."

Jax side-eyed me, but went along with the change of subject. "No alley access from the front," he said. "Probably from the far side, then?"

Titanshade buildings were laid out to maximize geo-vent openings, and consideration for minor issues like sanitation and utility access was secondary. At one point in its history, the entire city center had been raised to allow for sewers and utilities to be run under the cobblestone streets.

"Whoever papered the door got out somehow," I said. "Let's loop around back and see what we see."

The next street up was Kenbrook. We turned the corner, ambling down the sidewalk and slowing slightly when we came to an alley opening. It went straight back and jogged right. Classic Titanshade planning—a nod to the necessity of back-door access, while still managing to make life difficult for everyone involved. Worse, the L shape created a blind turn, making it impossible for us to know who or what waited for us at its end. We continued our trek around the block, but never saw another opening. That meant our only option was to go in and hope for no unpleasant surprises.

I stared down the dark corridor snaking between the buildings, considering that whoever might be in there could be the most wanted group of vandals in AFS history. Jax seemed less interested in that than he should have been.

"The reason I asked why you went to the festival alone," he said, "is that your conversation drifts a bit."

"Drifts?"

"Yes." He looked from the alley to me. "Like there's something you don't want to talk about, so you change the topic abruptly. Which is strange, considering you already told me about your powers."

"It's not a power," I said.

"Sure it's not." He waved a dismissive hand. "Thing is, I can't but help wonder what else you're holding back. I mean, what could be more sensitive than what you already told me?"

Scowling, I toed the exterior of the building, adding a new scuff to the multitude crisscrossing my shoe. I knew Jax was smart, I even knew he'd seen through my attempt to keep the manna threads a secret. So why had I ever believed that I could keep Gellica's magical nature from him as well?

He waited, staring me down.

"Maybe because it's not my secret to tell." I pointed at the alley. "Are we gonna do this or not?"

Jax clacked his jaws and let out a dissonant, jangly harrumph. But he let the topic drop, at least for the moment.

We made our way down the alley, relying on the wall-mounted lights to guide us. The sun was beginning to stay in the sky longer, but the tight quarters let very little light creep in between buildings, and the few rays present were too feeble to banish the darkness completely.

"If I ever meet the civil engineers who designed this town," I whispered, "I'm going to arrest them."

"What for?"

"I'll figure it out."

Noises were coming from the far end of the alley. The angle of the alley corner gave Jax a longer line of sight, and he signaled me to hold my position. I peered around the corner, catching a glimpse of two burly human men loading debris into a dumpster.

Jax walked toward them with his hands down and hidden. I hadn't seen if he'd drawn his weapon.

"Gentlemen! I'm wondering about renting some commercial space. You know anything about that?"

The pair immediately spread apart, the movements of men accustomed to fighting outsiders. Still in the shadows, I drew my revolver.

"We don't know nothing about rents," said the wider of them. His flannel shirt was mostly unbuttoned, revealing a chest thick with sweat-matted hair and elaborate tattoos.

"Fair enough," Jax said. "But you're here working for someone. You have the name of a supervisor, or someone I can talk to?"

The wide guy stepped forward. "I got nothing for you, pal. Get back to your office."

The fact that he didn't have enough experience with people in suits to tell a cop from a banker made me wonder if wide guy was a rig worker. The other man had dropped the trash he'd been hauling, but held on to a crowbar. That guy was all angles, and the flickering streetlamp added highlights to large, wet eyes.

"This is private property." Crowbar had a nasally voice, every bit as sharp and filled with angles as the rest of him.

Jax's shoulders rose and fell, a shrug that never revealed his hands. "It's not, actually. The building is private property, but this is an alleyway."

The men exchanged a glance, then spread apart, flanking Jax.

Jax brought his hands out from behind his back. I was immensely relieved to see his weapon and badge. The primary purpose of carrying a gun is to convince other people violence is a bad idea. In order to do that, you have to show it to them and prove it's real.

"Police!" he announced. The men halted. But something in their stance said they weren't cowed, and crowbar guy tightened his grip.

Desperate people, willing to risk attacking a cop, all in order to possibly get away with . . . what? The only thing I could think of was an intrusion into the vent system.

I slid out of the shadows and stood near the pool of light from the damaged streetlamp, a circular drop of light flickering and growing stronger, fading and dimming.

"I'd do what he says," I announced, making it clear that they didn't outnumber my partner. "He's had a bad day."

But that shift in numbers was fleeting. A figure emerged from the shadows to Jax's left, much as I'd done across the alley. This was another Mollenkampi, short and burly. I'd barely registered his presence before he plowed into Jax's lower back. My partner stumbled, dropping his badge but managing to hold on to his weapon and stay on his feet.

The little guy kept pumping his legs, pushing Jax to the center of the alley. It was too risky to fire into their entangled bodies, so I opted to control the other two. Weapon raised, I stepped forward. "Do not move!" I screamed the words, compelling them to focus on me and not the struggling men. I couldn't risking opening fire, but if the attacking Mollenkampi managed to pry Jax's revolver out of his hand, that math would change quickly.

Jax pivoted his hips, putting his left side into the guy's weight, stretching his right arm to keep his weapon out of his attacker's grasp.

"Stay where you are!" I kept my revolver locked on the guy with the crowbar, who could potentially throw his weapon. "Hands where I can see them!"

I closed in on Jax and the shorter Mollenkampi, rotating so that none of the men were in my blind spot. A few months earlier, I might have shifted my weapon and grabbed the assailant. But even with all my physical therapy, my left hand was still missing two fingers, and I didn't trust myself to fire a weapon with it.

The wide guy shifted his weight forward, and I swung my aim, snarling, "Don't do it, asshole!"

From the corner of my eye, I tracked Jax trying to bring his weapon around, but the short Mollenkampi kept batting his arm away, and the filth-slicked alley gave neither of them purchase for their feet.

Unwilling to drop my aim or to switch hands, I reached into the wrestling match with my left hand. I knew better than to try to grab the Mollenkampi near either mouth, so instead I locked my free arm with his. I pivoted, turning my back on the other men for a perilous second. But it was worth the risk. While I was rotating across my front, putting the strength of my entire body into the motion, the Mollenkampi was pulled backward, tipping him off balance and freeing Ajax from his grip even as he stumbled to the side.

Jax spun, weapon raised, covering the other two as he backed up to gain a little space. Breathing heavily, he half turned to assist me. But I was already taking the Mollenkampi to the ground, letting my greater height and weight pin him to the ground. He pushed upward, threatening to topple me over, and I struck him hard, three times, putting my full strength behind each blow. The heel of my left hand connected just below his ear at the start of his jawbone. His head struck the alley stones, scattering trash and debris before bouncing back up to be hit again. After the third strike I shoved the muzzle of my weapon into the base of his neck and screamed, "Don't move!" His jaws went slack and his eyes flickered rapidly. I looked away, keeping one hand on the short Mollenkampi's back so I'd have a warning if he began moving as I surveyed the alley.

Jax had the two humans under control. He directed them to their knees, then prone. The crowbar had been kicked to the side. Maybe it was seeing their friend taken down, or maybe it was the look in Jax's eye as he held them at gunpoint. Regardless, both men were complying.

I caught my breath. The wide guy was on the ground, arms spread out in front of him. His tattoos were in the light, and I noticed that one had the bear and salmon insignia of the Weathering Storm rig. It confirmed my suspicion that they were rig men, out of work and willing to do whatever it took to pay the rent.

Jax took two steps toward me, and I stooped and picked up his badge from the alleyway filth. "Think you can hold on to it this time?"

He didn't laugh. "I'll watch these guys. You go back to the car radio and air this out."

From inside the building, there was a clang and a screech of metal on metal. I stepped in that direction.

"Carter!" It was Jax, reining me in.

"Dammit, she's getting away!"

"So? Control this scene and we'll get her later. We need backup."

I snarled a curse. "You go. You're faster than me. Run like the imps are on your ass, then get back with patrol cops as fast as you can."

"I'll be right back." The slap of shoes on pavement, fading as he rounded the corner. I kept myself positioned where the three men couldn't see me, focused on the two humans with more fight in them. Occasionally I shifted my stance so that I could view them from different angles, the better to catch any hidden movements. The seconds stretched to eternity. With each heartbeat, I expected someone to come bolting out of the building, wielding a shotgun and screaming suicidal defiance.

So maybe that's my excuse for being surprised when voices came from the far side of the alley.

I spun, and found Vandie Cedrow and a tall Gillmyn woman frozen at the alleyway corner. They each held paper bags, and the Gillmyn was sporting treated canvas coveralls, the kind a welder might wear.

Vandie's hand was on the welder's back, as if they were sharing a joke.

I turned. Aimed at her center of mass. "Drop the packages."

They stared, eyes wide. I repeated the command, louder this time.

Vandie recovered first. "Do as he says." She spoke to her companion. Her initial surprise was turning into a calm control.

To me she added, "Are we under arrest?"

"You're detained," I said, "until I can control the situation."

"Control away, mister hero."

"Yeah, I feel real bad about breaking up your party. Hands on your head."

They complied, and I glanced behind them. No sign of Jax or any patrol. I was between the newcomers and the men on the ground. I placed my back to the alley wall, allowing me to split my attention between both groups.

"Now kneel," I said.

Vandie and the welder sank to the ground. I tilted my head toward the building door. "What are we gonna find in there, Vandie? And how are you going to explain it away? Oh, wait—let me guess. It's for *the greater good*. Why is it that the greater good always seems to be great for a select few while the rest of us simply get screwed over in new and exciting ways?"

"And the mess of a system we have now, where the wealthy sit around and get richer while the disadvantaged suffer in the cold?" She pulled her lips back, exposing her teeth. "Is that the system you want to protect?"

"I protect people, not systems." I glanced around the rest of the alley, wary of more surprises in the shadows.

"Don't kid yourself."

The Gillmyn turned her head, and I corrected her. "Eyes ahead."

She complied, and I continued. "So you listened to Heidelbrecht's notes. That's a great way to demonstrate how you're not a homicidal maniac like your uncle."

"My uncle was sick." Vandie's voice was a monotone. "But his heart was in the right place. He wanted to protect people, like you claim you want to."

I spit out a "Ha" with as much disdain as I could muster. I was pretty sure that I could control the situation for a few minutes more, but trying to watch all five of them simultaneously would only last so long. Eventually one of them would do something stupid.

Still on her knees, Vandie kept talking. "He was sick, and in the end he failed his own principles. He caused more sorrow than he saved. He wanted to protect the status quo. But the best way to help people is never by preserving the status quo. It requires radical change."

"And you didn't cause more sorrow than you saved?" She hesitated and I pressed the point. "You want to meet the survivors of your sinkhole? The kids who're missing a parent or two? Maybe the people without jobs now that their storefront slid into the ground?"

"That wasn't us."

I blinked. "That wasn't you? It's a coincidence that you're digging into the thermal vents, and then they collapse. We both know that's not true." I squatted, dropping low enough to look her in the eye. "What I want to know, Vandie . . . What's in the vents?"

She was silent.

"What's down there, really? Because this idea that you've inspired a bunch of roughnecks to become miners for liberty? It's laughable." I straightened and stepped back. "What do you have going on? And where did you get the money to do all this? Because the whole point of your little festival was to help you keep the lights on." I tilted my head. "Is there treasure down there? Did you think you were going to find the Titan, trussed up like in some kids' book about Titan's Day?"

"Why not?" she said. "You believe in humans and Mollenkampi, and Haabe-Ieath spending their lives burrowing below ground. Is it really all that crazy that the Titan's down there, watching, and wishing that we were making better use of his sacrifice?"

There was a shout from down the alley. I held Vandie's eye. Neither of us moved. I stepped closer. Dangerously closer.

"What's in the vents?"

"Vandie . . ." The Gillmyn whispered a warning, or a plea.

As the noise and shouts increased, the younger Cedrow sighed. "Don't you have to read me my rights or something?"

"You're not under arrest," I said. "But I got a hunch that when we see what's inside that building you're going to be. And how long do you think you'll spend locked up?"

"Vandie." The Gillmyn welder again. She'd turned on her knees, staring behind them, as the sounds grew louder.

"Don't you want to tell me what's going on? Don't you want to say it to my face?"

Vandie's eyes flashed.

I leaned closer. "Just like your uncle."

She lashed out, fist missing my chin. The big welder half stood, whether to protect Vandie or join in the attack, I never knew. She was brought down suddenly, tackled and handcuffed by Jax and a red-shirted patrol cop. The backup had arrived.

36

'VE HAD VERY FEW MOMENTS of vindication in my career.
Walking into that building was one of them.

The entry looked normal enough. There was a conference room, a chalkboard, shelves lined with cleaning supplies, and a wall covered with ladders. The kind of thing you'd expect from a facility management company. Enough to satisfy any curious visitors, or even workers who weren't privy to the real reason Vandie had purchased the company that managed the building.

That lay through a door labeled Employees Only. And it opened onto a whole other world.

This was a wider, more open area. The walls were still lined with chests of tools and bins of refuse, but the focus was the monstrosity in the center of the room. Paulus hadn't been lying about sealing up the entry. There was evidence of jackhammers and broken concrete. Paulus may have wanted to bury the portal, but Vandie had gotten access by buying up the facility management company that controlled access, and she'd used it to give herself access to the vents.

An iron-rung scaffold rose out of the shattered concrete like an oil derrick jutting out of the ice plains. It was almost sacrilegious, just seeing the thing. I didn't even have it in me to laugh at my partner's discomfort.

"Oof." Jax buried his nostrils in the crook of his arm.

Even with the airlock, the whole area was overly warm and smelled strongly of sulfur. It was like being a little kid and putting your face in a home's entry vent to see how long you could stand the smell.

"The scaffold's helping stabilize the opening," I said, "but it's mostly there to provide that walled-in enclosure." I pointed at the heavy vinyl tarps draped over crossbeams, a sort of miniature version of the festival tents. "An improvised airlock, to prevent disrupting the service to those around them and raising suspicion."

"Too bad it's not helping the smell."

"It's not going to stop me from enjoying this moment," I said. It was everything I'd hoped to find. With any luck, we'd have this wrapped up shortly, and the questions about the mummified bodies would be far less pressing. The kind of thing I could manage to keep from spilling over onto Gellica or myself. I took a deep breath of sulfurous air and grinned. Vandie would talk, maybe even cut a deal. And we'd learn who was behind her operation, and discover the real source of the buzzing and the sinkhole.

I strolled over to Vandie's office, with an internal window so she could gaze out on her engine of change whenever she wanted. The shelves were lined with ledgers and files, all of them being documented by tech teams before being categorized and moved to evidence processing. A heavyset Mollenkampi was photographing the contents of a desk: a reel-to-reel tape player and a box of tapes and notebooks that I recognized at once. They'd been at Vandie's residence at the festival.

It was just a matter of time before those were analyzed, and Gellica's secret exposed. Once that happened, the whole raft of lies and secrets would come crashing down. We needed to get the truth out of Vandie first.

I struggled to keep my composure. We had Vandie dead to rights. But getting her confession and closing the case had suddenly become a race against the clock, and only I knew it.

The Bunker was teeming with curious souls that night. The arrest of Vandie Cedrow meant that Paulus was likely about to be cleared of wrongdoing, and everyone wanted to say they were there to see the city's most famous detainee go free.

For myself, I wasn't excited about the thought of Paulus walking out the Bunker doors. But I had no illusion that she was guilty of collapsing the sinkhole. And a confession from Vandie would immediately take pressure off of Paulus, and through her, Gellica.

So even though there was no true call for a Homicide detective when the crime was technically disruption of utility services and endangering the lives of the public, I stayed close at hand. Before long, I proved my usefulness with my face. Anytime Vandie caught a glimpse of me, it set her off on another speech about how the city needed to put right decades of graft and corruption. Between her and the men from the alley, I was almost on a carousel, visiting each one in their respective interview rooms.

The star of the show, Vandie sat in room 7D and stared at the back wall with the patience of a wealthy person waiting for her lawyers to arrive. She was calm and unresponsive, except when I was in the room. Then the corners of her mouth pulled down and her jaw set, still silent but with burgeoning rage. The interrogating officer was a weary-looking guy named Vignolini, who talked with his hands as he tried a mix of threats and appeals.

"We know what you were up to." Vignolini dealt out photos like a card shark. Each one showed the interior of the warehouse, and the hole in the floor leading into the vents. "Crawling through the vent system like rats."

Smart rats, maybe. Vignolini threw down a spread of three more photos, showing the antechamber Vandie's crew had built around the hole. The whole thing was careful, ambitious, and clever. Much like Vandie herself.

"Who owns the building, Vandie? That's who's bankrolling your little operation, isn't it? You tell us that and we can make things go easy." Vignolini's hands fluttered, a verbal violinist. "We're gonna find out who it is anyway, so tell us now, while it's still worth our while. Once we figure it out, then your leverage is . . . Poof!" He spread his fingers, a pantomime of her evaporating time.

Unfortunately for Vig, I very much doubted he'd be figuring out the owner anytime soon. Paulus was no fool, and I'd seen this play out before in white-collar crimes. Whatever holding companies she'd created to hide behind, it would take our forensic accounting team months of digging to crack through the legal shell game.

Of course, I knew the building belonged to Paulus. But I could hardly tip my hand. Not to mention that would sabotage the whole point of the arrest, since she was absolutely not behind Cedrow's operation.

"C'mon, Vandie," Vignolini said, now making *come-here* movements. "Don't you want to help the good guys?"

Finally breaking her silence, Vandie turned her eyes on me and said, "I don't think there's anything good about you."

That, at least, we had in common. She closed her eyes and shut her mouth, so I clapped Vignolini on the shoulder. "Be back in a bit, Vig."

Then I walked across the hall to room 7F, where the wide-bodied guy with tattoos listened to his interviewers and drummed his fingers on the table.

"You know what her uncle did to the workers at his family's rig, don't you?" The interviewer was a detective named Jordan, who rolled up his sleeves as he spoke. "Practically turned them into animals. Used them as shields while he did his dirt. You know that?"

"Yeah."

"And you don't care?"

"I care." The wide man's voice rattled and wheezed, like a graffiti artist's spray cans. "But you know who doesn't? My landlord. I gotta eat, gotta pay rent. The military's shut down most drilling, and taking all the manna for themselves. Oil built this town, and now that we're in trouble, they're mumbling apologies while stepping over our bodies." He scowled, working himself into a proper rage. "So when I get a call about some rich lady who needs debris hauled out of a building, I don't ask questions. Besides, Cedrow's a name I know, and her money spends as well as anyone else. And what's she doing that's so wrong? Talking about taking care of her workers? Making it safer on the ice plains?" He hissed a curse between his teeth. "You want someone to roll on a lady like that, you keep on walking."

The next room over was 7G, where the slender human who'd swung a crowbar sat with shoulders hunched and hands on his knees.

"Why'd you swing on a cop?" Kurachek was short, even for a Mollenkampi, and she compensated with a direct, in-your-face style of interrogation.

"I didn't." The guy's shoulders didn't even twitch.

Kurachek whistled through her speaking mouth's needle teeth. "That crowbar you were toting says otherwise."

"I was working," he said. "You understand *work*?"

"And then your friend attacked the officer."

"He ain't my friend."

"Really? You've never seen him before?"

"Course I've seen him. He's some guy who works for Vandie C. That don't mean he's a friend."

"You took his side."

Crowbar sat back. "Let me ask you this. If you saw a cop you don't know getting into it with some drunk on the corner, are you gonna talk it through and find out who's in the right, or are you gonna go in swinging and ask questions later?"

No one answered.

Crowbar smirked and hunched his shoulders again. "That's what I thought. So yeah, he wades in, and I'm automatically on his side. You want to know why he did what he did, you ask him." He shooed us away. "Go on, ask him!"

In a room at the end of the hall, beneath a stenciled 7J, the Mollenkampi who'd so bravely waded into the fray pointed at his biting mouth, splinted and wrapped shut with white gauze. "When do I get this looked at?"

"You already did." The detective was a human named Rogers, and he was clearly running out of patience. "Medic said it's dislocated, so don't move it. What were you doing in that warehouse?"

The Mollenkampi was silent.

"Don't have anything to say?"

"Yeah." He leaned forward. "I want a lawyer."

Vandie Cedrow's lawyers had arrived in 7D by the time I returned. One human and one Gillmyn, both in expensive suits, they flanked her on the barrow table. And as much as they told her to save it for the jury, she just couldn't help herself when she saw my smirking mug stroll back into the room. That's when Vandie Cedrow let slip the real source of her money.

I stood in the back of the room, doing my best to be seen by our guest of honor. Vignolini continued the questioning.

"We know you were tampering with the geo-vents," Vignolini said. "We know you wanted to create a panic with the sinkhole—"

"This is a load of crap."

One of her attorneys, a particularly thin Gillmyn with yellowing eyes, whispered his counsel in her ear.

"Then why did you set up this elaborate operation?" Vig pushed the photos of the airlock across the table.

"Because she said we had to find—" Vandie broke off. Every cop in the room was stock-still, and I knew they were all fighting the same urge I had to lean forward.

"Who's 'she,' Miss Cedrow? Who forced you into this?"

The lawyer placed webbed fingers on her arm, but she shook him off.

Vignolini made a show of indifference. "That's fine. We have your men on assaulting an officer. They'll tell us what we need to know, or they'll do their time. I'm sure they'll be real popular with the guards at Sequendin."

Vandie squeezed the sides of her head. "They didn't have anything to do with this." She'd already tried to bargain for her employees' release, but the CA had refused, saying that she had to talk before anyone could be deemed worthy of prosecution. She was riding the line between hope and distrust, and the end result looked to be a stalemate, not to be resolved until the workers either turned on her, or she caved and gave us what we wanted. Unless someone was willing to break the deadlock.

"Thing is," I said, speaking loudly and causing everyone's head to swivel in my direction, "my partner and I were the ones assaulted, and it's been so difficult to remember the details."

The other cops in the room were growing increasingly uncomfortable. Vig dropped a hand on my shoulder and applied subtle pressure, as if he could slide me out the door. "Maybe it's time you got a break, Carter?"

"What are you saying?" Vandie stared at me, face composed. Vig's hand fell away from my shoulder.

"My old man worked the rigs," I said. "Ursus Major. After my mom died, I was mostly raised by other rig families. I saw a lot of spouses end up at funerals, and a lot of my friends end up missing a parent. There's a lot of people in this world I don't like," I was careful not to express a personal opinion about her in front of her lawyers, "but I admire any impulse that would make sure more roughnecks made it home safe to their families."

Vandie winced, and her head lowered. She was still carrying guilt for the riggers who'd died on her uncle's campaign of madness. It was what drove her campaign for reform, and it was the key to unlocking her mind.

"Fourteen," I said. "Fourteen kids have to stand for a parent at their funeral. Fourteen kids who deserve to know that whoever killed their parent is gonna pay. I'm not talking about the workers who dug an entryway to the vents, and I'm not even talking about the woman who gave the order. I'm talking about the person who pushed you into doing it, the person who made the sinkhole inevitable. Tell us who's behind your trip into the vents. That's who we want."

Vandie nodded, and her pale Gillmyn attorney perked up. "We'll need assurances," the lawyer burbled with excitement, "immunity, a full package in writing."

"Let's hear what she has to say first," Vignolini said.

Vandie stared at the corner of the ceiling. Then she shrugged. "She approached me a few weeks ago. I have no idea how she heard what I was up to, so don't bother asking."

"Who is she?"

This was it. The moment when everything changed. The truth was within grasp.

Vandie cleared her throat. "Paulus."

We all sat in silence for a beat. My stomach flipped, and it seemed like the truth had turned into a handful of snow melting through my fingers.

Vandie leaned across the table. "The AFS is causing all of this.

And next, they're going after the festival." She rotated her head, staring at us in turn, and ending with me. "I was trying to stop them when you assholes decided to arrest me."

It took about an hour for the details to be worked out with Vandie's lawyers. They were competent, but not in the same league as a legal mind like Jankowski. Ultimately they had to concede most of their points, and we all crowded round. Auberjois had joined the room. I was still there, too, over Auberjois's objections. "She talks more when Carter's in the room," Vig had pointed out, and Auberjois couldn't argue with that. So we settled into our places, started the tape recorder running, and Vandie laid it all out.

"This city's fundamentally broken," she said. "I was born here, but when I traveled I saw the world. Every city-state has problems, and gaps between the rich and poor. Only Titanshade is built so that the poor freeze to death if they can't pay their bills."

Vig said, "And you wanted to fix that?"

"It wouldn't take a feat of engineering to boost the supply to the Borderlands. All it takes is the willpower to get it done."

"And that's what you had, the will to destroy the system?"

"No. To show that it can be done. In order to do that, we had to get in the ground and make a true map of the vents, get measurements on air flow and temperature." As she dove into her explanation, Vandie pushed and pulled the photos from the warehouse, technical explanations of what was what. According to her, nothing was designed to damage the vent system.

"You didn't make a proposal, take it before City Council?"

She rolled her eyes. "This city is dying. It needs treatment. If someone stumbles into the emergency room half-coherent and bleeding out from a gut wound, you don't ask permission before stitching them up. If you see someone being robbed on the street, you don't ask their permission to intervene and arrest the robber."

"Arresting muggers doesn't cause sinkholes," I said.

Vandie smirked. "Neither did I."

Vignolini circled his hands in the air, clearing the air of our dislike for one another. "You saw the bodies?"

"The old ones? Yeah. But we didn't touch them."

That was a lie. How else would Jax's badge have shown up underneath one of them?

"Thing is," she said, "the bodies weren't the weirdest thing down there. There're parts of the tunnels where the temperature jumps up or down. There're parts where you don't need lights, because the walls glow orange. And every now and then we'd find the buzzing rocks."

"The what?"

"Buzzing," she said. "They were . . . It was strange. They were regular rocks, big ones. But they got warmer the longer you touched them. And then everyone around you would get angry." Her lips pulled back, perhaps with the memory of the feeling, perhaps with a general sense of disgust at being in that interview room. "It was the rocks that spooked Saul. After that, he wanted out."

"The rocks spooked him?" Auberjois said. "I don't understand."

She smirked. "Go down and see them for yourself."

"Well, that's not happening," said Vig, repulsion creeping into his voice. "Now that your operation is shut down, we'll be making sure that no one ever goes into those vents again."

"That's a mistake," she said. "This city's future depends on our activities in the vents."

All the detectives shifted uncomfortably. Even Vandie's lawyers seemed put out. The idea of *activities* in the vents was like nails on a chalkboard, even for a roomful of people who made a living bringing the darkest deeds of the citizenry to light.

"What changed?"

"I found an investor," she said. "Anonymous, at first. Someone contacted me about my work. All the issues we'd worried about, they were smoothed over, and I was told to contact them if we ran into issues."

"Issues?"

"Like Saul," she said. "The first time I contacted the backer, it was because Saul said he was leaving, and didn't think we should keep our work secret anymore. When I met her, she told me not to worry, that the work was too important to stop and that she'd take care of everything."

"And this was Paulus?" asked Auberjois.

"Who else would it be?"

That was the question. There was no rhyme or reason for Paulus to be involved with such a thing.

"So Ambassador Paulus volunteered to help you destroy the entire system that made her wealthy and put her into power? Seems like a bad financial move on her part."

Vandie rolled her eyes. "I don't know exactly why she did it. Maybe to get to the bodies we found? You'd have to ask her assistant. The one who's always in the background. What's her name, Gellica?"

I felt my arms twitch, a massive tell. In a game of poker, that'd cost me some cash. But in interview room 7D it did far worse. Vandie's eyes opened a little further, and she knew she had me.

"The sorcery was done by Paulus. And she had someone on the TPD covering up for them. I can't prove who it was, but I've got my suspicions." Vandie's gaze lingered on me. "Paulus indicated it was someone high profile."

She was playing to the room, and feeding all the conspiracy theories we held in our hearts. And of course it wasn't the truth, but it wasn't exactly lies, either. The strongest deceits are built on a foundation of truth, like a pearl grown around a grain of truth. I believed much of what she was saying, but I was almost certain that Paulus hadn't been involved. But that still left the question of who was the sorcerer behind Vandie? While I was pondering that, Auberjois and Vig were pressing Vandie for details.

"You said she'd fix it. Fix it how?"

"One of the guys got some snake oil. And no, I won't tell you who it was, so don't ask." She ran her fingers across the shaved sides of her head. "Paulus made a manna link between that and one of the buzzing rocks. I gave it to Saul, told him it was a gift, a thanks for keeping quiet."

"You knew Saul had an issue," I said. "You knew he struggled."

"Yeah, well, it turns out his financial issue was greater than his drug issue, wasn't it?"

I closed my eyes, remembering Saul's roommate, Donna Raun, and her comments about needing money for rent.

"He sold the snake oil," I said, "to Sheena Kathreese. And she sold it to Bobby Kearn. When Bobby used it, Sheena was the closest person around. And she felt all that anger. She lost control."

Vig waved his hands again. "Wait, wait, wait. If that's the case, why didn't it trigger the attack right away?"

"Because," Vandie said, "Paulus had some kind of firewall between the manna bond. It wouldn't go into effect until I snapped a wooden stick she gave me."

I looked at the only sorcerer in the room. "Is that possible?"

"It was a stopper spell," Auberjois said. He was getting excited. "It's a magical safeguard. Paulus put a wall between the snake oil and the buzzing rocks. Then she tied the stick to the magical wall; break the stick, break the wall. It's like pulling the cork out of a bottle."

"So you popped the cork," I said to Vandie. "Then what?"

"That was when I found out that Saul had sold the snake oil."

I remembered the manna threads running between Vandie and Bobby Kearn's corpse. I'd been sensing the remnant of her magical "cork." But I also remembered the pained look on Vandie's face when she'd seen the transformed body. My breathing slowed as understanding sunk in.

"You killed Bobby Kearn by accident."

"I didn't kill him," she said. "The dancer did. I just brought the buzzing to the room. It was . . ." Her voice faltered. "I didn't mean for that to happen."

Like getting someone drunk and sticking them behind the wheel.

"And the transformation?"

"I don't know. She—Paulus, I mean. She never said anything like that would happen. I have no idea what caused that." Vandie bit her lip, pinching the skin until it paled. "Maybe something wrong with the spell? I don't know."

"And when you didn't manage to kill Saul, did you give up?"

She exhaled loudly. "No. We didn't know what we were going to do, but then Saul called us. He demanded more snake oil, a bigger batch this time. He was blackmailing us."

"That must have been so hard for you," I said.

"Whatever. We had to try a second time."

"Weren't you afraid of getting it wrong again?"

"Yes." She sounded emphatic. "Hells yes. That's why she—Paulus—made the safeguard, the stopper spell or whatever, so that it would only work at shorter range. That way, if Saul had sold it, it wouldn't affect anyone else. She had to get close, but triggered the magic herself. It worked, and Saul was killed. Except . . ."

I may have been kidding myself, but I thought there was genuine remorse in her words.

"Except he'd already diluted it and sold it to other people," I said.

"Yeah."

"So the buzzing attacks all over the city, they can be traced back to you."

"To Paulus," she said. "And to the rocks from the vents. And to whoever she had working for her. Keep searching that sinkhole, you'll probably find something."

Auberjois underestimated Vandie, and now she was playing him like a pro. What really galled me was that I'd underestimated her as well. The brash young revolutionary had been surprised by her arrest, but thought so fast on her feet that she'd used it as leverage to tear down everyone she hated, including Paulus, Gellica, and myself. If Vandie was going down, she intended to take her enemies down with her.

"I'm telling you," she said, "Paulus just wanted to hide the bodies that were already down there. I don't even think she meant to set off the sinkhole. But it happened, and now she's desperate to cover it up."

Another lie. The planted badge proved that Vandie knew the sinkhole was coming. But I couldn't call her on it, because I was the one who'd convinced Jax to keep quiet, and I was the one who'd concealed the badge when I found it in the sinkhole.

"How's she gonna do that?" asked Vig. "What could possibly cover up the sinkhole?"

Vandie's voice lowered. "She's got something planned at the

festival. I don't know what, but she was all over me, trying to get security info out of me. I think she may have sent someone out to scope out the place yesterday."

I held in a snarl. She was good. That was when I'd gone up to the festival site. If anyone tried to do some digging, they'd have no trouble realizing it was me.

The trouble was, there might be hard evidence on Paulus. Everything in Vandie's warehouse office had been seized, including the audio tapes. It'd take weeks for the whole thing to be processed, but it would happen. And when it did, someone would listen to those tapes, and maybe they'd start connecting dots. What else had Heidelbrecht said? Was there something on there that would implicate Gellica as her mother's creation?

I pressed a hand against my temple. Vandie Cedrow had run rings around me.

"Why do you think she's targeting the festival?"

Vandie took a breath. "She's setting me up."

I couldn't help but laugh. "She's doing a pretty good job of it, considering we caught you right outside your little rabbit warren."

"Paulus wants a distraction. She wants the world to think I did all this on my own." Vandie looked around at the assembled cops and attempted to plead her case. "Look, I know I'm not without fault here. But Paulus is playing you, hoping that you'll hang the whole thing on me, and give you a reason to let her walk. She's so desperate, she's got Gellica and whoever else is working for her trying to pull off something even bigger."

"Bigger?" There was concern in Auberjois's voice, and maybe a hint of excitement.

"Yes!" Vandie pounced. "You're asking about her motive? It's the simplest one there is. She wants to save her ass. If there's an explosion or something at the concert while she's in jail . . . She told me once that whales used to sing to each other. Maybe she thinks it'd be ironic if she won her freedom during a song."

I focused on that wording. *Whale song?* Whales had been extinct for a century so who the Hells made comparisons to whales?

Serrow.

I blinked, then blurted out, "You keep saying 'she' but correcting yourself, *she—Paulus.*"

Vandie stared at me, blank-faced. Auberjois turned in my direction, mandibles twitching with irritation. It was possible I'd interrupted him when I asked my question. Then again, my question was more important.

"I was trying to be clear. For the record," said Vandie.

"You were trying to correct yourself. Because I know exactly one sorcerer who rambles on with some fairy tale about singing whales." I stepped closer to the table. "You didn't mean Paulus when you said 'she this' or 'she that.' You meant Serrow. Because that's who really helped you, isn't it?"

Even before I'd finished my question, Auberjois was speaking over me.

"Carter, you're done here."

I opened my mouth, but he cut me off. "I don't need anyone covering Paulus's backside during my investigation. You're done. Show yourself out."

I turned to Vig, hands spread, appealing the decision. He only shrugged. It wasn't worth going to the mat with a captain. I recognized the tension around me. Everyone was ready to roll out to that festival and tear it apart looking for whatever could cause another sinkhole. Despite the fact that there were no geo-vents on the ice plains. Despite the fact that the site was outside our jurisdiction. Despite the fact that all we had to go on was the word of a woman who was already facing a stint behind bars. Everyone else in that room would believe her story. Cops want to be heroes. We don't always live up to that standard, but it's how we see ourselves. And Vandie was playing into it, offering us a chance to save tens of thousands of lives in a single go. Who wouldn't want to believe that?

Only a broken cop who wouldn't trust the word of a killer.

I could only hope I wasn't the only broken cop in the building.

37

AN HOUR LATER I STOOD in Auberjois's office, a relatively sparse room with a desk, two chairs for guests, and a side table. Auberjois sat at the desk, Bryyh and Guyer were in the chairs. Ajax and I stood closer to the door, waiting for our superiors to come to some kind of group decision.

Auberjois was shredding an envelope into thin strips, the repetitive rips underscoring his words. "We've got to bring in everyone on this. This is too big for just us."

Bryyh sighed. "It's outside the city's jurisdiction. We don't have any standing to go out there and disperse people and search for—I don't even know what'd we'd be searching for. We've got to be invited, or it'll play as a violation of their rights and federal law. And that's all the justification the feds need to keep the manna strike under their control."

I coughed. It wasn't going to make me look good, but it was time to reveal my earlier strategy for justifying access. "Well, if there have been complaints from citizens—"

The door flew open and a woman in a tuxedo entered, closing it behind her with a frame-rattling thud. "I understand you have something for me?"

Auberjois blinked. "Who the Hells are you?"

The newcomer grinned, causing the glitter on her cheeks to sparkle. "I'm the person who knows that you're a baby captain with zero job security trying to punch above your weight class." She bent toward Auberjois, hands on hips, chin jutting out. "And I'm the woman

1

who canceled a night at the opera to come down and mop up the mess you left when you shit the bed on this one."

Bryyh leaned back in her chair and folded her hands over her stomach. "This is Assistant City Attorney Doyle," she told Auberjois, then glanced at Guyer, Jax, and me. "You three are excused."

I wasn't familiar with this Doyle person, but from Bryyh's reaction, we were about to witness a controlled burn.

Auberjois seemed slower on the pickup. "Flifex was in the loop on the entire Paulus operation. He's working point on—"

"He was," said Doyle, "and then you convinced him to make the worst decision of his possibly abbreviated career. So Flifex *was* in the loop, and now he most decidedly is not." She turned on a heel and surveyed the room, as if measuring the drapes. "You are not to speak to him again. Going forward, all ARC Division contact with the City Attorney's Office will be through me."

"I don't understand what's so complicated," I said. Bryyh covered her eyes. "We've got Vandie on the geo-vent tampering. She's also selling us an obvious distraction about a threat to the festival and covering for her accomplice." I took a step toward the center of the room. "Serrow murdered Taran Glouchester, a reporter for *The Titanshade Union Record*. The reporter's partner tells me they were working on a big story involving Barekusu funneling cash to radical groups. Honestly, I have no idea why we're still talking instead of finding handcuffs big enough to slap on a Barekusu."

Doyle's dark purple lipstick made the sneer she gave me even more effective. "Can you imagine something more disastrous than arresting an ambassador?"

I shifted my feet, knowing where this was going.

"Not enough imagination? How about arresting both an ambassador and a beloved religious figure for the *same crime*. Maybe tomorrow you can bust some orphans who held an unlicensed bake sale to pay for their teacher's heart medicine. Because that would have a better chance of going on to conviction than this paranoid Barekusu theory."

"Stop!" Bryyh didn't stand, but her voice was sharp and decisive. "My detectives do good work. What you do with the charges is your business, but you won't speak to them like that again." She kicked Guyer's now-vacant seat toward the ACA. "Sit down, Irene, and let's talk this through." They locked eyes, and the rest of us let ourselves out.

Once we were in the hall I grabbed Jax and Guyer by the arm, swiveling my head and making sure we were unseen as I pulled them into an open conference room.

"This whole thing is going to Hells," I said.

"I'd already picked up on that," said Guyer, "but thank you for the recap."

I paced the room's perimeter like a captive animal taking the measure of the cage. "Vandie didn't lie the whole time. What did we learn from her confession?"

Jax sat on the table's edge, his nicely shined shoes kicked up on the chair seat. "She explained where the buzz is coming from. If we believe her, that is."

"Magical rocks?" Guyer braced her hands on the back of another chair. "I guess that's possible."

Jax shrugged. "It does sound a little ludicrous when you say it like that."

"This from the guy who came up with whale ghosts," I said.

Guyer looked at me. "Whale ghosts?"

"Okay," Jax said. "If we accept the buzzing rocks for now, and that Vandie's sorcerer—"

"Serrow!" I said.

"—linked it to snake oil, it at least explains how people all over town are hearing it and being affected. And it fits the general pattern."

"What pattern?" asked Guyer. "I'd love to hear a pattern about now."

"I mean the order of events." Jax ticked the steps off on his fingers. "The buzzing showed up at the festival, then in several locations in town. What Cedrow described was a botched murder attempt at the festival, then another in town. But that one went wrong as well, and it spilled out to affect more people."

"Not exactly a criminal mastermind," I said.

"Exactly!" Jax pointed at me. "Which fits with Cedrow, who isn't an experienced criminal. Plus, let's face it—when people spin lies they usually make themselves look more competent, not less."

"She definitely gave us motive for the Petrevisch killing," I said. "I can see her getting squirrelly if she thought Saul was about to run his mouth. And all the other deaths were accidental casualties."

Guyer snorted. "Doesn't do much for her friend-of-the-worker persona."

"No," I said. "It certainly does not. And it doesn't make sense that she'd be working with Paulus."

Jax nodded. "Cedrow certainly seems to despise the AFS. And that makes Paulus her enemy."

"Even more than that," I said. "Paulus would have wanted the mummified bodies to disappear, and Vandie was hoping for them to be found."

"How do you know?" Guyer asked.

I glanced back at the door. "Because when I found the first body, I also found Jax's badge. Whoever planted it knew that they'd both be found."

Guyer crossed her arms. "You think Vandie opened a sinkhole to reveal the old bodies?"

"No," I said. "She wanted headlines about warmth distribution everywhere from the evening news to the tabloids. Vandie was betting on a big response to her big actions. If mummified bodies made us and the AFS look bad, that was icing on the cake."

"So." Jax leaned forward, elbows resting on his knees. "What don't we know?"

"If Vandie's telling the truth about the buzzing and the stopgap spell—"

"Stopper spell," Guyer muttered.

"The point is," I said, "we're agreed that Vandie wouldn't be working with Paulus. So how do we find out if Serrow is the real sorcerer behind the Petrevisch stopper spell?"

"And the transformations," said Guyer. "Is Vandie playing dumb about them? Or does she really not know?"

I was back to pacing the edge of the room. "The Barekusu could be related to the cause of the rock buzz . . ."

"You left off the most pressing item," said Jax. "Is Vandie lying about the festival? If there's a chance that Dinah McIntire and all those people could be in danger, we need to warn them."

"But if it's just a distraction," Guyer said, "then whatever resources go into dealing with it will be hours away. The entire city will be vulnerable."

The three of us stared at each other. The decision was out of our hands. For now, all we could do was wait to hear what our superiors decided to do.

A few hours later I sat in the hallway, my suit coat serving as an impromptu cushion under my rapidly numbing rear end. Guyer and Jax paced nearby. When the door to Auberjois's office flew open and Doyle stalked down the hall, we knew that at least a decision had been made.

"What's the word?" I scrambled to my feet and moved to intercept her.

The assistant city attorney had taken off her tuxedo coat, revealing a glittering pair of suspenders.

"The word is quite clear," she said. "There will be no warrant issued to search Serrow or any other member of the Barekusu caravan. I suggest you drop it entirely."

"We have—"

"You have speculation and conjecture, against physical evidence and Cedrow's statement."

"The unsubstantiated word of a woman desperate to take down anyone around her," I said.

"Vandie Cedrow used her uncle's research to enter the geo-vents without permission, and with great malicious intent. She was assisted by a sorcerer we believe to be former Ambassador Paulus. That's all we need, and thats as far as the investigation goes." Doyle paused. "There's no murder here, Carter. There's no dead body for you to champion, to feel like you know or that you can be the white knight on a golden steed. You found someone doing a crime, you brought her in, and she confessed. You did your job, good for you. Now get out of the way, so the rest of us can do ours." Doyle stormed away, leaving us in shock.

Vandie's accusations meant that not only wasn't Paulus going free, she was going to be facing additional charges. Vandie's audio tapes of Heidelbrecht would be analyzed, dragging Gellica into the light. And Serrow was going to walk free, for the second time in a week.

Guyer simply shrugged. But her feigned indifference didn't fool me. I recognized the anger simmering in her eyes. By contrast, Jax's mandibles shook and his fists clenched.

"We have to at least tell the festival about the threat," he said.

"We did." Bryyh entered the hallway, closing the door to Auberjois's office. "Did you think we were just sitting in there talking to ourselves?"

"And?" I dusted off my jacket, hoping for good news.

"And we're in a bad spot." Bryyh frowned, hands on hips. "The management company thinks Vandie Cedrow was set up. The out-of-town bands and the audience don't trust the police, and the military base is hesitant to help because we've alienated the AFS by arresting Paulus."

"What can we do?"

"Decisions are being made at a higher level than us. It's up to the mayor and City Council at this point. We'll mobilize to be ready at a moment's notice, but all we can do right now is put out a press statement. Maybe we'll pull enough media attention that we'll limit attendance, maybe even pressure the festival staff to work with us."

"All those people at the concert, and the best you can do is hope for favorable media coverage?"

Bryyh's sad smile held more sorrow than I could have expressed in an hour-long rant. "That's the power of the press," she said, and left us standing in the hallway.

Jax's hands ran over his head plates, kneading them, massaging away the same tension that boiled beneath my skin. "For everything we know about Serrow, we can't touch her. They've given more access to the paper where the dead reporter worked than the entire police force."

The power of the press, I thought, and watched Bryyh disappear down the corridor.

"I'm going to try something," I said. "I'll let you know how it turns out."

Guyer and Jax threw questions after me, but I didn't have any answers they'd want to hear.

I stalked the halls, my worn soles devouring vinyl tiles as if walking fast could soothe the anger inside. When I got to my desk, I sat very still, staring at the Bullpen and the cops who went about their business, trying to find killers and protect the innocent. And then I did something I never thought I'd stoop to.

I picked up the phone, dialed information, and said, "Yeah, can I have the number for *The Titanshade Union Record*?"

I SAT IN AN OVER-PRICED SANDWICH shop near the foothills of the Mount and waited. I'd already finished one coffee that had cost more than an entire meal in my neighborhood, and was seriously considering springing for a second, when the reporters arrived.

The human male was tall and dark haired, with a crisply trimmed beard. He wore a tailored suit in a rich green that matched his eyes, and there was a youthful spring in his step that made me feel exhausted just looking at him. Klare looked much as she always did, professional, serious, with eyes that took in everything and a camera slung over her shoulder.

She spotted me while her companion was still scanning the room. She headed my way, and he lengthened his stride to reach me first. Eager to impress and competitive. I filed it away for future reference.

"This is Jihan," said Klare. "He's the one writing this piece. Jihan, you know who this is."

His grin widened. "I do." He mock-bowed to the photographer. "Klare, when you told me you'd lined up security, I didn't realize what you had in mind. This is brilliant!" He turned back to me. "Pleasure to meet you," he said. "I didn't know what to think when Klare pitched me this idea, but I've got—"

"You knew to say yes," Klare spoke over him. "We don't have much time, so you go on outside, Jihan. I need a minute to make peace with the detective."

He nodded, and I heard him whisper "Brilliant!" on his way out.

When her compatriot was gone, I said, "You didn't tell your new partner? You must've spent a lot of capital at work to make this happen."

"All of it," she said. "And I didn't trust him to keep his mouth shut. But how could my editor pass up the idea of the dead man's partner photographing the scandalized Barekusu alongside the hero cop?"

"It'll sell papers."

"It might backfire. The press can't afford to be seen as bought and paid for. Unlike cops. Everyone knows you're corrupt already."

"Keep telling yourself you can make a difference snapping pictures," I said. "We'll keep risking our lives and putting away the bad guys."

Klare pushed into my space, the way she had at Mickey the Finn's. She stared me down, and her voice grew quieter, more intense. "When this is done, you'll lock Serrow up for what she did."

"If I can," I said, "I'll do it with pleasure."

"I'll hold you to that." Her biting jaws closed with a click, a sound not too distinct from the sound of a camera shutter closing. "Now let's go. Jihan gets nervous when I leave him on his own."

The Barekusu caravan had relocated, moving farther up the base of the Mount, away from the tragedy of the sinkhole. The camp was comprised of deceptively simple structures, wood and canvas tents with luxurious kusuma linings arranged in concentric circles around the center of the camp. The hum of generators indicated that they had electricity. A few Barekusu sat in a ring, playing instruments that were equal parts string and percussion, delicate fingers dancing along the necks, while powerful show hands thumped out a rhythm on the body. Several of the instruments showed signs of recent repair, likely damaged in the chaos of the sinkhole. Children frolicked around us or hid behind parents, reacting to strangers much like human children. The youngest were long-legged and awkward, their hair not yet grown out to the luxurious lengths of the adults.

As we walked through the camp, heads the size of my torso swung in our direction. They didn't appear to be shocked at our appearance or to perceive us as a threat. They simply followed our progress as we moved toward their leader. We had an appointment with Weylan.

Or rather, my companions did. Part of the fallout from Serrow's murder of Glouchester had been an agreement with the *Union Record* that they'd have a number of unfiltered interviews. Klare had managed to talk her superiors into letting her and me go and confront her partner's killer. Weylan had refused that, but agreed to meet with us himself. All the better for the PR moves. And me? I was simply working off-duty security, like a lot of cops. I'd been invited in along with Klare and Jihan, no warrant required. The power of the press at work.

We were led through the circles of tents and shelters. One tent was set aside from the rest, and a particularly broad-shouldered Barekusu crouched in front of it, massive show hands splayed in front of him, as if he were ready to spring forward. The tent flap was open, and I caught a glimpse of a familiar shape. Even if I hadn't noticed, the sudden stiffness in Klare's walk would have told me—that was where Serrow was confined for the time being.

Past the scandalized sorcerer's prison, we came to a larger-than-average tent and were left to perch uncomfortably on furniture built for Barekusu anatomy. There were a trio of low-slung, backless couches that looked like a cross section of an egg on a single pedestal. A side table held a pair of white rocks, each the size of my head and seated on sturdy wooden holders. The woodwork and upholstery on all the furniture was highly crafted, and would likely have cost far more than I could afford on a cop's salary. The reputation of the Barekusu as master traders was apparently well deserved.

In the center of the tent a small electric grill warmed a kettle of tea paste and a selection of dipping leaves. Shops in town had tried to capitalize on the caravan by selling Barekusu cuisine, but this particular snack's odor was pungently acidic, and I did my best to breathe through my mouth as we waited. Jihan flipped through the set of notes on a clipboard, while Klare took establishing shots. They both had a job to do, no matter what strings and pressure Klare had exerted to get them into this interview. Whereas I just had to sit back and prepare to throw a wrench in the works.

Eventually, the entry flaps pulled back, and Weylan's swaying bulk pressed into the tent. It was a larger space than most of the other tents we'd seen, and could easily hold several Barekusu at once, but it still felt tight with the larger being in such close proximity. Weylan moved over to the grill and scooped out a mug of tea paste, perhaps watching us or perhaps ignoring us completely—it was hard to say with the eye plates drawn tight.

He was medium-sized compared to the other Barekusu, though he moved perhaps a step less nimbly. It wasn't until he turned that I recognized the greenish fur, the fish stripes of black that ran along his back. This was the Barekusu who'd made eye contact with me during their parade into the city. And he was staring at me now, the bisected irises swirling and darting and refocusing on me. I reminded myself that I was there as a security guard, and was fully justified in studying his movements. So I did my best to give no thought to looking away. And when I did drop my eyes, I told myself that it was to make me seem less of a threat.

Both Klare and Jihan seemed to have a similar reaction. I wasn't familiar enough with Barekusu to read their body language, so maybe it was a pheromone or pure charisma, but Weylan had a presence that Serrow simply didn't match.

"I believe I am honored by your visit," he announced. "You may begin when you are ready to begin."

Jihan cleared his throat and glanced down at his notes. I stayed focused on Weylan. I'd met Serrow in tight quarters, and the smell had been strong, but here in the Barekusu guide's own tent it was far more intense. It wasn't quite hay, but it reminded me of a smell I'd encountered on a school field trip to a Therreau farm. Sweet, but undercut by something fetid. Weylan smelled like a perfumed beast of burden, bearing all our moral complications along the Path.

Finding his place in his notes, Jihan asked, "What are you looking forward to sharing with the citizens of Titanshade?" His first question was such a laughable softball that I almost thought it was self-parody.

"And what you do make of Guide Serrow's murderous rampage?" Klare asked her question from behind her camera, the lens no doubt providing a comforting barrier, as if Weylan couldn't reach out and crush it in the grip of his show hands, just like Serrow had crushed Glouchester's bones.

Weylan swiveled his neck, looking from one to the other. "Which is your question?"

Jihan was stone-faced. "I have a list of preapproved questions. Those are the only ones I can ask. What anyone else says, well," he shrugged, "that can be listed in the article or not, but it certainly may make for a more interesting conversation."

My estimation of the young reporter increased dramatically.

"Ah." Weylan rolled his neck, and sniffed the air. "I can smell the ambition on you, young man. And on your partner, rage."

"No one asked how we smell," said Klare. "And how evasive you are will be reflected in this write-up."

Weylan looked at her, and the shutter clicked, accompanied by a blinding flash. It was dark in the tent, and my eyes swam with the afterimages of Weylan and Klare. I blinked rapidly. Was she trying to use the camera as a weapon?

For his part, Weylan simply lowered his eye plates, and would no doubt be unfazed by another flash photo.

Jihan rubbed his eyes. "Yes. Well, okay. Next official question. Guide Weylan, what would you say are your three favorite places to visit in Titanshade?"

The Barekusu ignored him, his sly hands drumming a pattern on his mug of tea paste.

"And you, Officer? I believe that your reasons are your own."

"He's here to ask about Serrow." Klare popped in another flash. "Why you covered for her, and when you're going to stop."

"Serrow will be addressed," said Weylan. "She may be sent on a penance journey, or she may be ostracized. It will be decided in time."

"In your time, on your terms." Klare emphasized her disgust with low, threatening clicks.

"If she is ostracized, she will be shaved and left on the plains. It will not be a fate that anyone would care to share."

"Glouchester had information on you," she said, voice rising. "He knew you were corrupt, and he was going to expose you. And we're not going to let you get away with it!"

I clenched my hands into fists. This was the part I hated. I spoke slowly and at volume, saying, "I'm not here to talk about the murder."

Klare froze, mandibles quivering with silent rage. I looked away. There was no chance I could bring Serrow to trial for Glouchester's murder. But maybe I could prove that Serrow was the sorcerer behind Vandie's venture, and find justice for the victims of their buzzing madness and the nightmare transformations. Justice that both the dead and living deserved.

I did my best to not look at her. I was afraid that if I did, I'd beg for forgiveness. And I needed to focus on Weylan. "I'd like to talk to you about Vandie Cedrow."

Weylan threw his head back and lowed deep and resonant, a long note that would have exhausted my lung capacity. A few moments later a pair of Barekusu, even larger and more intimidating than Weylan, came in and pressed their heads against the reporters' backs. Furious, Klare stared at me as if I'd just betrayed her. Which, I suppose, is what I'd done.

The newly arrived Barekusu slid around the tent's perimeter, using their bulk to herd the reporters toward the entrance. Klare pushed back, even struck one of them with a balled fist, but she may as well have stood against an ocean wave.

She screamed at Weylan, "You agreed to be interviewed! You made a deal with the *Union Record*!"

For his part, Jihan looked just as frustrated, but kept his mouth shut. The Barekusu weren't overtly aggressive, but they were big. And he knew full well what had happened to the last reporter left alone with one of the caravan.

Klare shouted over her shoulder as they herded her out of the tent. "You know what? I think I can do it better than you after all. I think damn near anyone could do it better than you."

The Barekusu guards departed along with the media, leaving me alone with Weylan.

After a long moment staring at each other, the hulking guide spread his arms wide. "And now, Officer, I believe you have questions you'd like me to answer?"

39

"**Y**OU ARE THE HUMAN WHO lived through the manna strike," he said. "Are you here to kill me, little detective?"

I was taken aback. "No. I'm here to find the truth."

"Yet you might kill me, if I were to pose a threat."

"If you posed a threat, I would subdue you." This was not how I'd expected the conversation to go.

"And if I resisted?" He rose and stepped forward. Weylan wasn't large for a Barekusu but he still had almost twice my mass, and I'd seen firsthand how Serrow had crushed the life from Taran Glouchester. It took all my effort to not fall into a fighting stance. But the guide merely lifted the lid of the paste pot, refilled his mug, and settled back onto his couch with a sly handful of dipping leaves.

"Well," I said, "I'd attempt to deescalate. If not, and if you were a danger to me or others, then . . ." I left the imagery to Weylan. In all honesty, I wasn't quite sure what I could do if he got it in his head to threaten myself or someone else. I shrugged it off. "I don't think it'd do my career much good, so let's not put me in a situation where I have to explain a dead Barekusu to my boss."

"Hah." He spoke the word, rather than laughing. "Agreed." I wondered what Barekusu laughter would sound like.

"We are old, we Barekusu." Weylan stripped tea paste from the spoon with prehensile lips.

"Sure," I said. "You live a long time. Maybe what, five hundred years?"

His eye plates rose and fell, perhaps checking to see if I was mocking him or simply ignorant of Barekusu life spans. "Not quite that old," he said, "though on the walk here, I certainly felt it."

I kept my comments to myself.

"I believe I meant our species, Detective. We Barekusu are the oldest of the Families. We awoke on Eyjan, and wandered its valleys and mountains, its barren lands of salt and ice. We did not remember our history, of what had come before. But we learned of the Path. And we walked it alone. Until we found our first siblings, the Mollenkampi in the north and the Yaw to the south."

Barekusu, Mollenkampi, Yaw . . . That litany triggered a memory.

"Believe Me, Young Eagles Have Such Great Holidays." I couldn't remember the dirtier version Hanford had composed all those years ago.

Weylan rocked to one side. "I do not believe I follow that statement."

"It's a memory trick," I said. "Something we're taught in school to remember the order of the Family awakenings. We do the same thing for the planets and colors of the rainbow. My point is, you can skip the history lesson and answer the question."

"And this trick is how you remember things?"

"Depends on what it is. Some things we can't forget," I said, "even if we try."

Weylan's mouth worked, chewing over my words and the bitterness to be found in them. "I believe you have known great loss."

"I've mourned," I said, unwilling to give personal details.

"This is how we mourn," he said. Delicate sly hand fingers plucked a braid of hair along his shoulder. The gray and green pattern shone with an undercurrent of reddish-gold. Two different colors. "This is a cutting of my friend's mane. Woven into my own hair, close to my body. I carry her and her memory with me."

I nodded. "She's always with you."

"Wherever I journey, she is there," he said. "But not for always. Her hairs are entwined with mine. Over time, the coat grows out and falls away. Over time, the same with sorrow. We carry them until they are shed, as all things eventually shall be."

I'd felt something like that myself. It had taken me a long time to say goodbye to Jenny. And I'd carried a connection long after her death.

I stepped to one side, tilting my head as if getting a better look at the fur, making note of the speed with which Weylan tracked my movements. The aging Barekusu was able to follow me easily. I didn't think it would be impossible to get the jump on him, but near enough to make the idea useless.

"When you spoke of Serrow," I said, "you said she'd be ostracized, shaved and abandoned."

"I believe I did."

"So she'd lose her loved ones' hair as well as her own."

"You begin to understand."

"Not really," I said. "I don't understand why Serrow was helping Vandie Cedrow. But I think she wouldn't have done that without your instruction. So that's my question, Weylan. Why did you help Vandie alter the geo-vents? What's in those vents that you wanted to find?"

The amount of governmental protection draped over the Barekusu meant I might not be able to arrest him, but I sure as Hells could push him for the truth.

"We found the other Families over the centuries as they awoke." He was back on the history lecture. "Though they woke with missing memories, scattered thoughts, and shattered languages, we helped them unite. Through it all, the way of the One True Path was a beacon."

"Tell me what's in the vents. What are you looking for?" I stepped to the side, stooping slightly to peer up in between the eye plates. The movement seemed to shock Weylan and he reared back, sliding off the couch and raising a thick-fingered show hand between us. But the motion was defensive, and I had no fear he might strike out. Not then.

"Why do you want to know what's down there?" I held my ground. "Validation of your faith? Proof that the Path is great and glorious and eternal?"

"For a detective, I find that you do not listen as well as you might."

"Insults won't distract me. I want to know what you came here to find."

"We are here because of the manna strike, as everyone knows," he said. "And when everyone believes such a thing, it must be true."

There was something different in his voice. I didn't have enough experience to read Barekusu body language and tones, but even I could tell that the idea of belief versus truth was a sore spot. An interesting hang-up for a guide.

"You came into the city singing a song," I said.

"'Requiem for the Titan's Hade,'" he said. "You weep for the Titan, correct? It seemed a respectful choice."

"Respectful is a funny term, considering you paid to burrow into his tomb."

He ignored the jab, humming a low note as he lifted the white rocks from the table, one in each show hand.

"What's in the vents?" I asked.

"Evidence, Detective. Something you should appreciate."

He was getting on my nerves. "Evidence of what?"

"Evidence of absence. There is nothing there but foul-smelling hot air. There is no Titan. There never was a Titan. You and I and all of us are playthings for whatever it is that watches from the shadows, laughing and weeping at our failures in equal measure."

Stunned, I found myself falling back on grade-school lessons. "The Titan blazed a trail. He's a sain—"

"A saint of the Path? A forgotten god? A divine being who somehow can't get out from under a pile of dirt and rock?" Eye horns creaked, and four irises spun and separated, studying me as he lifted the pair of white rocks from the table, balancing them like the scales of justice. "No, little detective, your mythical friend blazed no trail, and did not create the Path."

"Then what did?" I struggled slightly to keep my tone level. I hadn't realized how much Weylan's self-righteousness angered me.

"We are all stray pups," Weylan lowered one of the rocks, allowing it to disappear behind the fringe of fur, "plucked up by forces we don't understand."

"What kind of forces? Saints, demons, or sorcerers?"

"That is the question, little detective! That is the question indeed. Perhaps it is something alien, or perhaps mere superstition." He raised the other rock overhead. "The first Barekusu on Eyjan were alone and scared, so they created a methodology. Having no memory of what had come before or what was ahead, they decided that behind and ahead were merely more of the same. An eternal path, looping back on itself. Think what it must have been like, when my grandmother's great-grandmother awoke. The Path let her focus on the moment. And that was needed. And when we found the Mollenkampi, what did we do? These small but powerful warriors who lived in the far northern reaches, who had no memory and were just as confused as we had been?"

"You taught them." The words came automatically, a recital of the simple lesson taught in every school around the world: The Barekusu taught the Families about the Path. In Titanshade it was as ubiquitous in textbooks as drawings of a handsome Titan, chained beneath the Mount.

"Not quite. They asked questions and we encouraged them to come to their own answers." He drew his right arm back from underneath his fur, the three grasping fingers of his show hand empty. A bit of stage trickery. He'd no doubt transferred it to the sly hand on that arm. "Telling isn't effective. Skillful teaching is to let others come to conclusions on their own, never knowing they've been guided. And the most skillful of teachers convince the students that the questions are theirs, as well. A beautiful lie that reveals the truth."

"So you're saying . . ." At some point I'd clenched my fists so tight that the knuckles ached. "What *are* you saying? That the Path isn't real?"

"I believe I am one of a few guides on all of Eyjan who has access to the oldest of our records. I wove my knowledge from scraps of documents and oral tradition. Like the pages of a book scraped clean of ink, the original sources for the Path are scrubbed of the truth. But if we take that book and reconstruct the white space, what remains are the ink-black letters. So too the forms of the truth take shape." Weylan stretched the empty show hand backward, revealing the sly hand. It was empty as well. I blinked. *Where the Hells is that rock?*

"Why are you telling me this?" The idea of this pompous, condescending deceiver implying that we were similar, that we were anything alike made me so angry, so furious that he'd come to our city and betrayed our trust, betrayed *me* . . .

"You said it yourself. You are here for the truth. You and I are alike, Detective. Kindred hearts who never stop digging, even on holy ground, when we might upset order, and threaten the wealthy and powerful. Plus, we both have the public's good graces, at least for now. We can bring the public to pursue the truth. Though it may take a bit of deception to get them there. Just as the Path brought stability and peace."

I tried to focus on his argument. "What about wars? What about everyday cruelty? Where's your peace and prosperity when I start each day with fresh homicides?"

He was unnervingly still, almost vulnerable. "Perhaps it is superstition, or perhaps it is an unknowable force. There are those who believe the Path encompasses many worlds and many walkers. They believe that Dream Sight allows us to see through great distances, glimpses of what is and what should never be. For those, Eyjan is a spiritual fulcrum, and the paths of all the worlds hang on the ability of the eight Families to live in harmony. They believe that of all the many worlds, Eyjan is the chosen one. And of all the many walkers of the Path, there is one chosen to help right the scales." He ruffled his sly hands through the fine fur that fueled the Barekusu economy.

I pressed harder. "You tell me there's nothing in the vents. If that's so, then there's no reason to dig, no reason to bankroll Vandie Cedrow's operation. No reason for any of it."

"Poor little Vandra Cedrow. She's made a great medicine of revenge, hoping to cure her grief. You should understand that, Detective, as one who has done the same."

"Opening a sinkhole is a far cry from weaving a loved one's fur into your coat," I said.

"Yet Vandie is caught, and has announced that Ambassador Paulus is her ally. Now all that's required is to let the dominoes fall. Do your job, Detective, and all will be well."

"I doubt that very much."

"The reason I came to Titanshade," he said, "is that sometimes, someone is chosen to capture a moment. Moments such as this." He raised his left arm. When I hadn't noticed, he'd transferred the second rock to that sly hand. It was a simple deceit, but it infuriated me so much I almost doubled over. I realized what was happening even as I stepped toward him, hands rising. Talking to me alone, the buzzing rocks, the vulnerable, open stance.

Weylan wanted me to attack him.

With his size and strength advantage, I was unlikely to kill him, but an attack would make him a sympathetic figure. A martyr wounded for his cause. I forced myself to hold my position, then to fall back a step.

We stared at one another, me breathing fast, him working his great lips, almost ready to speak. I counted to ten and focused on my breathing. I used every trick the department shrinks had given me to work with, teetering on the edge between rage and restraint.

Then I thought of Talena and her mom, of Jax and Hanford, Guyer and Bryyh. Of Gellica. I thought of all the people who'd suffer if I lost control. I found my center and sucked in a deep, cleansing breath. The buzzing began to recede.

"The chosen, huh?"

I thought of the manna strike, and how I'd been touched by the iridescent rain of manna spraying up from far below ground. I thought about how it pried into my head, whispered things I didn't want to hear. I thought of the way Weylan had paused during the parade and stared at me in the street, and the way he tried to entrap me now.

"No." I was sick of being labeled a hero to sell newspapers, sick of being whispered about and speculated about. And damn sick of being manipulated by the buzzing hunger of manna. "I'm not chosen for anything. I'm not special."

The Barekusu stepped back, irises swirling. He shook his head rapidly, like a dog shedding water. His ears tips flapped and his lips puckered, as if he were singing a silent *ooo*. I stared, realization dawning that this is what he looked like when he laughed.

It took a moment for him to compose himself, during which he set the white rocks back in their cradles. The buzzing cut off immediately. "Hah. No, little detective, you are not chosen. You are a novelty. A brief-lived human who happened to be in the proximity of great events."

"I was the first living thing touched by the manna." For someone who'd just insisted he wasn't special, even to my ear I sounded offended.

"Were you? Even in the ice plains there are insects and bacteria. Even below ground worms tunnel through the earth. Are any of them touched by fate, any bacteria with a special connection allowing them to alter the course of history?" He shook his head again, though less violently this time. "No. Your thought is endearing, but misguided. You are not the one who has been chosen." He raised his eye plates and stared at me. "I am."

"Chosen for what?" I said. "Why are you even here?"

"To find the truth," he said, "and to drag it out into the light, kicking and screaming." His nostrils flared, and the heat of his breath moved over me. "To shove it into the faces of the people, and make them look at it. How they choose to reconcile their hearts with it is out of my power."

"All you wanted was to show people an empty hole."

"The furthest thing from that. I believe everyone on the Path must dig for their own truth. For that to happen, there must be study, must be research, must be excavation."

"Excavation?"

"Of one's own psyche, of course." Weylan dragged a sly hand through his chin hairs. "Though one must wonder, *why* are you people so averse to digging? You don't bury your dead, you barely dig foundations for your buildings. It's as though you've transferred all your instinct for the ground into the oil wells. Don't you appreciate the secrets that lie beneath your feet?"

I stepped past Weylan, no longer fighting off the sense of anger and betrayal. Moving toward the rocks on their pedestal, hand stretched out. "And you were willing to let people die for that?"

The guide's hairy forearm blocked me from getting too close. No doubt he feared I'd touch them, and make him lose control. It'd have been a death sentence for me, as well as for his plans.

"How many people have died in your various pursuits of the truth?" he asked.

I gave him my most condescending smile. I hadn't been reaching for the rocks. There were manna threads on the rocks, plummeting straight down, linking to something beneath our feet. Weylan was using next gen manna. That meant I could sabotage it.

"A lot fewer than died in yours," I said, and lowered my hand.

"Perhaps," said the aging Barekusu. "Perhaps that's true." He turned his head, and stared upward, as if looking through the tent ceiling at the Mount. "But what is it worth to break our mental shackles? We need to fly, Detective. We need to *soar*. But the lies we tell ourselves will always tether us back to the ground." He rounded on me, the thick horn of his eye plates rising once more. "It has been a long time indeed since I visited Titanshade. When this is done, I don't believe I shall return. Go home, Detective." He breathed out a great huff of air, riding on a low, humming note. "Go home, seeker of light. You don't belong here any more than I do."

I started to protest, to tell him he was wrong. But Weylan had already turned away.

He threw back his head and lowed, a deep and resonant note that reverberated in my chest. From all around, the rest of the caravan echoed the tone. I stepped back, uncertain how to react. Weylan's sly hands danced in quick rhythm, and his lowing picked up a half-step, turning into the first notes of the song the caravan had sung as they entered town. "Requiem for the Titan's Hade."

I walked away. And the song named for a dead god who'd never existed echoed from the sacred hills as I descended into the filth and corruption of Titanshade.

40

I LEFT THE FOOTHILLS OF THE Mount in a daze, only passingly aware of my path as I wandered the streets of the city. I hopped a bus, and took a seat across from a guy determined to alert everyone else on the bus that we were all worms raveling through the corpse of a giant, and that the key to truth was encoded on the back of breakfast cereal boxes. He rattled on, until a woman across the aisle finally had enough and told him to shut up. He pushed her; she hit him with her purse. Other passengers stepped in, and the prophet of worms and destruction soon found himself cowering beneath the seats, shielding himself from the kicks and blows of the crowd. It occurred to me that if the guy had been wealthy or influential, it would have gone different. Maybe in a week the talking heads on the news would be debating our inherent worminess.

Weylan was a fanatic. Maybe he wasn't born one, maybe he hadn't been one for the entirety of his centuries-long reign as one of the continent's spiritual guides, but at some point he'd become convinced that he had the one single truth.

I wasn't a religious guy. Never have been. But I observed the old practices, and found comfort in the notion that though our steps were unique, we were all on one true Path, each of us merging into a single great journey.

Reluctantly, I stood and announced myself, badge held high. I slid between the combatants, and asked if the woman was hurt. She wasn't, and once things calmed down, I asked the driver to stop and kicked worm man off the bus. I told him he was lucky to walk away with only a bloody nose and bruised dignity. He shot me an obscene gesture as the doors closed. The bus lurched forward with the hiss of hydraulics and a plume of black exhaust, and I rode on.

Eventually, I got off at the Sylvan neighborhood, a spot on the southeast edge of the Borderlands. I walked briskly, both because of the chill in the air—I hadn't brought my overcoat to the warm-weather meeting in the Barekusu camp—and also because I had no desire to attract any of the desperate characters clinging to the shadows at alley mouths. Not to mention that I had a specific destination in mind.

Still, I almost missed it. The small green and white sign over a narrow doorway looked like an apartment walk-up entrance, rather than a commercial property. I stood in front of it for a long moment, wondering if I was making a mistake. But of all the people I knew, at that moment there was only one I truly wanted to talk to. I pushed open the door, crossed the threshold of the Sylvan Community Center, and asked for Talena Michaels.

A young woman welcomed me, and asked me to wait in the common area while she consulted with Talena. As she walked away it dawned on me that she'd pulled loose her curls and braids, letting her hair flow as free as Dinah McIntire had at the festival. I wondered how quickly fashion trends traveled the globe.

While I waited, I stared at the walls, covered with hanging files stuffed with informational brochures. Voting rights, renter's rights, free clinics, and guides to the city for newcomers fought for space with support networks for any one of a dozen different addictions, traumas, and fears. Almost all the brochures highlighted some sort of inspirational prayer—Talena's activism had always been tied to her fervent faith. Any free space was festooned with photos of smiling clients at rallies and picnics, protests and religious ceremonies. All of them wore the ba, the symbol of the Path. It was like the Bullpen, but the workers were twenty years younger and the photos were beaming faces rather than corpses and mug shots. It would have been moving, if Weylan hadn't made me doubt everything it was based on. From across the room the woman I'd spoken to waved me over.

Talena didn't have a separate office. Her desk merged in with all the others. But the respect and deference the others showed her was evident by the glances they sent my way, as if warning this aging stranger that he'd better not have ill intentions toward their leader. The child I'd helped raise had become a woman whose influence was growing as fast as the list of people she'd helped. And I was about to tell her it was all based on a lie.

She didn't stand as I approached, but she did look up from a list of names on her desk. Most likely she'd been doing some fundraising.

"I don't know why you always think I can help with your cases," she said. "Contrary to your way of thinking, not everyone in this city knows each other."

"No, I . . ." The open layout meant that anyone could potentially overhear us. But what Weylan had told me wasn't the kind of thing I could keep to myself. "Is there somewhere we can talk privately?"

"Is this serious? Because I've got a lot to do tonight. And the last time we talked, you were halfway into one of your barroom black-outs."

"It's serious," I said.

She sighed, but called out across the room, "Hey, Elaine, is there a consult room available?"

A petite Gillmyn in thick-rimmed glasses responded without looking up from her filing. "Room B is open."

"Follow me," Talena said, moving to the rear of the center, passing Elaine on the way.

There was a table and three chairs, one of which Talena plopped into before propping her elbows on the table. "What do you want to tell me? Or do you want me to do some kind of favor for you?"

"I just got back from talking to Weylan," I said. Her eyebrows went up, probably as close to impressed as she'd be willing to give me. "And I need to tell you about it."

I told her everything.

As I spoke, Talena began to look away. Her eyes moved around the room, to the volunteers and information and photos, none of which would be around if not for her faith in the Path. By the end, she simply stared at the table between us. When I was done, she was quiet for a long, long time. Finally she raised her head.

"Do you remember when I was a kid, and kept sneaking out to the arcade? Mom flipped her shit at the idea of me going out alone."

"Oh, I remember." Jenny's temper had been fierce, and the idea that anyone would put her daughter at risk, even if it was Talena herself, made her quick to fury.

"Yeah, so remember what she told me?"

I did. "Grannie Greenteeth."

"Grannie Greenteeth who lived in the sewer, waiting for little kids walking alone at night." She trailed off for a heartbeat, then smiled. "When Mom got it in her head to be colorful, she could get downright harsh."

I remembered Jenny's colorful language when she was upset with me. "Yeah."

Talena pushed back a loose shirtsleeve and rolled it tight against her forearm. "Granny Greenteeth wasn't real, but the danger was. If we can use things like that to steer kids right, why can't we use a story to steer all of us in the right direction? And if someone did, some Barekusu con man storyteller who figured that all these new species popping up and threatening the world needed some guidance, is that a bad thing?"

"It isn't real," I said.

She grinned. "You know what's real? This." She pointed at the walls of the community center, and the letters and pictures that lined them, each one a story of loss and hope and redemption. It was unchanged from when I'd seen it earlier, but now instead of a litany of false promises, I recognized it as a catalog of real, verifiable change for the better. A hundred candles lighting the night as a blizzard raged all around. "Every one of these stories is true, Carter, no matter what inspired them. And those stories? They're what can change the world."

"Everything you do, everything you risk. Can you honestly say you'd still do that if you'd have known that the Barekusu were making it all up, that there's no Path, no Titan, none of the saints and demons and things that matter?"

She looked away, lips twisted, as if she were truly giving it some consideration. When she spoke, it was with complete confidence. "What do you think I'm going to do when you leave here? Do you think I'm going to stop?"

I half smiled. The thought was ludicrous. "No. But—"

"Carter!" She leaned forward, shaking her head. "I don't help people because I have faith. I have faith *because* I help people."

"Faith in what?"

"In the ability to create change. To make things better, one tiny step at a time." Talena raised a hand, preventing me from interjecting. "Look, I'm not saying I enjoy hearing about this conversation with Weylan, but . . ." She hesitated. "Did you tell Jax?"

"No."

"Don't." She bit her lip before continuing. "At least not now. It'd distract him. That man has more on his mind than he should, and he doesn't need a theological crisis right now."

"But you go to guideposts," I said. "And all those books you read about the Path and the Titan . . . They're lies."

"The ones that showed him as a big buff guy in chains? Honestly, I never thought of him like that." She chuckled. "Books, saints, guideposts . . . They're great, but they're just aides. Rituals to help me remember something important."

"Like the order of the Families." There was something about that, something I was right on the edge of grasping.

"You mean Believe Me, Young Eagles . . . ? I guess so." She cocked her head, staring at me like a puzzled dog. "I mean, you know there's no actual eagles on holiday, right?"

But I was staring at the far wall, toward the Mount, toward my apartment where stolen audio tapes and torn notebook pages held answers I'd failed to recognize.

"A mnemonic device." I practically heard the puzzle pieces snap into place. "Laughing Larry. It's not a poem or a code. Hells below."

I bolted from her office. I wasn't sure what I believed, but I had a riddle to unravel. And that was something I could get my head around.

IT WAS LATE EVENING BY the time I left Talena's, and all the government offices were long since closed. So I had to wait until the morning to get into the MEB.

The Municipal Engineering Building was located farther leeward than the Bunker, but that wasn't a reflection of their respective influences. The police investigated crimes and had the power to imprison. The MEB held the reins of progress. Without their approval, no construction could happen, no development could occur. The department was notoriously fickle, and it was a commonly held belief that its employees operated mostly on bribes and kickbacks rather than direct salary. The contractors I drank with at Mickey the Finn's told twenty different jokes about inspections, but they all had the same punchline. "Is it gonna pass? MEB-e yes, MEB-e no."

The waiting room was a study in false wood paneling, with orange carpet and dingy yellow fluorescent lights. Shockingly modern design for a government building.

Next to the take-a-number stand a hand-written sign read: *Temporary Geo-Vent Map, ten taels (cash only).* The geo-vent layouts were complex and not fully understood, but a combination of old record-keeping and echo-location helped MEB ensure that there was little to no disruption of the vents during construction work. Now everyone was scrambling to understand what impact the sinkhole would have on this system. But the revised maps weren't what I was after.

I took a number and waited with a group of equally long-faced patrons. After a period of painful inactivity punctuated by the occasional customer service event, I was called to the front.

"I need a copy of the pre-sinkhole geo-vent map," I said.

The woman at the counter pointed at the sign. "New ones are ten taels."

"I understand, but I want the old one."

She turned and shouted into the back room, "Karl! There's a man here, wants a copy of the *old* geo-vent maps."

"We got the new ones printed!"

"I told him! The man wants old."

There were footsteps, and an aggravated human with rambunctiously hairy eyebrows peered at the woman, and then me.

"Old map's no good." His voice was a combination of disbelief and annoyance. "Use the temporary map, until the fixes are final. Then come back and buy the finalized version. Only thing you can do."

"It's for a historical survey," I said.

The wiry salt and pepper of his eyebrows twitched. "New map's already printed."

"I understand. I need the old—"

He turned and was gone. The woman called out the next number.

"Hold on," I said, "is he coming back, or do I—"

"Wait over there. Next!"

She'd indicated a separate waiting area, this one without even the pretense of seating. But I shuffled and stood, and eventually the man reappeared. I paid the two tael copy fee, wondered briefly about the price difference, then set it out of my mind as I made my escape back to the Bunker.

The Bunker was a blur of activity. Vandie Cedrow's warning about the festival was the worst-kept secret in department history. In the day and a half since Vandie had indicated that the festival was a target, the grounds had been visited by representatives from the military encampment stationed at the manna strike. All of which had turned up nothing. The festival promoters steadfastly refused to allow a police presence. With its location outside the city's sphere of influence, the TPD couldn't force their way in. The military might have been able to, but considering that the charges against Paulus reflected back on the AFS itself, it was essentially a no-win situation for them. If they found something, its presence would be blamed on them, and if they failed to find something the eventual disaster would be blamed on them as well.

Now the city government was trying to walk a political tightrope. If they showed too much aggression they risked a response from the federal military encampment. If they didn't respond immediately to any call for assistance from Titanshade citizens, they'd face being voted out of power.

Vandie claimed that the attack was planned for the climax of the festival's final night, during Dinah McIntire's set, just as the clear southern window of the tent was to showcase the moon cresting the Mount. Not wanting to cause a panic, the city had begun to urge concertgoers to return early, or skip the final night. It barely moved the needle. Now we were on the penultimate night of the show, the last chance to put together a plan before time ran out.

To do that, I had to talk to Guyer. I spotted her in the hallway and I jogged to catch up.

"I'm busy, Carter." She had an armful of folders and a scowl that made it clear she was about to walk into an unpleasant talk. I matched her pace.

"Look," I whispered, putting my hand on her shoulder, redirecting her from the meeting room she'd been headed for. "You wanted to hear how I got this connection? Fine. I'll tell you everything."

She frowned, but allowed us to coast past the room. A group of impatient techs glared at us through the open door.

"What's the catch?"

I took a breath. "I need you to cover for me at tomorrow's medical exam."

Guyer squinted at me. "You want me to write you a note? I'm not your doctor."

"No, but you do have the clout to keep Baelen from sniffing at my heels for a day or two."

One of the techs stuck his head out the door. Guyer waved him off with a curt, "One minute!"

"Guyer, I need a little freedom, and Baelen can't be peering over my shoulder right now." Exasperation was creeping into my voice. I gathered myself and continued. "Come on, the department's going in circles because no one can figure out how to deal with the festival, and Vandie Cedrow's real conspirators are running loose."

She opened her mouth to protest, and I added, "Please."

Guyer exhaled through flared nostrils as she sized me up.

"Can you have this wrapped by Friday?"

"One way or another," I said. I didn't mention that the other option might see me dead.

She leaned back, her shoulders to the wall, arms crossed between us. "Fine. I'll come up with something that will keep Baelen busy for a couple days. Happy?"

"That's all I ask." I hesitated, and she frowned.

"What is it, Carter?"

"Well, there is one more thing." I gave her my most winning smile. "What are you doing this evening?"

When I saw Jax I asked him to come by my apartment as well, then I put in a call to Jankowski, Paulus and Gellica's lawyer. Next I grabbed some takeout and hustled home. I had a few hours to eat and prepare before anyone arrived. When the first knock came on my door, I opened it up and let Ajax inside.

"I hope this is worth it," he said. He took a seat on the couch, where Rumple immediately began parading back and forth along the back cushions, as if showing off the apartment to a friend.

"It has to be," I said. "Vandie says the next attack is tomorrow, the last day of the festival."

"Since when do we believe her?"

"I think she's lying about where, but not when," I said. "She wants as many people out of town as possible on that specific date and time. There's a reason for that."

Another knock at the door, and I rose to let Guyer into my home. She waved hello to Ajax, then did a slow pirouette in the center of the room.

"I knew people who lived like this in school. At least the couch is nice." She flopped down on the easy chair and held up a hand for Rumple to sniff in greeting. "So you got me here. Congratulations. Now what's the big secret you want to talk about? Are we going to have to drag it out of you?"

"No, the time for secrets is long past." I cocked my head. "Did you hear something?"

The sound came again. A tap, rather than a knock, and not from the door. I crossed to the room and opened the blinds. Gellica stood on the fire escape, arms crossed. I raised the window sash.

"I wasn't sure you'd come," I said, stepping back.

"Not sure why I did." She kicked a leg up and over the window ledge, entering my apartment.

Gellica took two steps and paused at the edge of the room. Maybe it was seeing Jax and Guyer. Maybe it was seeing the couch she'd given me as a breakup letter. Maybe it was because the whole thing just kept getting weirder.

Jax's biting jaws clacked. Rumple was no longer prowling the couch behind him. "Surprised to see you, Acting Ambassador. That's an unusual way to make an entrance."

"Hello, Ajax." Gellica nodded to him. "I had to slip away from the press, as well as some of your colleagues who are watching me."

"Well, I'm glad you did," I said. That surveillance was the reason I'd reached out to her through Jankowski. I took a moment to prop the window open, then took the only open seat, on the couch beside Gellica. "This is almost everyone we need."

"Almost?"

"Enough to get started." I made introductions between Guyer and Gellica. They looked at each other for two uncomfortable breaths, the DO with her head tilted, the diplomat straight-backed and calm.

"Huh." Guyer turned back to me. "Interesting company you keep."

I chuckled. "Weylan said something similar to me yesterday."

All three of them stared.

Guyer held up both hands in a stop-right-there motion. "You spoke to Weylan?"

"Yeah."

"What's he like?"

"He's a regular person. Just another asshole whose ego is going to get people killed." I cleared my throat. "Speaking of which, Vandie Cedrow has everyone in the Bunker and City Hall panicked about an attack on the festival."

"Not everyone," said Guyer. Jax nodded agreement, rolling one of Rumple's glittering toys across his palm.

"She's got no reason to mess with the festival," he said. "She wants change in the heat distribution, not to hurt people."

"That hasn't stopped her so far," Guyer said.

"She hasn't done any of this on her own," I said. "And she's not the one who poses a danger now." I brought them up to speed on my conversation with Weylan, and his particular flavor of self-important delusion.

"Does he just want to destroy the city?" asked Guyer.

Jax had been silent during my recap, but he spoke up now. "I think Weylan wants us to dig. He's been pushing for it in all his public appearances. If he's desperate to find the truth, he may think it's buried under Titanshade. The Titan is one of the few stories that the Barekusu didn't help form. Weylan wants to know what's under our feet, but the city has so many moral proscriptions against digging inside the city limits. He thinks the only way we'll do it is if he starts the hole himself."

"Someone needs to stop him," I said. "And it's looking like that someone is us."

"Carter," Gellica said my name like a parent about to tell their kid that the street-corner imps on Titan's Day aren't real. "I'm a diplomat." She pointed at Guyer. "She interrogates dead people. You and Jax arrest murderers in alleys. You need a spelunker with demolitions expertise." She dropped her hands onto the couch, as if perplexed by the whole question. "Don't you have a bomb squad or something?"

Jax chimed in. "There was no sign of explosives at the first sinkhole. There's no reason to assume they'd change their methodology at this point."

"There's no reason to assume they won't, either."

"Alright," I said. "We'll just call up the bomb squad and let them know that they need to ignore their orders to go to the festival so that they can tag along for a forbidden excursion into the geo-vents that might get them killed, but will almost certainly end their career."

"Wow," said Guyer. "You really know how to sell me on this, don't you?"

"This isn't police work," I said. "This is knowing that people are going to die, and there's only one way to stop it." I turned to Gellica. "The sad truth is that you've got more pull in the department than we do."

"Used to, maybe," she said. "After you arrested Paulus, any influence I had faded like morning fog. No one wants to stick their neck out for an ambassador sitting in jail. Or her lame-duck placeholder." She traced the flower pattern on the couch that had once been hers. "No, until Paulus is released, we're in this alone."

"There's another reason I don't want to bring in more players," I said. I was kneeling by the side table, and now pushed myself onto my ass. Jax and Guyer had a professional respect, and the trust of one cop for another. But I also needed them to trust Gellica. And while I couldn't tell them her secret, I could make it clear I trusted her with my own. "The three of you know about my . . ." I waved my left hand, displaying the missing fingers. "My knack for feeling manna in the air."

"A knack you said you'd explain," Guyer said. "And tell us how it started."

"It's just a best guess." I cleared my throat and began. "I noticed it about five years back. With my ex."

"Your wife?" said Guyer. To my right, Gellica stiffened almost imperceptibly.

"We never got around to formalizing it." I paused, then added, "We weren't exactly together when she got sick. But people can matter even if you can't make a relationship work." Gellica looked away.

"Good news for you, considering your track record with relationships." Guyer said it with a smirk.

"She had cancer."

Guyer's smirk faded. I'd be lying if I said I didn't take a little satisfaction in that. It was irrational, but on some level I wanted the entire world to feel Jenny's loss. "When she was getting real sick, we tried an operation. Marrow transfer. Experimental treatment."

The others said nothing.

"It bought her a little time. I was grateful for that, and I was grateful to the place that gave that gift." I took a breath, and pressed on. "After the surgery the staff shifted her room unexpectedly a number of times. Because of "turnover" they said. I always managed to find her, even when the staff gave me bad directions. We used to joke that she was a magnet, pulling me home. But that's exactly what she was. We were linked."

I looked around my circle of friends.

"After she died, she went up the Mount, to be taken by the Sky Shepherds." The broad-winged birds rode the thermals around the Mount, and carried the remains of loved ones back into nature's embrace. "But they missed part of her." I squinted, eyes stinging slightly. "And I felt it. For years, I felt her up there." I cleared my throat. To tell any more would be too much. More than they needed to know, and certainly far more than I was willing to share.

"The place that treated you," said Jax. "That created this bond . . ."

"The Cedrow Care Center." I forced my jaw to relax. Even saying the words enraged me. Jenny's suffering had made us both Harlan Cedrow's first round of lab rats. "We were the early tests of the human compasses that eventually led to the discovery of the manna well."

Guyer stared at me, mouth open. "Why haven't you told the world about this?"

"Because I had zero proof," I said. "Beyond a literal feeling in my bones. And now even that's gone. The point is that Jenny and I had a manna bond. So all this talk about next gen manna and the strike? I don't know if it's even relevant."

Guyer exhaled, a long, exaggerated breath that made it clear she thought all of this may be irrelevant.

"When you were in that C3 lab," Gellica was restrained, her arms and legs tucked tight to her body, and there was urgency in her voice, "how many others were in there?"

I spread my hands. "Dozens. No idea if they got the manna bond or not. No idea if they're affected now or not. Maybe there's many people out there just like me."

Beside me, Gellica winced, and I knew she was wondering how many other people shared our connection to magic. But Jax sat forward, a college kid happy to wrestle with a mental puzzle.

"Probably not," he said. "The buzzing and associated killings have happened around the city. But the transformations have only occurred when you're in the area."

"We don't know that's even connected to me," I said.

Jax nodded. "And we don't know if Vandie is lying about the festival being threatened. But here we are."

I took a breath. "Okay. I don't know what's causing the transformations. But I'm not doing it consciously, and it doesn't feel like it's going through me. The connection I have is more than feeling the threads. I'm like a battery for next gen manna. I can absorb it and redirect it into other threads made with next gen manna."

"What if . . ." Guyer rolled her head, fingertips dragging along her jawline and down her neck. "What if Carter was primed by the early Cedrow experiment, then triggered at the strike site?"

Jax sat forward. "That would explain why no one else seems to have the same ability to affect the threads. Some were primed but not inundated, others inundated but not primed."

"Like being soaked in kerosene and handed a sparkler," I said. "Neither one will kill you, but the combination is explosive."

The others stared at me. "Look, I don't know the whys or the hows. But I've told you everything I do know. The three of you are the only ones who know about this."

Gellica tensed. "And you're sure no one else has this kind of extra-sorcerous connection?"

She was wondering if I'd betrayed her own magical origin story.

"As far as I know? Absolutely not." I held her eye for a moment, and her shoulders eased downward, relaxing.

"In fact," I said, "as far as we know, Heidelbrecht never told Vandie's dear old uncle Harlan exactly what he was doing that exposed the geo-vents. We'll probably never know for sure, and it doesn't matter. Because what we've got right now is Vandie distracting the entire city's resources while an untouchable religious figure is pulling some kind of delusional savior trip."

"We can't roll into their camp and arrest Weylan," Jax said. "Even if we could convince some judge to sign off on a warrant, he wouldn't be charged. Look at how Serrow walked away from murder, and that's with a body *and* a confession. There's nothing we can do, unless we witness him altering the tunnels with our own eyes."

I smiled. "Luckily, I know where they're headed next."

Jumping up, I stalked into the kitchen, returned with the map, and spread it flat on the coffee table. Guyer and Jax leaned forward to get a better look. Gellica was on the couch, still idly tracing the flower pattern. I pulled my attention away from her and back to the map.

"Okay, Paulus's old warehouse that Vandie occupied is here. Jax, hand me that pencil, please."

He did, and I marked the warehouse under a big W.

"This is an old geo-vent map," I said. "Which means it was current when Heidelbrecht made his report to the dearly departed Harlan Cedrow. And when Vandie wrote this." I showed them the page of notebook and the sentence about Laughing Larry.

Gellica rubbed her brow. "Who's Laughing Larry?"

"Not who, where." I grinned. "It's a mnemonic device. Because if you get lost, you need something to help find your path."

"To where?" Gellica asked. She smelled like sandalwood and proilers, which I did my best to ignore.

"They can't create a sinkhole just anywhere. They need another cavern, like the first one. The mnemonic is a set of directions from here." I tapped the geo-vent map, where I'd written a W. "This is Paulus's warehouse. Laughing, Larry Doesn't Rightly Realize, and so on. Left, left, down, right, right." I traced the route's dozen-odd steps across the vent map. "Look where it ends up."

I moved my hand, revealing a spot in the city center, not far from the Bunker itself.

"Think about the destruction from the first sinkhole," I said. "Now consider how many people are in apartments and office buildings, how many lives will be shattered if it happens there."

They stared at the map's confusing array of squiggles and marks. Slowly, I watched realization spread across their faces.

"Are you sure?" Jax asked. One mandible tapped a beat on his jaw.

"Pretty sure."

"Any chance you could get more specific?" Jax said.

"On a scale of one to ten?" I raised all my fingers. "About an eight."

Guyer interrupted us. "Okay, even if this is right, what you do want to do about it?"

"I want your help to stop Weylan."

She sat back, arms crossed.

"I saw you in Auberjois's office," I told the DO. "I saw the anger. You know this is bullshit, and you know that we need to do something about it."

"No, we don't. Someone does, but that doesn't mean—"

"Oh, well, let's just wait around for *someone* to step up and do the right thing. Because we all know how well that works, right? Just look around at the city, and see all the people stepping up to do the right thing." I pointed at Jax. "That double homicide with all the witnesses? I'm sure they'll come forward any day now, so that the CaMachios' parents can know that their sons' killers have been caught."

"I get it."

"Or hey, maybe someone will step up and do something about Serrow, after she snapped a man's spine and dumped his body on the floor of the guidepost. I'm sure that'll happen any day now."

"Imp's blade!" She hissed out a breath. "Just come out with it. What do you want us to do?"

"We need someone here." I pointed at the spot in the heart of the city, where Vandie's mnemonic directions led. "Watch and wait. If the Barekusu show, do what you need to do. I'm going to go in the hole and follow the Laughing Larry directions." I looked at Jax. "I wouldn't mind not going alone."

Jax's eyes crinkled. "You definitely need help. And since I came to this damn town, it's basically been one long downhill slide anyway."

"Do you really think they're planning another sinkhole?" Guyer stood and began to pace.

"Oh, Weylan definitely is. He's got Serrow as a true believer, and maybe a handful of others, but I don't think he's infected the rest of the caravan with his chosen one nonsense. There were Barekusu deaths during the first sinkhole, and I doubt they'd be on board for round two."

I paused. "I need to go in there." Guyer and Gellica's faces were strained. The thought of going in the geo-vents was taboo, and created a deep sense of unease in them, just as it did for me. I pushed on, making my case.

"I sensed next gen manna at the Barekusu camp. We know that Serrow and Vandie used next gen manna to eliminate Saul. If Weylan is using next gen manna to create the sinkholes, then I can drain whatever he's doing it with and redirect it."

"I don't know," said Guyer. "There are . . . Oh, come *on!*" She snatched something off the windowsill. The window slammed shut, rattling in its pane. Guyer spun to face me. In her hand was the weathered paperback, *Your Death and You*. "Really, Carter? You're using it to keep a window open?"

I waved it off. "Just for a little bit."

Jax cleared his throat and tried to redirect the conversation. "You said they have manna?"

"They have at least some," I said. "I felt it when I was at the camp. Since I could feel it, that means that it's next gen manna, and that means—"

"You can put the whim-wham on their spell!" Jax clapped his hands.

"That might work," said Gellica.

I stared at Jax. "Whim-wham?"

"It's never going to work." Guyer tossed the book aside and returned to the couch. "You drain manna, and then you immediately need to use it, right?"

I nodded. The cold and hunger it brought made holding the magic for long periods intolerable.

"So where do you put the excess while you're underground? I have to be up top, since you need someone on a bike who knows the territory. We'd need two sorcerers," she said. "One on ground level, one below."

I repeated her words, hoping that I wouldn't have to spell it out. "We need two of you."

Gellica broke in. "I've told you before, I'm not a sorcerer. I've learned a couple linkages, but that's not the same thing."

"Not you," I agreed. "And Guyer's right that we'll need her in the tunnels. We need someone else we can trust, and who can navigate the streets quickly, like on a scrambler."

Guyer frowned. "What the Hells are . . ." Her brows unfurrowed, and her eyes widened. "Oh, no. Don't you drag him into this."

"Harris is a cop. He wants to save lives."

She advanced on me, jabbing a finger at my chest. "You suck everyone around you into your bullshit."

"Is that what this is?" I indicated the room and the group gathered around to save the city. She pulled back her lips, as if she were about to list all the reasons she didn't trust me. I pressed my palms onto the map of the geo-vents. "If you really think there's nothing to this, then fine, leave Harris out of it. But if you do, if you even *think* I might be right, then you know we need him."

"And you want me to talk him into it?"

"I want you to ask him. If he doesn't want to go through with it, you can leave." I sat back. "I just didn't want you to feel like I snuck it up on you."

"As opposed to how I feel right now?"

Across from us, Jax was studying the map of the vents. "Covering this whole area is going to be tough."

"Gellica knows that neighborhood, but she'll be on foot," I said. "That's why we need someone on a bike up top. Her and Harris? We couldn't ask for a better team up top."

Jax wiped his hands on his knees. "It should work."

"It *might* work," said Gellica.

"It has to." I sat back. "Because if not, a whole Hells of a lot of people are going to die so that Weylan can satisfy his curiosity."

"Well," said Gellica. "Here's hoping that our faith in you isn't misplaced."

42

HARRIS AND I MET UP on the edge of Estante, the shopping district that housed Vandie Cedrow's geo-vent entrance. We stood at the corner a block from the building, acting as if we were old friends.

"What's in the sack?" He pointed at the backpack slung over my shoulder.

"A few toys," I said, "to help us find the way home."

He didn't press for details, focusing instead on scanning the street. The poor guy was nervous.

"Are you sure you're okay with this?" He'd been eager enough, even volunteering before Guyer could ask for his help. But actually staring a quasi-legal action in the face is a different matter entirely.

"Not exactly," he said. "But then, I haven't been okay with most things since I came to this city." He craned his neck for a view of the Mount, which stood in stark relief in the early evening sunset. "I was there at the hardware store. I was at the sinkhole. Do you really think that I'd let another Cedrow tear this city apart?"

We stood for a moment in amiable silence. As usual, I couldn't keep my mouth shut.

"I asked you this before . . ." I began.

"So why ask again?"

"Your answer keeps changing." I shifted the backpack to the other shoulder. "Why'd you come to Titanshade?"

He sighed. "I fell in love. Big, beautiful guy named Davey. Out of school I hired in as a divination officer in Gibston. Cushy job, good benefits. But Davey was a dreamer. He was convinced that Titan-shade was going to go through an energy revolution, and the ice plains would be transformed into wind farms. He sunk all his money, and a good chunk of mine, into starting up a windmill service company. I quit my job and followed him. But the wind farms never materialized, and the drilling freeze shattered the last of Davey's hopes. He decided that the real money was in solar panels. He moved out west."

"You stayed."

"Had to. I'd shot myself in the foot with that quick transfer request out of Gibston. No other department will touch me if I leave a second job in as many years. They won't think I'm serious." He shook his head. With his bucktoothed smile and large ears, he looked like a taxi with both doors open. "The things we do for love, hey?"

"Tell me about it." I spotted Jax's familiar figure, still a little way off but making his way toward us. "Speaking of, are you and Guyer . . ." I let it trail off.

"Well, we sorta are." Harris shrugged, almost bashfully. "We're a good pair. I needed someone fun to show me around town." As he talked about Guyer, his grin settled into something warmer, a genuine affection. "And she's a good match for a farm boy like me. You can see it when she gets done up to go out on the town—her heart's not in it. She thinks she needs to be at galas and receptions, but she'd rather be on a dirt bike, kicking up dust."

Jax was almost on us. I waved, and Harris turned, surprised. He was still new enough that he didn't have cop radar. Another reminder of how skilled Jax was with only a few months of experience.

Harris wore dark jeans and a biker jacket. I was dressed in jeans and a black pullover, topped by a dark canvas windbreaker. Jax was wearing tan slacks and a green button-up shirt that looked like it had been freshly ironed. I shook my head.

"Kid, it's a good thing you carry a gun, because otherwise this city would chew you up and spit you out."

He snorted. "There's no dress code for this kind of thing."

Guyer pulled up on her bike. She wore jeans and a dark shirt with a leather jacket. Jax looked away, pretending not to notice.

"Where's your little friend?" Guyer asked me. "I thought she was going to cover the city center with Harris."

"Gellica's there already." I turned to Harris. "You won't see her. But trust me, she'll be watching." There was no time to explain Gellica's ability to slip into the shape of a large cat creature. Besides, I had enough trouble keeping my own secrets straight.

Harris climbed onto his bike and turned his easy smile toward Guyer. "Fine. I'm not planning on letting anyone see me, either."

I spoke a little louder. "Okay, are we all clear on the timeline? We're about to be out of communication, so we have to hit this like clockwork." There was no chance that walkie-talkies would work that far below ground, nor would pagers get a signal.

"Actually, I've been thinking about that," said Guyer. "You still have that notepad you're always carrying around?"

I pulled it out of my back pocket.

"Great." She handed me a half slip of carbon paper.

"The twin of that carbon slip is in here." She flashed a similar notepad, then tossed it to Harris. "Whatever you write on one pad will appear on the other."

"Huh." I slipped the carbon paper beneath the top sheet, then grabbed my pencil and tried it out.

Harris glanced at his pad, then looked at me. "You never even met my mother."

"That was expensive," Guyer snapped at us. "Use them in emergencies, and if the paper gets hard to read, slip the carbon onto a new sheet." She dropped her kickstand and dismounted.

Harris unzipped a pocket, dropped the notepad inside, and came out with two small silver objects. "I worked a little magic myself." He held one of the objects out to Guyer. The streetlights gleamed on the reflective surface. "Paired bells."

Guyer squinted. "Is that wax on the clapper?"

"Yep." Harris closed his jacket pocket. "It's a stopper spell."

"Clever!" Guyer said. To me, she added, "The connection between the bells won't take effect until the wax is pulled off one of them. It's like a bottle stopper, or the safety on a gun."

"I've heard of them." Of course I had. They'd been used by the sorcerer who helped Vandie Cedrow kill Bobby and Saul.

"Once they're active," Harris said, "the bells will ring louder the closer they are to each other. I figured it might come in handy if we all get separated."

Of course, he hadn't given one to all of us. If the light had been better, I might have thought Guyer was blushing.

"Be careful," she told him.

"Always am," Harris said, then pursed his lips as if reconsidering. "Mostly." He grinned his goodbyes, winked at Guyer, and roared off on his bike.

"Well. That was sweet," I said.

Guyer shoved the bell into her hip pocket, and opened a side saddle on her dirt bike. She traded the leather jacket for her cloak, pinned up with a brooch into a kind of poncho, giving her more freedom of movement. "Something else about that carbon paper. It's bound with next gen manna. You can still do your battery trick. In case something happens to me."

I wanted to tell her that wasn't necessary, that we were all going to walk out of this fine. But I still remembered Klare's look of contempt in Weylan's tent, and I wasn't quite ready to make another round of empty promises.

The three of us made our way toward the back access alley where we'd confronted Vandie's workers a few days earlier. A dozen paces away, a dingy white box truck sat idling at the curb. I caught the driver staring at us through the side-view mirror, a saucer-eyed human no more than twenty. He looked like a roughneck, with a broken nose and overly thick coat.

"Hey Jax, how did you say the Barekusu would need to get around without being seen?"

We paused at the alleyway; the driver gunned the engine and departed. Streetlights reflected on the side of the truck, revealing a slightly different sheen where an old logo had once sat. We watched as the box truck reached the end of the block and turned the corner.

Jax whistled and said, "That's ominous."

"Do you remember if we've seen anything like that at the transformation sites?"

He hesitated, then shook his head. "There's so many cars and trucks on the street. I don't know for sure."

The three of us exchanged a glance. "There's nothing to do for it now," Guyer said.

I grunted my agreement, and we moved on until we reached the building's back entry. We paused at the door, each of us staring at the shreds that remained of the scarlet crime scene tape, dangling impotently from the shattered door frame. We were clearly not the first to arrive.

Jax spoke low. "Are we still doing this?"

I nodded. "If someone else thought to get in here, then it's even more important that we go ahead."

He pulled up his shirt and freed his revolver from the pancake holster that nestled against his abs. Jax dressed like a guidepost volunteer but he was lean and muscular, the perfect build for someone about to go trudging through a tunnel system. I was none of the above, but there was no time to fix that.

I drew my weapon as well, and together the three of us entered the building.

Inside, the lights were off, and the walls echoed with our steps. I ran my hand along the wall until I located the light switch. The fluorescents blinked awake, showing us the scene much as we'd left it after arresting Vandie and her crew. The shelves had been picked over, and the items were in disarray. But more importantly, the door to the back section stood open. The warmth and smell of the vents was heavy in the air. Through the doorway, we could see that the entry to the vent system was breeched. Whoever had come before us had either looked in and left it open, or had descended themselves.

Jax and I separated, keeping our backs to the walls and covering each other's blind spots as well as looking for any telltale sign of movement. Jax stayed silent, slipping into the shadows, as I called out, "Police! Announce yourself and do not move!"

There was no answer, but far below us, echoing up from the hole, a metallic rattle as if a table had been overturned. I suppressed a groan. We not only had an unknown trespasser, we had a competitor in the vents.

Jax looked at me, and I spun an index finger. We made a quick loop of the building, and verified that we were alone. Whoever had come before us was below.

"Well," I said, "at least this means we don't have to worry about our backside." Jax only glared. I made my way to one of the standing tool chests near the girders. "C'mere and help me block the door. Better safe than sorry."

Together we carry-dragged the tool chest to the door, at least putting some kind of barrier between us and anyone who might follow.

I pulled open the backpack. It held three metal-cased flashlights, three cans of spray paint, and the vent system map.

I shoved a flashlight in one jacket pocket, a spray can in the other, then passed the backpack to Guyer. "We get separated, use the paint to mark where you've been."

Guyer took one of each and handed the bag to Jax, who slipped it over his shoulder.

"You ready?" he asked.

"Much as I'm gonna be." I looked at Guyer, and she looked at the hole. She and I had a deeper hesitation than Jax. We were about to shatter a taboo we'd been taught since infancy.

I pointed at the ladder disappearing into the hole. "Go ahead, Jax. Youth before beauty."

"That's not how the saying goes."

Guyer cut between us with a muttered, "Boys," and headed to the shaft opening.

She descended the ladder rapidly, and by the time I reached the bottom, she was staring into the darkness, hands overlapped at the wrist, sidearm tracking the beam of her flashlight. I was about to say something but swallowed my words as I stepped away from the ladder. The air was thick with invisible webs. I shook my head and blinked, doing my best not to pluck them like guitar strings.

"You okay?" It was Jax. He'd descended in near silence, and now peered at me, a mandible wavering in the flashlight beams.

"Yeah," I said. "It's a manna thing."

"This battery trick of yours seems to have a lot of drawbacks," said Guyer.

"No shit." I focused on the beam of our flashlights, and the glint of metal on the ground. A knee-high crate had once held a metal tray with the welder's tools. It had been dumped on the floor, metal tools scattered ahead of us. Undoubtedly, this was the work of whoever was ahead of us, and the cause of the clatter we'd heard earlier. There was also an array of safety markers, ropes, and flashlights. From the look of them, they'd been used and returned. Whatever Vandie had been doing with the tunnels, it was an ongoing project.

"We'll need to keep our eyes open." I lifted one of the ropes from the floor, inspected it, then wrapped it into a coil. "Only pull out the map if we need it."

"We're headed into an unexplored tunnel system," said Jax. "Pretty sure we're going to need it. And judging from the equipment here, maybe a little more."

"Put this in the bag." I handed the coiled rope to Jax. "You remember the rhyme, don't you?"

I'd insisted we all recite it together, like a parent obsessing over their kid's homework, until we had it memorized.

"Laughing Larry. Yeah, we got it." Guyer peered into the darkness. She didn't say it was the point of no return. She didn't need to.

We turned left and entered the tunnels.

The stink was overwhelming. I wished for some kind of face mask, but anything other than a full-on gas mask would probably have still let in the stench of rotten eggs and damp soil. But that was expected. What was more surprising was the occasional light source. Much of the tunnels were in total darkness, but there were strange sections lit by an amber glow, as if there was a bank of lights just on the other side of the tunnel wall. The light was warm to the eye, and the atmosphere was even warmer. I kept my jacket on so that I could keep the spray can with me, but I was sweating heavily and wishing I'd brought water, or other liquid sustenance.

The vent walls varied in texture. Sometimes they were packed dirt, sometimes jagged rock, sometimes something soft and almost velvety. But always, they were warm. The whole thing felt as if we were walking through an animal's den or a massive insect hive. Or maybe not so massive; with nothing to provide perspective, my sense of size was thrown off, and I had trouble remembering we were in large tunnels, and had not been somehow shrunk, and wandered into narrow halls of an ant's nest. It was made worse by the intricate strands of manna thread. I couldn't avoid them, so I did the only thing I could. I pressed on like I was stumbling through a cobweb-infested attic crawl space.

We paused at a branching path. Ahead, tunnels wound in a half-dozen directions. The main path continued straight ahead, while offshoots darted left and right, as well as sloping down, and a hole directly above us. The three of us stared at it.

"So, when we've got to go up," Jax said, "I don't suppose you've got some way to make that climb?"

"Nope."

Jax exhaled loudly. "Let's hope it doesn't come to that, then."

"It won't," I said. "That's what the Laughing Larry rhyme is for. Vandie's already mapped out a path to get to the site and back."

"I think he's right," said Guyer. "The safety equipment at the foot of the ladder had ropes but no climbing gear. Whatever we're headed toward, it's probably walkable."

We crouched on our haunches as I shook the rattle can and marked our divergence. There was no place to rest, and no further sounds of our predecessor. I stared down the tunnel, where the beam from my flashlight faded into nothing.

"Think that's Weylan out there in front of us?" I asked.

"Could be. Could be one of Vandie Cedrow's workers, or a reporter who wants to break the story of lifetime. Could be a couple teenagers were in the building on a dare, then got spooked when they heard us announce ourselves."

"You believe that?"

He hesitated. "No." He raised his weapon once more, and we pressed on.

We got lucky, in that we didn't have to make a vertical ascent. However, it wasn't long before we came to a hole in the ground that corresponded to the "Duck" in the mnemonic rhyme. Our lights traced the rim, revealing fresh scrabble marks on the far side. Our predecessor was still ahead of us.

I peered over the edge, weapon ready, as Jax lit up the tunnel. The bottom was disturbingly distant, a vertigo-inducing view, like peering down from a second-story roof. If we were following Weylan, as I suspected, then he'd have been able to prop himself between the walls. I wasn't sure how well a Barekusu would bend into a narrow opening like that, but I didn't see a body at the end of the shaft, so I had to assume he'd made it through alive.

"For the record, this is the stupidest thing you've ever asked me to do."

"Noted."

It wasn't quite a straight vertical shaft, so we opted to hold the rope in reserve. I was heaviest, so I went first. We figured if I slid out of control, there was no reason to crush anyone beneath me. I scooched feet-first as far down as I could, clinging to the hole's edge, and then to Jax, as Guyer held on to him from above. Using my partner as a kind of ladder, I continued my descent. I was able to slide the last stretch without worry, and then catch him as he released. The two of us caught Guyer when she dropped down.

Jax looked back at the slope. "Can we get back up this way?"

"I think so."

"As far as confidence builders go," he said, "that's pathetic."

After the dip, we had a long, long trek of winding back and forth, gradually rising in elevation. As we got closer to the surface, the tunnels grew tighter, and there were more frequent small runs leading off of the top or side of the tunnel. It seemed like these were the finger vents that would ultimately lead up to the indoor vents and innumerable outdoor fissures that kept the city habitable. We were in the source of the city's life, creeping single file toward our destination.

I was in front, and paused when we came to a fork. I called over my shoulder. "Is it 'Leaves Righteous Lawyers'?"

"No," said Jax. "It's Leaves Lawyers Running. I can't believe you're the one who insisted we memorize the thing."

"Oh, for . . . Turn around, Ajax." Guyer dug out the map and pressed it flat against Jax's back. She peered at it in the illumination of the flashlight beam. "Take a right."

I shuffled ahead, progressing past a series of dark alcoves, each one of them a side tunnel that led us far off our path. "Are you sure? I thought it was Righteous Lawyers."

Behind me, Guyer laughed. "Have you ever heard of a righteous lawyer?"

I looked over my shoulder, past Jax, just in time to glimpse the massive furry arms reaching from the alcove to seize Guyer by the neck. I spun, and my flashlight beam bounced off of Serrow's eye plates.

"I believe you'll put down your weapons." Her shadow spread dark and looming across the geo-vent corridor. "Before we all get hurt."

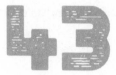

JAX DROPPED INTO A LOW crouch, his weapon already drawn, giving me clearance to fire over his head. But that wasn't going to do any good.

Guyer was a living shield, held firmly in place by Serrow's thick-fingered show hands. The Barekusu's bulk filled the side tunnel, giving no room for flanking. We could only take her from the front, and to do that we'd need to go through Guyer. I showed my hands, holding no weapon, armed only with my voice.

"Okay. Alright, Serrow. You're in charge. What do you want us to do?"

One of Serrow's show hands wrapped around one of Guyer's hips, the sly hand hidden behind the DO's back. Her other show hand held Guyer's head, ready to crack it like an egg. That arm's sly hand gripped Guyer's hand, holding it high and away from her sidearm. Guyer's opposite hand was unhindered, but fluttered ineffectively near her throat, as if panic were setting in.

"I want you to believe me." The Barekusu's voice was still far lower than a human's but higher than when I'd heard her speak before. I wondered if it was a sign of stress, or of madness.

"I do," I said. "I do believe you. You cast the spell on the angel tears to kill Saul Petrevisch. And that got out of control."

Serrow was breathing fast, eye plates open, multiple pupils swirling as she looked for surprise attack.

"Other people were affected by the angel tears. Including you, right? At the guidepost, you heard a song, didn't you? A buzzing song, that made you act. Made you do things."

"It made me do things. But not that."

"Not what?"

"We're on the verge of something magnificent," she said. "Weylan and I are about to uncover a truth that's been hidden for millennia. If it's rushed, then it will retreat once more."

"You said the buzzing made you do things, but 'not that.' What did you mean?"

"You're a detective," she said. "You don't arrest people before you can convict. The truth can't come out before there's proof." She panted, her tongue a speckled pink shape peeking out past the fur draping her muzzle. "That was why Mr. Glouchester needed to be silenced."

The muscles along my jaw clamped shut, and I focused on my breathing. I'd felt bad for her, believed that she was forced to strike out. But that was another lie. She'd fooled me, or I'd fooled myself. Either way, Glouchester's death wasn't an accident, and Klare had been more right than I realized.

"No," I said, whether to her or myself, I wasn't sure. "I've heard the buzzing. We've all heard it. What is that noise, Serrow?"

I watched Guyer from the corner of my eye. The hand that had seemed to flail ineffectively was actually stretching with purpose, toward the brooch on her cloak. The same brooch that was linked to her baton.

I spoke again, louder. I wanted Serrow's attention focused on me. "What is it?" I asked. "What is the buzzing that's trapped in these rocks?"

The Barekusu's panting was heavy. "The sound of empty lies coming to light. I believe that I'd—"

Guyer gripped the pin, pulling it free, and in response the baton leapt from her belt, dancing, controlled by the manna that linked it to the brooch. She angled her hand and jabbed backward, plunging the pin into Serrow's hand. In a perfectly matching arc, the baton darted between Serrow's eye plates.

The Barekusu sorcerer howled from pain and surprise. She lunged forward, propelling Guyer in front of her. Jax rolled to one side, but I was slower. She swung her hand, crashing into the vent wall.

Guyer's baton struck again, and this time Serrow released her hostage, shoving her toward me and Jax while she clawed at her eye plates.

Stumbling behind Serrow's momentum, Guyer collided with me and we toppled to the warm stone floor. Serrow closed in, massive show fists swinging as she shouted, almost chanting, "Betrayal, betrayal, betrayal!"

In the midst of her ravings and swinging fists, I glimpsed the sly hand that had been obscured behind Guyer. It carried a simple wooden rod.

Guyer rolled, pulling me with her. A hairy show fist grazed my shoulder, numbing it to my elbow before crashing into stone still slick with my sweat. But there was something else I felt—the tangled cobwebs of a manna bond, wrapped around the wooden rod. I twisted back and pawed the air. *There.* I gripped it tight and pulled on it, drawing the energy into myself. It was like plunging my arm into deep water. The numbness and cold spread up my arm and over my body while the ringing in my ears dropped in pitch, becoming a resonant hum that surged through my bloodstream. But in all of that, I smiled, like a man sitting down to a steak dinner. I stared up at Serrow, past her eye plates, to the look of shock and wonder in her large eyes.

"I don't believe," she said, all her attention turned to me. Maybe that was why she didn't see Jax.

He came in low, still crouched, dipping beneath Serrow's head before springing upward and putting the whole of his body's strength behind the double-handed strike to Serrow's jaw. Her head shot up and struck the tunnel ceiling with a dull thunk. Her eyes rolled back, her eye plates clicked shut, and she went limp, collapsing on top of Jax with a heavy *slumph* like a load of laundry striking the ground.

Guyer pushed herself up and crawled past me, pulling at the unconscious Barekusu's head and shoulders and screaming, "Pull him out!"

I scrambled to my feet, head reeling from the strikes and from the sulfur-tinged heat. Jax was conscious but shaken as we dragged him out from beneath Serrow's limp form. We stayed there, leaning against the tunnel walls, breathing hard and staring at the unconscious Barekusu.

"What do we do with her?" Guyer asked.

"I don't know." We couldn't carry her out, and we didn't have handcuffs that would fit her.

Her eyes widened, and she pointed behind me. "The rope!"

I scrambled back to the backpack, and pulled out the rope we'd taken from the base of the scaffold. Guyer and I trussed Serrow's arms and legs while Jax nursed his head.

"You sure you're okay?"

He glanced up, wincing. "Does it matter?"

My nose was dribbling blood, and I wiped it away with the back of my hand. "I suppose not."

Guyer stood in the main tunnel, staring at her watch. "We lost time. McIntire's set already started."

"Dangerously Dropped Under Lower Levels." Jax shook his head, pointing back the way we'd come. "Are we at *lower* or *levels*?"

Guyer responded, but I couldn't make it out. I was thinking about the flow of manna that I'd absorbed. It was delicious. "Serrow had a link to something down there. Might be more."

"More what?"

I licked my lips. *"More."*

"We don't have time."

I ignored her and pushed past Serrow's unconscious form, stepping over the Barekusu as though she were a lumpy rug. Jax grabbed my shoulder, and I turned unfocused eyes on him.

"Are you with us, Carter?"

"I'm hungry."

Jax looked past me. "Guyer! You still have that next gen manna? He needs to release what he took in!"

I was aware of them moving around me, but my focus was down the hall. I could smell the manna down there, as if it were the first thing I'd been aware of all day, and for a second I was a little kid, waking to the smell of cooking bacon and a father who was off-shift from the oil rigs. I dragged a hand across my mouth, and it came away wet. I thought that I'd split my lip in the struggle, but the liquid was clear. I realized I was drooling.

Guyer was there, digging in a pocket, and suddenly the smell was there, too. It dripped from the baton and the pin.

"It's ready," she said. "Now what?" But I was already plunging my hand into the threads that entwined the baton. I felt the tasty deliciousness of the threads, and had an image of myself at the center of a vast web, a spider scurrying toward tasty flies wrapped in thread. I blinked, and looked away, repulsed.

But I didn't let go of the threads.

Instead, I exhaled and pushed the cold and cotton that packed my head into the threads. The hunger drained away with it, and I was left sweating, shocked by the sudden heat of the tunnels. Guyer jerked backward, and the baton whipped through the air, narrowly missing our heads as it collided with the wall, sending a shower of stone chips through the air.

"Imp's blade," she whispered, staring at the pin in her hand. Guyer tried to recall the baton, but the sudden burst I'd put into it had used up the manna that created the link, like kerosene speeding a bonfire. Once the manna was gone, the link turned on the materials themselves, and Guyer cursed as the plastic and metal crumbled to dust.

I tried to speak, but my throat was constricted. I swallowed and tried again. "Magic eats itself."

Guyer only stared at me.

"We should go," I said, and pushed down the hallway. Neither of them moved. I turned to face them. "There's no time!"

I stepped closer. "That manna thread goes farther down the tunnels, not toward the entrance, and not to ground level. We didn't run into Serrow on her way to the site." I raised my voice as I began to walk away once more. "We ran into her coming back."

I MOVED DOWN THE CORRIDOR. THE thread from Serrow's staff had been drained but wasn't extinguished. I followed it, walking with my left hand raised, as if following a safety lead on an oil rig. I'd gotten no more than a half-dozen steps when I was pulled backward. Jax clasped the collar of my lightweight jacket.

"Carter, the rhyme leads the other way."

"But Serrow was down here." I took another step, legs wobbling, still exhausted from the exhilarating rush and subsequent crash of channeling manna. "We need to trace her route."

I slipped out of the jacket, abandoning it to Jax's grasp, and pushed ahead.

Jax and Guyer hesitated, but not for long. Jax complained, but marked our way with spray paint anyway. Guyer retrieved my jacket. She pulled out the notepad and began trading a flurry of notes with Harris.

"There's a dozen Barekusu on the street above us. So much for your theory that Weylan is a lone wolf. He says—" She swore viciously, like a parolee learning about activity restrictions. "I'm running out of room. Should've made more of these things."

"Sure," said Jax. "Less efficient than a phone call, and a couple million times more expensive. I'm sure they'll catch on."

The tunnel sloped gently upward, and we crossed into a space much larger than the others we'd been in. It had a domed ceiling, lined with hairline cracks and fissures. Our flashlight beams traced its dimensions, showing a width and height similar to the cavern that had opened up beneath the city center. The fissures were old, but indicated some structural weakness. It was another sinkhole, waiting to happen.

Gradually our flashlights converged, coming to rest on the center of the room. A single white rock the size of my head sat on the cavern floor.

I plucked the quivering, invisible thread in the air and imagined where its path led. "It's connected to the rock. Could be something next to it, or maybe above it?"

"The other end of this thread," said Guyer, "was it connected to Serrow herself, or to something she was carrying?"

I hesitated. "Probably that wooden rod she had."

She spoke through clenched teeth. "You didn't check?"

"You didn't ask me to. Hells, you're the sorcerer!"

"And you're the anomaly that defies everything we learned in school. So forgive me for not covering your mental lapses."

"Guys," Ajax said. "Look at the rock."

In the pale yellow of three flashlight beams, the rock wiggled slightly from side to side.

"I'm going to check it out," I said, already walking toward it, aware that the stone beneath my feet and over my head was intended to collapse. With each step, I could see the stone in the room's center more clearly. For a simple rock, it looked surprisingly familiar. I slowed as I approached, bringing my hands closer, and felt the tingling sensation of manna threads. There were wispy threads to the sides, and a full network of them above it, reaching up and widening, like the branches of an ancient oak.

"It's connected to the ceiling," I called. "But, there's—it's like a knot in the thread."

"A knot?" Guyer repeated. "Okay. I think I know what they're doing! Can you actually see the connection being blocked?"

"No. But I can feel it."

"It's a stopper connection, like the bells Harris gave me." She almost laughed. "And you can touch it? This is amazing."

"I don't care what it is. How do we kill it?"

"Do we want to?" said Jax.

"Hells yes," I said.

"No, he's right! If the stopper bond is waiting on Serrow to sever it, then we'd trigger the sinkhole immediately. That'd be bad."

Jax stepped forward, raking his light up and down the natural grotto. "Okay, first thing, this isn't where we thought they were headed. So is their plan different?"

Guyer nodded. "That might affect how we turn it off."

I tugged at my lower lip. The stopper spell had been the same one used by Serrow to kill Saul Petrevisch. I turned to my friends.

"It's tied to the wooden rod! Like the one Vandie used when she killed Bobby Kearn by mistake." It took a sorcerer to create manna bonds, but anyone could use them. "We have to find that wooden rod, and keep it safe!"

"I believe it is quite safe, little detective." I pivoted, reaching for my weapon as Weylan's voice echoed across the room.

A shape appeared at the far edge of the chamber. The Barekusu guide drew closer, lit by our trio of flashlights. "We are still gathered to share the truth. The only change is that we won't be alive to see its impact on the world. One way or another, we'll find what lies beneath this city."

He stood on his hind legs and one show hand, and held Serrow's wooden staff in the other. My mouth was dry. You didn't need to be a sorcerer to *use* manna-linked devices, only to create them.

Jax kept a bead on Weylan, and Guyer circled in the other direction, flanking the religious leader who'd lost his faith, only to be born again in self-aggrandizing delusion. He'd even lectured me on justice when he'd held those two boulders in his—I blinked.

I'd been so obsessed with disarming the sinkhole, I hadn't considered why the rock in the center of the room looked familiar. It was one of the two buzzing rocks that Weylan had used to demonstrate the sleight-of-hand trick in his tent. The ones he'd said held "the weight of the world" or some other bullshit. A pompous self-aggrandized ass like him couldn't help but flaunt the tools of the city's destruction in front of me.

The weight of the world.

Weylan began talking again, but I'd stopped listening. I studied the manna-bound rock in the center of the room. Spreading my arms, I wove my fingers through the invisible web linking it to the ceiling, until I found a separate, much thicker, thread leading directly up. One that angled up and away, in the direction of the Mount.

I turned and interrupted whatever he was ranting about. "You made an easy-to-carry totem," I said, moving my hands through the air above the rock, plucking the manna threads like the strings of a harp. "Something you could bring down here for Serrow to bind with the ceiling." My left hand was entangled in the multitude of thin threads connected to the cavern ceiling, while my right still held the thicker thread that had the stopper spell. "You get a safe distance away, snap those rods, and this boulder transfers the weight of the Mount to the ceiling. The cavern collapses like a too-heavy anchor dragging a boat down to the bottom of the sea. The rock gets buried, and you've got a sinkhole that looks totally natural."

His eye plates rose and he stared at me with all his swirling pupils. "There is nothing you can do. Not even death can stop me from breaking this bond."

"You'd be surprised at what I can do," I said, and began to feed.

The threads that connected the rock to the ceiling were legion, and they were delicious. There was a pop and the flapping sound of fabric pulled taut on a grand scale. I exhaled and let my eyes shut, and for a moment pressure wrapped me like a shroud, as if I'd been embraced by giant arms, tender and oh so cold. But the reverie was short lived, shattered by another crack, this one timed with a buzzing roar.

I forced my way through the layers of cold, rising from the depths and breaching the surface. I stumbled forward, eyes open wide, taking vast hungry gulps of air and exhaling like a whale sending spouts of hot air streaming high into the clear blue skies.

The room came back into focus. Aware of my surroundings again, I studied Weylan. He'd turned his attention away, probably assuming that I was trying to distract him. The hunger was unbearable, and I was both ravenous and engorged. I felt I might vomit, and then devour that as well, a dog eating his own sick or a murdered teenager devouring his intestines through an unnatural, gaping mouth.

Weylan snapped the rod. With the stopper spell broken, the mass of an entire mountain passed through the thread in my other hand, channeled into the tiny footprint of the rock, which immediately sank through the stone floor. And that was all that happened.

Weylan stared at the intact ceiling and made a deep, throaty noise of confusion and raw rage. I grinned at him like a wolf grins at a hare. I'd drained the threads leading to the ceiling to almost nothing, and the link was no longer enough to pull down the ceiling. I'd stopped the sinkhole from happening.

But with the magic came the cold, and the pressure was building. My vision dimmed, and the cold penetrated my very core. When my knees buckled, I realized the magic I had drawn was more than I could bear. I had to release it or it would destroy me. And I had nowhere to put it, except the thread that connected the Mount and the stone.

With no time to consider, I poured everything I'd just consumed into the connection between the white rock and the mass of stone on the surface. I wept with release as the energy coursed out of me, a force multiplier that amplified the white rock's mass exponentially. It plunged even further, cutting through the pocked stone of the geovents like a drill head through the ice plains. A thunderous crash numbed my ears. Six sharp shots sounded, tiny and impotent in the midst of the chaos.

I closed my eyes, and for a moment I was a child, playing as my mother put new sheets on the bed. She'd throw the sheets in the air and snap her hands sharply, spreading the fabric with a *crack* and letting it bell out over me, tinting the sunlight and creating my own private wonderland. Lazy days with my mother had been few and far between. She'd been a cop, and that meant getting up and going after the bad guys.

I sat up, vision dancing with dark spots. Dust and dirt filled the chamber, choking me, and turning my friends' flashlights into pale yellow cones that appeared almost solid.

Forearm pressed over nose and mouth, I struggled to my feet. The dust-filled air clung to my sweat-slicked T-shirt and eyes, turning to mud. My flashlight was on the floor, and I picked it up, swinging its beam, and finding the hole in the floor that I'd almost tumbled down into. I veered away, dizzy, struggling to breathe. Someone was at my side, and I jerked away, arms raised to defend myself. It was Guyer. She was yelling something and pointing. I looked, and grasped the sorcerer's arm with my free hand.

Weylan stood at the edge of the precipice and peered down. His long fur dangled down past his drawn eye plates, hiding his expression, but his sly hands twitched and spasmed, like a child twining their fingers in nervous anticipation. Blood streamed from his shoulders; the sharp cracks I'd heard during the explosion had been Jax or Guyer opening fire, trying to stop Weylan's last, destructive impulse. Maybe it was his bulk, or maybe it was the plain stubbornness of a man who'd lived for centuries, but he was still on his feet. There was a single wooden rod in each of his show hands, both of them snapped in half. He swayed on his feet, and first one then the other rod fell into the hole left in the boulder's wake.

"Two rods," I said, as Guyer tugged on my shirt, pulling me away from the hole. Weylan had held two rods because there were two remaining control points. The one we were in, and the one Vandie's rhyme would have led us to if not for Serrow's ambush. We'd stopped one, but not the other. The other . . .

I turned to Guyer and yelled, "The others! Gellica and Harris!," but she was focused on Weylan.

When the first few single strands of fur began to pull away from his face, I knew that something was wrong. As the hole began to brighten, I stepped back, pushing Guyer behind me, as if I could do anything to save her.

The wind grew to a furious, unnatural howl. More of Weylan's fur lifted away, and I remembered a demonstration in school, children pressing our hands against a metal ball while a static charge lifted the hair from our heads.

Weylan's entire body floated, hovering over the hole, almost soaring as he stared down into the depths, eye plates wide open in a way that would leave him exposed to even the most simple-minded of predators. His outstretched fur rose and waved on the warm air flooding up from the hole, looking for all the world like Dinah McIntire's tasseled red dress. With each rise and fall of his fur, he grew thinner, consumed from within.

"I am chosen," he said. Then, screaming, "I am chosen!" He kept screaming, but the words switched to Barekusan, and the low rolling bass notes held no meaning for me. Before long I doubt they held any meaning for him, either. He hung in the air, emaciated and wild-haired, and then he was gone, sucked into the hole, disappearing like a spider into a vacuum.

There was silence, and then the red light extinguished.

"What was that? You want to tell me what the Hells that was?" Guyer screamed in my ear, her voice cracking, wheezing, as we both struggled to breathe.

I shook my head, too winded for words, too confused for explanations. She and I clung to each other, limping a slow circle around the room's perimeter, trying to find our way out. A new ringing distracted me, the sound of a bell coming from her pocket. I thought it one more audio hallucination. But then a clear and familiar voice rang out from farther down the tunnels. "Guyer! *Guyer!*"

It was Harris, entering through the sinkhole we'd failed to stop. My light touched on him as he emerged from the same opening where Weylan had first appeared. He raised a hand and called Guyer's name once more.

"Go," I said to Guyer, and gave her a gentle shove in his direction. "Get help. I'll find Jax."

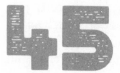

MY FLASHLIGHT BEAM SLICED LOW arcs through the dust, but I still almost missed Jax. I found my partner seated on his ass, his back straight and legs splayed out. "Carter?" He'd apparently lost his flashlight in the chaos, and he pressed a hand to his head as he spoke, glassy-eyed and confused.

I turned the light onto my face, showing him it was me. "Let's get you on your feet." I pulled him upright.

A new light appeared in the chamber. Harris and Guyer were already gone, so that left one possibility.

"Gellica?"

She was beside us in a rush. She gripped Ajax and took the bulk of his weight. Her hands left dark, wet marks across his once-tidy shirt.

I tripped over a cloth. My flashlight beam sliced through the darkness and lit up Guyer's black cloak. The glyphs along the trim gave me pause. I knew how expensive it was, and seeing it in the dirt was a reminder of how much Guyer had put on the line for me. The least I could do was pick the damned thing up.

"Get him out of here," I said. "I'm right behind you."

I stooped, gathering the cloak in my arms. Guyer and Jax were not more than three paces ahead of me, and I could catch up with them easily. But as I grasped the cloak, concealed shards of glass sliced into my left hand. A tingle danced over my palm and up my arm, a charge of energy that I recognized immediately. In the struggle and darkness, Guyer's vial of next gen manna had shattered, and now the liquid I couldn't seem to escape seeped into my bloodstream.

I realized I'd slowed, lagging behind Gellica and Jax. It didn't matter. They were only a half-dozen paces away. I could still catch up.

But the sound of a sigh brought me to a full stop. It was the exact sound my old man used to make as he slipped into his easy chair and settled in for a night of cheap beer and reruns.

To my left, the red light was back, cresting like whale spout from the newly hewn shaft in the middle of the room.

"There is no way in Hells," I muttered, and stumbled after my friends, away from whatever was in that hole.

It wasn't going to let me get away that easily.

The ground trembled, and I fell, knees striking the rock-strewn ground. The cut in my hand throbbed as if infected, and I was filled with buzzing rage. Where was Jax? Where were Guyer and Gellica? They'd *left* me there, abandoned me to rot in that pit. Their betrayal pierced me to my core, and I wanted to shake them, to make them understand how they'd hurt me. If I could just get my hands around their throats, pin them down and beat their weak skulls against the rocks, then they'd know how I was the real victim.

I threw my head back and screamed my rage, but even in the full grip of my anger, I knew it wasn't right—the rage I felt wasn't mine. It was real, but it wasn't *true*.

I staggered to my feet, took three stumbling strides to the lip of the red-lit hole, and screamed into it.

"Get out of my head!"

The light in the pit shifted, from red to a shade I didn't recognize. A moment later I saw something else. It was fuzzy and unclear, the way the manna-laced glyphs on Guyer's cloak defied focus. Dirt slid down my forehead, falling into my right eye. I blinked, and the shape of the thing transformed, becoming sharp angles and crisp lines.

I pawed at my eye, wiping the dirt away. The thing returned to its nebulous state. I covered my right eye with my hand, and immediately I saw the angles and lines return. I switched my hand to my left eye, and saw delicate swoops and spirals, pulsing and spinning at countless different rates. I dropped my hand, and both eyes only saw the fuzzy, furry cloud in the center.

And then it changed.

It was a woman, belly swollen with life. It was a Barekusu guide, shaven and abandoned on the side of the road, then a road-kill ice hare crushed and forgotten, belly swollen with the gases of decay. It was an incomprehensible question whose truth I could feel deep in my bones. It was a fungus blooming from a discarded rind, its freshly birthed spores set free to ride the breeze and weave in the winds, pulled into a loose figure eight before landing on the entwined hands of a Mollenkampi couple, their foreheads touching, whispering multi-toned words of love as remnants of their meal rotted in their teeth and squeezed through their stomachs. Death for life, life to death in an eternal prison that meant freedom and I was shouting, screaming words I didn't know, wishing the thing would let me go, let me go, *let me go.*

I managed to push myself backward, or pull myself forward. It was impossible to say for certain. Because all I could look at was the thing in the hole below, and the incessant whirl of transformations that reduced the warped bodies of murder victims into dull echoes by comparison. It shifted again, a sudden flurry of activity at its fringes, like fur suspended in air, each strand wiggling in a separate direction yet somehow all pointing at me, tracking me like the multifaceted eyes of an insect.

"Car-ter." A singsong whisper.

My head throbbed like no hangover I'd ever had. The voice pinched my sinuses and made my teeth ache, but I couldn't turn away. I blinked, realizing that tears were rolling down my cheeks even as thicker drops hit my lips, bringing the tang of copper. My nose had started to bleed.

I took an unsteady step backward, waving a hand to catch my balance. I struck the thread that led down to the boulder sitting somewhere in the shaft, no doubt being devoured by manna rot.

I blinked, and the shape pulsed inward-up and vibrated faster. The buzzing got louder, the invisible barber now forcing the shears inside my ear, shaving thoughts off my brain and letting the clippings fall to the rough rock floor. I reached up, covering my face with Guyer's cloak. Near the strand that led to the hole were the faintest threads of the spell meant to cause the collapse on the surface.

"Carter!" A human voice caught my ear. Harris's voice. I turned, my hands still caught up in the threads tied to the cracked ceiling, a web of destruction I'd helped prevent from collapse. Harris was closer, flashlight illuminating the way to freedom, to a path of justice, that could give clarity for the dead, and closure to families. Everything I worked for. All I had to do was tell the world about the thing in the pit. *Tell them, and bring them back, and watch them pay for abandoning me.* I snapped my head back and forth, banishing the thoughts.

Harris drew closer, near enough for us to make eye contact. Something about my face must have given him pause, because he slowed and came no closer. The look in his eye was unmistakable, a swirling transformation of confusion into fear.

Guyer's cloak fell away, fluttering to the tunnel floor like a dead bird. My hands were in the air, one grasping the thread leading to the red-tinted shaft, the other entwined in the dozens stretching upward, to the tons of dirt and rock that would bury the thing beneath the Mount once more.

I worked my lips, but could find only one word.

"*Run.*"

I was already moving, and maybe that's what spurred Harris to move as well. As I moved, I drew the last of the manna thread leading into the depths, and fed it back into the threads reaching up into the cavern roof. It collapsed with a roar, far exceeded by the sound of rage and betrayal from the thing beneath the vents.

I ran as fast as I could, not even slowing as my stomach forced my lunch up and past my lips. Vomit and sweat and blood and tears were all the same, and I was vaguely aware of the jagged shapes of rock gouging my hands as I neared the surface. Then I was through, and the air was still and cold and fresh, and it took a long moment before I realized the buzz in my ears wasn't from that thing underground. It was the sound of my own screaming.

Harris was beside me, covered in dust and bleeding from countless small wounds. Someone ran into me. I was so weak on my feet that I stumbled forward. I turned, raising a hand. A woman in her mid-twenties, skin coated in soot and dirt, stared at me and worked her mouth, though no sounds came out. She shook her head and walked away, mouth still moving, silently objecting to the reality around her. Harris grabbed my shoulder, breathing hard, and whispered, "Oh, no."

We'd emerged into the very chaos we'd hoped to prevent. Hundreds of people ran through Titanshade's city center, screaming as a blend of commercial space and high-end living plunged into the sinkhole.

Twin holes had opened their hungry mouths to devour buildings and people alike. The first had been caused by Weylan, and had allowed Harris and Gellica to find us. The second had been caused by my attempt to bury the thing below. As of yet it was small, only taking up the center of the street. But it was spreading. And if we didn't evacuate the area, people would die because of what I'd done.

From the building on my right terrified faces peered out the windows, some screaming, others staring blankly at the chaos. Screams and sirens filled the air, but then even they were muffled by a rumble of stone and collapsing dirt. The hole was expanding, reaching toward the sidewalks and creeping closer to the buildings. If those storefront facades fell into the hole, I wasn't sure where the destruction would stop.

A hand gripped my arm. Harris pointed through the crowd at Gellica and Guyer and Jax. They were already helping the injured evacuate the area.

"This way," I said, or perhaps it was Harris. We moved in their direction, but stopped when the electrical service flickered, then gave out, streetlights and neon signs going dead, plunging us back into the darkness. Something rumbled, and the hole expanded again. The building nearest us shuddered. Its structure began to slip, and the faces in the windows turned from shock to terror.

I stared, unable to help. Then material rose from the sinkhole and slammed into the façade, supporting it for a few precious moments. Metal sheets flew from the roof of a neighboring building, strengthening it more. On the sidewalk a group of divination officers controlled the objects, doing their best to slow the destruction and allow occupants to escape. Even in that chaos, people were helping one another.

We fell into a rhythm then, evacuating the crowd, as sorcerers stripped empty buildings to support the next as occupants were evacuated and survivors were plucked from the sinkhole. Gradually, the scene stabilized. More first responders entered the area. They carried flashlights and headlamps, each one as fragile as a candle in an ice storm. But together they lit up the night. I helped as long as my legs would hold me. Eventually I stumbled to the side, crawling onto a semi-stable mound of debris shed by one of the surrounding buildings to get a scope of the event as the rescue continued around me.

Lying on that pile of rubble, panting for breath, I stared at the ravenous hole in the ground. Even as the city's residents rallied to help those in need, that vengeful, shifting thing was still below us, buried but not dead.

Whatever was trapped beneath the city of Titanshade, it was beyond our comprehension. It was angry. It was awake.

And it knew my name.

46

I DROVE ACROSS THE ICE PLAINS in a rented snow-runner. It was worth the price to not have this trip on the official TPD record. Early on in the drive, I passed one tour bus after another, all of them headed south. Maybe Dinah McIntire peered out from behind one of those tinted windows. Maybe not. Within another hour I was passing large trucks laden with the stage and support beams, the last remnants of the Ice on Her Fingers Festival, beating a hasty retreat to the south. As they passed by, the radio news slipped in and out of static. "New sinkholes . . . few casualties reported . . ." I snapped it off. Our small team hadn't attracted attention emerging from the new sinkhole site, not in the chaos of that night. But I'd heard more than enough for now.

The Shelter in the Bend site had been radically transformed once more. The tents were gone, leaving the rig-work unearthed and exposed to sunlight. Whatever had been left by the performers and audience was abandoned, the remaining trash rapidly being reclaimed by the ice plains. With Vandie in jail and her management company shut down, it seemed as if cleaning up the mess was no one's job.

I parked near the rig and hopped out of the snow-runner. I sucked in a breath and winced as the biting cold snaked into my bones, making my bruises and bandaged cuts ache. I hoped I wasn't too late. I'd been delayed by the traffic snarl caused by the sudden departure of the Barekusu caravan. The crowd that watched the Barekusu leave was just as silent as the one that had welcomed them. Weylan had disappeared, presumed lost in the sinkhole. That, combined with the scandal surrounding Serrow, was the official reason the caravan was leaving early. Serrow herself would be shaved and ostracized, left to die of exposure on the route back over the ice plains.

Shivering, I pulled a cardboard box from the rear of the snow-runner. Nearby movement made me jump. A form longer than I was tall flowed past me like a shark. I clutched the box to my chest but held my ground. With a swish of its tail, the big cat padded by as if I were inconsequential. White on white, her passage was totally silent. I followed her, the sun at my back pressing my shadow ahead of me. The cat had a shadow as well, though hers was shaped like a woman. Then cat and shadow both turned a corner and disappeared from sight.

Ducking my head against the wind, I walked faster, and found myself facing an outbuilding that looked familiar. I shouldered past the door and moved down the hall until I came to another familiar room. It was the office that Vandie Cedrow had used as a residence. The smell of the cat was heavy in the air, but it was Gellica who stood near the desk, staring out over the vast, icy plains.

Among the casualties of the new sinkhole were about a dozen badly wounded Barekusu guards. They told half-coherent tales of a roaring, slashing beast almost as large as them. These tales were written off by rescuers, but I knew better. Whatever ancient predator had spurred the evolution of the Barekusu's herd behavior, Gellica was worse. The Barekusu's primal fear ran deep, and the ice-white cat that managed to be everywhere at once was likely the cause of their quick retreat from the city as much as anything else.

The woman standing at the desk was a creation of magic, broken off from the world she sought to serve. I figured we had a lot in common.

I approached to within a few paces and leaned against the desk. The office views had been restored by the removal of the tent, and we could see the Mount to the south and sweeping, relentless ice plains to the north. Gellica didn't take her eyes off the north-facing window as she spoke.

"Why did you want to meet here?"

I shrugged. "It seemed like far away." I plunked the box on top of the desk.

"Tell me about it," she said. "The Titan."

I pulled off one glove, then the other. At least the festival crew had thought to leave the heat running inside the rig buildings.

"What do you want to know?"

"What it was like, seeing a saint of the Path?"

"It wasn't divine. It . . ." My eyes flicked across the ice plains, and to the skies above. "It was alien."

"Like it didn't belong?"

I surprised myself by responding with a humorless laugh. "No. It made me feel like *I* didn't belong. Like none of us belong here." I winced to hear my own nonsense. I was getting worse than Hanford.

She was silent, then asked, "What do we do now?"

I thought of Talena, and her faith in faith itself. "We go on. It means that we do what we can to help people." I slid the box closer to her, then shoved my hands back in my pockets. The heat was running, but that didn't make it warm.

"The other reason I came up here was to return these to where they came from." I thumped a heel into the desk, peppered by Vandie's stickers and slogan of optimism.

Gellica frowned and yanked the box top open with one hand. Inside were dozens of reel-to-reel audio tapes.

"Those are Heidelbrecht's reports to Harlan Cedrow," I said.

"Isn't this evidence?"

"Evidence locker still has the same number of tapes. They're just blank." I cleared my throat. "There's more than enough evidence to link Vandie to tampering with the geo-vents. Between her confession, the statements from her workers, and the warehouse with the big hole in the ground. This wasn't needed."

"I notice you didn't destroy them, either."

"This way you see them, know they're here. You can destroy them yourself. Or you can listen to them. See if there's something in there that's useful to you." I shook my head. "I don't blame you for not trusting me."

She started to say something then covered it by faking a cough. "It was never about me not trusting you. The problem is that you can't trust me. Or anyone else, for that matter." Her lips pinched tight. "You hate having to trust the living. It's why you prefer working your murder cases. You think the dead can't disappoint you."

I shook my head. "Look, it's not that I hate trusting people—"

Gellica closed her eyes and laughed. "Yes, you do, Carter. Yes, you do."

I fell silent, staring at my snow-crusted shoes. After a few heartbeats she leaned back against the desk.

"Let's try again." She tapped the box. "You broke the law and risked your job. In exchange for what?"

"For helping me. For saving lives. For . . . Hells, I don't know. For justice, I guess."

Her lips curled into that smile I liked so much. "That's what I've already done. What else are you angling to get?"

"I need to know what that thing is below the city. I need to know how it's tied to me, and I need to know fast."

"I don't have answers."

"But you at least know the right questions, and who to ask." I placed myself between her and the window, blocking her view. "This isn't something that can linger over my head. Whatever's down there? It changes everything."

Her gaze drifted over my shoulder, thoughtful. "Does it?"

I stared at her like she'd lost her mind. She ignored me and went on.

"Whatever you saw, whether it was the Titan or something else, it isn't new. For all we know, it's been there longer than any of us have been alive. The only difference is that now we're aware of it."

"No," I said. "The difference is that it's aware of us. And it can affect the world above. The buzzing rocks that drove people to murder? Dead bodies changing shape and trying to hunt down their killers? All just reflections of the magic and thirst for vengeance we witnessed in the tunnels." I widened my stance and held out my hands, like a city attorney appealing to a jury, trying to persuade myself as much as her. "The bodies weren't transformed by my connection to manna. They were echoing that thing below ground."

She didn't reply, and I stared through the window on the opposite wall, at the Mount and the city that huddled in its arms. I fought the urge to upend the desk. "How many damn secrets are hidden beneath this town?"

"I don't know. Maybe if we'd stop burying them, they'd stop coming back to the surface." She lolled her head. "Okay. You want to know what's under the Mount and how you're connected. Is that all you want?"

"Not even close. But I may have burned that bridge to ashes."

She ignored that comment.

"I don't know that I can help you," she said. "I don't have the influence you think I do. And since Paulus's arrest, I have even less."

"Paulus is a free woman," I said. "She walked out of holding this morning."

"Paulus is weakened and desperate, a diplomat under house arrest. There are questions about her involvement, and the process to replace her is already well underway. If she's going to stay in power, she's going to need to do something dramatic, that will be seen and respected both here and in the capital."

"She'll do whatever she has to."

Gellica drew her arms in tighter. When she spoke, her voice was small. "That's what I'm afraid of." She shivered, the first sign I'd seen of her reacting to the cold. "She told me that I was the only one. Of all the takwin she tried to create, I was the only one who lived. But that photo you gave me, of the girl in the sinkhole. She was like me. Born and grown before I even existed."

I faced her head on. "Are you willing to cross her?"

"What if there's more survivors like me? What if I have sisters out there?" Gellica raised her dimpled chin toward the world beyond the rig. "I'll do what I need to, as well."

"Paulus didn't cause the sinkhole, but we both know the old bodies down there are hers," I said, arms crossed. "I want to see her pay for that. Can you accept that? You've always stood up for Paulus before this. Said she was trying to do the right thing."

"She was. But so were Weylan, and Vandie. Hells, even Harlan Cedrow thought he was doing the right thing. You thought you were, when you stole this from the evidence room, right?" She smacked the cardboard box of audio tapes. "Everybody thinks they're doing the right thing."

"No," I said. "Some people know what they're doing is wrong. Even if they have to do it."

"Okay, fine. Pretend I said *most*, if that makes you feel better. My point is that the whole world's turning their attention to this town right now, and every one of them thinks they know what's best for us."

I chuckled. "*We* don't even know what's best for us."

"Exactly." She stared at her hands, fingers folded as if in prayer. I reached out and she gripped my hand, fingers entwined with my own.

"You know I tend to screw things up," I said, surprised to feel my throat constrict.

"I noticed." I was even more surprised to see the wetness in her eyes.

Without thought, I pulled her hand, and she stepped in to me. Her free hand snaked up my neck, tilting my head down to reach hers. We kissed, a silent moment of warmth and support. When we broke off, she didn't step away.

"This can't end well." Her breath against my neck was as warm and full of life as the geo-vents. "People like us don't get a happily ever after."

"So let's not worry about endings."

We held one another silently, taking a moment to relish in the feeling of not being alone. Light from the ebbing sun bathed us from behind, throwing our silhouettes through the northern window, a pair of black blades on the ice. I told myself that her shadow was that of a normal human, and that it was only a trick of the setting spring sun that made it look like the great white cat who appeared shortly before dire catastrophe.

ACKNOWLEDGMENTS

WRITING THE CARTER ARCHIVES IS a joy, and I'm immensely indebted to everyone who helps make this dream come true. Writing the acknowledgments, however, is always a bit intimidating. I feel like I could go on indefinitely and still manage to leave someone out. So, given the limitations of ink and page, here are some of the many, many people who have my gratitude.

My mom was hugely influential in getting me to read, and she had unceasing faith that I'd end up as a writer. I'm still proud every time I can tell her that I've sent another story out in the world.

Mandy Fox is a brilliant teacher, master storyteller, and almost unspeakably patient with my nonsense. I can't thank her enough, and I'm a little stunned at how lucky I am to have her in my life.

My agent Nat Sobel is amazing. Always willing to answer my questions, his comments and feedback are invaluable. My thanks to him and the whole team at Sobel-Weber: Judith Weber, Adia Wright, and Sara Henry.

It's a real privilege to be part of the DAW family. Sheila Gilbert has helped steer each of The Carter Archives books into safe harbor, and I'm continually stunned by her insight and understanding of narrative. Huge thanks as always to Sheila, Betsy Wollheim, Katie Hoffman, Joshua Starr, Mary Flower, and Leah Spann.

My initial drafts are inflicted on my fellow writers, both in Writeshop: Catherine Vignolini, James Wesley Rogers, Jeannine Jordan, Jerry L. Robinette, and Sandra J. Kachurek, as well as the Pineapple Hedgehogs: Jodi Henry, Paul Nabil Matthis, and Stephanie Lorée.